THE ROAD TO COMPIÈGNE

THE ROAD TO COMPIÈGNE

JEAN PLAIDY

LARGE PRINT

Oxford

Copyright © Jean Plaidy, 1957

First published in Great Britain 1957
by
Robert Hale and Company

Published in Large Print 2011 by ISIS Publishing Ltd.,
7 Centremead, Osney Mead, Oxford OX2 0ES
by arrangement with
The Random House Group Limited

British Library Cataloguing in Publication Data
Plaidy, Jean, 1906–1993.
    The road to Compiègne.
    1. Louis XV, King of France, 1710–1774 - - Fiction.
    2. France - - Kings and rulers - - Paramours - -
    Fiction.
    3. France - - History - - Louis XV, 1715–1774 - -
    Fiction.
    4. Historical fiction.
    5. Large type books.
    I. Title
    823.9'12–dc22

ISBN 978–0–7531–8838–5 (hb)
ISBN 978–0–7531–8839–2 (pb)

Printed and bound in Great Britain by
T. J. International Ltd., Padstow, Cornwall

Contents

1. The Road...1
2. The Marquise 4
3. The Royal Family 15
4. The Apartments of the Marquise..............44
5. Madame Seconde....................................66
6. Comtesse de Choiseul-Beaupré.................83
7. La Petite Morphise................................109
8. Unigenitus 121
9. The Repentant Marquise 138
10. The Parc aux Cerfs 160
11. The Affaire Damiens.............................167
12. The Coming of Choiseul 211
13. Mademoiselle de Romans 225
14. The Last Journey to Paris 259
15. Marie-Josèphe 280
16. Death at Versailles................................300
17. Madame du Barry.................................329
18. The Presentation of Madame du Barry........361
19. Choiseul and Madame du Barry 382
20. The Defeat of Choiseul.........................397
21. The End of the Road 408
    Bibliography 429

CHAPTER
ONE

The Road

All through the hot days the people in the bustling city talked of the road. They joked about the road; they sneered at the road; they snapped their fingers at it and they hated it.

Because it was the habit of the people of Paris to sing songs about that which they particularly loved or loathed, they sang songs about the road.

When the bakers of Gonesse came into the city twice a week with their load of bread — which they must sell to the citizens as they were not allowed to take it back beyond the Barrier — they discussed the road with the peasants who were making their way to Les Halles, that great circular space with six busy streets leading into it. Extolling the qualities of good bread, of fish, meat and vegetables, they found time to discuss the road. The coffee-women standing at the street corners, their urns on their backs, called: "*Café au lait*, two sous the cup. *Café au lait*, with sugar, my friends!" And while their customers stood by to drink from the earthenware cups, they would joke with the coffee-seller about the road.

The barbers, running frantically to keep their appointments, flourishing wigs and tongs, their clothes white with powder, called to each other the latest news of the road; the lawyers on their way to the Châtelet referred to it gravely; the clerks hurrying early to their work found time to whisper about it.

It was discussed by lords and ladies in their carriages, by the sweating passengers huddled together in the lumbering *carrabas* travelling back and forth between Paris and Versailles at the rate of about two miles an hour, and by those who, not being able to afford a carriage and despising the *carrabas*, must travel in those comic vehicles which Parisian humour had christened *pots de chambre*.

In the Palais Royal the prostitutes and the gallants introduced themselves by a comment on the road, while the agitators there made of it a subject for fierce controversy.

Men and women, cautiously picking their way through the streets to avoid the sulphurous mud, joked about it; those who halted by the Pont-Neuf for a brushing-down spoke of it with the *valets* of the streets.

The road to Compiègne, the Route de la Revolte, had caught the imagination of the people of Paris. It was a symbol between them and their King. It was the retort of Louis XV to the criticism of Paris. "You no longer call me Louis the Well-Beloved, so I have built a road to skirt your city. I shall never again come for pleasure to Paris, but only when my duties demand that I should do so."

And the people of Paris laughed and sang about the road to Compiègne because they wanted their King to know that they could match his indifference with theirs — and show their hatred if need be.

CHAPTER TWO

The Marquise

The Marquise de Pompadour sat before her mirror and, while her maids dressed her hair and painted her face, received visitors in her apartment. It was the hour of the *toilette* when the most important lady of the Court was free to listen to the conversation of her visitors.

Graciously she smiled. With cheeks and lips carmined, with her hair piled high above a face which was piquant rather than beautiful, she was indeed attractive; but there were many among those who attended her *toilette* who declared that beneath the serenity and cosmetics was a jaded, weary and apprehensive woman. It seemed hardly possible, to those who saw her at this time, that this could be so. Yet all knew that the Marquise was a brilliant actress.

How gracious she was! Never, even towards the most humble, did she show anything but kind attention.

Her enemies whispered: "See how cautious she is! Is that because she knows that her power over Louis is diminishing?"

"Does she know it?"

"She must, if she is not a fool. And how could a woman, born plain Mademoiselle Poisson who has become the Marquise de Pompadour without the aid of friends at Court, be a fool?"

"She gives no sign."

"Does she not! Note the grim determination of that delicate jaw. Louis is exhausting her, and she knows it. She cannot last."

The beautiful eyes of the Marquise were bland. It did not seem possible that she could be aware of the whisperings.

"My mirror," she murmured to her woman; and she held it delicately and elegantly that she might view her face from every angle.

She smiled at the company. This one wanted a post at Court for himself, that one for his son. Here was a man who desired a command in the Army. Here was a woman who sought a place for her daughter. Here was a merchant who wished to sell her a beautiful vase; he knew the taste of the Marquise was perfect. Here was another with yards of beautiful satin in one of the delicate shades such as had become associated with her.

So to Madame de Pompadour they came, because the Marquise was charming and kind; it was her policy to make no enemies and to help where she could; and of course her word carried more weight than that of anyone else with the King.

"For the moment!" her enemies would whisper gleefully. "But wait. Let some bright young charmer appear. Remember de Mailly. The King was faithful to her for years. He would never have rid himself of her, even though he was tired of her. But when Madame de Mailly's sister, Madame de Châteauroux, said, 'Dismiss that woman from Court,' poor Madame de Mailly had to go."

So would it be with the Marquise.

For the time being she remained because Louis had found no one who appealed to him sufficiently to make him want to replace her; but the time would come, and then: woe to the Pompadour.

Now she was smiling at a man who had asked for a command in the Army.

"Monsieur," she was saying in her gracious way, "I feel sure that we shall be able to grant your request."

We! She had the effrontery to use that word which linked her with the King. She did it continually. "We shall leave for Marly, Choisy, Fontainebleau." And she meant "the King and I".

Louis heard and he did not protest. He was too lazy, too anxious to avoid unpleasantness. Yet everyone believed that the time would come when Madame la Marquise would be asked to leave Court.

She could not completely disguise the fact that she was an unhealthy woman; and a woman needed the vitality of ten to keep pace with Louis XV of France.

While they clustered about her the King arrived. Now they fell back, the men bowing low, the women sweeping the floor with their gowns, as Louis made his way to the *toilette* table.

The Marquise had risen, she curtsied with grace. Everyone was alert, but if Louis was tired of the

Marquise he gave no sign of this. All must be aware of the brightening of his face as he took the hand of this charming woman and said: "Madame la Marquise, how are you this day? I wish to hear your news."

He did not dismiss those who had assembled in the room, but the etiquette of the *Château* demanded that they retire at once. He had glanced neither to right nor to left as he had made his way to the Marquise, which meant that he expected to be immediately left with her.

When they were left alone the Marquise gazed at him tenderly. He was not looking well; there was a yellowish tinge on his skin which had not been there a few months ago. Still, Louis was a very handsome man. His eyes were of such a deep blue that they seemed very dark, and his white wig accentuated their colour. His movements and gestures were of such grace and dignity that the Marquise often thought that, had she never seen him before and been asked to pick out the King from a crowd, she would have selected him.

She was in love with him. Even before she had met him she had had a strong conviction that she would one day be his mistress, and as soon as she saw him she had known that no other person could be so important to her as he was.

If only, she thought, I could have had his child. It was impossible now. She had had several miscarriages, but her doctor, Quesnay, had told her that she could have no more children.

It was so unfortunate. Son or daughter of Louis XV and the Marquise de Pompadour! Nothing would have been too good for that child, no honours too high. And what a bond it would have been between them! But it was not to be.

He looked a little melancholy now and she wondered whether he was thinking of the previous night, which she believed had not been completely successful for him.

The thought of her deficiencies in the bedchamber often terrified her, and she knew that the time when she must face this problem could not be far away.

However, the night was behind them; and during the day, on every social occasion, Louis could not have a more delightful and entertaining companion than the Marquise.

"You look charming," Louis told her.

"And you, Sire, are in the best of spirits."

It was not so; but she had found that by suggesting that he looked well and in good spirits he often could be wooed to such a state.

"Eager to hear your plans for the day."

"I had hoped I might have the pleasure of entertaining Your Majesty at Bellevue this afternoon."

"Nothing could delight me more."

"For this evening I have planned a little entertainment. A play, Sire. One which will amuse you."

"Written by your old friend Voltaire, I doubt not."

"Well, Sire, there are many people writing worse plays, and few better."

The King laughed. "As we do not have to see the author we shall doubtless enjoy seeing his play. Have you heard news of him in Berlin?"

"Yes, Sire. He writes now and then."

8

"It is a pleasure to remind ourselves that we have one lunatic less at Court."

The Marquise forced herself to laugh lightly, but she was disappointed. She had hoped to put many honours in the way of her old friend, François Marie Arouet de Voltaire; alas, genius though she considered him to be, he lacked those manners which would make him acceptable at Versailles.

"I think Your Majesty will enjoy the play."

"I am sure of it. You, my dear Marquise, are taking a part?"

"An important one. But do not ask me to talk of it. I would have it a surprise for Your Majesty."

He took her hand and lightly laid his lips to it. He was thinking how delightful she was. She always talked good sense. No matter what topic he raised he could be sure that she would throw herself wholeheartedly into it. But she rarely suggested a topic. She waited for his lead. She was a wonderful woman. If only she were a more satisfactory bedfellow, she would be perfect.

He was finding his glances straying very often nowadays; and he would feel faintly annoyed with himself. The Marquise was such a good woman, and he did not want to give her enemies the satisfaction they were looking for.

The Marquise was now smiling at him tenderly, giving not the slightest sign of the alarm she was feeling. During the five years she had been the King's mistress she had studied every mood of his so that she was often able to read his thoughts.

9

His next words terrified her. "My dear Marquise, I am a little anxious about your health. Can you assure me that you have consulted Quesnay on this matter which is of the utmost importance to me?"

She laughed. None would have guessed that she had begun to feel sick with the apprehension which had seized her. Then tears came suddenly into her eyes. "I am so deeply touched," she said, "because Your Majesty is concerned for my health. Yet, my dearest, you will forgive me if I laugh. I never felt better."

"I thought, my dear, that last night you were a little tired . . . a little too easily tired."

"Nay, my dear Sire, not I. But do you remember that frightening occasion when you were taken ill in my bed, and Quesnay said that *you* must take care? Forgive me, Louis, but I cannot forget that occasion and often it sets me trembling."

"Death!" murmured the King. "Who knows how near any of us are to it?" He shook his head mournfully, and the beautiful blue eyes held hers quizzically. He never seemed to tire. Was that what he was telling her?

She smothered a cough and said: "What a melancholy subject, and death is far, far from *us*. We are young yet."

"Let us hope that it *is* far away," said Louis.

"Oh, but I meant to make Your Majesty laugh, and here we are on this melancholy subject. Sire, have you heard of Richelieu's latest love affair?"

"No, my dear," said Louis. "But tell me. The fellow is so outrageous. How does he manage at his age to remain like an eager boy? Tell me that."

The Marquise laughed lightly. "We should remember, Sire," she said, "that these stories of his prowess are invariably related by himself. This could mean that the powers of Son Excellence are even more amazing after the event than during it."

Now the King was laughing with her, the Marquise was relieved.

She remembered other scandals with which to amuse Louis, and when he left her he was a great deal brighter than when he had come. It was often thus. He would mount the stairs to her apartment in a melancholy mood, and retire with raised spirits, very often smiling to himself on recalling some amusing anecdote.

Left alone, the Marquise lay down on a couch and tried to suppress the cough which she had been fighting during the interview with the King.

As she lay there the door of the apartment opened and a woman tiptoed in.

"Is that you, Hausset?" asked the Marquise.

"It is I, Madame."

"And you were in your little alcove scribbling away while the King was here?"

"Within reach, should you have needed me, Madame."

The Marquise smiled rather wanly; there was no need to keep up appearances with her confidential woman who was also her good friend.

Madame du Hausset threw herself on her knees and took the hand of Madame de Pompadour. "You'll kill yourself. You'll kill yourself," she declared passionately.

"Poor Hausset, then you will be dismissed from the Palace; and how will you then continue with your memoirs? I suppose you could continue with them, though they would not be so interesting, would they? Now you can write about the King and your mistress who is also the King's. I wonder for how long that will be."

"That's no way to talk," said Madame du Hausset.

"No way indeed. But I am aware of it all the time, you see.

Those people at the *toilette* . . . did they think I could not read their thoughts?"

"This dieting of yours, Madame — it is no good to you," said Madame du Hausset. "Nothing you eat can make you a match for the King. Few women could be."

"I fear, Hausset, that I am not a very sensual woman. I must tell you something. There have been nights when the King has slept on the couch in my room. What does that mean?"

"It means that he has a great regard for you, Madame."

"He says, 'I will not disturb you.' What does *that* mean?"

"That he considers your comfort."

"For how long, Hausset, does such a man continue to consider the comfort of his mistress?"

"It would depend on how deep was his affection for her. Can Monsieur Quesnay do nothing for you?"

"He has given me drugs and pills, but I remain . . . as has been said . . . as cold as my name."

"Then, Madame, take my advice. Give up truffles and diets and doctors' pills. Eat heartily and what you fancy. I feel sure that will bring you good health more quickly than anything; and with health will come that warmth which the King asks of you."

"My dearest Hausset," said the Marquise, "I am glad to have you with me. I can speak to you as to no one else."

"Madame, you know I am your friend."

"Then pity me, Hausset. The life I lead is not to be envied. Such moments as this are rare, as you know. I have never a minute to myself. I must think constantly of my duties. There is no rest. You should pity me, Hausset, from the bottom of your heart."

Madame du Hausset nodded slowly. "I pity you, Madame la Marquise. I do pity you with all my heart. Everyone else at the Court, in Paris, in France, envies you. But I who see most have only pity for you."

"My good Hausset, it gives me great comfort to have you with me and to think of you in your alcove room scribbling away concerning the day's doings. Do I figure much in those memoirs of yours? Does the King?"

"Very much, Madame. It could not be otherwise."

"No. I suppose not. But what am I thinking of? I must change my dress. I am to entertain the King at Bellevue this afternoon. Come . . ."

She was seized with a fit of coughing which she could not suppress. She held her handkerchief to her mouth, and when she had finished coughing lay back exhausted, while Madame du Hausset took the bloodstained muslin from her hand.

Neither of them mentioned it; it was a secret which so far they kept between them; but both knew that such a secret could not be perpetually kept.

The Marquise was suddenly gay. "Come," she said. "There is no time to lose. I must be at Bellevue in time to greet His Majesty."

CHAPTER
THREE

The Royal Family

When he left the Marquise Louis went to the *petits appartements* which he had created for himself round the Cour des Cerfs. It was here that he could enjoy solitude and the pursuit of his hobbies; here he felt that he could achieve one of his ambitions, which was to separate Louis de Bourbon from Louis XV of France.

He wished now that he could cast off his mood of melancholy. Life seemed to have nothing of real interest to offer him. It was a wearying round of ceremony and adulation; of brilliant entertainments which were so like one another that he could not remember which was which.

He was forty years old — not such a great age; and yet he felt that life had nothing fresh to offer him. He was jaded and there were very few people who could rouse him from his melancholy. The Marquise was certainly one; Richelieu was another; his daughter Adelaide could amuse him because she was such a wild and unaccountable creature; his daughter Anne-Henriette could touch his pity because she was so fragile and as melancholy as himself.

Poor Anne-Henriette, she still mourned for her lost lover, Charles Edward Stuart. It would have been folly to have allowed such a marriage, yet he could not help feeling a twinge of conscience every time he saw Anne-Henriette. It was for this reason that he avoided seeing her; he hated to have his conscience stirred.

Adelaide interested him more nowadays. She was eighteen and still pretty; it was amusing to listen to her talking of State matters. She really believed that she had a great influence over her father. Perhaps that was why she was so fond of him. She was indeed fond, and no one dared criticise him in her presence, so he had heard. If she suspected any of doing so, she would scream in anger: "Take that creature away to the dungeons!"

At Court people were beginning to wonder whether the violent and vivacious Adelaide was mentally unbalanced. They were asking whether the King intended all his daughters to remain unmarried. There was Anne-Henriette now twenty-three, Victoire seventeen, Sophie sixteen, and Louise-Marie thirteen, all — as eighteen-year-old Adelaide herself — marriageable, and yet the King did not stir himself to make marriages for them.

There were naturally those who looked on the King's relationship with his daughters with some suspicion. Particularly as Adelaide was so blatantly and passion-ately devoted to him. But Louis did not care. He had grown lethargic. He did not care what was said of him either in the Court or in that sullen city of Paris which had withdrawn its affection from him since whenever possible he had avoided visiting it.

He liked to have his daughters at Court. It was pleasant to see how devoted they were to him and ready — no, almost eager — to neglect their mother for his sake.

Oh, there was intrigue in plenty going on about him. He did not mind in the least. There was even some amusement to be drawn from it.

He was disappointed in the Dauphin, who had now become a fat, rather self-righteous young man of twenty-one. Quite obviously he was in the grip of the Jesuit party, and the Dauphine with him.

Strange how such an unattractive young man had managed to inspire devotion from both his wives. It seemed that Marie-Josèphe, the present Dauphine, was as much in love with her husband as her predecessor, Marie-Thérèse-Raphaëlle who had died in childbirth, had been.

Louis could see that as time passed the Dauphin might be an embarrassment to his father. If he was going to support the Jesuits, and through them the Church, against the *Parlement* — and there had been controversy between Church and State in France since the Bull Unigenitus had been issued by Pope Clement XI in 1713, and particularly so when this had been condemned by the civil authorities in Paris in 1730 — he might place himself at the head of a powerful party and thus cause serious friction in the country.

Louis did not wish to look ahead at such unpleasantness. He preferred to live from day to day.

Still he could not help his thoughts going back to his family. He did not consider the Queen. He rarely thought of her now. He had long tired of her since she had come to France, much to the astonishment of all Europe, a penniless daughter of the exiled King of Poland, to mate with the King of one of the greatest countries. But he had loved her in those first years because he was an inexperienced boy of fifteen, and she was the first woman he had known. She had borne him ten children, seven of whom were living; so they had both done their duty to the State and need not concern themselves with each other. Let her continue with her devotions, her incredibly dull life, her infantile efforts on the harpsichord and with a paintbrush; let her go on leading her pious life among her own court which was made up of people who were as uninteresting as herself.

He would go on his way, his melancholy way, desperately seeking to chase away boredom in the company of such gay spirits as Madame de Pompadour.

When he compared his mistress with the Queen he told himself that he could never exist without her. Dear Jeanne-Antoinette, his little fish. Ah, fish! It was a pity she was so cold — yet fortunate that he understood such coldness was by no means due to her feeling for him.

He longed for a mistress who would share his eroticism and at the same time be as charming a companion as his dear Marquise.

18

Was that possible? Perhaps not. That was why he must be content with his dear friend who charmed him so completely in all ways but one.

Perhaps it was not possible to find complete satisfaction in one person. He loved Anne-Henriette but her melancholy for the loss of her Bonnie Prince Charlie irritated him besides bothering his conscience. He had quickly tired of Victoire when she had come home from Fontevrault; Victoire was really a silly little thing; as for Sophie she was sillier. Louise-Marie was brighter but, poor child, she was not very prepossessing with her humped back. No, Adelaide was his favourite daughter at the moment — mad Adelaide who could always be relied upon to amuse by her very outrageousness.

And thinking of his family and his mistress he was reminded of the animosity between them.

It was natural enough perhaps that they would resent the Marquise. But why could they not behave with the dignity and decorum which she displayed?

It was incredible. She, with her humble beginnings, could behave as a lady of the Court, and if she felt any rancour towards these young people how successfully she hid it!

He was ashamed of his family: Adelaide's wild schemes for turning the Marquise from Court, the stupid acquiescence of her sisters, who could do nothing it seemed but wait for their cue from Adelaide. As for the Dauphin, he had behaved like an ill-mannered schoolboy. The King had actually seen him put out his tongue at the Marquise's back.

Yes, when he considered his family, he was not very pleased with their conduct. He was even glad that Madame Louise-Elisabeth, Anne-Henriette's twin whom they always considered the eldest member of the family, had left Versailles, although when she had arrived on a visit so recently he had been delighted to have her with him.

Compared with their sister, known as Madame Infanta, the other girls seemed *gauche*, and he felt ashamed of them and of himself for not more seriously considering their educations.

Adelaide had immediately become jealous of the attention he paid Louise-Elisabeth, and in her wild way had formed a party to work against her. Moreover Louise-Elisabeth had made friends with Madame de Pompadour — perhaps to spite her sisters and brother — and thus had given further pleasure to her father.

But very soon he understood that it was the ambitions of Madame Infanta which were largely responsible for the affection she had shown for her father. She longed for a throne; she was disgusted that a daughter of a King of France was asked to be content with the Duchies of Parma and Placentia which had come to her through the Peace of Aix-la-Chapelle. She had grandiose ambitions; she would like to see France go to war once more in order that conquests should be made and a throne secured for herself; and she wanted Joseph, the son of the Empress Maria Theresa, as a husband for her little daughter.

They had made a statesman of his daughter at the Spanish Court. But finding her so demanding, such a disturber of his peace, in spite of his joy in the reunion, Louis could not but be relieved when she left Versailles.

Now he would take coffee with his younger daughters. It was a little ritual which never failed to amuse him. Moreover he must discover how far the Dauphin was carrying on his intrigues under cover of his sisters.

He went to the kitchen of the *petits appartements* and prepared coffee. When it was ready he put it on a tray, and himself went to Adelaide's apartment by way of the private staircase.

Adelaide's eyes shone with pleasure when she saw him; with a gesture she dismissed the woman who was with her. She curtsied vehemently — all her gestures were vehement — and Louis thought she looked a little wilder every time he saw her.

"Coffee . . . dearest Sire; this has made my day happy."

"My dearest daughter," said the King, "do not grow so excited. I beg of you, rise. It is in the pursuit of informality that I come to you thus."

"Dearest Papa!" Adelaide laughed. "I must ring for Victoire. But first let us enjoy a few moments alone . . ."

"Alone," repeated the King. "Is it possible to be entirely alone? It seems that, even when we imagine ourselves to be, there are those to watch unseen and listen."

Adelaide put her fingers to her lips. "Intrigue . . ." she murmured. "Intrigue all about us!"

21

"My dear, how you thrive on it! But let me give you some coffee."

"Dearest Papa, no coffee tastes like the coffee you brew."

"You flatter me, daughter."

"That would be impossible. Whatever pleasant things were said of you and all you do, could only fail in truth because they did not praise enough."

"Why, you are learning to pay very flowery compliments, Adelaide. How goes intrigue? What do you ask of me today?"

"Leniency for those poor Jesuits, Sire. Are they not holy men? I know Madame de Pompadour hates them and wishes to see them robbed of their power. That is natural enough, is it not? She fears the men of the Church. Why, were they to succeed in making you repent she would get her *congé*."

"Oh," murmured Louis, "no doubt if I listened to the men of the Church I should not indulge in what I have heard called 'orgies' with my charming daughters."

Adelaide stamped her foot angrily. "Orgies . . . what nonsense!"

"I am very fond of you," murmured Louis. "Perhaps we drink too much at our little suppers — our intimate suppers which we and we alone share."

Adelaide continued to stamp her foot. Her face was flushed scarlet. "Nonsense! Nonsense!" she cried.

"Now, my dear, ring for your sisters. Their coffee will be cold."

Adelaide pulled the bell which was connected with Victoire's *appartements* next to her own, and in a few minutes Victoire came hurrying in. Adelaide watched her sternly while she curtsied to their father.

"And you rang for Sophie?" asked Adelaide.

"Yes, Adelaide."

"Well, my dear, I have made this coffee. Come," said the King. "Sit beside me and tell me your news."

It was five minutes later when Sophie appeared.

She curtsied to her father and Louis was amused to see how her eyes turned to Adelaide as though she were asking what she must do next.

"You rang for Louise-Marie?" asked Adelaide. Sophie put her hand to her mouth. "You have forgotten again," scolded Adelaide. "Then go back and ring for her immediately."

Sophie shambled away. Louis avoided looking at her; he was not very proud of his daughter Sophie. Even Victoire did not attract him very much. She was by no means gay and of course completely dominated by Adelaide.

"What were you doing when you heard the bell?" Louis asked her.

Victoire looked at Adelaide as though for inspiration. Adelaide said sternly: "Go on. His Majesty has asked a question and expects an answer."

"I was sitting in my *bergère*," said Victoire, glancing anxiously at Adelaide to see that her answer had met with approval.

"Sitting," said the King. "And reading perhaps?"

"Oh no," answered Victoire. "I was eating. It was chicken and rice." Her eyes sparkled at the memory.

"And you would rather be there in your *bergère* now, eating chicken and rice, than taking coffee with your father?"

Victoire looked at Adelaide. "Certainly you would not," said Adelaide. "You appreciate the great honour of drinking coffee which is not only served but prepared by His Majesty."

"Oh yes," said Victoire.

"Make the most of the honour," said the King. "I fear it is all you can enjoy. The coffee itself has grown cold through such delay. And, ah, here is Sophie."

"Did you ring for Louise-Marie?" Adelaide asked her.

Sophie nodded.

Of all his daughters, Louis thought, Sophie was the most unattractive. It appeared that she could not look him straight in the face, for she had an irritating habit of peering at him sideways. Adelaide said it was not at him only that she looked in this way. People frightened her, and often she did not speak a word to anybody for days at a time. Sometimes she threw herself into the arms of her waiting-women and wept, but when she was asked why she did this, she was not sure.

"Come, my child," said Louis now, "you would like some coffee?"

Sophie looked at Adelaide. Adelaide nodded, and Sophie said as though making a great effort: "Yes, Your Majesty."

Louis was aware of Adelaide's eyes on Victoire. Something was afoot, he realised, and wondered what.

Evidently Victoire had some duty to perform and Adelaide was reminding her of this.

"Well, Victoire?" he asked.

Victoire hesitated, glanced at Adelaide and then said as though she were repeating a lesson: "Maman Putain has a very bad cough. It grows worse. Only she keeps it for when she is alone."

Anger showed momentarily on the King's face. He resisted an impulse to box the stupid child's ears. How dared she refer to Madame de Pompadour in his presence as 'Madame Prostitute'! It was not only an insult to the Marquise but to himself.

He remembered though that Victoire probably did not understand what she had said; she was clearly obeying Adelaide's orders, and if he were to be annoyed with anyone it should be with Adelaide.

Anxious as he always was to avoid unpleasantness he attempted to do so now. He looked coldly at Adelaide and said: "Your sister presumably refers to some acquaintance of hers. I pray you explain to her that such epithets are not suitable on the lips of a young Princess."

Victoire was stolidly looking at Adelaide like one who has completed a set task. Sophie, having just enough intelligence to sense that something was wrong, looked from the King to Adelaide.

"I see," said Louis, "that it is time I prepared for the hunt. I will say *au revoir* to my daughters."

At that moment Louise-Marie appeared. It had taken her all this time to cross the rooms which separated her apartments from those of her sisters because of her deformity.

Louis, gazing sadly at her, wished that she had Adelaide's looks, for she was a bright little thing, the most intelligent of his daughters. It was so unfortunate that the poor child was deformed. He raised her from her curtsy and embraced her in sudden pity.

"I am sorry, my child," he said, "that you have come precisely at the moment when I am about to take my departure."

"If Adelaide would ring for us all simultaneously when Your Majesty wishes to see your daughters, I could arrive before you are about to leave."

Adelaide said sharply: "You forget that you are the youngest. You must consider the etiquette of Versailles."

"Adelaide's etiquette," Louise-Marie amended with a little laugh. "Not 'Versailles'. Perhaps Your Majesty would order how it should be done."

Louis touched her cheek with the back of his hand.

"My dear," he said, "do you want me to displease Madame Adelaide?"

He had had enough of the angry looks of Adelaide, the defiance of Louise-Marie, the laziness of Victoire and the stupidity of Sophie.

"*Adieu*, my children. We shall meet again soon." And when at a sign from Adelaide, they curtsied, he returned by way of the private staircase to his own apartments.

His daughters could do little to relieve his melancholy. Then he remembered that the afternoon would include his being entertained at Bellevue by the Marquise; and his spirits lifted.

In her apartments the Queen was at prayer. She knelt before a human skull which was lighted by a lamp and decorated with ribbons. She prayed for many things: for the health of her husband and a return to his favour, that her daughters might find good husbands and bring credit to their family and their country, that Madame de Pompadour might be cast aside and the King be made so fearful of the life hereafter that he would return to his wife.

It was alarming to contemplate the power of the King's mistress. Recently Comte Phélippeaux de Maurepas had been dismissed because he had written scurrilous verses about her. Maurepas was a friend of the Queen and the Dauphin; and his departure was a great loss to them.

"Holy Mother of God," prayed the Queen, "show the King the error of his ways."

She was not asking for a miracle. Louis, in spite of his great vitality — he could ride many a horse to exhaustion and remain in the saddle longer than any of his friends, and she had had unpleasant experience of his uxorious demands — had been subject to frequent fevers and could therefore be made to ponder on sudden death.

In fact she believed that his melancholy was in some measure due to his awareness of the fact that at any moment he might die with all his sins upon him.

She trembled for Louis' soul, and whenever she had an opportunity let him know this. There were not, of course, many opportunities now. They rarely spoke to each other, except in public. If she wished to approach him on any matter she did so by letter. It was the only way in which she could be reasonably sure of claiming his attention.

She rose from her knees and sent for her favourite ladies, the Duchesse de Luynes, Madame de Rupelmonde and Madame d'Ancenis. They were all soberly dressed, as she was, quiet decorous ladies, kindred spirits of the Queen.

"I think," she said, "that we will read together."

As Madame d'Ancenis went for the book on theology which they read aloud together, the Duchesse de Luynes said: "I had hoped that Your Majesty would play for us."

The Queen could not hide her pleasure. "I will play, since you ask me," she said. "We will read later."

Her ladies sat round her while she stumbled through her pieces on the harpsichord, a smile of contentment on her face because the music sounded delightful to her ears.

Madame de Luynes, watching her, thought: poor lady, it gives her such pleasure and it is not much for us to endure.

Afterwards they studied the mural which the Queen was painting in one of the small chambers. She showed her delight in this as a child might, not seeing the faults. Madame de Luynes noticed that her painting teachers had been at work on the mural and had to some extent improved it, but it was still a poor piece of work.

The ladies exclaimed at its beauty, but Madame de Luynes knew that the others, like herself, were eager to bring some joy into the Queen's life and were prepared to suppress a little honesty for the sake of doing this.

She had had her pleasure; now she would return to duty. The book was produced and each lady read a little while the others sat at their needlework.

None attended to the dreary lecture, yet they all sat, their heads on one side, appearing to listen intently.

Each lady's thoughts were far away. The Queen was thinking of the past, for she had had a letter from her father only this day. These letters from Stanislas, who now ruled the Duchy of Lorraine and who had once been King of Poland, brought the brightest moments to her life. From her father, alone in the world, she had constant love.

To herself she repeated the opening phrase of that letter: "My dear and only Marie, you are my other self and I live only for you . . ."

They were no idle words. Her father loved her as did no one else. Often she thought of that day when he had burst in upon her and her mother and told them that she was to be Queen of France. She could never do so without bringing tears to her eyes and, oddly enough, the tears were not for the loss of joys which she had believed she would hold for ever, but because she missed her father, for naturally they could not meet as often as they wished.

So life went on, she was thinking, each day very like the previous one. She with her little court, which was not the King's Court, lived according to the pattern she had laid down for herself: prayers, interludes with her ladies such as now, playing the harpsichord, doing a little painting, playing cards in the evening and retiring early to bed.

Louis never visited her there now, and for that she was only mildly regretful and very thankful. Another must now suffer those onslaughts of passion. Poor Madame de Pompadour, how was she bearing the strain!

She found that she was speaking her thoughts aloud. "I thought the Marquise looked a little tired today."

There was a feeling of relief in the little group. The Duchesse de Luynes looked up from the book.

"I have heard, Your Majesty, that she suffers often from exhaustion," said Madame d'Ancenis, "and that she is subject to fainting fits."

"Only Madame du Hausset knows the truth," put in Madame de Rupelmonde, "and she guards the Marquise and her secrets devotedly."

"I am glad," said the Queen, "that Madame de Pompadour has such a good friend and servant." She smiled affectionately at the trio. "I know what such friendship can mean."

"The lady is so unpopular with the people," murmured the Duchesse de Luynes.

"Such ladies often are," added the Queen.

"If," said the Duchesse, "you, Madame, were seen more often in the company of His Majesty, they would be pleased. I have heard that in the city they talk continually of the road to Compiègne. This quarrel between the King and the capital — it makes me uneasy. One hears tales of what is said . . ."

"Oh," put in Madame d'Ancenis fiercely, "if only His Majesty would dispense with the Marquise and be as he was with Your Majesty in the beginning . . ."

The Queen's fingers tightened on the shirt intended for some poor man of Paris, and she forgot this apartment, she forgot the present moment, for she was back in the past; she was arriving for the first meeting with the King at that little place not far from Moret, which had ever since been known as *Carrefour de la Reine*. She was stepping out of her coach to meet her fifteen-year-old husband, the handsomest young man she had ever seen in her life; she was experiencing the great joy of knowing herself beloved — penniless daughter of an exiled king, nearly seven years older than her husband though she was. Those ecstatic days were long past; and there was no going back. Therefore it was a weakness to brood on them.

And what were her women talking of? The conversation was becoming dangerous. The Pompadour. The road to Compiègne. These were no subjects for a Queen who upheld the etiquette of Versailles more rigorously than anyone else.

The softness left her face and her mouth was a firm straight line.

"I pray you," she said to the Duchesse, "continue with the book."

★ ★ ★

At the *château* of Bellevue Madame de Pompadour awaited the arrival of the King.

What peace there was in this beautiful place! She would have liked to come here with only her little daughter Alexandrine and Madame du Hausset, and lie lazily in the shade under the trees in the quietest spot of the garden. That was impossible. She had worked hard to attain her position and must work equally hard to keep it. Never must she relinquish her hold on the King; none could be more fully aware than she was how many were eager to take what was now hers.

She had driven from Versailles half an hour before, to make sure that all was in readiness for the King's visit. Fortunately Bellevue was not far from Versailles. Unfortunately it was not far from Paris; thus the people of the capital could comfortably wander out to look at this latest extravagance of the King's mistress.

She looked at the gilded clock and noted the time. Very soon the King would be with her.

She wandered out into the gardens, for the sunshine was inviting. There was no stirring of the wind, and the silence and warmth gave an atmosphere of timelessness to the place. Thus it will be, she thought, long after I am gone. People will come to Bellevue and say, "This is the house which was built by the King for Madame de Pompadour." They would think of her, the most successful woman of her period, little guessing the whole story.

"Alexandrine," she called to the little girl who, in the company of a boy a few years older than herself, was watching the goldfish in one of the ponds.

Her daughter came running towards her. How ungainly was little Alexandrine! But she was only seven, and there was time for change; all the same she would never be a beauty such as her mother was.

Perhaps, thought the Marquise, she will find contentment instead of adulation, peace instead of the continual need to excel.

"Ah, my child," said the Marquise, kissing her daughter lightly on her cheek. "You are looking after your guest?"

"Oh yes, Maman; he thinks the gardens here so good for hide and seek."

"Do not overheat yourself, my darling," said the Marquise anxiously; the sight of this daughter, her only child, always aroused the utmost tenderness within her. How she wished that her father had been Louis instead of Charles Guillaume Lenormant d'Etioles. She would have felt much more at ease regarding the girl's future if that had been so.

The gardens seemed no longer so peaceful; she was once more conscious of the need to hold her place, to fight the exhausting disease which every day forced itself upon her notice; the future of her beloved daughter must be assured.

"Maman, is His Majesty coming today?"

"Yes, my dear. But when he comes you must continue to entertain your guest and not approach us unless I call you."

"Yes, Maman."

"Go now and play with him. I must go into the *château*. His Majesty is due to arrive at any moment now."

Alexandrine hurried back to the boy, who had been watching them with great interest. Lightly the Marquise wondered what gossip he had heard about her. He had no doubt been told that he must do all in his power to please her.

Madame du Hausset was coming into the garden to call her.

"The carriage will be here in a very few minutes, Madame. I have already heard it on the road."

Now she must compose herself; there must be no sign of anxiety. In Bellevue he must feel that he could throw aside all formality, that at any moment he could be plain Louis de Bourbon, and with the same speed become the King if he so desired.

She was waiting, smiling, hands outstretched because she sensed at once that there was to be no formality. She saw that he had had a dreary morning and she guessed it was due to those stupid daughters of his. Therefore she would not refer to them during the few hours he was at Bellevue. Some would have sought to profit from his irritation towards them; not so the Marquise. She wanted him to feel that in Bellevue, away from the Court, he could relax completely; this afternoon she was not so much his mistress as the friend who never failed to amuse and entertain.

"My dear," said the King, kissing her hand, "how enchanting is Bellevue. What peace there is in this house. Are you not delighted with your *château*?"

"Never so much as at this moment when clearly it provides Your Majesty with what you seek."

He continued to hold her hand. "I would we might stay here a week. Alas, I must return to Versailles this very day."

"Would Your Majesty like to take tea or coffee? Or would you prefer wine? Shall I get Hausset to make it, or would you like to do so? Or shall we do it together?"

"I will prepare coffee myself," said the King.

Madame du Hausset had already appeared to inquire the wishes of her mistress. She made a deep curtsy, and the King said to her: "Rise, my dear. We have escaped from ceremony this afternoon. I am now going to show you how to make coffee. Come, you shall watch me and taste my brew."

With a charming gesture he linked arms with both women. Madame du Hausset flushed slightly, and an expression of intense happiness crossed her face. It was not that she was overwhelmed by this sign of the King's regard so much as that she could tell herself that this afternoon need not be too exhausting for her mistress.

"You are gracious indeed, Sire," said she.

"Nay," said the King, "you are the good friend of my very good friend. That is enough for me. Shall I tell you what the Marquise said to me the other day? 'I have the utmost confidence in dear Hausset. I think of her as a cat or dog, and I often behave as though she is not there. Yet I know that, should I put out a hand to her, she will be immediately at my side to discover my need.'"

"The King repeats me word for word," said the Marquise, smiling across Louis at Madame du Hausset.

"The Marquise," began Madame du Hausset emotionally, "is my very good friend."

"The King shares in her affection," murmured Louis. He decided that when he returned to Versailles he would arrange that Madame du Hausset should be given four thousand francs as a sign of that friendship, and he would see that she received a present every New Year's Day.

"You must show His Majesty the present I gave you," said the Marquise, reading his intentions.

"An exquisite snuff box, Sire," said Madame du Hausset.

"And what pleased her most, Louis," added the Marquise, "was the picture on the lid of the box."

"And the picture was?"

"A portrait of Your Majesty," said Madame du Hausset.

"Naturally," added the Marquise graciously.

They had reached the kitchens and the servants, bowing low, disappeared. They knew of the King's interest in the kitchens and they guessed that he was going to prepare coffee.

When they had drunk the coffee and Madame du Hausset had left them they studied plans for a Hermitage which they were to build at Fontainebleau. They had recently built one at Versailles, but the Marquise thought it would be an excellent idea to add to this new Hermitage a poultry house and a dairy.

The King was pleased with the idea and told her that he was thinking of designing a livery for her servants here at Bellevue, as he had for those at Crecy.

The Marquise was delighted for, while he showed such absorption in her affairs, he must feel as affectionate towards her as he ever had.

Afterwards they wandered into the gardens when he expressed a desire to see a new statue which had been erected since his last visit.

The Marquise felt relaxed and happy in the sunshine. Now she had no doubt that she held the King, for surely the pleasant hours they had spent together this afternoon meant more to him than fleeting sexual satisfaction. *That* he could find in profusion; but where in his Kingdom could he find a friend, a companion who would devote herself to his interests as slavishly as did the Marquise de Pompadour?

She felt intoxicated by the warm scented atmosphere and her sense of achievement. She decided that afternoon to have Alexandrine betrothed to the boy who had been invited to play with her. She could be sure that such a betrothal would make the future of Alexandrine secure, because the boy was none other than the King's own son by Madame de Vintimille, for whom he was said to have had as much affection as he had ever had for any woman.

The Marquise could feel an odd envy of the Duchesse de Vintimille, who had come stormily into the King's life, dominated it, and died before one jot of her power had waned.

Even now Louis spoke of her with some emotion. It was so much easier to reign supreme for a short period than to try to hold a position for many years. Would Madame de Vintimille have been as successful as the Marquise if she had not died in childbirth?

They were strolling on the terraces when they saw the children. Obeying instructions, neither Alexandrine nor her companion appeared to notice them.

The Marquise was aware of Louis' eyes on the boy. Was that tenderness for the child or for his dead mother?

"I fear," she said with a little laugh, "that they have failed to realise they are in the presence of royalty. Shall I call them to order?"

"Let them play," said Louis.

"Do they not make a charming pair, the handsome little Comte de Luc and my own not quite so handsome Alexandrine?"

"They are charming," agreed the King. "And clearly absorbed in each other."

"I wonder if they will continue, all their lives, to be so aware of each other that they are not conscious of the presence of others? I could hope so."

The King was silent. Anxiety touched the Marquise. Was this after all the moment to pursue the subject? Was she coming near to irritating the King?

"I have a fondness for the young Comte," she said. "His appearance delights me."

The King did not smile, and she was not sure whether he understood her meaning. His illegitimate son was amazingly like him; there were the same deep blue eyes, the auburn curls. Louis at ten must have looked very like young Monsieur de Vintimille, the Comte de Luc.

The Marquise continued: "He is so like his father."

The King stopped. His brows were drawn together. Was it against the light or was it a frown? Then he spoke. "His father?" he said. "Did you then know Monsieur de Vintimille well?"

It was as though a cold wind had suddenly sprung up to spoil the warm sunshine of the peaceful gardens. Fear touched the Marquise. She had irritated the King. He was not going to accept the boy as his son; he was not prepared to discuss the desirability of a marriage between him and Alexandrine. This was a reproach for the Marquise. Had the pleasant intimacy of the afternoon been part of a plot to wring a promise from him? Was she a place-seeker like the rest? Had he been mistaken in thinking that she offered him disinterested friendship?

"I have seen him," she said lightly. "Sire, may I have your opinion on the English garden I am intending to have made here? I was wondering who would be the best man to take charge of such operations."

The King's expression cleared. It was only a momentary darkening of the perfect sky. But, thought the Marquise trying to quieten her fluttering heart, how quickly a storm could blow up.

One must choose carefully each word, each act.

The King and his intimate friends were preparing to leave Versailles for the *château* of Choisy. Louis was

39

thoughtful, for Choisy had many memories for him. Now he was thinking of Madame de Mailly, his first mistress, who had loved him so dearly. Poor Madame de Mailly, she was still living in Paris — he believed in the Rue St Thomas du Louvre. He did not ask; her existing state made an unpleasant subject. He had heard that she lived in great poverty and found it difficult to find food even for her servants.

And once he had loved her. She had been the first of his mistresses, and in the early days of his passion he had thought he would love her to the end of his life. But her sisters, Madame de Vintimille and Madame de Châteauroux, had supplanted her; it was strange that those two, such vital human beings, should both now be dead, and poor little Louise-Julie de Mailly living in pious poverty in his detested city of Paris.

It was for Madame de Mailly that he had acquired the Château de Choisy — a charming dwelling, beautifully situated in a sheltered position overlooking the wooded banks of the Seine. He remembered the pleasure he had had in reconstructing it. Now it was a *château* worthy of a King of France with its blue and gold decorations and its mirrored walls.

There he could live in comparative seclusion with his intimate friends, headed by the Marquise. They would hunt by day and gamble in the evening. Everything about Choisy was charming; even the servants fitted perfectly into the blue and gold surroundings. Their livery was blue — of the same azure delicacy as that which was so prominent in the *château* decorations. He

40

himself had designed the blue livery for Choisy as he had the green for Compiègne.

Thinking of the delights of the *château* he was impatient to be off.

"I am ready," he said to the Duc de Richelieu, First Gentleman of the Bedchamber.

Richelieu bowed. "The Marquise and the Court, Sire," he said, "are assembled in readiness, knowing Your Majesty's impatience for your azure Choisy."

"Then let us go."

"To Choisy," murmured the Duc, "most delightful of Your Majesty's *châteaux* . . . made to reflect our pleasures . . ." He gave the King that lewd look which could be said to hold a glint of insolence. "Alas," he went on, "there are some of us who lack the prowess of Your Majesty."

The King smiled faintly, pretending he did not see the allusion to the Marquise.

He turned to the Marquis de Gontaut and murmured: "Son Excellence should not feel envious of others who lack his years. Would you not say he has had his day?"

Richelieu (universally called, somewhat ironically, Son Excellence since his return from his embassy in Vienna), turning his eyes to the ceiling, murmured: "Sire, I did not express self-pity. I cannot reproach myself or my fate, for I have found the secret of perpetual pleasure, which does not flag through experience, but gains from it."

"I trust you will share your secret with us."

"With none other than Your Majesty." Richelieu put his lips close to the King's ear. "Variety," he whispered.

"I shall insist," said Louis, "that you share this secret with no other. I would not have the morals of my Court worse than they already are. Let us go."

They left the King's bedchamber and, as they came into the Oeil-de-Boeuf, the King stepped on a paper which lay directly in his path.

He paused to look at it. Richelieu stooped to pick it up. He glanced at it and was silent. He would have screwed it up had not the King held out his hand for it.

"I see," said Louis glancing at it, "that it is addressed to me."

"Some foolish lackey has put it there," said the Duc. Louis read:

Louis de Bourbon, once you were known in Paris as Louis the Well-Beloved. That was because we were then unaware of your vices. You are now going to Choisy to be with your friends. It is the wish of your people that you were going to Saint-Denis to be with your ancestors.

Louis stood still for a few seconds. So, he was thinking, there were some among his people who hated him so much! It was incredible that such a short time ago he could do no wrong in their eyes. He thought fleetingly of his return to Paris after he had been with the Army in Flanders; he could still hear the applause of the people ringing in his ears; he could see the smiling faces of the crowd, the adoration they had shown for their handsome King. Then they had blamed his mistresses for his extravagances, his Ministers for his State policies. Now they blamed the Marquise de Pompadour for everything; but they blamed Louis also.

It was the reference to the tomb of his ancestors which momentarily unnerved him. They wished him dead. He was afraid of death, afraid of dying suddenly, before he had had time to repent.

They had spoilt his sojourn at Choisy. While he was there in those delicately blue, gold-mirrored rooms, he would now and then be reminded of his ancestors who had once lived as luxuriously as he was living now, but whose corpses now lay in the tomb at Saint-Denis.

His dislike of Paris was intensified. How glad he was that a road was being built to skirt the city.

Never would he enter his capital unless forced to do so. He had said that he would not, perhaps in a moment of pique; but events such as this strengthened his determination.

He screwed up the paper.

"Come," he said; "to Choisy."

CHAPTER
FOUR

The Apartments of the Marquise

In the Dauphin's apartments on the ground floor of the Palace of Versailles his friends were assembling in accordance with their custom.

It could be said that there were three courts at Versailles: the King's, the Queen's and the Dauphin's.

Young Louis was in his twenty-third year; and his character was entirely different from that of his father. In appearance he was more like the Queen. He lacked Louis' good looks and courteous manners, was too plump, and took little exercise; he was extremely pious and more than a little self-righteous.

For this reason he had a great dislike of Madame de Pompadour, which, even had she not possessed such influence with the King, he would still have retained. It was shocking, he thought, to see a relationship, such as that which existed between his father and the woman, allowed to be carried on openly; and that she, not highly born, should be more or less First Minister of France was scandalous.

It was natural that the woman should be ranged against him. *He* wanted to see a return to power of the Jesuits, for he believed that the Church should hold sway over the State. She was bitterly opposed to such a policy because a Court in which the Church reigned supreme would very soon make the position of a woman such as herself intolerable.

Watching his guests — who treated him on such occasions as though he were already King of France — he felt a deep resentment against his father. He had forgotten the days of his childhood when the greatest pleasure he could experience was a visit from his kindly and handsome father. The King was no longer proud of his son. In fact he saw the Dauphin through cynical eyes and had accused him of dreaming of the day he would be King, as he sat with a theological book before him.

"You like people to think you read serious books," the King said smiling, "far better than you like reading them. Why, my son, you are even lazier than I am!"

This was disconcerting, especially as there was an element of truth in the remark.

But the Dauphin knew what he wanted. He wanted to form a court in which the utmost decorum was practised. Such people as the treacherous Richelieu could have no place in his court. If men had mistresses, no one should know about it, although the Dauphin deeply deplored the fact that any man should take a mistress.

He had been very fortunate in his wives. Both had been physically unattractive women but what they lacked in beauty they made up for by their devotion to duty. Bitterly he had mourned the death of his first, Marie-Thérèse-Raphaëlle, who had died in childbirth after two years of marriage; but Marie-Josèphe of Saxony, his present wife, was as virtuous as her predecessor. She was now pregnant and he had great hopes that she would present him with a son this time. Her first child had been a girl, but they felt that they, both deeply conscious of their duty to the State, would have many children.

When his sisters, Anne-Henriette and Adelaide, arrived, the Dauphin and Dauphine greeted them with the utmost affection. They had decided that while the approval of the Queen could help them very little, these two girls could be very important to their schemes.

The King had a great affection for his daughters and it pleased the Dauphin to make use of them as spies who were welcomed into the other camp.

"My dearest sister," murmured the Dauphin, "I pray you sit beside me and tell me your news."

Adelaide was loquacious as usual, Anne-Henriette silent. The latter seemed more fragile than ever beside the Dauphin. It was as though she still hankered after Charles Edward Stuart, which was foolish of her. Yet, thought the Dauphin, her listlessness was to his advantage. She was ready to do and say all that was asked of her, because she did not seem to care what happened to her.

In his two sisters he had two allies, and for two entirely different reasons; the diffidence of Anne-Henriette and Adelaide's love of intrigue were equally advantageous to the Dauphin's party. And it was odd that their great love of their father enabled him to use them to work against him. The fact was that these two Princesses were above all jealous of Madame de Pompadour's influence with their beloved father.

"Maman Catin grows more unhealthy every day," Adelaide told him delightedly. "I am sure she cannot live long. Oh, what a good thing it would be for France and the King if she were dead! I cannot think why — since so much good could come of it — someone does not . . ."

The Dauphin laid a hand on her arm. "You are overheard. Be careful what you say."

"What do I care!" cried Adelaide. "I say what I mean."

"If anything should happen to her, and it was remembered that you had uttered such words . . ."

"Our father would never blame me for anything."

"You are becoming too excited, Adelaide," said Anne-Henriette soothingly.

"What our father needs, since he must have mistresses, is a new one every night. The next morning they should be decapitated."

"What our father needs," said the Dauphin reprovingly, "is to return the affection of the Queen and live with her honourably as befits his state."

Anne-Henriette nodded; and at that moment the Curé of Saint Etienne-du-Mont was brought to the Dauphin and introduced to him. The Dauphin received him with pleasure, for this man, who was a canon of Sainte Génévieve, had already made a name for himself by refusing the sacrament to Jansenites. Fearlessly he had proclaimed his Ultramontane opinions and had been on the verge of arrest, which could have resulted in imprisonment and deprivation of his office; but there were powerful men of the Church to uphold such as he, and the outcome of the struggle was by no means certain. His Archbishop had intervened and the Curé went free. Such men looked forward eagerly to the day when the Dauphin became King of France and they would have the support of the crown.

"Welcome," said the Dauphin. "You are a brave man, Monsieur Bouettin. Our dissolute country has need of such as you. I know that should a similar occasion arise you will meet it as bravely as you have already."

"Your Highness may rely upon me," answered the Curé.

"Allow me to present you to Madame Anne-Henriette and Madame Adelaide," said the Dauphin.

The ladies received him graciously, Anne-Henriette quietly listening to what he had to say, Adelaide stating her own views with vigour.

The Dauphin could not help feeling a twinge of uneasiness as he watched his sisters. The Dauphine watched her husband anxiously, reading his thoughts.

"Perhaps," she whispered, "it would be advisable to let them help only in this matter of expelling that woman from the Court."

The Dauphin grasped his wife's wrist in a gesture of affection.

"As usual," he said, "you speak good sense."

"To rid ourselves of her should be our first task," went on the Dauphine. "For while she holds her present place the Church party will be kept in subservience."

The Dauphin put his face close to his wife's and whispered: "She cannot long keep her position. Those who are watching tell me that she spits blood, that there are times when she is completely exhausted. How can a woman in such a state continue to satisfy my father?"

"But when she is gone, there will be others."

"He is very fond of my sisters," he replied. "Adelaide delights him more than Anne-Henriette since she has grown so melancholy."

"But should there not be a . . . mistress?"

The Dauphin's eyes were veiled. He had heard rumours concerning the alleged incestuous relationship of his father and his sisters. Such thoughts were too shocking for a man of his convictions to entertain: all the same he must encourage his sisters to please their father. He and the party relied upon them to work for them from an advantageous position.

"It is to be hoped," said the Dauphin, his mouth prim, "that the King will remember that he has a virtuous and affectionate Queen."

The Dauphine nodded. She agreed with the Dauphin in all matters.

The Marquise sat back in her carriage as it was driven along the road from Versailles to Paris. She felt relaxed and happy because she believed that a few hours of freedom from duty lay before her.

She was going to visit Alexandrine whom she had placed in the Convent of the Assumption, where she was receiving an education which would prepare her for the life of a noblewoman. It was pleasant to plan for Alexandrine, and the Marquise realised that she owed some of the happiest hours of her life to her daughter.

Thus must her mother have felt about her. She could smile remembering the schemes of Madame Poisson, which had seemed so wild in those days and yet had all been realised. They had considered then that being the King's mistress was a matter of accepting homage and presiding at grand occasions; they had not dwelt on the other duties.

But I am happy, thought the Marquise. In spite of this exhausting existence I am indeed happy.

Paris lay only a short distance ahead now. She was beginning to feel a little apprehension when she thought of the capital. Louis might snap his fingers at Paris, but she could not do that. She must remember those days when she had driven in the Champs Elysées and the only people who had turned to look at her had done so to admire her beauty. Then they had said: "What a charming creature!" and they had smiled pleasantly. Now the people of Paris would say: "It is the Pompadour!" and there were scowls instead of smiles.

She wanted to be free to ride through the streets of Paris once more unnoticed, to smell its own peculiar smells, perhaps to wander along the Left Bank, past the Roman remains near the Rue Saint-Jacques, to ascend the hill of Sainte Geneviève.

She recalled old days in the Hôtel des Gesvres when she had presided over her *salon* there and had entertained the wits of the day. Then she had not considered each word she uttered; she had not felt this need to watch her every action.

No, her little Alexandrine should have a more peaceful life than her mother's. She should be well educated so that she could enjoy the company of wits and *savants* like Voltaire and Diderot. Yet she should never have to feel this apprehension, this uncertainty: the inescapable fate of a King's mistress.

Before going to the Convent of the Assumption she had arranged to dine in the Rue de Richelieu with the Marquis de Gontaut.

She was approaching the city; and she could now see Notre Dame, the roofs of the Louvre, the turrets of the Conciergerie and the spires of several churches.

She felt a slight tremor of emotion to contemplate this much loved city in which she had spent so many happy years, dreaming, with her mother, of the glorious future. It seemed strange that, now the glories were realised, she should feel this nostalgia for the old days.

The streets were more crowded than usual, it seemed, and the carriage must slow down. She wondered why so many people were out this day. Was it a special occasion? It was a Monday, a day when there were no executions in the Place de Grève, but the Fair of the Holy Ghost was being held on that gruesome spot. There was great excitement as the women tried on the second-hand clothes, the sale of which was the purpose of the Fair. There was always a great deal of noise and ribaldry, for the women must necessarily try on the second-hand clothes in public. But that weekly event could not account for so many people in the streets.

Perhaps Monsieur de Gontaut would be able to explain over dinner.

The carriage was almost at a standstill now and, when a woman looked in at the window, she saw a grin of recognition.

"The Pompadour!" cried the woman; and the cry was taken up by others in the street.

She drew back against the rose-coloured upholstery. There was no need to tell the driver to drive on as quickly as he could. He too sensed the excitement in the streets today. He wanted no trouble.

It was a sad thought that when the people of Paris called her name it must be in enmity, never in friendship.

She was relieved when she reached the Rue de Richelieu and found the Marquis de Gontaut waiting for her.

"There is much excitement in the streets today," she said. "What has happened?"

As he led her into his house he said: "Madame de Mailly is dead; they have been assembling outside her house in the Rue St Thomas du Louvre all day. They are saying that she was a saint!"

"Madame de Mailly, Louis' first mistress . . . a saint!"

"The people must have their saints, no less than their scapegoats. They say that she encouraged the King to good works when she was with him, and that since she has been cast off and neglected by the King, she has devoted herself to the poor."

The Marquise laughed lightly. "I wonder whether when I die they will be as kind to me."

"I beg you, Madame, let us not consider such a melancholy subject. Shall we take a little refreshment before we dine?"

"That would be delightful, but we must not linger, for my little Alexandrine is waiting for me at her convent."

The Marquis led his guest into a small parlour and gave orders that wine should be brought. The girl who brought it was young — not more than fourteen — and very pretty.

Her eyes were round with wonder as they rested on the Marquise, who gave her the charming smile she bestowed on all, however lowly they might be.

When the girl had gone, she said: "A pretty child . . . your serving-maid."

"Yes, she is still an innocent young girl. It will not be long before she takes a lover. That is inevitable."

"Because she is so pretty?"

"Yes. And she will be acquiescent, I doubt not."

"There is a certain air of sensuality about her," agreed the Marquise. "Well, she is young and healthy . . . and it must be expected. But tell me your news, Monsieur de Gontaut."

He was about to speak when a manservant hurried into the room. The Marquise looked astonished at the intrusion.

"Monsieur le Marquis . . ." began the servant. He turned to the Marquise and bowed. "Madame . . . I beg you to forgive this intrusion, but the alley at the back of the house is fast filling with the mob, and they are shouting that they will break down the doors and force an entrance."

The Marquis turned pale. "Madame," he said, "you must go to your carriage immediately, while there is yet time."

"But my daughter . . ."

"It is better that she should see her mother another day than never again," muttered the Marquis grimly.

"But you think . . ."

"Madame, I know the mob."

The Marquis had taken her firmly by the arm. He signed to his servant. "See if they are gathered about Madame's carriage."

The servant left to obey. He came back in a second or two. "No, sir, there are few people in the street as yet."

The Marquis then hurried his guest out to her carriage. "Whip up the horses," he instructed the driver. "And . . . back to Versailles with all speed."

As they drove through the streets, the Marquise heard her name shouted when the carriage was recognised. She sat erect looking neither to right nor left, wondering whether some bold agitators would rush to her carriage and stop its progress. What then? What would they do to the woman whom they hated so bitterly?

Why do they hate me so much? she asked herself.

They had read those scurrilous verses which had been composed about her — those *poissonades* as they had been called; they sang songs about her; they blamed her for the weakness and extravagance of the King.

She had too many enemies. She knew that in the Dauphin's apartments plots were concocted against her. The Queen naturally had no love for her. The Princesses looked upon her as their rival in their father's affection. Richelieu and his friends watched for any opportunity which might be used to bring about her downfall.

When she and her mother had planned her glorious future they had not taken into account such enemies.

She felt exhausted; and it was when she felt thus that those fits of coughing, which were becoming more and more distressing, could be imminent.

That reminded her that of all her enemies her ill-health was the greatest.

How relieved she was to leave the city behind her; now the horses were galloping along the road; now she could see the great honey-coloured *château* before her.

She knew suddenly that the time had come to take drastic action. She had long put off taking this step, not only because it was dangerous, but because it was repellent.

Yet at this moment she was certain it was imperative that she should take it.

Her thoughts were now on the ripe young girl — as yet innocent, but for how long? — who had waited on her in the house of the Marquis de Gontaut.

★ ★ ★

Louis was overcome with remorse. These were the moods which the Marquise feared more than any others, for it was when repentance and the desire to lead a virtuous life overtook such men as Louis that such women as herself might be considered not only redundant but a menace to their salvation.

If her plan worked she would have little to fear in the future. But it was such a daring plan. Could it succeed? If she discussed it with her friends they would say she was mad.

Her dear friend Madame du Hausset was extremely worried. She was the only one with whom she had dared talk of her plan.

Dear old Hausset had shaken her head.

"I would not, Madame. Oh no, I would not."

"If I had not been bold I should not be where I am today," replied the Marquise.

And this night the plan was to be put into operation. If it failed, what would the relationship between herself and the King become?

But it must not fail. It merely needed delicate handling, and she could trust herself — and Louis — to see that it received it.

Madame du Hausset hovered about her, pale and tense, wondering how long it would be before they left Court for ever. The Marquise could smile, contemplating her companion.

"Something has to be done," she said. "You know matters cannot continue as they are. You yourself have told me often enough that I am killing myself."

"But this . . ."

"This, dear Hausset, is the only way. I know that. If it were not, rest assured I should not take it."

"But what position will you, a great lady, be putting yourself into, that's what I ask!"

"A great lady," mused the Marquise. "The outcome of this matter may well decide my greatness. So far I have done little but raise myself to an envied position and amuse the King."

Madame du Hausset said: "How is the King?"

The Marquise smiled sadly. "He is deeply repentant of his behaviour towards Louise-Julie de Mailly."

"The saint of Paris!" murmured Madame du Hausset cynically.

"Oh, she was good to the poor. She visited them and sewed for them . . . and had so little for herself."

"She did not visit them nor sew for them when she was in favour with the King, did she?"

"My dear Hausset, amusing the King, as you know, gives a woman little time for aught else. Now do not look so despondent, I beg of you. Let me tell you this: when I was nine years old a fortune-teller told me I should be the King's mistress. That came true. Sometimes I think that between us my mother and I made it come true. Now I will tell you something else: I am going to die, the King's very dear friend. I am as certain of that as I was that I should one day be his mistress. And oh, Hausset, I could so much more happily be his dear friend than his mistress. I would be his *confidante*, the friend to whom he would come to discuss everything . . . State matters, scandal, plans for building . . . everything. That is what I would be to the

King, Hausset. And at night I would retire to my apartment here in Versailles, and sleep and sleep that I might be fresh the next day to entertain the King."

Madame du Hausset shook her head. "There would be those to provide the nightly entertainments, and they would be the ones who would get their wishes fulfilled. Depend upon it, the first of those wishes would be to have you dismissed from Court. Did not Madame de Châteauroux, who seemed secure in his affection, demand the dismissal of Madame de Mailly, even though she was her own sister?"

"There is no need, Hausset, to follow in the footsteps of one's predecessors. One travels along untrodden paths. Therein lies success." The Marquise laughed, but Madame du Hausset detected a note of nervousness in the laugh. "My enemies are all about me. My reception in Paris . . . to what is it due? To the *poissonades*. And who writes the *poissonades*?"

"We said it was the Comte de Maurepas until you had him dismissed from Court."

"Depend upon it, he writes them still. He can do so as easily in exile at Bourges as he could in favour at Versailles. Others no doubt write them too. The Dauphin's party are my enemies. They circulate stories about me in the streets. They plan to have me ousted from the Court."

"If you drew the King's attention to those meetings in the Dauphin's apartments . . ."

"I should merely irritate Louis. He knows of the meetings. He is angry because the Dauphin and he are no longer good friends. It is not my task to remind the

King of what he wishes to forget. This is my battle —
mine alone, Hausset; and alone I must fight it."

"And the Church party is against you!"

"The Church party is the Dauphin's party, and at
times such as this — Holy Year itself, with the Jesuit
Père Griffet preaching his sermons at Versailles — I am
uneasy. The determination of Paris almost to canonise
Madame de Mailly does not make life easier for me. Do
you not see that it is all part of the plot against me?
They wish to bring Louis to a repentant mood, to make
him review his life — and my part in it — and see it as
a deadly sin in his life. They want to bring him to such
a state of repentance that he will have no alternative but
to dismiss me from Court."

"Dismiss you! He could not do it. Whom does he
turn to when he is tired and bored? To you . . . always
you."

"Yet he dismissed Madame de Châteauroux when he
was at Metz."

"That was because he thought he was dying and in
imminent need of repentance."

"The life of the King's mistress is full of hazards,
dear Hausset. Yet the life of the King's dearest friend
and *confidante*, who was not his mistress, could, I
believe, be a very pleasant one."

"It terrifies me," murmured Madame du Hausset.

"And now we are back at that point where we
started."

"And His Majesty is with your enemies; they are
telling him that Madame de Mailly was a saint, that he
should be repentant. That although her soul has been

washed white over years of piety, his is stained with his recently committed sins."

"Poor Louis, they will make him very melancholy."

"They'll drive him to repentance."

"It is possible that his melancholy will be so great that he is ready to employ any means to disperse it. If that is so, we shall hear him mounting the stairs to my apartment."

"And you will comfort him."

"I and another. Have you prepared her?"

Madame du Hausset nodded.

"How does she look?"

"Pert."

"And pretty — very pretty?"

"She looks what she is — a serving-slut."

Madame de Pompadour laughed. "That, my dear Hausset, is exactly how I would have her look. I believe I am right. Listen! Do you hear footsteps on the stairs?"

"He is coming," cried Madame du Hausset; and her face was illumined by a smile. "Try as they might," she muttered, "they would never keep him from you."

"I arranged that we should be alone," she told him, smiling gently. "I guessed your mood. Hausset of course is in her little alcove room."

Louis nodded. "I cannot forget Louise-Julie," he confessed. "Memories assail me continually. She was living in that poor place, and I hear that she had not enough to feed her servants adequately."

"Doubtless she was happy."

"Happy, in such a condition?"

"She was a saint, we hear. Saints are happy. They do not ask for worldly possessions. They only ask to mortify their flesh and do service to others. She was happy, happier than you are now, so you have nothing with which to reproach yourself."

He looked at her and smiled. "You were always my comforter."

She took his hand and kissed it. "I would ask nothing more than to continue so for the rest of my life."

"My dear, is it not significant that in this mood of depression I must come to you, and when I have been with you but a few minutes I feel my spirits rising?"

"May it always be so. Will you do something to please me? I have had a little supper prepared — for the two of us only. We will eat *bourgeoises* tonight if you will have it so. And while we eat I would have you forget Madame de Mailly, but only after you are reassured that there is nothing with which you could reproach yourself. You made her happy while she was with you by your favour; and afterwards she made herself happy by her exemplary life. What a fortunate lady she was! Hers must have been one of the happiest lives ever lived."

"I cannot forget the way she looked at me when I dismissed her from Court."

"She would have understood. It was her sister, Madame de Châteauroux, who dismissed her — not you."

"It was I who spoke the words. She looked at me with anguish in her eyes and then she looked away because she knew that her sorrow would give me pain."

"Come, I am going to have supper brought to us. I have a new maid — the prettiest creature you ever saw. I am eager for your opinion of her."

"My opinion?"

She laughed. "It is amusing, is it not — the King of France to give his opinion of a humble serving-maid? But . . . she is innocent at the moment, yet if ever I saw a wanton it is that girl." She rose and called to Madame du Hausset. "His Majesty is supping with me. We shall be alone. Is all ready?"

"Yes, Madame."

"Then will Your Majesty come to the table? I have had it set in one of the anterooms. It would be more cosy there, I thought."

"You have a surprise for me," said the King. "My dear Marquise, it is so like you to seek to divert me."

"This little diversion meets your Majesty's needs tonight rather than a grand entertainment. Moreover had I planned a masque or a play, Père Griffet would have railed against me more than ever."

"He has certainly brought an air of melancholy to us . . . but perhaps we need it."

The Marquise had led him into the small room and they had sat down.

She signed to Madame du Hausset, and the serving-girl appeared.

The Marquise, watching intently, saw the immediate interest in the King's face. She had known that this girl, with the peculiar mingling of innocence and sensuality, could not fail to inspire it. She had chosen wisely. So far her plan could succeed, but she must act with the utmost wariness. Madame de Pompadour must retain her dignity. She must not appear as the King's pander. Everything that followed must be gracious and performed with the utmost delicacy.

The girl showed no awe of the King. She bent over him as she served him; she smiled her innocent yet sensual smile. Louis patted her arm and the Marquise noticed that his hands lingered on the girl.

When she had gone, the Marquise said: "You must forgive her. She does not know who you are. She has never been to Versailles before. Louis, I am going to ask a favour."

"It is granted," he told her.

"You would say that before you have heard what it is?"

"My wish is to please you. I sincerely hope that it will be in my power to grant this favour."

"I wish to leave this apartment."

He was surprised. They had planned its decorations together; it was a delightful set of rooms and worthy of the King's mistress.

"There are rooms on the ground floor of the north wing . . ."

His eyes seemed to glitter as they met hers. He knew the rooms to which she referred. Madame de Montespan had occupied them when she had ceased to be the reigning favourite of his great-grandfather, Louis Quatorze.

He remembered that his great-grandfather had allotted that apartment to Madame de Moutespan when he had married Madame de Maintenon.

The eyes of the Marquise were pleading with him; they were wise, serene and very loving.

How like her to act with such delicacy! He understood perfectly.

She was resigning her place as mistress because she knew she could not adequately fill it. She wanted to devote her days to his comfort and her nights to the rest she so desperately needed.

Indeed she was a wonderful woman — so wonderful that she made virtues of her inadequacies.

He was excited. The pretty little waiting-girl who did not know he was the King could be dismissed from the Palace with a present which would be more than she could earn in a lifetime. It would all be discreet and sedate; he could trust the Marquise to arrange that.

What a situation! Who but the Marquise could have conjured up something which was so necessary to them both and planned it with such finesse? Who but the Marquise could have brought about such an exciting and amusing state of affairs?

Nothing could have drawn him out of his mood of brooding melancholy more quickly than this little plan of Madame de Pompadour's.

He took her hand and kissed it. His eyes were shining with amusement.

"My dear, dear friend," he said "Never did I have such a good friend. Remain so, I beg of you, while we both have life in our bodies."

The Marquise laughed lightly.

The first step had been taken. Now she had started the new way of life. Nights of glorious rest and peace lay before her. Each day she would rise — fresh, full of vigour, ready to be the King's good friend and *confidante*, ready to help in State affairs, ready to plan his pleasure.

CHAPTER
FIVE

Madame Seconde

There was all that excitement in the Palace which attended a royal birth. It was a great occasion, for the Dauphine had been brought to bed and this time she had not disappointed all those who had wished for a boy; on the twelfth day of September in the year 1751 the little Duc de Bourgogne was born.

The Dauphin and his friends were delighted. So were the King and Queen. Marie Leczinska had treated her daughter-in-law very coldly when she had first arrived in France, because Marie-Josèphe was a daughter of the man who had taken the throne of Poland from Stanislas. However, the gentle manners of the Dauphine, her piety and her determination to win the affection of the French royal family had very quickly overcome the Queen's prejudices.

The King was fond of her too. He found her intelligent and, although she was by no means an attractive woman — her teeth were very bad and her nose of an ugly shape — she had a comely figure and a clear complexion and when she became vivacious, which she did often in the company of the King, she was quite charming.

Her sense of duty was very strong, so after having had a daughter and a miscarriage she had taken the waters of Forges because she believed that these brought about fertility; she was eager to give birth to a boy.

Now she had achieved this and orders were given for general rejoicing throughout France.

All came to admire the new baby who promised to be healthy and full of vitality.

The Dauphin declared he was the proudest father in France and insisted on carrying the baby about the apartment himself while Marie-Josèphe looked on with pride and affection; her desire to please her husband was always with her and on such an occasion she could feel that she was succeeding admirably.

The Marquise came to pay homage to the baby. She was very eager for the Dauphin and Dauphine to know that however much they might malign her, she bore them no ill-will.

"Why," she cried, "this little one has the eyes of his grandfather."

It was true. The small Duc de Bourgogne was coolly surveying her with eyes that were dark blue in colour.

The Dauphin could not bear to see his son in the arms of the Marquise, and himself took him from her. The Marquise smilingly relinquished him, giving no sign that she resented his brusqueness.

As usual she was determined if possible to conquer her enemies with smiles rather than threats, to set herself on their side rather than against them. She was deeply aware that a woman in her position needed friends in every quarter and she believed that by ignoring enmity it could sometimes cease to exist.

Having taken the child from the Marquise, the Dauphin left his wife's apartment and went to that of his mother.

"The very thought of the association between my father and that woman sickens me," he told her. "She behaves as though she were the Queen. She has been so gracious to my son! This woman of low birth . . . of no breeding . . . to take my son — an heir to the throne of France — and comment on his appearance! It is beyond endurance."

"My son," answered the Queen, wrapping her shawl more tightly about her shoulders, "do you imagine that I view her elevation with pleasure? One must accept these humiliations. One must bear one's burdens with resignation for the glory of God."

"If I were King I would make an example of women such as that one."

"You do yourself little good by railing against her; it displeases your father. The only way in which you can deal with such a situation is to refuse to speak to her."

"I do that. Do you know, my father arranged that she should ride in my carriage only yesterday. Neither the Dauphine nor I spoke to her."

"To be treated as though one is not there is so much more unnerving than to be abused," said the Queen. "Now tell me what festivities you and the Dauphine are arranging to celebrate the birth."

"There is to be, as you know, a thanksgiving service at Notre Dame."

"The people will want processions, dancing in the streets, free wine."

"They shall not have it. The people are suffering now from too much extravagance. I propose to give a dowry to six hundred girls who shall be selected for their virtue."

The Queen smiled. This son of hers, was a man after her own heart.

"One day," she said, "the people of France will rejoice to call you their King."

The Dauphin let his lids fall over his eyes; he did not wish his mother to see the flash of hope that was there; he did not wish to recognise it himself.

He believed that the people of Paris were longing for that day when the cry would go up: *Le Roi est mort. Vive le Roi!* He would not admit to himself that he too was longing for it; yet it seemed to him that by making the Church party strong, by dismissing such women as the Pompadour from the Court, France would be a happier country.

The royal procession made its way to Notre Dame. This was an occasion when Louis *must* enter his city of Paris.

His people watched him sullenly. They wished him to know that they were no more eager to have him in Paris than he was to go there.

He met with bland charm the gaze of those who looked into his coach. There was about him a dignity which demanded their respect even though they had determined to withhold it.

It was not easy to shout abuse at the King when he was among them. There, in his robes of State, he was an impressive figure; and the Queen beside him, lacking that dignity, a plain stout woman with very little that was royal in her manner, made them proud of their King in spite of themselves.

They remembered that he was Louis de Bourbon, belonging to a great family of Kings, a descendant of their beloved Henri Quatre, who, they had to admit, had had as many mistresses as — if not more than — any King of France. They might remind themselves later that Henri Quatre, lecher though he was, loved his people and served them well, but as the carriage passed on its way to Notre Dame they momentarily forgot their hatred of the King.

But the old resentments were not sufficiently suppressed for them to show pleasure at seeing him. They had complained against him too much among themselves. The road to Compiègne had been too recently made. It was not easy to forget that this occasion was one of those when he could not avoid visiting Paris.

Thus there were few to call "*Vive le Roi!*" as the procession passed along the road from Versailles to Notre Dame de Paris; and it was said that those who did so had been paid by certain members of the Court, in order to rouse enthusiasm in the crowd.

So on rode the King, to give thanks to God for the birth of his grandson, blandly serene as though oblivious of his unpopularity, as though he had forgotten that he had ever been received with joy by the citizens of Paris who had once called him the Well-Beloved.

The Dauphine sat back in her carriage, the Dauphin beside her.

This, she was telling herself, should be one of the happiest days of her life. The husband, whom she had sought to please, loved her and the whole of France was celebrating the birth of their son, who might one day be King of France.

This was the very purpose for which she had come to France as a little girl of fifteen — a very frightened little girl who had been told that she must please the royal family of France, because to be accepted into it was the greatest honour she could hope for.

She would never forget her cold reception by the Queen and her future husband. He had hated her because he had so loved his first wife that he would have resented anyone who attempted to take her place. If it had not been for her sister-in-law, Anne-Henriette, she would never have understood. She would always love Anne-Henriette for explaining to her; she would always love the King for being kind to her.

She wished that there need not be this rift between the King and the Dauphin; she would always serve the interests of the Dauphin, but she was very fond of the King, and he of her. Although he knew of those gatherings in their apartments which she attended, he bore no resentment towards her. He understood her need and wish to follow the Dauphin in all things, and she knew that, fond of her as he was, Louis thought her

71

a little dull because she had neither the wit nor charm of women such as the Marquise de Pompadour.

The fact that she and her husband were voted dull by all the brilliant people of the King's Court accentuated the kindness of the King towards her, for he always listened to what the Dauphine said, as though she were being as amusing and witty as the Pompadour.

"How fortunate you are," the King had said to her, "to possess such a faithful husband."

Fortunate indeed. There were few faithful husbands at the Court of France, and it was a secret dread of hers that one day the Dauphin would conform to fashion and take a mistress.

There should not be such fears on such a day. But all was not as it should be. How silent were the people! They did not shout as the King's carriage went by. They stood staring in sullen groups.

She noticed how thin some of them were, how ragged their clothes. It was said that there was great poverty in Paris and that this was due to the high taxes. The price of bread was continually rising and there were many stories of riots outside the bread shops.

They had left the church and were making their way back to Versailles when, approaching the Pont de la Tournelle, she noticed that the crowds were greater. The coach, carrying the King and Queen, drove on in a silence which could only be called hostile. The Dauphine involuntarily moved closer to her husband.

There was a murmur among the people, and the Dauphine, glancing out of the window, saw that the crowd was mainly composed of women who were trying to come nearer to the coach; and it was all the guards could do to restrain them.

Then one of the women disengaged herself from the crowd and threw herself at the carriage; she clung to it, her face pressed close against the window.

"Bread!" she cried. "Give us bread. We are starving."

The guards would have removed her, but the Dauphin restrained them.

"Throw them money," he commanded.

"Money!" The crowd took up the cry. "We do not want a few louis, Monseigneur. We want bread."

"Bread!" chanted the crowd. "Bread!"

The Dauphin put his head out of the window and said: "I understand your sufferings. I do my best to serve you."

There was a silence. The people had heard of the piety of the Dauphin. He did not live extravagantly; he did not fritter away money, wrung from the people by taxes, on building fine *châteaux*. It was said that he gave a great part of his income to the poor.

One woman shrieked: "We love you, Monseigneur. But you must send away the Pompadour, who governs the King and ruins the Kingdom. If we had her in our hands today there would be nothing left of her to serve as relics."

The Dauphin said: "Good people, I do what I can for you." He then commanded the Captain of the guard to scatter money among the crowd, and the carriage passed on.

The Dauphine was white and trembling. She had difficulty in restraining an impulse to throw herself weeping into her husband's arms.

The Dauphin however was sitting erect against the satin upholstery thinking: that woman spoke for the people of Paris. She said, "We love you. Send away the Pompadour."

This was proof that these people had transferred their allegiance from his father to himself. He knew that his father could win back their respect, for the King had a natural charm and dignity which the Dauphin did not possess. Even now it was not too late for the King to change his mode of life, to let his people see him often, to wipe out the implication of the road to Compiègne.

If his father did that, if he worked for his people, if he showed himself ready to be a good king then they would not turn so eagerly to the Dauphin.

But he would not do it. He had decided on the road he would take. He had decided when he made the road to Compiègne.

And now the people are waiting, thought the Dauphin. They are praying that soon it will be my turn.

It was a cold winter and the east winds sweeping across Paris brought sickness to the city. The Palace was not spared.

Since the exile of Charles Edward Stuart, Anne-Henriette had become more and more frail. Her father and her sisters remonstrated with her. They tried to make her eat but she had little appetite. There were times when she would remain looking out of the window, across the gardens or the Avenue de Paris in those big draughty rooms, seeming not to feel the cold.

Those members of her family who loved her — and all her sisters did so very dearly, even Adelaide whom her listlessness irritated — grew more and more worried concerning her health.

The Queen was the least sympathetic. She deplored the weakness of her daughter which had made her give way to her feelings so spinelessly. If life were difficult one should meet the disappointments with prayer. That was the Queen's advice.

Anne-Henriette listened respectfully to her mother's advice but nothing could bring her comfort.

From a window of the Palace, Adelaide saw her in the gardens one bleak February day, inadequately clad, walking in the avenues as though it were a summer's day.

Accompanied by Victoire and Sophie, Adelaide went out to insist on Anne-Henriette's return to the Palace.

Anne-Henriette allowed herself to be led to Adelaide's own apartments, where a huge fire warmed one of the smaller rooms.

"Why, you are shivering," she cried, taking her sister's hands. "How could you let yourself get so cold!" Adelaide shook her head in admonishment, and Victoire and Sophie did the same.

But on this occasion Anne-Henriette did not smile at them; she lay back in the chair into which Adelaide had pushed her, and her eyes were glazed.

She felt so tired that she was glad to rest; there was a pain in her chest which made it difficult for her to breathe, and the faces of her sisters swam hazily before her. She was not entirely sure who they were. For a time, when she had been in the gardens by the ornamental pool, she had thought that her twin sister, Louise-Elisabeth, was with her and that they were waiting for a summons for one of them to go to their father who would tell the one who was called that she was to go to Spain as a bride.

She had imagined that the call had come to her and it was she who was going to Spain. The Duc de Chartres was heart-broken; but then she was not sure whether it was the Duc de Chartres or Prince Charles Edward Stuart.

"Not for me," she murmured. "I am unlucky for lovers . . ."

"What are you saying?" asked Adelaide.

"What is she saying?" whispered Victoire to Sophie; and Sophie as usual looked to Adelaide to supply the answer.

"It does not matter," said Anne-Henriette, "I am unlucky for lovers. But it is no longer of any consequence."

Louise-Marie, the youngest of the sisters, came slowly into the room. She walked with some difficulty but her face was vivacious; yet when she looked at her eldest sister the smile left her face.

"Anne-Henriette," she cried and hastening to her sister she took her hand, "what is wrong? Her hands are burning," she cried, turning to Adelaide. "She has a fever. Call her women. Call them at once. Let her bed be warmed. She should be in it, for our sister is very ill."

Adelaide resented the interference of her youngest sister and haughtily raised her eyebrows, but Louise-Marie cried: "This is no time for etiquette. Our sister is ill . . . so ill that she frightens me."

Adelaide then commanded Victoire to go to Anne-Henriette's apartments at once and warn her women.

"Now," said Louise-Marie, "we will take her there. Anne-Henriette, sister, do you not know me?"

Anne-Henriette smiled so patiently that Louise-Marie thought hers was the sweetest smile she had ever seen.

"You see," said Anne-Henriette, swaying in the arms of her sisters, "there was no lover for me. I brought bad luck to lovers. But do not let it concern you. It is of no significance now."

"Her mind wanders," said Adelaide.

"No," said Louise-Marie. "I think I understand."

Then she began to weep quietly, and the tears ran unheeded on to the satin of her gown.

Anne-Henriette was unaware of her sisters as she was half carried from the room.

Louis looked at the Marquise and his face was blank with sorrow.

"She . . . so young . . ." he said. "My little Anne-Henriette . . . dead."

"She has been ill for some time," said the Marquise. "She was never as healthy as we could have wished."

"I cannot imagine what life will be like without her."

"My dearest," said the Marquise, "we must bear this loss as best we may. You have lost one whom you loved and who loved you; but you are surrounded by others who love you no less and who, I know, are loved in return."

The King allowed his mistress to take his hand and kiss it gently.

He looked at her, so elegant, so charming. And he thought: she is part of my life. My joys are hers, my sorrows also. How could I endure this tragedy if my dear Marquise were not here to comfort me?

Seated before her illuminated skull, the Queen prayed for her daughter's soul. She prayed also that this tragedy might turn the King's thoughts from debauchery to piety. It should be a reminder to him that death was ever ready to strike. It had carried off this young girl; perhaps it was not so very far from her father. Perhaps he would ask himself whether he should not seek a remission of his sins while there was yet time.

"If he should do this," she told the Dauphin, "the death of Anne-Henriette will not have been in vain."

The Dauphin nodded; he was regretting the death of his sister. He loved her gentle disposition, and Marie-Josèphe often said that her sister-in-law was the best friend she had ever had. He remembered too that she had been a useful member of that little community which gathered in his apartments and won certain privileges from the King for the Church party. Often some little post would be asked for one of its members, and there could not have been an advocate more likely to succeed with the King than his beloved Anne-Henriette.

"Her death is a great loss to me," he told his mother; "it is perhaps a great loss to the Church."

The Queen understood and agreed. Her grief at her daughter's death did not go as deep as that felt by other members of the family. She had often fought against the jealousy she had felt for her daughters, whom their father loved so much more than he did their mother. There had been times, Louis having summoned his daughters to the *petits appartements* to share an intimate supper with him, when she had knelt for hours in prayer, trying to quell the turbulent jealousy which possessed her.

She would never forget her coming to France and those first months of the King's undivided attention, when they had been lovers and she had appeared to him to be the most beautiful woman in the world.

It was not easy even for the most virtuous of women to love others — even though they were her own daughters — who could please the King as she so longed to do, and never could.

Adelaide violently mourned her sister and shed stormy tears. Victoire sat in her *bergère* and was more melancholy than usual. Sophie watched first Adelaide then Victoire as though to decide how long it was necessary for her to mourn her sister.

Louise-Marie was heartbroken. She did not storm nor weep, she simply said: "If they had left me a little longer at Fontevrault I should never have known Anne-Henriette. Oh, why did they not leave me at Fontevrault?"

And Sophie suddenly ceased to wonder how much Adelaide expected her to mourn her sister, and ran away into a quiet corner to cry alone.

In the streets of Paris the death of Madame Seconde was freely discussed.

The verdict was that the loss of this beloved daughter was God's vengeance on the King for his dissolute way of life.

"How could it be otherwise?" the people asked each other in the cafés and the markets. "God would punish him for his neglect of his people and his absorption with the Marquise. This is his just reward."

"This is the result of offending God and displeasing the people. God has taken from him the daughter he loved best."

The Church party encouraged such observations. The sooner the King was made to realise how offensive was his conduct in the eyes of God — and the Church party — the better.

There was hope in the apartments of the Dauphin.

"Such a disaster could bring about the dismissal of the Marquise," said the Dauphin.

Louis himself was very apprehensive. He was beginning to wonder whether there was some Divine warning in this loss. She was a young girl. It was true that she had been frail; but she was too young to die.

His doctors had told him that she had no will to live, that she had refused their medicines; she had refused the food which had been prepared for her; she had turned from all her family and friends to look beyond them into the unknown.

He dared not think of her unhappiness. There were many who would say that she had died of a broken heart. Twice she had loved, and twice been frustrated. Marriage with the Orléans family had been distasteful to Fleury and therefore had not taken place. Her love for Charles Edward Stuart had been deeper perhaps, but how could the King of France give his consent to their marriage after the defeat of the '45? That had happened nearly seven years ago. Had she mourned a Prince, who was not even faithful, all that time?

She died because she had no wish to live. They were tragic words to describe the passing of a young woman. It distressed him and there was only one person who could cure him of sadness such as this; yet the mood which had been engendered by the people of Paris and certain members of his Court led him to doubt whether he should seek that solace.

Death . . . so close to them all! Who would be its next victim? What if it should strike at *him*, and he should suddenly pass from this world to the next — an unrepentant sinner?

He wanted to confess his sins, but he knew that before he could receive absolution he must swear to sin no more.

The Marquise occupied the suite of Madame de Montespan now, but she was still known as his mistress. He knew that the confessors and the bishops, aided and abetted by the Dauphin and the Church party, would withhold the remission of his sins until he had dismissed Madame de Pompadour from the Court.

He sent for Adelaide; he embraced her warmly and they wept together.

The King looked at this vivacious but unaccountable young woman. She was twenty years old and her beauty was already beginning to fade, but he still found her company stimulating.

From Adelaide he could take comfort which at the moment he felt too apprehensive to take from the Marquise.

"You must fill your sister's place," he told Adelaide. "You must be both Adelaide and Anne-Henriette to me now."

"Yes, Father," cried Adelaide; and there was no mistaking the adoration he saw in her eyes.

"You shall have an apartment nearer to mine," said the King. "We will rebuild a part of the *Château*. It will mean destroying the Ambassador's staircase . . . but we will do it . . ."

Adelaide knelt awkwardly and embraced her father's knees.

"I will be all that you ask of me," she cried; and her eyes were gleaming with triumph; she had already forgotten the death of Anne-Henriette.

CHAPTER
SIX

Comtesse de Choiseul-Beaupré

Death seemed to be hovering over Versailles that year. The hot summer had come and the King with Madame de Pompadour was staying at his *château* of Compiègne for a spell of hunting.

One morning early the Dauphine awoke with a sense of foreboding, perhaps because it had been a restless night. Several times she had awakened to find the Dauphin muttering in his sleep; and when she had spoken to him he had answered incoherently.

Touching his forehead she had thought it to be over-hot; thus she had spent a very disturbed night; and as soon as the light was strong enough she sat up in bed and studied the sleeping Dauphin.

His face was flushed, and she had no doubt now that he had a fever. She rose, called his servants and sent for his physicians.

In a few hours, the news spread through the Palace and beyond. The Dauphin is suffering from small-pox.

83

There was scarcely a disease more dreaded — highly contagious, swift in action, it had been responsible for the end of thousands.

The Dauphine was terrified. She could not imagine her life without her husband; and she was fully aware of the danger in which he lay.

The physicians told her that she must leave the apartments. Already she may have caught the disease. She must understand that by remaining at her husband's bedside she was courting death; and even if she escaped death she might be hideously marked for the rest of her life.

She said firmly: "It is my place to be at his side. More than any other I belong here, and here I shall remain."

She would allow no one to dissuade her and, dressing herself in a simple white dress, she performed all the necessary menial and intimate duties which were required. Her lips were firmly set; she had not wept, but she constantly murmured prayers as she moved about the apartment, and again and again she said to herself: "If I do everything for him I shall save him, for I shall do these things better than any other. I must, because I love him so much." Then she began to say: "I *will* save him. He *shall* not die." And with that a great peace came to her because she believed that anyone who wanted to succeed so much and who put every effort into her task could not fail.

Again and again she was warned to leave the sickroom; again she was reminded of the horrors of the disease, of its terrifying results; and she merely smiled wanly.

"What price would be too great to pay for his recovery?" she asked.

And after that they knew it was no use trying to dissuade her.

The news was carried to Compiègne and reached the King when he had returned to the *château* after the hunt.

Louis was horrified. "I must return at once to Versailles," he declared.

The Marquise ventured: "My dearest Sire, there is great danger at Versailles."

The King answered sadly: "Madame, my son, the Dauphin, lies near to death."

The Marquise merely bowed her head. "We will prepare to leave immediately," she said.

Death! thought the King. It is like a spectre that haunts me. It hangs over my family — a grey shadow from which we cannot escape. Only in February I lost my dearest daughter; am I now to lose my son?

He was glad that he had built a road from Compiègne to Versailles. At such a time the covert looks which implied "this is the retribution" would have been intolerable. The people would attribute the illness of the Dauphin to the same Divine wrath to which they had credited the death of Anne-Henriette. No, at such a time he could not bear the sly triumph of his people.

If the Dauphin were to die, the heir to the throne would be the baby Duc de Bourgogne. And if he, Louis, himself died, there would be another boy King of France. The Dauphin must not die.

The Marquise sought to comfort him on that journey back to Versailles.

"I have heard," she said, "that a doctor named Pousse knows more about small-pox than any man living. Would Your Majesty consider sending for him? He is a *bourgeois* and will know nothing of Court manners and procedure, but since he is considered to have saved more from small-pox than any other doctor, would Your Majesty have him brought to Versailles?"

"We must seize every opportunity," agreed the King. "No matter what this man's origins are, let us send for him."

"I will order him to come without delay," said the Marquise.

Louis sat at the Dauphin's bedside. He had waved aside all those who would have reminded him of the risk he ran.

My son, he thought. My only son! I wish that we could have been better friends.

How deeply he regretted those differences which had grown up between them. He tried to remember at what stage they had begun to grow apart. He saw himself going into the royal nurseries in the days of the Dauphin's boyhood, and he remembered how the little boy would fling himself into his arms.

Then, thought the King, he loved me as he loved no other. Now he is indifferent to me as a person and even antagonistic to me as King. There must be moments when he thinks of being in my place. Does he then look forward to the day when I shall no longer be here?

How sad was life!

If only we could say to time, "Stop! Let it be thus for ever." Then he would remain young — a young husband, a young father, a young King at the sight of whom the people cried, "Long live the Well-Beloved!" Looking back he saw the road to Compiègne like a riband dividing his life, separating the first half from the second. The sowing, one might say, and the harvest.

Here at the bedside of his son he felt a great desire to be a good man, a good King, beloved of his Court and his people. But he had grown too cynical. He knew too well these moods of regret and repentance.

They passed as inevitably as time itself.

Dr Pousse swept through the Dauphin's apartments like a whirlwind. He did not ignore etiquette; he was merely unaware of its existence. He did not know the difference between a Comte and a Duc; he had no idea how deep a bow was required of him; and if he had known he would not have cared. He had one aim in life, to cure patients of the small-pox. It mattered not to him if they were heir to the lowest eating-house in the Rue des Boucheries or to the throne of France — he saw them only as patients on whom to practise his skill.

There was only one person of whom he approved among those surrounding the Dauphin. This was a quiet young woman dressed in white.

"You!" he cried, pointing at her. "You will remain in attendance on the patient. The others will do as you say."

He liked her. She worked without fuss; she would do anything that was asked of her with a quiet efficiency.

"H'm," growled Pousse, "when this young man is well again he will owe his recovery to two people: his doctor and his nurse."

When he barked orders at her she obeyed with speed. They had the utmost trust in each other, these two.

"Now child," he would say, "make sure that the patient rests. Nobody is to disturb him, you understand. Not even his papa."

"I understand," was the answer.

Pousse patted her arm affectionately. "A good nurse is a great help to a doctor, child," he said.

The Dauphin's condition was giving the utmost anxiety, and the King came to the sickroom to sit at his son's bedside.

Pousse approached Louis and, taking hold of a button of his coat, drew him to one side.

The few attendants who had accompanied the King to the sickroom stopped to stare at this unheard-of familiarity, and Pousse was aware of their surprise.

He smiled grimly and allowed his attention to stray temporarily from his patient as he spoke to the King.

"Now, Monsieur," he said, "I do not know how you expect me to address you. To me you are simply the good papa of my patient. You are anxious because your son is very ill. But cheer up, Papa! Your boy is going to be well soon."

Louis laid his hands on the doctor's shoulders and said emotionally: "I know we can trust you. You respect no persons — only the small-pox."

"I have a great respect for my old enemy," said Pousse, his eyes twinkling. "But I have him beaten. I and the nurse have got the better of him this time."

"His nurse," said the King, "is the Dauphine."

"The patient's wife, eh?" said Pousse; and a slight grin formed on his lips. "I have no doubt that I have not addressed her as a lady in her position expects to be addressed. But Papa, I have a fondness for my little nurse that I could have for no grand lady. I shall send the noble Parisiennes to her when their husbands are sick, that they may learn what is expected of them. She is a good girl. And I am shocking you, Monsieur, by my lack of respect for the members of your family."

"Save the Dauphin," said the King, "and you will be my friend for life."

There was great rejoicing throughout the Court, for the Dauphin had recovered. This was due, it was said, to the skill of Dr Pousse and the unselfish devotion of the Dauphine.

No one could have been more delighted than the Dauphine. She felt that this illness of her husband had bound them closer than ever; she rejoiced because, since she must always be a little jealous of her predecessor, she could say to herself: Marie-Thérèse-Raphaëlle never nursed him through small-pox at a risk to her own life. Now she had an advantage over that first wife who had commanded the young affections of the Dauphin and had died at the height of his passion after only two years of marriage, so that she was engraved for ever on his memory — perennially young, beautified by distance, an ideal.

As for Dr Pousse, he received a life pension for his services.

The Marquise de Pompadour added her congratulations to those of the Court, but these were received coldly by the Dauphin and, because she deplored his determination to regard her in the light of an enemy, she decided that she would be more ostentatious than any in the general rejoicing.

So she planned a *fête* at Bellevue.

The entertainment was to be more lavish than anything hitherto achieved. Fireworks were always popular and could be very effective; the Marquise planned a lavish display with a pageant to symbolise the Dauphin's recovery.

There was to be a Dolphin (the Dauphin) among sea-serpents and other monsters of the deep, which were to breathe fire over the Dolphin. The fire, explained the Marquise, was to represent the small-pox. Apollo would appear to smite the fire-breathing monsters, and the Dolphin would then be seen among charming nymphs.

The Dauphin had lost none of his dislike for the Marquise during his illness; indeed he had emerged from his ordeal even more puritanical. He was not to be wooed by such pageants. However he could not refuse the invitation to Bellevue and, while the pageant given in his honour was in progress, he sat, watching it, surrounded by his friends.

90

"The Dolphin bears some resemblance to yourself," said those companions, who greatly feared a friendship between the King's son and the King's mistress, "but how hideous the creature is! It is a caricature, meant to bring ridicule on Your Highness."

"Look at the sea-monsters! They breathe fire. They are meant to represent the people. This is monstrous. The people love the Dauphin. Madame Catin will never persuade the Court otherwise, however much she tries."

"Depend upon it the lady is trying to make the Dauphin look a fool while she pretends to honour him. This is a trick worthy of her."

The Dauphin listening allowed himself to grow more and more furious with the Marquise.

When the pageant was over he abruptly left Bellevue for Versailles, and everyone knew that this attempt of the Pompadour to placate the Dauphin had been a miserable failure, because the Dauphin was determined not to be placated, and was going to carry on the war against the Marquise until his or her death or her dismissal from Court.

All waited for the retaliation to what he chose to consider as an insult to his dignity.

It came a few days after the *fête* at Bellevue, when the Marquise, attending a reception in the Dauphin's apartments, was kept standing — for she could not sit without the Dauphin's permission — for two hours.

Never before this had the Marquise allowed the Court to observe her physical weakness. This time it was impossible to do otherwise. She was almost fainting with fatigue at the end of two hours.

The King was annoyed when he heard what had happened, for he knew that, in arranging the *fête*, the Marquise had had no thought but to win the Dauphin's friendship. That burst of affection, which he had felt for his son when he had thought he was dying, was petering out. He felt irritated with the self-righteous attitude of his son towards his father's mistress.

There was only one way of preventing the repetition of such an occurrence. That would be to bestow the highest honour at Court upon the Marquise — the *tabouret* — which would enable her to sit in the presence of royalty.

The King hesitated. To bestow such a high honour on the Marquise would cause a rumble of discontent through the Court. He was unpopular in Paris; he did not wish that unpopularity to extend to his immediate circle.

A *tabouret* for the Marquise! He must brood for some time on such a matter for, dear as she was, he must remind himself of her origins.

There must be an official celebration of the Dauphin's recovery, which would necessitate another journey into Paris.

There would be the ceremonial drive from the *château* into the city, and the thanksgiving service at Notre Dame. The King's ministers, knowing the trend of opinion in Paris and the fast continued growth of the King's unpopularity, hastily reduced the price of bread, hoping that by so doing they could ensure a loyal greeting from the Parisians.

Louis set out without any enthusiasm for the journey. Heartily he wished that he was taking the road to Compiègne instead of the one through Paris.

The Queen in her carriage came behind him. She had no such fears, for she knew that the people regarded her as a poor ill-used woman, and that the more they hated the King, the greater was their sympathy for her.

A few people at the roadside shouted "*Vive le Roi!*" as the King drove by, but that happened outside the city; as soon as they entered the streets of the capital there was nothing but sullen silence.

The service over, the drive back began, and again that sullen silence was encountered. The King's carriage passed, and as the Queen's came near to the Pont-du-Jour a man with haggard face and ragged coat broke through the guards and leaped on to it.

He threw a piece of black bread into the Queen's lap and shouted: "Look, Madame! This is the sort of bread we are asked to pay three sous the pound for!"

The Queen stared at the bread on her lap while the man was dragged from the coach.

The horses were whipped up, a sullen murmur broke from the crowd. The King and the Queen heard the words: "Three sous the pound for bread we cannot eat! Bread . . . bread . . . give us bread . . ."

It seemed that there could not be a royal visit to the city these days without some such demonstration.

★ ★ ★

When the Infanta, Louis' eldest daughter, arrived at Versailles on a visit, he was delighted.

She would comfort him, he said, for the loss of his dear Anne-Henriette. Adelaide, observing the affection between them, was jealous, for since the death of her sister she had felt herself to be firm in the role of the King's favourite daughter.

It was difficult however to compete with the fascinating and worldly Infanta. Louis revived a pet name of her babyhood and referred to her as his Babette. Babette was wiser than Adelaide and immediately consolidated a friendship with the Marquise, which pleased the King.

She now had a son and daughter and was therefore to be allowed to spend a year at Versailles. "My home," she said, "for which I have never ceased to long."

In the first weeks of her return the King was so delighted with her that he forgot his depression; but once she had charmed him, Babette could not help showing that there were ulterior motives in this great show of pleasure in being with her father.

"I am your daughter," she told Louis, "your eldest daughter. And I am condemned to spend my days in that dismal hole of Parma!"

Louis promised that, if he could do anything at any time to raise her state, he would do so.

She was dissatisfied. Her ambitions were limitless. Now she had children for whom to plan, she wanted a throne for her son and nothing less than the Imperial crown for her daughter.

Young Joseph, son of Maria Theresa, was the husband she needed for her child. Imperiously she suggested that, if need be, France should go to war to bring about this marriage.

Louis might listen to his daughter's plans with an indulgent smile, but he began to grow a little restless in her company.

He was heading for one of those moods of melancholy from which it seemed only the Marquise could save him.

But many were speculating as to the change in the relationship between the King and the Marquise who, they noted, was now significantly installed in the rooms which had once belonged to Madame de Montespan; could that mean that nothing but friendship existed between her and the King?

It was said that young girls — often of the lower classes — were brought to his apartments in secret.

Could such a state of affairs go on?

Quite clearly it was time some enterprising and ambitious person brought to the notice of the King a woman who could take the all-important role of *maîtresse-en-titre* which Madame de Pompadour seemed so gracefully to have abandoned.

The Comte d'Argenson believed that he could bring about the dismissal of the Marquise, and he discussed the matter with his mistress, the Comtesse d'Estrades. The Comte, who was a younger brother of the Marquis d'Argenson, the diarist, was at this time Minister of War and in high favour with the King; he feared the

Marquise, and moreover, should a new mistress reign in her place, like most of those about the King he realised what great advantage could come his way if she were a protégée of his.

It was his scheming mistress who called his attention to the very pretty, frivolous and newly married Comtesse de Choiseul-Beaupré.

The Comtesse d'Estrades called on the young lady to discover whether she would be amenable, and the two ladies began by discussing the Marquise.

"It seems," said Madame d'Estrades, "that the woman grows older as one watches her."

"Indeed!" cried Madame de Choiseul-Beaupré. "She must be quite ancient. What the King finds to admire in her it is beyond my wits to discover."

"The King," her companion added, "is a man of habit. So long has he been making his way to the woman's apartments that it has become a ritual. Someone should break him of an unnecessary habit."

"Is it true," asked the young woman, "that he no longer sleeps with her?"

"That is said to be the case."

"If His Majesty fell in love with someone else she would doubtless be dismissed."

"There is a great opportunity for some clever woman."

The Comtesse d'Estrades eyed her companion speculatively. The shaft had struck home. Madame de Choiseul-Beaupré was twittering with excitement.

The King's mistress! Someone like Madame de Montespan. What glory had come to *her*! It was true though that she had been displaced eventually by Madame de Maintenon, who had even *married* Louis Quatorze.

But Louis Quinze had a wife; still perhaps the Queen would die. Madame Anne-Henriette had died, and the Dauphin had recently come very near to death.

The young Comtesse felt almost giddy, contemplating the power which had come to the Nesle sisters. Only Madame de Mailly had suffered; the other two had died, but the King had doted on them even as he had doted on Madame de Pompadour.

"How . . . would it be possible?" she asked.

"If a young lady were pretty enough, charming enough, amusing enough and eager enough . . . there would be many to help her. Perhaps Son Excellence himself. I can vouch for Monsieur d'Argenson. They discuss the charms of women with the King. They would whet his curiosity and then . . . a little supper party. After that it would rest with the lady herself. The King is affectionate, courteous, helpful . . . and you must admit, extremely handsome."

"I do admit that," said the young Comtesse clasping her hands together and looking into a future which seemed to her glorious.

Louis was interested in the accounts he heard of the pretty young Comtesse.

He had been told that she was deeply in love with him and that her greatest wish was to have an opportunity of proving to him the depth of her affection.

Louis was bored. He needed a diversion and, since the Comtesse so earnestly desired an interview, he declared it would be churlish to deny it.

The interview was arranged and was very successful. The King found the Comtesse not only charming but a passionate companion. Clearly one such interview could not satisfy him.

The young girls who had been brought to him were amusing for a very short time. For intellectual companionship he relied on the Marquise. He now felt how charming it was to combine lust with Court manners; the Comtesse had come at the right time to supply a needed change.

The news of the King's latest love affair was not yet spread about the Court. The power of the Marquise was great and it was very necessary that she should remain in ignorance of what was happening until the time when the Comtesse could demand her dismissal.

D'Argenson and his friends chuckled together, dreaming of the day when the Marquise would receive her *lettre de cachet*.

Quesnay, the doctor who had worked for Madame de Pompadour and had often attended the King, was also a friend of d'Argenson and Madame d'Estrades.

When he heard of the plot to destroy Madame de Pompadour he was deeply distressed.

"Have no fear," d'Argenson told him. "It shall make no difference to you. You shall not lose your place."

The doctor shook his head. "I have worked for Madame de Pompadour in her time of prosperity," he answered gravely. "If she is dismissed from Court I shall go with her that I may work for her in her adversity."

Such loyalty filled the plotters with dismay.

It was very necessary, they decided, that Madame de Pompadour should be quickly vanquished while the passion of the King for the Comtesse de Choiseul-Beaupré was at its height.

At the same time they bore in mind the need to act with the utmost caution.

Madame de Choiseul-Beaupré herself believed she knew how to bring this about. Her husband's cousin, the Comte de Stainville, had recently come to Court.

"He is the cleverest man I know," she declared. "He hates the Pompadour. He will tell me what I ought to do."

The Comte de Stainville was a young man with a face somewhat resembling that of a pug-dog; but his appearance was all that was unattractive about him. Brilliant, witty, charming and belonging to one of the noblest families in Lorraine, he seemed made for distinction. He was a patron of the arts, entertained lavishly, gambled excessively — and was, undoubtedly one who was certain to make his way at Court.

When he was very young he had rarely been seen at Versailles. He had belonged to the Army and had had a great love for Paris itself, and thus had not often visited Versailles.

He seemed suddenly to have come to the conclusion that his talents were more suited to a political life than a military one, although at the time of the Peace he had become a Lieutenant-General.

Like many an ambitious man he had cast a wary eye on the Marquise, and he had decided that he could climb to power more easily if she were not continually at the King's elbow advising him what to do.

He enjoyed writing verses, and what more natural than that these verses should be concerned with Madame de Pompadour.

He was very interested therefore when his cousin's wife asked if she could see him very privately because she had something of the utmost secrecy and importance to convey to him and was eager for his advice.

He granted her an interview. He thought her physically attractive and mentally repulsive.

"Well, my child," he said, "what is this secret matter?"

"I am loved by the King," she said.

He raised his eyebrows and smiled at her cynically.

"You do not believe me, I see," she said. "The King tells me he loves me. Madame de Pompadour is going to be dismissed from Court. I shall ask it, and the King has already said that he can deny me nothing."

He continued to study her in silence, and she stamped her foot impatiently. "So you still do not believe me. Look at this. It is a note from the King which le Bel brought me today. Read that and then say whether you believe me."

The Comte de Stainville took the letter and languidly read it.

The King was certainly enamoured of the woman, to write to her so indiscreetly, and there was no doubt that the letter was from the King. What a situation! Poor Madame de Pompadour, her days were certainly numbered.

So this woman, who had managed to arouse such passion in the King, was going to demand the dismissal of the Marquise as the price of further favours. It had been done before. Madame de Châteauroux had caused good Madame de Mailly to be dismissed.

"I want you to help me, cousin," she was saying. "I am going to answer this letter. And I want to make my intentions clear. The Pompadour has become a habit and . . . I dare say one should be careful how one asks a man of habits, like the King, to rid himself of the creature."

"One would need to be very careful," said the Comte.

"You are clever with words. You would know how to express what I want to say."

"I have an idea," said the Comte. "Leave this letter with me and I will compose a reply for you. The reply should not be delivered immediately. His Majesty must not think that you are too eager."

She nodded. "And you will do this for me?"

"Certainly I will, little cousin. You may safely leave this matter in my hands."

She nodded briskly. She had no doubt that her future would be brilliant, with men such as Monsieur d'Argenson and her kinsman Stainville to guide her. All she had to do was smile and be pleasant, accept homage and jewels, grant favours; and these brilliant men would look after all else.

The Comte de Stainville read and re-read the letter. He was very thoughtful.

His cousin had married an extremely pretty woman but an excessively foolish one.

Poor little Comtesse! She had reached the King's bed, but how long would she hold her place in it? One week? Give her two. Perhaps, with great good fortune, three.

Could she achieve the dismissal of Madame de Pompadour in such a short time? Perhaps. The King's passion was intense, even though, Stainville was sure, with such a partner it must be brief.

He would be short-sighted indeed to entangle himself with such a fool as his silly little kinswoman. Alliance with the Marquise would be a very different matter. She might be past her first youth, but she was still a very beautiful woman; as for diplomacy and sound good sense, knowledge of the world, intelligence — the Comtesse was a fool to imagine she could compete in those fields. When he considered the Marquise he wondered whether every woman at Court would not be foolish to compete with her.

She was passing through what could be the most difficult stage of her career. She had become the King's friend and had abandoned the role of mistress. That was a very bold and dangerous step to have taken — though a necessary one, he could well believe — and a woman would need a great deal of courage to take it.

But added to her other qualities the Marquise was possessed of great courage.

He made up his mind.

He sent a messenger to the apartments of Madame de Pompadour asking if she would see him immediately on a matter of great importance.

Madame de Pompadour coolly surveyed the Comte de Stainville.

She knew that he was the author of damaging verses, and she believed him to be her enemy. She gave no sign of this, but received him with the utmost graciousness. He admired her more than ever and congratulated himself on his astuteness in taking the line he had decided upon.

"Madame," he said, "knowledge has come to me which could deeply concern your welfare."

"Yes, Monsieur le Comte?"

"It is a letter, in the King's handwriting, to . . . a certain lady."

"You wish to show me this letter?"

"I do not carry it with me. I felt it to be too important a document."

"Why . . . do you tell me of this?"

"Because I felt it was a matter on which you should be informed."

"I should understand better if you showed me the letter."

"I may find it in my power to do so."

"You are . . . asking some . . . reward for this document?"

"Madame," he said, "it would be enough reward for me if I might consider you my friend."

"Have your sentiments towards me changed then, Monsieur le Comte? Oh, forgive me. Am I too blunt? You see, this information you offer me . . . it seems so unaccountable, coming whence it does."

"I understand," he told her. "There have been differences between us in the past. But it has occurred to me that, in the future, these differences might be smoothed away."

"I am delighted to hear you say this. I have no wish to be your enemy, Monsieur de Stainville."

"Perhaps we may be friends. Perhaps we may work together. You, Madame — if you will forgive my impertinence in expressing myself so freely — are an extremely intelligent woman. I believe I myself am not without that valuable asset. We are alike in our ambition, which is to serve His Majesty with zeal and prevent his falling a prey to . . . worthless people."

"I see, Monsieur de Stainville, that we are indeed of one mind."

"I am deeply grateful for this interview, Madame. Perhaps I may be allowed to see you tomorrow, when we may discuss this matter further."

She bowed her head in assent, although he was aware of a fierce curiosity within her to understand more of what he was hinting.

He had frightened her. That was what he wanted. She must be made to realise the significance of this matter. He wanted her to remember in the future what he had done for her. To have produced the letter immediately would have made the affair of less importance. Let her spend hours of uncertainty. Let her doubt his motives. When she realised that he was truly eager to set himself on her side, she would be all the more appreciative.

It was three days later when he gave her the letter which the King had written to the Comtesse de Choiseul-Beaupré. By that time she was in a state of nervous exhaustion, for all that Stainville had told her confirmed her suspicion that the King was enamoured of a woman of the Court, and that this woman and her enemies were working for her own dismissal.

With the letter in her hands she was exultant. She knew now how to act.

She went immediately to the King's apartment.

"How are you, my dear?" he asked. "You look strange. Has something upset you?"

"This," she said, "has been shown to me."

Louis read it and flushed angrily, immediately presuming that the Comtesse de Choiseul-Beaupré, boasting of her conquest, had shown his letter to Madame de Pompadour.

The Marquise said slowly: "I recall the Comtesse de Choiseul-Beaupré — an extremely handsome creature, but clearly frivolous and not to be trusted."

"As usual you are right," said the King. He put the letter into a drawer. She knew that he would choose an opportunity to destroy it.

"I trust," said the Marquise gently, "that you will not be too angry with the Comtesse. She is young and foolish."

105

"My dear, I fear *I* have been made to appear the foolish one."

"If that were possible it would be . . . quite unpardonable. You know, my dear Sire, that you may trust my discretion in all things."

"I do, I do!" cried Louis. "There are times when I believe you are the only person in the Court of whom I could say that."

He went to a desk and began to write. She looked over his shoulder as he did so.

It was an order to Madame de Choiseul-Beaupré instructing her to leave Fontainebleau before the next morning.

He would not see her again.

The Marquise smiled serenely. But she was fully aware that she had emerged from a very dangerous situation. Oddly enough she had that strange Comte de Stainville to thank for it. She would not forget what he had done. He was a brilliant man, and she would see that he received his dues. Moreover it was comforting to know that she had, as a friend, one who might prove to be a brilliant statesman.

She did spare a little pity for Madame de Choiseul-Beaupré; but not very much. The silly little creature would never have been able to hold her position at Versailles. Little idiot! Did she not realise all the anxiety and exhaustion which went into maintaining the role of King's mistress?

She was more sorry for her when she heard that she was already pregnant. The Comtesse was not allowed to see the King again; her glory had been very brief, as her life was to be. She died nine months later in childbirth.

The King felt he must make amends for the pain he had caused his dear friend by the affair of the Comtesse de Choiseul-Beaupré. Recently the Dauphin had required the Marquise to stand for two hours at a reception. Louis made up his mind that Madame de Pompadour should never again suffer such discomfort and indignity.

To the delight of her friends and the consternation of her enemies, Louis declared his intention of bestowing on Madame de Pompadour the *tabouret*.

Now she had the right to sit at the *Grand Couvert* and any Court ceremony; she was to have the privileges of a Duchesse and to be known as the Dame, Duchesse, Marquise de Pompadour. Never before had such an honour been accorded to one who was not of the nobility.

The delighted Marquise immediately ordered that her ducal coronet should be displayed on all possible occasions.

D'Argenson and his mistress, Madame d'Estrades, were apprehensive, and terrified lest the part they had played in the *affaire* Choiseul-Beaupré should be discovered by the Marquise.

No one however was more furious than the Dauphin, who had the temerity to reproach his father.

"Never, never," he cried passionately, "has such a low-born person been so elevated."

"That may be the reason," retorted the King coldly, "why we have so many dullards at Court."

"I shall refuse to speak to the woman — Duchesse though she may be."

The King shook his head sadly. "You should pray," he told his son, "that I may live for a long time. You have so much to learn before you could be King of France."

With that he dismissed his son, but the coldness continued between them. It had never been so marked, and everyone at Court was aware that the rift had been widened; they wondered whether it would ever be bridged while Madame de Pompadour remained at Court.

The Marquise herself was enjoying a new vitality. She had come through a battle with great honours; yet she did not forget that, had her enemies been more subtle, she might so easily have lost it.

She believed now that she could measure the King's affection for her. This affair had taught him a great deal. He would not again think of lightly abandoning her in favour of a pretty woman. He had learned that he could trust the Marquise as he could few others. They had passed into a new phase of their relationship.

The Marquise did not forget the man who had been of infinite help to her. She was ready now to cultivate the astute Comte de Stainville. Some service should be done for him; and she looked forward to a time when she and this man, who her intuition and experience told her would be a worthy ally, should be working together to their mutual advantage.

CHAPTER
SEVEN

La Petite Morphise

There were riots all over Paris. On this occasion it was not poverty which had aroused the wrath of the people.

Bouettin, the curé of Saint-Etienne-du-Mont, had been asked to administer the last sacrament to Abbé Le Mère who was a Jansenite priest. Bouettin declared that Le Mère had opposed the Bull Unigenitus and for this reason he refused him the last sacrament.

To deny the last sacrament to a dying man seemed, to those people who did not hold Ultramontane views, an act of callous criminality and, when the Abbé was buried, ten thousand people followed him to his grave.

Protests were made to the Archbishop of Paris, Christophe de Beaumont, whose reply was that those who did not accept the Bull Unigenitus were in his view heretics and therefore not entitled to the sacrament.

The protagonists were clearly determined to make an issue of this case. Even before the Abbé had died the magistrates had called on the King at Versailles and had extracted his promise that the Abbé should receive the sacrament.

Since Bouettin, under the protection of the Archbishop, refused to administer the sacrament, the *Parlement* decided that their authority would be flouted if they did not protest; but as the Archbishop was too important a man to be attacked, they contented themselves with issuing a warrant for the arrest of Bouettin.

Louis realising that, in issuing such a warrant without his consent, the *Parlement* was flouting his authority, quashed the warrant.

Thus the *Parlement* was brought into conflict with the King, and dissension spread from Paris to the provinces.

The President of the *Parlement* called on the King to warn him and to remind him of what could happen to kings who set themselves against their parliaments.

The name of Charles I of England was not mentioned, but the case of the King who had quarrelled with his Parliament and lost his head as a consequence was in everyone's mind.

Louis' answer was that it was the duty of the *Parlement* to acquaint him with acts of dissension, but for him to judge them.

By this attitude he had won the approval of neither side. The *Parlement* considered that the King was obstructing it in its duties; the Ultramontane clergy knew that the King was not with them, and that they must rely for their support on the Queen, who was powerless, and the Dauphin, from whom they hoped a great deal.

The *Parlement* pointed out that since Louis had ascended the throne forty-two thousand *lettres de cachet* had been received by people who would not agree to the Bull Unigenitus.

Louis grew tired of the wrangle and sought to divert himself by increasing his pleasures. Meanwhile all over the country there were quarrels between those who accepted the Bull and those who did not. It was not safe for priests to walk in the streets, as the very sight of priestly garments was enough to inflame a certain section of the people.

The riots continued. The Dauphin watched the progress of events with eagerness.

The King protested that he was weary of such dissensions.

"Let me hear no more of this matter of administering the sacraments," he pleaded.

To escape from the controversy all about him the King paid a visit to the artist, François Boucher, whose work he greatly admired and whom he had employed to decorate walls and ceilings of certain of his *châteaux*.

He insisted that Boucher take him to his *atelier* that he might see his latest work, and while he was there his eyes fell on a portrait of a child. She was in her very early teens, and Louis paused before the portrait in admiration.

"That," he said, "is not a true picture of the model. You have idealised that creature. No one could be so perfectly beautiful."

111

The artist was about to protest but he hesitated, and the King saw a wary look come into his eyes.

"You are right, Sire," he said. "It is an idealised portrait."

"Yet," said Louis, "so lifelike that, if such a perfect child existed, one could imagine her stepping out of the picture."

"Your Majesty is gracious to commend my work. Allow me to present you with this picture."

The King laid his hand on the artist's arm. "No, my friend," he said. "I read your thoughts. It would grieve you greatly to part with that picture. It would be like losing a friend."

"Your Majesty is mistaken . . ."

The King raised his eyebrows in surprise; it was necessary to accept blunt words from these artists who did not understand that in the etiquette of Versailles it was impossible for a humble workman to tell the King he was wrong.

Boucher stumbled on: "Nothing would give me greater pleasure than for Your Majesty to accept the picture."

The King shook his head. "So there was no model," he said. "That perfect child never existed outside the artist's imagination. It is a sad thought, Monsieur Boucher."

"Very sad, Your Majesty."

The King was smiling when he left the *atelier*.

When Louis returned to Versailles he summoned his *valet de chambre* Le Bel.

Le Bel had become one of his most valued servants, and this was due to the peculiar duties which he performed with astonishing skill.

Since he had been introduced to a serving-girl in the apartments of Madame de Pompadour, Louis had found such types greatly to his taste. It was stimulating to cast off all need for *finesse*, to escape from the etiquette of the Court which insinuated itself even into the bedchamber. With young working-girls etiquette was ignored simply because they were unaware of its existences.

Le Bel had made it his cherished duty to find such girls who could administer to the King's pleasure. He was indefatigable; he would discover them in market or shop, tempt them with such a fortune to be earned in a few days as would not have been theirs after years of hard work and parsimonious living. In almost every case Le Bel's propositions were irresistible; and thus a stream of little *grisettes* found their way up the private staircase to those very secret rooms in the north wing of the Palace, which to the knowledgeable had become known as *le trébuchet*.

Here in this "snare for birds" Louis received these young girls, who pleased him for as long as they could and then were dismissed with a present which made them a very suitable *partie*, and so would ensure a life of comparative comfort.

"Le Bel," said Louis, "I want you to find for me a certain dark-eyed girl. She cannot be more than fourteen, I'll swear."

"Her name, Sire?"

"That I cannot tell you, for I do not know it. The only clue I can give you is that there is a painting of her in Boucher's *atelier*. I have a suspicion that you may find her there hidden away somewhere. Boucher prefers to show his canvases rather than his little mistress — and it does not surprise me."

Le Bel was delighted. Such a quest was what he enjoyed.

"Sire," he said, "I can assure Your Majesty that it will not be long before Boucher's goddess steps from her canvas into your arms."

"I am glad to hear you say that," said Louis. "I feel very impatient."

The next day found Le Bel drinking in Boucher's studio.

He greatly admired the painter's work, he said, and he wondered if he might take a closer look at some of the pictures.

It was easy, with a little flattery, to win the artist's confidence; and Le Bel was astonished and delighted when a young girl came into the *atelier* to serve them with wine.

Le Bel, connoisseur as he was, thought he had never seen such a beautiful child. Enormous dark eyes sparkled in her oval face, and her heavy bluish-black hair was caught back with a red riband.

She was clearly delighted to be working for François Boucher.

When she had left them Le Bel said: "Now that is a pretty creature."

"Pretty!" cried Boucher indignantly. "Louise is beautiful."

"I see you have painted her. It is certainly an arresting picture."

"Yet," said Boucher, "even I cannot do justice to Louise's beauty. I have painted her over and over again in an endeavour to satisfy myself."

"You are fortunate to have such a model. She seems a good and docile girl, too."

Boucher nodded. "Poor Louise, life is not easy for such as she is. She thinks this place luxurious after the home she comes from."

"Was it so bad then?"

"Bad, my dear sir? When I tell you that her rapacious old mother has sold — yes literally sold — her sisters, you will know what I mean. My beautiful Louise was brought up in a second-hand clothes shop not far from the Palais Royal. Madame O'Murphy could not sell her old clothes dearly enough, so she sold her daughters as well."

"O'Murphy. It is a strange name."

"The father was an Irishman. He was a soldier at one time, and a man of low character. They put Louise with Madame Fleuret when she was twelve. She is only fourteen now."

"Madame Fleuret. Is she the dressmaker?"

"She carries on a profitable business under the guise of dressmaking. Her place is nothing less than a brothel. And so, to her, for a consideration, the old-clothes-woman sent her all her daughters. I

115

discovered Louise there. I brought her away with me. I can tell you she was delighted to come."

"I can well imagine it."

Louise came into the room again. Le Bel, watching her, knew that she was aware of his eyes upon her.

Le Bel said: "Ah, what a relief it is to relax in an artist's *atelier* after all the etiquette of Versailles."

She was an intelligent creature. She had pricked up her ears. She was ready to be interested in the man who lived at Versailles, the great Palace which would seem fabulous to such as she was.

"Fill Monsieur Le Bel's glass, Louise," said Boucher.

"Thank you, my dear," said Le Bel. His eyes held those of the girl; they were warm and full of admiration.

Le Bel rose to go in due course and when he descended the stairs to the street he did not immediately leave the neighbourhood. He believed that she would understand he wanted to speak to her privately and would find some excuse for leaving the house shortly after he did.

He was right.

He had only to wait five minutes when, a shawl over her blue-black hair, Louise came into the street.

"Mademoiselle O'Murphy?" called Le Bel.

"Why!" she cried, feigning surprise in such a way that it amused him. She had a certain sense of humour, this girl. Daughter of an old-clothes-woman she might be, but it was possible that she possessed a certain wit as well as astounding beauty. "It is Monsieur Le Bel of Versailles."

"I have waited to see you, Mademoiselle. I have something to say to you."

"Could you not have said it in Monsieur Boucher's *atelier*?"

"No, I could not have said it there. You are very beautiful. You must know this."

"I have heard it said that that is so," she answered pertly yet gravely.

"I could make your fortune."

"Many have offered me fortunes."

"I could offer you one more glowing than any you have yet been offered. I could take you to Versailles."

She mocked him in the *argot* of the streets. "I know, Monsieur Le Bel. You are the King in disguise."

"You could be nearer the truth than you think."

Her smile was mocking, yet he could see that she was alert.

"Listen to me," he said. "I will bring a carriage to the end of the street this time tomorrow. Be there. I will take you to Versailles . . . and fortune."

"How do I know that you can do this, or will?"

He took a ring from his finger. "See this. It is a diamond. It is worth more than you could possess if you spent the rest of your life in Monsieur Boucher's attic. I will lend it to you until you have so many jewels that this will seem a worthless bauble."

She took the ring. Its sparkle fascinated her. But she was no fool; she had all the cunning of the streets in her, Le Bel guessed that if she had helped her mother in the old days she would have struck a hard bargain in the Monday market on the Place de Grève.

He knew that tomorrow she would have the ring tested, and when she discovered its value she would be waiting to step into the carriage he would have brought for her.

He was right.

She was there, the shawl over her magnificent hair.

Le Bel smiled at her delightedly. He greatly enjoyed such commissions. They delighted Louis and they were extremely profitable to himself. People were beginning to say that Le Bel was one of the King's most valued friends.

As he took the girl's arm and helped her into the carriage he wondered whether to warn her that the person to whom he was taking her was of very high nobility. Perhaps that would not be wise. Louis particularly enjoyed the outrageous remarks and behaviour of the little girls who were brought to *le trébuchet*. Indeed there were occasions when he himself would make use of a phrase which was indigenous to the St Antoine district and afforded him great amusement because it could never have been heard before in the royal apartments at Versailles.

Le Bel smiled at her, well pleased. She would be a success, he was sure. She was almost unbelievably beautiful and by no means shy. She would be impressed by the grandeur even of the secret apartments, yet not overawed.

"I must tell you," he said, "that I am presenting you to a nobleman who has heard of your attractions."

She nodded. He noticed that she was twirling the ring round and round on her finger.

Certainly the King was going to be very grateful for his adroitness in the case of Mademoiselle O'Murphy.

They left the carriage and entered the Palace by the door which led to the private staircase. If any noticed them they were wise enough to make no comment. Le Bel, hurrying into the Palace with a muffled figure, was not such an unusual sight.

The King was waiting for them in the small apartment under the roof of the Palace, where a table was laid for two. Louise O'Murphy had never seen anything so luxurious. But her attention was all for the nobleman, who believed himself to be sombrely clad but to her seemed magnificent.

He was the most handsome man she had ever seen, although he seemed old in her fourteen-year-old eyes. She was fascinated by his movements, and his voice was the most musical she had ever heard.

He took the shawl from her and threw it to Le Bel who caught it and stood as though waiting.

"Thank you, my friend," said the King. "Mademoiselle and I are grateful to you. Goodnight."

Le Bel retired, grimacing at the shawl in his hands.

The King meanwhile drew Louise towards the table.

"You are even more beautiful than I believed possible," he told her. "Your picture does not do you justice after all."

Louise laughed suddenly — rather harsh laughter it was — and said: "Yours does not do you justice either."

Louis looked surprised but very interested.

"You know who I am then?"

She nodded. "Your picture is on all the coins," she told him.

CHAPTER
EIGHT

Unigenitus

While the King sought to forget the controversy over the Bull Unigenitus in the company of Mademoiselle O'Murphy, the *Parlement* was not idle. Its President sought an interview with Louis and warned him that there was the utmost danger in the present state of unrest.

"Sire," he said, "schisms such as this one need small forces to dethrone great Kings, whereas great armies are necessary to defend them."

"I am weary of this matter," said Louis.

"Sire," was the answer, "you cannot afford to be weary."

Still the King declined to take any action, while the supporters of the Bull continued to refuse the sacrament to the Jansenites, and the Jansenites continued to protest.

Many of the King's ministers felt sure that from such a situation revolution could grow. They impressed this fear upon the King who at length decided to act. He was firmly convinced that the power of the State was invested in the crown, and determined therefore to deal with the matter in accordance with his own views.

Rarely had he acted so energetically. On a certain May evening he had *lettres de cachet* delivered by his musketeers to the members of the *Parlement*, ordering them to leave Paris immediately for certain places which had been assigned to them.

The members of the Grande Chambre were not included in the list of exiles but decided that they would follow the *Parlement* into retirement as a protest to the King. They reassembled at Pontoise.

From Pontoise the Grande Chambre made itself heard. The *Grandes Remonstrances* were drawn up and published. Farsighted men read them and gravely shook their heads. It was as though the shadow of revolution had appeared on the horizon.

The gist of the *Remonstrances* was that if his subjects must obey the King, the King must obey the law. They would not allow a schism to triumph which could not only strike a blow at religion but at the sovereignty of the State. They were resolved to remain faithful to the State and the King, even if they suffered through such fidelity.

The end of Charles I of England was now openly recalled and the fact emphasised that a parliament could condemn a king to the scaffold. The King was being weighed against the State, and the people of France were beginning to tell each other that nations came before Kings.

It was the hot breath of revolution. Nation above the ruler; Church above the Pope. That was the propaganda which was spreading throughout the country.

Tension was particularly high in Paris. One careless step now, and up would go the barricades and the revolution would begin.

The Marquise was earnestly watching the conflict. Her health had improved considerably lately, and she congratulated herself on the step she had taken. Now she was able to rest each night, knowing that the King was safe with some little working-girl who probably lacked the education to write her own name.

The latest, Louise O'Murphy, to whom he had been faithful for many months, was a typical example. The girl must be unusual to have amused Louis all this time; she was more than pretty, being a real beauty, and her ribald wit was proving very amusing to the King.

She no longer lived in the secret apartments of the bird-snare, for Louis had installed her in a little house not far from the Palace, where she had her own servants. Thus he could call on her whenever he felt the inclination to do so, at the same time using the *trébuchet* for other little birds.

It was impossible to keep the existence of a mistress of such long-standing entirely secret, and the Court had long since begun to speculate on the "Petite Morphise", as they called her. As for Louise herself she was so delighted with life that she bubbled over with good spirits and, having her own carriage, could not resist the temptation to ride out every day, expensively clad, with jewels flashing on her person, smugly content and more strikingly beautiful than ever.

She was so pleased with her good fortune that she attended the Church of St Louis regularly to give thanks to the saints for bringing her to the King's notice.

She had recently borne a child and was overjoyed by this event.

The Marquise was delighted with the Petite Morphise, who was clever enough to know that she could never aspire to the position of *maîtresse-en-titre*, and had no wish to do so. She was completely happy as she was, and no doubt had the good sense to make provision for the days when the King's favour should not shine so continually upon her.

The Marquise could therefore look back on the dangerous step she had taken, with some complacency.

Madame du Hausset brought her news of the Petite Morphise from time to time, and she was always kept informed of the young girls whom the indefatigable Le Bel conducted to the secret apartments.

"The only danger," she had confided to Madame du Hausset, "is that a lady of the Court should take the place of these little girls."

"That," agreed Madame du Hausset, "we must indeed watch for and guard against."

"But," said the Marquise, "at the moment the King is too deeply immersed in this wretched affair of Unigenitus. He is determined to be firm though and I am sure he is right in this."

"It is dangerous, though, Madame, for a King to dismiss his *Parlement*."

"If Louis is strong he will come well out of this matter," mused the Marquise. "You know, Hausset, I have often thought that Louis needs adversity to bring out his strength. He can be wise, calm . . . he has all the qualities of kingship. The point is that he does not exert himself to use them."

She smiled tenderly.

"You are as much in love with him as you were when you first came to Versailles," Madame du Hausset told her.

"One does not fall out of love with Louis," said the Marquise. "I think, dear Hausset, that we shall, through this affair, be rid of some of our ministers, and there will be new ones to take their places. I should like to see Monsieur de Stainville holding a high post."

"He would be your friend. We could be sure of that."

"He has shown me that he is."

"And you have shown yourself his friend, Madame. What a brilliant marriage it was that you arranged for him!"

"The little Crozat girl, yes, one of the richest heiresses in France. Monsieur de Stainville is somewhat extravagant. Such a gambler! He was certainly delighted with that marriage and, although she is but twelve, she will grow up, and she adores him already, I have heard."

"Poor little thing!" murmured Madame du Hausset.

"Poor little thing to be the wife of a man who in a few years' time — I promise you this, Hausset — may well be France's most important minister!"

"I was thinking of all the mistresses he will have. I know his kind."

"She will forgive him. He has great charm. I could wish that he had not gone to Rome. It was his great desire to have had the post of Ambassador. I believe he has Vienna in mind. He is prepared to be very friendly with the Austrians. I am sure he will do well, but I should like to have had him here in Paris. One has not so many friends that one can lose them without regret."

One of the Marquise's women appeared at the door with the news that a messenger had come to see her and had stated that the matter was urgent.

"Bring this messenger to me at once," cried the Marquise and, when she saw that it was one of the nuns from the Convent of the Assumption, she felt faint with apprehension.

"Alexandrine . . ." she murmured.

"Madame, your daughter was taken ill a short while ago. We think you should come to her at once."

The Marquise stood by the bedside of her ten-year-old daughter. She did not weep. There was nothing she could do to bring her child back to life.

Alexandrine, in whom all her hopes were centred, had been the only child left to her. And there would never be another; she believed Quesnay was right when he had told her that.

The Mother Superior came to stand beside her. "Madame la Marquise," she said, "this is a great shock to you. Pray let me conduct you from this room, that you may rest awhile."

"No," said the Marquise, "leave me with her. Leave me alone with her."

When the Mother Superior and the nuns retired, the Marquise went to the bed and took the rigid little body in her arms.

Yesterday this child had been alive and well. Today she was dead. There seemed no reason for this. It was one of the cruellest blows which could have befallen her. A seemingly healthy little girl suddenly taken with convulsions, and within a few hours dead!

"Why?" demanded the Marquise. "Why should I suffer so?"

The people of Paris would say it was retribution for her sins. She had left this child's father to go to the King. Was it because of this that she had lost her son and her daughter? Would the people of Paris be right when they said — as she knew they would — that this was the punishment of a sinful woman?

"No," whispered the Marquise, putting her lips against the child's cold forehead. "There was no denying my destiny. It was my fate. It was planned when I was born. Alexandrine, my little love, it would have happened even had we been living with your father in the Hôtel des Gesvres, even if I had never gone to Versailles."

She sat by the bed, still holding the child, thinking of the future she had planned for her and how different it would be from the reality.

She would never again plan for little Alexandrine, never feel that relief because the child was not beautiful, never say, I wish her to find the peace which was denied me. There would be no future on earth for little Alexandrine.

The Marquise went to Bellevue to mourn her daughter, taking only Madame du Hausset with her. The little girl had been buried with great pomp. It was necessary that this should be so; otherwise it would be thought that the Marquise was losing her power. Deep as the present anguish might be she must constantly bear the future in mind. So the ceremony took place and was all that could be expected for the daughter of the Marquise; and now Alexandrine lay in the Church of the Capucines in the Place Vendôme.

Louis came to visit her at Bellevue.

She was touched, for she knew how he hated the thought of death and sought always to avoid unpleasantness.

"My dear, dear friend," he said, embracing her, "I have come to mitigate your sorrow."

She looked at him with tears in her eyes. "Then," she answered, "you are indeed my dear friend."

"Did you doubt it?"

"I thought that it might be too wonderful to hope that you would come to see me here."

He himself dried her tears.

"Come," he said, "let us walk in the gardens. I want to see the flowers."

So she walked with him and forced herself to think of matters other than that small figure lying in its tomb. Louis had come to her; he had offered solace in her grief; but he would not expect her to mourn long.

128

"We miss you at Versailles," he said. "Pray come back to us very soon."

It was a command. It was a necessity. If she did not continue to fight for her place she would surely lose it.

Within two weeks she came out of retirement and returned to Versailles.

Back at Court the Marquise sought desperately to forget the death of her child. She began to consider, more deeply than she had hitherto, this desperate state to which the country was being led by the conflict between Ultramontanes and Jansenites. She could see that revolution was in the air and, although it seemed impossible that these rumblings could shake the great foundations of Versailles, she believed that much which was unpleasant could ensue.

She herself was the most unpopular woman in the Kingdom, and she sought to win the regard of the people by studying affairs and wisely advising the King.

The Dauphin and his party were firmly behind the Ultramontanes; the *Parlement* were for the Jansenites; and the King seemed to be hovering uncertainly between the two — determined that France should not come under the sway of the Papacy, yet equally determined not to become a tool of the *Parlement*.

The Dauphine gave birth to another son during the hot month of August — this was the Duc de Berry — but such was the state of ferment in the country that this event seemed insignificant and the ceremonies, which heralded the birth of a possible heir to the throne, were dispensed with.

It became clear that some determined action would have to take place soon, as Christophe de Beaumont, the Archbishop of Paris, had become firmer in his resolve to suppress all those who did not support Unigenitus. He began by depriving confessors of their power if they failed zealously to carry out the instructions he had laid down. The Jesuits sent one of their number, Père Laugier, to Versailles with orders to preach against the *Parlement* in the presence of the King, and to demand its abolition. The Protestants of France foresaw a return of those conditions which had preceded the Massacre of the St Bartholomew and many Huguenots prepared to leave the country.

The conflict showed itself in several forms and, when the Opera Buffa came to Paris from Italy, quarrels broke out as to the merits of French and Italian music, which were a reflection of the great quarrel as to whether France should stand aloof from the Church of Rome or be governed by it.

The King often made his way to the apartments of Madame de Pompadour; the Petite Morphise and the visitors to the *trébuchet* could give him only very temporary relief from his anxieties; it was the company and opinion of the Marquise that he ardently sought.

When de Maupéou, the chief-President of the *Parlement*, asked for an audience the Marquise was firmly behind the King's agreement to see him and, as a result of this meeting, the *Parlement* was recalled to Paris. Louis had seen that the state of unrest could not be continued and that he would be wiser to recall his *Parlement* than to place himself firmly on the side of

130

Rome. The quarrel between King and *Parlement* was patched up, the conditions being that silence be maintained on the matter of the Bull Unigenitus and that the magistrates should deal appropriately with any who refused to keep that silence.

Thus Louis had adroitly kept his position between the two antagonists. He had recalled his Parliament to power and at the same time had made no quarrel with the clergy by renouncing the Bull.

It was a masterly stroke, and Louis was aware that his dear friend the Marquise had been instrumental in helping him make it.

With the *Parlement* recalled, the Ultramontanes were not prepared to maintain silence over the Bull, and cases of the sacrament's being refused to dying Jansenites again began to disturb the people.

Then Louis acted with strength. Christophe de Beaumont received his *lettre de cachet* which ordered his immediate retirement to his estates at Conflans.

This was one of the biggest blows yet struck at the Ultramontane party; the Dauphin was filled with rage, the Queen with sorrow. They both believed that Madame de Pompadour was responsible, and they declared that it was not even a matter of principle with her, which might have been more forgivable; the woman was merely afraid that the domination of the Church would mean her dismissal.

The Bishop of Chartres came to Versailles to protest to Louis about the exile from Paris of Christophe de Beaumont.

"Sire," he said passionately, "surely a bishop should reside in his diocese."

Louis looked at him coldly and replied: "Then I suggest you go to yours without delay."

The *Parlement* then announced that the Bull Unigenitus was not a rule of faith, and the clergy were forbidden to treat it as such.

With the Archbishop in exile and the *Parlement* in Paris the tension relaxed.

At this time Madame Adelaide had become astonishingly subdued, and her cunning Mistress of the Robes, the Comtesse d'Estrades (the woman who had failed to replace Madame de Pompadour with the Comtesse de Choiseul-Beaupré), determined to exploit this situation. Certain suspicions had been aroused and, recalling an occasion when, during a theatrical performance at Fontainebleau, Madame Adelaide had fainted, Madame d'Estrades believed she knew the reason for the change in the Princesse.

"I was overcome by the heat; it was unbearable," Madame Adelaide had moaned.

But, reasoned Madame d'Estrades, the other ladies had not been overcome by the heat.

Madame Adelaide's very full skirts could be concealing. Was it possible that the King's beloved daughter was about to bring scandal to the Court?

She was not of course the only one to notice this change in Adelaide; and when the latter left Versailles for a month or so there were many to suggest the reason.

132

"Was it not inevitable?" asked certain members of the Court. "Adelaide was adventurous; the King refused to arrange a marriage for her, and it was, if one considered all the circumstances, only to be expected. But a scandal! Particularly if . . ."

But it was unwise to continue with such a conjecture.

Others said: "They say it was the Cardinal de Soubise. He and Adelaide have become very friendly indeed."

"The Cardinal de Soubise! But that is very shocking."

"Yet not so shocking as . . ."

Eyebrows were lifted; fingers were put to lips; that was something which might be *thought*, but which it would be more than one's position — perhaps one's life — was worth to put into words.

So Adelaide returned to Court, a little less vivacious, a little cautious, not quite the hectoring princess who had amused them before.

The King's attitude appeared to have changed. It was clear that he no longer felt the same affection for her. Perhaps she herself was more unbalanced than she had been; perhaps she had ceased to be very young, and that outrageous behaviour which was amusing in a young person could become exhausting and wearying in an older one.

Louis revived old nicknames for his daughters. Adelaide was "Loque", Victoire "Coche", Sophie "Graille" and Louise-Marie "Chiffe". When they were children these unflattering names had been given affectionately; now it seemed that the affection had been withdrawn and they expressed Louis' growing contempt for his daughters.

The attitude of the King could not fail to have its effect on the Court, and many were becoming not quite so respectful to Madame Adelaide as they had once been.

The King made a habit of inviting her to play on various instruments for the amusement of himself and a few friends. Like her mother, Adelaide was no musician and, also like her mother, she believed she performed excellently.

Adelaide would sit at the instruments, playing with vigour and producing a great deal of noise, while the King applauded with apparent enthusiasm; and the more inharmonious the sounds produced, the louder was the applause. The courtiers followed the example of the King and applauded with him, while Adelaide smiled complacently, refusing to believe that she was not a great musician.

Louise-Marie implored her not to allow herself to appear so foolish, at which Adelaide tartly retorted that her sister should curb her jealousy. Whereupon Louise-Marie merely shrugged her shoulders and turned away.

This was an example of how the King's feelings had changed towards his eldest daughter; and Madame d'Estrades decided to make the most of the situation.

Her lover, the scheming Comte d'Argenson, had not given up hope of driving Madame de Pompadour from Court, and his mistress shared his determination. Adelaide seemed a good tool to be made use of.

Madame d'Estrades therefore began to feel her way in that direction. As Mistress of the Robes she had her opportunity.

One day Adelaide declared her intention of wearing one of the most costly of her dresses — a rose-coloured satin gown embroidered with stars and trimmed with gold ornaments.

The dress was not in her wardrobe.

"Then where is it?" Adelaide demanded petulantly.

"You have forgotten, Madame," said the Comtesse d'Estrades, "you gave that dress to me."

"I . . . gave it to you! But I am sure I did not."

"Oh yes, Madame." The Comtesse looked sly. "It was at that time when you were planning to leave Versailles . . . for a spell. You may have forgotten. I have not. The skirt of that gown was a little tight . . . I think."

Adelaide's eyes flashed in the old manner, but a cautious look crept into her face.

"I see," she stammered. "I . . . had forgotten."

After that clothes began to disappear from her wardrobe, and although she hated the Comtesse d'Estrades, she was afraid to dismiss her.

This state of affairs went on for some time, and Adelaide no longer appeared in the flamboyant dresses which had once delighted her. Madame de Pompadour noticed that her shoes were quite shabby and that she sometimes went without stockings.

It was not difficult for the Marquise to find out what she wanted to know. She despised Madame d'Estrades and she did not forget what part she had played in the

Choiseul-Beaupré affair. She would not wish to appear to take revenge on the woman for that, because she preferred to let the Court think that the matter was of so little importance to her that she could afford to ignore it. However she now saw a way of ridding the Court of an undoubted enemy and at the same time turning another enemy into a friend.

She asked Madame Adelaide to receive her. It was significant of the changing personality of the Princesse that she agreed to do so; and the Madame Adelaide whom the Marquise found waiting for her was a different person from the haughty, headstrong young woman of not so long ago.

The Marquise behaved as though they had been lifelong friends instead of enemies; and Adelaide, who had been reduced to a state of nervous tension by the cruel Madame d'Estrades, felt almost affectionate towards the kindly Marquise.

"Forgive my coming to you in this way," said Madame de Pompadour, "but I believe you are less happy than you used to be, and I would like to consult you about a certain evil woman in your service."

"Pray continue," said Adelaide eagerly.

"I refer to Madame d'Estrades."

Adelaide clenched her hands and seemed to hover between an outburst of fury and a collapse into tears.

"I believe her to be intriguing with her lover," went on the Marquise. "I do not think she is a woman to be trusted. But she is your Mistress of the Robes and I hesitate to use any influence to have her removed without your permission."

136

Adelaide sought to retain her dignity. "If this woman is guilty of intrigue, I should put nothing in the way of her removal."

"Then I have Your Highness' permission to proceed with my inquiries and, if I find my suspicions to be well founded, to have her removed?"

"You have my permission," said Adelaide; and her eyes were shining with joy at the prospect of being released from a position which was becoming more and more intolerable.

A few weeks later Madame d'Estrades was ordered by the King to leave Versailles for Chaillot. Her dismissal from Court was brought about with great care; for it was not forgotten that she was the mistress of the powerful Comte d'Argenson and that she was privy to secrets of Madame Adelaide's. Therefore she was given a large pension with her dismissal and she retired in some state.

Adelaide, free of her, began to recover some of her old vigour; but she could not recapture the position she had once occupied. The beauty she had once possessed had left her during the strain of the last months; she still had the power to dominate her feeble-minded sisters but no one else. Poor Loque, Coche and Graille had become figures of fun at Court. As for Chiffe, intelligent as she was, she could only inspire pity for her deformity.

The King's family no longer afforded him much pleasure. He must look elsewhere for an escape from his ever-increasing *ennui*.

CHAPTER NINE

The Repentant Marquise

The Marquise was suffering from a great deal of anxiety through aspirants to the role of *maîtresse-en-titre*.

Madame du Hausset had played a large part in preventing one young woman from attaining that position. This was the wife of a very rich financier who had, at a ball at Versailles, to which those not of the highest nobility had been invited, succeeded in catching the King's attention.

The lady wrote to the King after this encounter and received a reply; fortunately for the Marquise this reply fell into the hands of the financier who, appalled at the thought of his wife's becoming the mistress of any other man, even the King, was determined to put a stop to the affair.

He took the letter to Madame du Hausset and asked her advice. Madame du Hausset immediately showed the letter to Madame de Pompadour.

The Marquise was too wise to hurry to the King with the letter, for the case was too similar to that of

Madame de Choiseul-Beaupré. She decided to bring this matter to a close without appearing to know anything about it.

She summoned Monsieur Berryer, the Lieutenant-General of the Police, and asked him to submit the letter to Louis without telling the King whence he had received it.

Berryer, eager to please the Marquise, did so, and Louis was shocked to learn that such a private letter had, so he thought, been allowed to pass from the hands of the one for whom it had been intended, and believed that the woman had been boasting of his interest in her.

Women who were so indiscreet could never find favour with him; so that was the end of that aspirant.

The Duchesse de Narbonne-Lara, a very beautiful and undemanding young lady of the Court, had pleased him; she asked for nothing in return for her submission but very quickly became pregnant. Louis had an aversion to pregnant women unless he was deeply in love with them; and the Duchesse left Versailles for Parma where she served Louis' eldest daughter, Madame Première.

Another woman — and this one gave the Marquise far more anxiety than any other — was the Marquise de Coislin.

This was a woman of great ambition determined to receive the highest honours from the King and, knowing that she could not reach the height of her ambition while Madame de Pompadour had his confidence, her plan was to bring about the dismissal of the Marquise.

The Marquise was thrown into a panic by this woman, who did not hesitate to flaunt her success before the whole Court, and to make sly allusions during card-playing of her intentions.

But once again good luck came to the Marquise. Madame de Coislin was a vulgar woman, far too sure of herself. Her demands were outrageous and, after a few weeks of the King's favour, she was winning special honours for her family and supporters.

This meant that the Marquise was not the only member of the Court who viewed the rise to power of Madame de Coislin with alarm.

Naturally comparisons were made between Madame de Pompadour and Madame de Coislin, and the courteous manners of the former were remarked upon. Her habit of regarding everyone as her friend until they showed themselves to be her enemy was applauded, and there were many at Court who began to say: "If it is a choice of two evils, let us choose the lesser, who is Madame de Pompadour."

All letters which passed through the post were submitted to censorship, and the King could read any that he wished. Thus one written by a member of the *Parlement* to a friend fell into his hands. In this letter the writer had discussed the new mistress at some length and compared her with Madame de Pompadour. He pointed out that no one expected the King to be without a mistress as most Frenchmen felt they had a right to indulge themselves in that way; but the King

would be ill-advised to leave the one he already had —
who was a kindly woman already rich — for one who
was far from kindly and had her fortune to make. Such
a woman, went on the writer, could in time rule the
King and so would bring him once more into bitter
conflict with his ministers.

When Louis read this letter he was deeply impressed.
He recalled the years of his affectionate relationship
with Madame de Pompadour. The Comtesse de Coislin
was attractive enough, but she was demanding; and he
could not really like anyone who so blatantly showed
herself to be the enemy of his dear friend the Marquise.

Very shortly after that letter fell into his hands,
Madame de Coislin was no longer to be seen at
Versailles.

But such alarms were very distressing to the
Marquise. Her little plan for bringing working-girls to
the King's notice, while being moderately successful,
was not entirely so. Perhaps it was because she had not
given sufficient thought to this matter and had left it
too much in the hands of Le Bel.

Louis was insatiable. She must remember that. He
could tackle his little *grisettes* in the *trébuchet* and any
Court lady who might win his favour.

She must give the matter the attention it demanded.

La Petite Morphise had at last lost her hold on the
King's attentions and Louis had found a husband for
her in the Sieur Beaufranchet. Little Louise O'Murphy
had come a long way from her mother's old-clothes
shop, and there were many girls in hungry Paris who

remembered her childhood there and the destiny which would have been hers had she not been so fortunate as to win the King's affection.

There were mothers who said to themselves, what happened to young Louise O'Murphy could happen to my Jeanne, my Marie, my Louise.

Le trébuchet in the attics of Versailles was no longer a secret place. The snared birds were apt to sing rather noisily, and it could not be expected that such young songsters would remain subdued. Madame Adelaide's apartments were near those of the King. Often the high spirits of the girls brought them to her notice.

It was well known in the Palace that the *trébuchet* existed, but the etiquette of Versailles demanded that its existence be ignored. Yet it was not easy to ignore something which forced itself upon the attention.

The Marquise called Le Bel to her one day to discuss this matter.

"There is too much noise coming from those apartments under the roof," she told him.

Le Bel spread his hands helplessly. "Madame, it is impossible to preserve silence in them."

"I know. That is why I think it would be a good plan to empty them."

Le Bel looked startled. "It is the wish of His Majesty . . ." he began.

"We have not yet discussed it," said the Marquise. "But I am sure the King will see the desirability of transferring the inhabitants of those apartments to another place. You might consider this."

"Yes, Madame," said Le Bel; and he retired thoughtfully.

In a very short time Le Bel had found exactly what he was looking for. He brought to the King's attention a little house in the Parc aux Cerfs district of Versailles, near enough to the Palace to be reached without fuss, in a secluded spot hidden from idle sightseers.

The house had only one storey and was divided into a few separate apartments, each complete in themselves.

Le Bel gave himself to the task with relish. He could see that providing the King with a private brothel was an excellent idea, and that many an embarrassing moment which he had suffered when conducting giggling working-girls up and down the private staircase at Versailles would now be avoided.

He decided to use his reliable housekeeper, Madame Bertrand, to take charge of the establishment, knowing that he could entirely trust not only her capabilities but her discretion.

He discussed the matter with her and asked for her advice.

"You will need," he told her, "to have absolute command over the girls."

"You may trust me for that, Monsieur, and if I may make a suggestion . . ."

"Pray do, Madame Bertrand."

"These girls, I presume, will come from every class in Paris. They may be of the *bourgeoise* class, they may be merely *grisettes*, dressmakers' assistants, milliners . . ."

"They will be selected, not for their social standing, but for their physical charms."

"If they know that they are maintained by the King, Monsieur, they will give themselves airs."

"It is very likely."

"They will scheme among themselves . . . against each other . . . Let us keep them apart as much as possible; and I think, Monsieur, that they should be under the impression that their benefactor is a wealthy nobleman."

"It is an excellent idea, Madame Bertrand, and one I am sure which will appeal to the King. The girls will all be very young indeed. The King prefers them to be young. He is unhappy with those who may have had too many previous adventures. You understand he is continually apprehensive regarding his health."

"You may trust me, Monsieur, to look after their health, and to preserve the necessary secrecy."

"Madame Bertrand, I am sure you will earn the gratitude of the King."

"I know what is expected of me and I shall do it," was the answer.

Madame Bertrand proved that she meant what she said; and very soon the little house in the Parc aux Cerfs was ready for its first occupants.

She carefully divided the house into its series of small apartments, arranging that each girl should have two servants — a manservant and a maidservant; she ruled them sternly and never allowed them to leave the house unless chaperoned.

Madame Bertrand however realised the need to keep her charges occupied when the King did not visit them; she therefore arranged that they should be taught to dance, paint and sing, and teachers were sent to the house to give them lessons. On occasions they were allowed to visit the theatre, but they never did so unchaperoned. A special private box was allotted to them, and here they sat with their chaperon who guarded them well from the amorous attentions of young men and the too curious eyes of the audience.

Many of the girls who were brought to the Parc aux Cerfs by the energetic Le Bel had come from very poor homes. To live in such a place seemed to them the height of luxury, and the charming courtesy of their benefactor, who was such a contrast to the rough-mannered and often brutal people among whom they had spent the greater part of their lives, won their instant affection.

Moreover when a girl's services were no longer required in the Parc aux Cerfs, she was given a present which would seem fantastic wealth for her; and if she were pregnant she would be married to some citizen who felt himself fortunate to take her and the handsome dowry which went with her.

The Marquise, considering the establishment in the Parc aux Cerfs, believed that she had set up a strong resistance to such women as the Comtesse de Choiseul-Beaupré and the Marquise de Coislin who threatened her security.

The death of Alexandrine had had a marked effect on the Marquise. She abandoned a great many of her frivolities, spent less time at her *toilette* table and attended Mass twice a day.

The whole Court now knew that she had ceased to be the King's mistress, but she occupied the equally important role of friend and adviser.

She now held sewing parties at which were made garments for the poor. Her enemies noted the change in her habits with sardonic smiles. "The Marquise's health is declining even more rapidly than we thought," they told each other. "See, she is preparing to leave this world in an aura of sanctity after the manner of Madame de Mailly."

There were some who recalled Madame de Maintenon. Could it be that the Pompadour hoped for the death of the Queen and marriage with the King?

"The Queen should take care," whispered the most venomous of her enemies.

The Marquise ignored the comments and continued in her mood of piety.

The Jesuits however could not forget that she was their enemy.

They blamed her — unfairly — for the conflict surrounding the Bull Unigenitus which had not turned out satisfactorily from their point of view. Following the decree of the *Parlement* that the Bull Unigenitus was not a rule of faith, Pope Benedict XIV had declared that all had the right to receive the sacrament. This was a blow to those who had fought so earnestly to uphold the Bull; naturally the Jesuits were not pleased and, as they felt the Marquise to be largely responsible for all the decisions reached by the King, they were decidedly unfriendly towards her.

Now she sought their help in bringing about her reformation.

She began by modelling her life on that of Marie Leczinska. There were the same sewing parties, the reading of theological books, the prayers.

Marie Leczinska, while not receiving these advances enthusiastically, did not repel them. She watched the Marquise with envy not untinged with admiration. How could she honestly not admire a woman who was showing her how she might have successfully maintained her position had she been as shrewd and far-sighted. Madame de Pompadour, unable to satisfy the sensuality of the King, yet remained his friend and the most important person at Court. Was it possible that, had Marie Leczinska been equally wise, she might have occupied the position which was held by Madame de Pompadour today?

All eyes were on the Marquise. All wondered what the outcome of this new phase into which she was entering would be.

The King was happily occupied with his Parc aux Cerfs. Madame de Pompadour was deeply concerned with her soul. There was no doubt that, when she was recognised as a reformed and saintly character, the King's respect for her would not be diminished but increased. Perhaps he would follow her example.

Meanwhile it was necessary for Madame de Pompadour to be absolved from her sins and to be allowed to partake of the sacrament; so she sent for a priest to pray with her and instruct her in the ways of repentance.

She chose Père de Sacy, the King's confessor.

Meanwhile the clouds of war were beginning to gather over France.

The Peace of Aix-la-Chapelle had been more profitable for the English than the French, and that fact continued to rankle. The British Government kept a wary eye on French affairs; the Peace had meant the passing of Madras from French into British hands, but the British were covetously surveying other territories in Asia.

They watched in particular a French merchant, Joseph Dupleix, owner of a factory at Chandernagore who had become Governor of the French settlements. He now held sway over land from the River Narbada to Cape Comorin; but an enterprising Englishman, Robert Clive, who had gone to India as a clerk in the service of the East India Company was determined that the British should be supreme in India. Clive was a more brilliant administrator than the Frenchman and he had greater support from his Government than Dupleix had from his; moreover the French, very eager to keep on good terms with their neighbours across the Channel, again and again gave in to British demands in India.

Not only were the British determined on supremacy in India but they were equally anxious to dominate Canada; constantly on the alert to increase trade, they felt that the French in Canada were a stumbling-block to their progress, and in June of 1755 the English admiral, Boscawen, seized two French frigates, even though there had been no declaration of war between the two countries. The French, taken by surprise, lost three hundred ships in the battle which ensued; as a result the French ambassadors in London and Hanover were immediately recalled to Paris.

There had to be retaliation. Richelieu, who had distinguished himself at Fontenoy, was put in charge of troops who were sent to Port Mahon, capital of Minorca. They stormed and took this fortress. This was a victory for the French to equal that of the English in Newfoundland. As a result the English recalled Admiral Byng, who had failed to prevent the French victory, and he was shot for treason at Portsmouth, "*pour encourager les autres*", as Voltaire commented.

Before the French could enter into a major war with her enemy across the Channel she must make sure of peace in Europe.

Maria Theresa saw in this state of affairs a possibility of recovering Silesia, which she had lost during the War of the Succession.

Her Ambassador, the Prince von Kaunitz, had been long seeking to make an alliance with France. Kaunitz, outwardly something of a fop, was in fact a shrewd statesman and he had quickly seen that the best way of bringing success to his efforts in France was to win the friendship of Madame de Pompadour.

This he had attempted to do, but Maria Theresa was torn between political expediency and her conscience.

She felt it far beneath her dignity to have anything to do with a woman who, in her eyes, was a sinner.

But Maria Theresa was always one to consider the needs of her country rather than those of her conscience. Her husband however, the Duke of Lorraine who had been given the Imperial crown at the close of the War of Succession, rarely interfered in political matters, but could not help smiling cynically at the thought of his pious Maria Theresa's becoming an ally of the notorious Madame de Pompadour.

He had laughed because she, Maria Theresa, the haughty and pious Empress, should consider acquiring a woman of easy virtue, and of *bourgeoise* origins also, as an ally. It was not as though she were on good terms with the Church. It was impossible, said the father of Maria Theresa's sixteen children, to have anything to do with a woman of the Pompadour's reputation.

It may have been that these views had been communicated to Madame de Pompadour, and that this was the reason why she was so eagerly seeking a new way of life.

In any case it was with great delight that Kaunitz reported to his Empress that the Marquise was on the point of being converted to a life of piety.

The Dauphin was watching events with interest.

He was as determined as ever to bring about the Marquise's dismissal from Court.

He was at the moment emotionally disturbed. Always he had deplored the morals of his father, and it seemed incredible to him that he himself could become involved in a love affair with a woman not his wife; yet this was exactly what had happened.

One day he had gone to see the work of Fredon, a painter whom he admired, and in the *atelier* of this man he had met a woman. She was young and very beautiful and he had paused to talk to her about the artist's work, which she also admired.

He had had such faith in his own virtue that he had not at first been alarmed by his interest in this woman who told him that her name was Madame Dadonville and that she was a great admirer of art.

They should meet again in some artist's salon, suggested the Dauphin. Perhaps at Fredon's? It would be very interesting if they did, she answered.

They met several times, and suddenly the Dauphin realised how much these meetings were beginning to mean to him, and that it would be advisable to discontinue them.

He did discontinue them, only to discover that they had been a great deal more important than he had imagined.

But he was a virtuous man. What harm could there be in an occasional meeting? he asked himself.

A little later he asked himself further questions. A man could not be called a libertine for taking one mistress. When he looked around him and studied the lives of other men he could smile at these qualms which beset him.

He thought of Marie-Josèphe. She was a good woman; she adored him, but there was no denying the fact that he had been forced to marry her.

151

Why should he deny himself this pleasure? That was what he was asking himself. What made temptation irresistible was that Madame Dadonville was asking it also.

Thus the Dauphin had, for the first time, been unfaithful to his wife; and after the first time there was a second, a third, a fourth . . . and then he lost count of the number of times. How could he do otherwise? He was in love with Madame Dadonville.

Now they were meeting regularly.

This lapse did not make him feel any more lenient towards Madame de Pompadour. His father had a score of mistresses. His own affair was quite different; he was sure of that; and he was still as determined as ever to drive Madame de Pompadour from Court.

Therefore, when he heard that she was proposing to begin her reformation through the services of Père de Sacy, he sent for the priest.

"So Father," he said, "I hear you have a new penitent."

"It is so, Monseigneur," answered the priest.

"And you will shrive her and make of her a virtuous woman?"

"It is what she wishes."

The Dauphin laughed. "You will bring your cloth into ridicule, *mon Père*, if you offer her absolution while she continues her way of life."

"I have heard, Monseigneur, that she now lives virtuously, has given up her carnal life and is merely the King's good friend."

The Dauphin again laughed. "So you would make friends with a woman who has been a bitter enemy of the Jesuits."

"If she is truly repentant . . ."

"Repentant!" cried the Dauphin. "Why, Father, where is your good sense? Do you not know what this parade of piety means? She is eager to make an ally of the Empress Maria Theresa. She is as determined as ever to bring about the downfall of you Jesuits."

Père de Sacy bowed his head. He could see that if he gave the Marquise what she wanted he would mortally offend the Dauphin, and since their defeat over Unigenitus the Jesuits looked very eagerly to the Dauphin for his support. They believed that when he was King their position would be made very secure in the land.

It was imperative not to offend the Dauphin.

Père de Sacy bowed his head before the Marquise.

"Madame," he said, "I deeply regret that I can be of no use to you. It is you who must take the first step before I can absolve you from your sins."

The Marquise smiled. "But, *mon Père*, I have taken that step. I have renounced my sins and asked for forgiveness. I am prepared to live virtuously from now on."

"Madame, there is only one way in which you can do this."

"I do not understand you. I have already . . ."

"No, Madame, the Church would demand that you show your true repentance to the world. There is only one way in which you can obtain absolution."

153

"And that is?"

"You must leave the Court, renounce your position here, return to the husband whom you deserted when you came to Versailles, and live quietly with him."

This was one of the rare occasions when the Marquise lost her temper.

"I see, Monsieur," she said, "that you are truly a Jesuit."

"Madame, I am indeed. And you knew this when you sent for me."

"Jesuit!" cried the Marquise. "You are gloating in your power over me . . . or what you imagine is your power. Your Society wish for nothing more than to see me leave Court. Now let me tell you something, Monsieur Jesuit: I shall never leave Court of my free will. Only would I leave to please His Majesty; never would I go in order to serve the purpose of the Society of Jesus. You forget that I have as much power at Court — nay more — than you and your Society. While that is so you are foolish to think to dictate to me."

"Madame, I merely told you the price of salvation."

"And I merely tell you to leave my presence at once."

Père de Sacy retired immediately; and when he had gone the good sense of the Marquise overcame her anger.

Why lose her temper with the man? All she had to do was send for a priest who *would* hear her confess and give her pardon without naming his conditions.

This was not difficult to do.

The Marquise publicised her conversion by erecting a gallery in that convent which was the resort of

154

fashionable penitents: the Capucines in the Place Vendôme.

Maria Theresa now felt that her conscience no longer stood between her and Madame de Pompadour. She was at liberty to negotiate with the lady whom all knew to be, although not in name, the First Minister of France.

Maria Theresa signed the first Treaty of Versailles in May of 1756. Frederick of Prussia meanwhile had signed a treaty with George II against France. Thus war on two fronts was threatening France who was already at war with England. Then Frederick invaded Saxony without warning — a direct attack on Maria Theresa.

The powers of Europe were lining up for a major conflict. The Seven Years War had begun.

The Dauphine was an unhappy woman during those days.

Her father had become a victim of war and, at the approach of Frederick's armies, had escaped to Warsaw, leaving her mother behind in Dresden to negotiate with the envoys of the King of Prussia.

This was a bitter blow indeed to Marie-Josèphe; but one which hurt her more had fallen upon her.

She believed she must have been the last one at Court to learn of her husband's infidelity. That knowledge did nothing to alleviate her sorrow.

That which she had always feared had happened. He loved someone else, really loved her, not because she had been forced upon him, not because she had determined to do her duty, but simply because she so charmed him that there was no help for it.

The Dauphin was in turn melancholy and truculent.

Sometimes he was so tender, calling her his dear little Marie-Josèphe, recalling the time when she had braved death or disfigurement to nurse him through a dangerous illness. Then she had to leave him as quickly as possible, for she feared she would burst into tears and implore him to give up this woman.

At other times he would strut about her apartment, almost as though it was no concern of his that she suffered, rather indeed that he thought her a fool to suffer, not to understand that every man must have his mistress.

Her women shook their heads philosophically. The Dauphin had been faithful so far, and that had been quite remarkable. How many women did she know with husbands who in the course of many years took only one mistress! they implied.

One is as hard to bear as ten would have been, she thought; perhaps harder. If he had been as his father, I should have become accustomed to his infidelities.

The Queen, realising what was happening, took to spending more time with her daughter-in-law.

She herself remembered too well those days when she had first discovered the King's infatuation for Madame de Mailly.

Poor little Marie-Josèphe suffered even as Marie Leczinska had done.

The Queen would dismiss her women when her daughter-in-law came to her; she would make the

Dauphine sit at her feet and lean her head against her lap while she stroked the young woman's hair.

"Weep if you wish, my daughter," said the Queen to her one day. "There is no one to see you but myself. It is good to weep sometimes. It cleanses the mind of bitterness."

So the Dauphine sobbed until she was exhausted; then she sat quietly at the feet of the Queen.

"It will pass," said Marie Leczinska. "It always passes."

"I did not think it would ever happen . . . to us. We were different."

"We are all different, or so we think until we make the discovery that we are all alike. You are as I was, my daughter. The Dauphin is as his father."

"With the King there are so many."

"In his youth he might have been called a faithful man. It was only later that there began to be so many."

"You mean that my Louis will be . . ."

"Who knows, child? It is well to be prepared for any eventuality."

"I think I should die."

"You would live, as I have lived."

"Your Majesty gives me great comfort."

"Perhaps *you* comfort *me*. My grief was so like yours. But weep no more, for it is useless to weep. Queens . . . Dauphines . . . they learn to accept what is thrust on them, you know."

"I know, Your Majesty."

"When he comes to you, you must give no sign of resentment. You will remain his friend, and if you are wise, you need not lose his affection."

157

"You do not understand," cried the Dauphine vehemently. "It was once a perfect thing, and now it is . . . besmirched."

"But give no sign of your resentment, my child. Take my advice. Had I been a wiser woman I might have been a happier one. I will show you something. This day I had a letter from the King. All our communications are by letter. He no longer cares to converse with me." The Queen's voice trembled slightly. "But this letter . . . shall I tell you what it contains? It is a request from the King that I make a certain lady one of my *dames du palais*."

"And this lady is?"

"Madame de Pompadour of course. You see it is not enough that *he* honours her on every occasion; I also must do so."

Marie-Josèphe had sprung to her feet. "I would not do it. If he were to bring that woman to me . . ."

"Let me tell you how I answered this request, my child."

"Yes, Your Majesty."

"I wrote to my husband that I had a King in Heaven from whom I drew strength to endure my burdens, and that I had a King on earth to whom I should always offer obedience."

The Dauphine clenched her fists and cried: "You do not love him as I love the Dauphin."

"My dear child, calm yourself," answered the Queen. "In time you will learn forbearance . . . even as I have. You will understand that women like us are born to endure without complaint."

158

Then the Dauphine fell to her knees and in silence buried her face in the Queen's lap.

Marie Leczinska smiled sadly as she laid her hand tenderly on the head of her daughter-in-law.

The people were bewildered. The French at war, and the Austrians were their allies! Such a reversal of policy could not easily be understood, for the Austrians had been their enemies for a long time and they did not trust them.

France was committed to a war in their colonies and war in Europe, and wars meant taxation. They did not want war; they wanted bread.

Moreover Madame de Pompadour had been made a *dame du palais* in the Queen's household and was parading her piety before the world. They did not trust Madame de Pompadour; they did not respect the King.

Madame de Pompadour was the First Minister of France, it was said; and France was now engaged in a bitter struggle on two fronts.

Depend upon it, said the people of Paris, this is a sad day for France.

CHAPTER TEN

The Parc aux Cerfs

The King found great solace during these days of stress in being able to slip from the Palace into the little house which had become known as the Parc aux Cerfs, where one, two or even three little charmers would eagerly be waiting for his arrival.

It was pleasant to enter that little house as a petty nobleman, and call Louise . . . Jeanne . . . or whatever the name of the favourite of the moment might be, and then hear the light running footsteps, to see a charming child — none of them was much more — running to greet him and fling herself into his arms in an access of joy.

It had been a brilliant inspiration to select these young girls from the poorer quarters of Paris. It ensured their gratitude. Le Bel was a connoisseur; he spent a great deal of time prowling about the streets of Paris, selecting likely candidates for a term in the little house.

Already the good fortune of some of its inmates had become known, and mothers were asking each other how their daughters could be received into this establishment which ensured them not only meals which were more than adequate, fine clothes, a life of luxury for as long as they were considered to deserve it, but finally a handsome present and possibly a good marriage.

Le Bel seemed to have no difficulty in keeping up the supply, for there were rarely more than three girls living at the Parc aux Cerfs at one time. There was not really sufficient room for more, and the King had no wish that the place should resemble a harem. Three was a pleasant number and, since the girls could be dismissed when they began to pall, there could not have been a more satisfactory arrangement. There was one very charming child in residence, and the King was spending a great deal of time with her. He had given her a name of his own — Louison; he was addicted to nicknames, and, as his little friends did not know who *he* was, he liked them to preserve their anonymity.

Louison had bright intelligent eyes; she was observant — a characteristic which might not have been so appealing had it not been accompanied by such a charming appearance. She could be as passionate as he could wish and sometimes she seemed like a child; she would sit on his knee and examine his clothes. They were very fine, she said; she knew because it had been a custom of hers to go to the Place de Grève on Mondays when the sale of second-hand clothes was being carried on.

She would take the cloth between her fingers and feel it, her head on one side.

"It must have cost a great deal," she would say. "It is a fine piece of cloth. My lord, you must be a very rich man indeed."

But that was obvious. Only a rich man could afford to keep an establishment such as the Parc aux Cerfs.

One day the King arrived wearing the order of the *cordon bleu* — which was immediately noticed by Louison.

She did not mention it however, because she knew that her patron could grow impatient of too many questions, and when he was a little irritated, although he rarely showed it, he might send for one of the other girls either to share his company or to monopolise it completely, and so result in Louison's being dismissed.

That was something which Louison found very hard to bear. She was engrossed in her new life; she found the Parc aux Cerfs luxurious in the extreme, but she could only be completely happy when the owner of the establishment called and she was with him, for she had fallen passionately in love with him.

She had never dreamed there could be such a person. He bore his years with grace, and if he lacked the freshness of youth he well made up for that by his tender and courteous manners. Never had Louison heard such a musical voice; never had she seen any person move with such grace. His habit of taking her hand and kissing it when they met made her aware that she had stepped into a world far from the crudity of the *faubourgs*.

Here were all the trappings of romance. The spiriting away from a garret to what seemed like a miniature palace; after having slept on a sack to sleep on a bed which was shaped like a sea-shell and trimmed with pale pink satin; to wear beautiful clothes; to have jewels;

to have food and wine and learn the accomplishments of a lady; but chiefly to be loved by a man who was surely too gallant, too charming to belong to this world. Being more imaginative than her companions, Louison often wondered whether she had died and gone to Paradise.

Once she said to Madame Bertrand: "If this is what happens to you when you are dead, and people only knew it, everyone would long for death."

Madame Bertrand was shocked. She hastily crossed herself. There, she thought, is one who must be watched a little more carefully than most.

After the King's visit, Louison said to Madame Bertrand: "*Ma Mère,*" (the girls regarded Madame Bertrand as their Mother Superior and addressed her as such) "I noticed that my lord was wearing the *cordon bleu* today."

"Your eyes are a bit too sharp, my child," retorted Madame Bertrand.

"But it *was* the *cordon bleu*. I am sure of it."

"Well, what if it was?"

"I wonder who he is, to wear the *cordon bleu*."

Madame Bertrand made a sudden decision then; she believed that a girl as sharp as Louison might garner too much information, put two and two together and make the discovery. She decided therefore to put her on a false track.

"He is a great gentleman, very rich, very important," she said.

"As I know," murmured Louison demurely.

"I will tell you something more. He comes from Versailles."

Louison nodded. She had guessed it.

"And," said Louison, "he is a great friend of the King's."

Madame Bertrand looked at her sharply. "What makes you say that?"

"Because he is so distinguished that even the King must notice him and make him his friend."

"He is a Polish Count," said Madame Bertrand quickly. "He is a member of the Queen's family. As you know, the Queen is Polish."

Louison nodded, and Madame Bertrand saw that one of the other girls had appeared and was listening to the conversation.

From that day the girls referred to their benefactor as the Polish Comte.

Madame Bertrand reluctantly confessed to Le Bel what had happened; and Le Bel informed the King.

Louis was amused, and was content to be regarded as a member of his wife's household, perhaps even a relative of hers.

There came a day when the King arrived at the Parc aux Cerfs and spent the few hours he was there with a girl who was not Louison.

At such times she was desolate.

It was useless for Madame Bertrand to try to keep the girls apart in order that they should not know that one enjoyed more favour than another. They were always aware when the King was in the house; the manners of Madame Bertrand seemed to change. There was an atmosphere of ceremony about the place which was impossible not to sense at once.

Particularly was Louison aware of this and could be sure that he was in the house, although she had not heard his arrival.

She crept out of her apartment. She could hear the sound of voices coming from the rooms of another girl. That was his voice.

If only, she thought, this were my house, only mine; and he came regularly to see me . . . only me.

She felt so wretched, she could not stay in her own rooms, and she crept down the staircase to the small reception hall.

Now she had no doubt that he was in the house, for he had taken off his coat and it lay on a table.

She went to it and let her fingers caress the fine cloth. She lifted it to her lips and, as she did so, she heard the rustle of paper in a pocket.

Louison was by nature curious and, during her stay in the Parc aux Cerfs, she had learned to read a little. She put her hand in the pocket and felt what she was sure were letters. She looked about her.

No one would see her if she took those letters from the pocket and read what they contained. Furtively she touched them. He would not be pleased if he knew that she had read his letters, and Madame Bertrand, if she discovered, might feel it her duty to tell him.

Louison knew this, yet she found the temptation irresistible.

165

There were two letters. Her eyes glanced over them and somewhat stumblingly she tried to read the contents.

They both began "Sire", and there were references to "Your Majesty".

"Your Majesty's most humble servant," she read.

They were addressed to the King. One was signed with a name which was not unfamiliar to her: D'Argenson. He was an important minister, and he signed himself "Your Majesty's humble servant".

Louison thrust the letters back into the pocket.

She had made a great discovery. The owner of the Parc aux Cerfs, her lover, was not a Polish Comte; he was the King of France.

Hastily she ran back to her own apartments. She shut herself into her room. Although she was uneducated she was intelligent. She pictured herself falling to her knees when he next came, calling him Sire and telling him that she was His Majesty's humble servant.

But wait. He had not wished to be recognised as the King so he must never know that she had discovered his identity.

Louison was wise enough to realise that his secret must be hers also.

CHAPTER
ELEVEN

The Affaire Damiens

That winter was one of the coldest within the living memory of Frenchmen. Even the rivers were frozen; and people were dying, not only in Paris but in the countryside, of cold and hunger.

The war was an added burden. The price of bread soared and taxes were levied on all food entering Paris.

Public opinion was against the war. Frenchmen refused to accept the Austrians as allies. It was said in the streets that the Marquise had persuaded the King to this alliance because of her friendship with Maria Theresa, who had flattered her by calling her "dear friend and cousin". Louis was reputed to have been further seduced into this unnatural alliance by his desire for a marriage between his granddaughter — Madame Première's child — and Joseph, the son of Maria Theresa.

Machault and d'Argenson had strenuously opposed the Austrian alliance. Machault had proved himself a zealous Finance Minister when he had succeeded Orry in that post. He had planned necessary reforms, but the clergy had declared him to be impious when he had endeavoured to close many convents and prevent new ones being founded, when he had stated that the development of trade and agriculture was of more importance to the nation. Louis had been unwillingly obliged to relieve him of that post and transfer him to the Ministry of Marine; and the transfer put an end to financial reform in France. Louis had great respect for this man; yet he had acted against his advice in this matter of the Austrian alliance.

D'Argenson, who was now Minister of War, had long been a favourite of the King's. He was every inch a courtier and quite different from the diarist, his far from handsome brother the Comte d'Argenson who was known as *d'Argenson le bête*, to distinguish him from his handsome younger brother, the Marquis.

Since blame for the war could not be laid on the shoulders of the ministers, the unpopularity of the King increased.

It had been impossible to keep completely secret the existence of an establishment such as the Parc aux Cerfs. It might have been advantageous, from the King's point of view, if no attempt at secrecy had been made, for what the people did not discover concerning this place they made up for in their imaginations.

There were too many mothers, who could not feed their families, seeking to place their daughters in a home where they could be sure of food and warmth. Many of these young girls were destined for prostitution; indeed many had been brought up with this career in view. How much better for them to be inmates of the King's private brothel, in which they

168

were well treated, and when they left, were given a dowry.

Thus, while the citizens of Paris screamed their disapproval of the Parc aux Cerfs, many were seeking admission for their daughters, and it was because they could not find it that their anger against the King increased.

Wild stories were circulated throughout the capital.

"Citizens, guard your children," was the cry. "They are being spirited away to pander to the lust of a lecherous old man."

"He insists on youth. They say he prefers ten-year-olds. Ten-year-olds! Is it not a scandal?"

"How much does it cost, think you, to maintain such an establishment? Millions! Oh, my friends, while you are crying out for a few sous' worth of bread Louis is wasting millions on his pleasures."

Never had the King been so unpopular. He avoided going to Paris even on State occasions. Adelaide had grown more hysterical than ever and was constantly on the alert for would-be assassins. She tried to revive a medieval law which allowed only those who could prove that their nobility went back over three hundred years to approach the King.

Adelaide was scoffed at and assured that the ancient nobility were no more to be trusted than any others.

Meanwhile the rumours persisted. There were by now nearly two thousand girls established in the Parc aux Cerfs, it was said. The King bought them as might any Sultan.

He had cornered the wheat in order to find the money for these transactions.

"Citizens, the higher the price he demands for his wheat, the more money he has at his disposal to buy his girls."

The King ignored these rumours. He continued to find intellectual pleasure in the apartments of the Marquise, and that of a physical nature in the Parc aux Cerfs.

In the *cafés*, the state of the country was freely discussed. The war was deplored; the price of bread considered; the dismal prospect contemplated of a city in which it was no uncommon thing for people to faint in the streets from hunger, and die on the cobbles.

There was one man who went from *café* to *café*; he would sit listening avidly to all that was said, his eyes gleaming, his head nodding; now and then he would add a remark to what was being said.

One day when he was seated at a table, listening as usual, one of the party turned to him and said: "You . . . what have you to say about this? Are you with us? What do you think of France today, eh? What do you think of a King who spends millions on his pleasure-house and sends his scouts out to bring in little children from the streets?"

Then the man rose; he clenched his fists.

"This," he said, "is what I think. It should not be allowed to go on. It should be stopped."

"And who will stop it, eh?"

"He who is chosen might do so."

"Come! Do you suggest we should form ourselves into a society and choose one among us to teach the King a lesson?"

"Perhaps," said the man, "God will choose him."

His companions looked at each other and smirked. Here was a fanatic. It might be amusing to hear him talk.

"God, you say, my friend?"

"Yes," was the answer. "I said God." He turned to face them all. "I have seen a great many injustices in my life. I was once servant to Monsieur de la Bourdonnais. Have you heard of him, gentlemen? He was at one time Governor of India, and he served his country well. His reward? Ruin, my friends, after three years' imprisonment in the Bastille. I was servant to Monsieur Bèze de Lys. He was a good man who tried to abolish this cruel practice of *lettres de cachet*. His reward? A *lettre de cachet* which took him to the Pierre-Encise. You gentlemen of Paris do not know the Pierre-Encise? It is near Lyons, and is one of the cruellest prisons in France."

"You have seen much injustice," cried a man at the table. "So have we all. Look . . . just look at the streets of Paris today. Would you not say that the people of Paris suffer even as these men you served?"

"Ay, my friend. The King must be warned. He may have many years before him. A warning now, before it is too late . . . that is what he needs."

"And who will give this warning to a Sultan who thinks of nothing but his harem?"

"Someone must," was the softly spoken answer.

Then the man rose and left the *café*.

It was time he returned to his work in the house of a certain lady who was the mistress of the Marquis de Marigny, brother of Madame de Pompadour.

"Why, you are late back, Damiens," said one of his fellow servants. "What have you been at?"

"I stopped to talk in a *café*," he said.

"*Café* talk!" was the answer. "What are they saying in the *cafés*?"

"That which makes your blood boil with indignation and your heart bleed with pity for the misery of the people."

"Oh, you always were a lively one. There's soup ready for you if you want it."

Damiens sat at the table and sopped his bread in his soup.

"Here," he said, "we eat plenty because we are supported by the brother of the wickedest woman in France, while outside in the streets the people die of starvation."

"Then you ought to thank your lucky stars you're in a good place, that's all."

"It is the injustice . . . the cruel injustice . . ." murmured Damiens. "But something should be done. God will decide one day that something must be done."

His fellow servant left him, to confide in another that Damiens grew madder every day.

The big rooms at the Palace of Versailles were not easy to make warm and comfortable in such wintry weather,

172

and the King decided that the Court should go to Trianon.

Adelaide came to her father, accompanied by Sophie. The King raised his eyebrows in astonishment; Adelaide rarely appeared nowadays without her two sisters in attendance. They would walk behind her as though they were her ladies-in-waiting, and her manner was very haughty towards them.

"And where," said Louis, "is our Coche this day?"

"Madame Victoire is in her bed, Sire," said Adelaide, "and I fear that she will be unable to leave it. I have in fact forbidden her to do so. She has a fever, and the cold air would be very bad for her."

"Poor little Coche," said Louis; "how will she fare alone at Versailles without her Loque and Graille?"

"We shall visit her each day," said Adelaide.

"I am relieved to hear it. And you are ready to make the journey now?"

"Quite ready, Sire."

So the Court moved to Trianon during that bitter January, and Victoire was left behind at Versailles to recover from her fever.

Robert François Damiens knew that he had been chosen. He did not yet understand what he was to do, but he believed that when the time came that would be revealed to him.

He could no longer remain in the household of Marigny's mistress. He could no longer eat food supplied by the brother of Madame de Pompadour, while the people of Paris were starving.

He left Paris, and it seemed to him that his footsteps were guided along the road to Versailles.

When he arrived there it was dark, and he found an inn where he put up for the night.

He joined the company there and asked if there was any hope of seeing the King.

"The King is at Trianon," he was told. "Only Madame Victoire, of the royal family, is at Versailles. The court moved to Trianon a short while ago. It is warmer there."

"Trianon," cried Damiens. "That is not far from here."

"Just across the park," said the hostess.

"Then I might be able to see the King."

"Monsieur, you look strange. Are you ill?"

"I feel ill," said Damiens. "Perhaps I should be bled. I hear queer noises in my head. Is that a sign of fever? Yes, perhaps I should be bled."

"Nay," said the hostess feeling his forehead. "You have no fever. And surely you would not wish to be bled in such weather as this. What you need, Monsieur, is a hot drink and a warm bed. You are a fortunate man, for you have come to the right inn for those comforts."

Damiens took his candle and lighted himself to bed, but in the morning he was up early. He stayed in all the morning but in the afternoon when he went out his footsteps led him to the park.

It was deserted and the wind was biting, but near the Palace he met a man who, like himself, appeared to be waiting for someone.

"Good day to you, Monsieur," called this man. "What bitter weather!"

"I had hoped to see the King," said Damiens.

"I also wait for His Majesty. I have a new invention, and I wish to show it to him. The King is interested in new inventions."

"So you are waiting here for the King. I was told he is with the Court at Trianon."

"That is so," said the inventor, "but he will be coming later in the day, so I heard, to visit Madame Victoire who is at Versailles suffering from a slight fever. I fear I myself shall be suffering from a fever if I loiter about in this bitter wind. It may also be that His Majesty will decide not to visit his daughter after all. One cannot be sure. You too have business with the King, Monsieur?"

"Oh yes," answered Damiens. "I also."

The inventor gazed at the man in the long brown coat and slouch hat which hid his face.

"You seek his help?" asked the inventor.

"No," answered Damiens, "I seek to help *him*."

Clearly, thought the inventor, the man was a little strange, and the wind was growing wilder every moment.

"I do not think I shall wait," murmured the inventor. "I feel sure His Majesty will not face this wind today. I will wish you good day, Monsieur, and the best of good fortune."

"Thank you, my friend," said Damiens. "God be with you."

Left alone in the park, Damiens strolled about, seeking the protection of the trees from the wind, rubbing his cold hands to bring back the circulation. From his pocket he took a penknife; he opened it; it had two blades, a big and small one.

While he stood there he heard the sound of carriage wheels coming across the park. Hastily he put the penknife into his pocket and, as he saw the coach rattling by on its way to the Palace, he began to run after it.

It was now about half past four and growing dark. By the time Damiens reached the Palace the King had already entered with those who were accompanying him, and a little crowd of people had gathered in the Cour Royale to see Louis.

The King's coach was drawn up and the postilions were chatting with the little group of people in the faint light from the *flambeaux*. "He'll not stay long," said one of the postilions conversationally. "'Tis Madame Victoire whom he is visiting."

Someone murmured that he would have stayed longer if the invalid had been Madame de Pompadour.

Damiens leaned against the wall waiting.

Louis was bored, although Victoire suffering from fever was far less irritating than Victoire in good health. She lay still in her bed and merely smiled faintly at her visitors, so there was no need to attempt to make conversation with her.

He had brought Richelieu with him to enliven the company, together with the Duc d'Ayen, one of his intimate friends who occupied the post of Captain of the Guard. The Dauphin was also present. In fact it was due to the Dauphin that he had come, for he was not going to let that self-righteous young man set himself up as a model of virtue who braved the January winds to visit his sick sister. The King was determined to prove that he was as good a father as the Dauphin was a brother.

They stayed for two hours, chatting at Victoire's bedside, before preparing to return to Trianon; and it was nearly half past six when Louis came down the Petit Escalier du Roi on the east side of the Cour des Cerfs and crossed the Salle des Gardes on the ground floor of the *château*.

The Dauphin walked beside him, and Richelieu and the Duc d'Ayen were immediately behind followed by four of their attendants.

As Louis stepped down into the Cour Royale a man suddenly pushed his way out of the group waiting there, and pressed against him.

Louis cried out suddenly: "Someone struck me."

He put his hand to his side and felt that it was wet and sticky. "I have been wounded," he declared. "It was the man wearing a hat."

The Dauphin cried: "Seize him! Seize the man with the hat."

The guards were already seizing Damiens. Someone knocked his hat from his head.

"That is the man," said the Dauphin. "He did not remove his hat when the King appeared. That is the man. I noticed him because of the hat."

Damiens was led away.

177

★ ★ ★

Supported by the Dauphin, Richelieu and d'Ayen, the King was helped back into the Palace and up the staircase to the *petits appartements*.

"So . . ." he moaned, "they have determined to kill me. Why do they do this to me? What have I done to them?"

"Sire," murmured Richelieu, "preserve your strength."

"Call the doctors immediately," ordered the Dauphin. "Let there be no delay. Every moment is precious."

The King lay on his bed and the coat was cut away from the wound. By this time the first of the doctors had arrived and it was discovered that the wound was not deep; the knife could have been but a small one and, owing to the weather, there were several layers of clothing for it to penetrate.

Louis was certain that he had been assassinated. He recalled the death of his ancestor, Henri Quatre, who had been struck down by the mad monk, Ravaillac, in the prime of his life.

"This," he cried, "is often the fate of Kings."

Now more doctors had arrived; the Queen and Princesses, informed of what had happened, crowded into the bedchamber.

The King must be bled, said the doctors, and this was done. Meanwhile rumour spread from Versailles to Paris.

"Louis has been assassinated. He was attacked by a murderer at Versailles this day."

The news was carried from house to house and people came out into the streets in spite of the cold to talk of it. Now that they believed him to be dying they discovered that they did not hate him as much today as they had yesterday.

He was led away from his duty, they said; led away by that woman. He was our King. He was a good man at heart. And now he is dying, struck down by a murderer.

Louis, thrown into a panic as he considered his many sins, asked for Extreme Unction. This was like the realization of that perpetual nightmare: that he would be struck down before he had had a chance to repent.

"Sire," said his doctors, "you are going to recover. The wound is not a deep one and none of your doctors thinks it is fatal."

"You are deceived," said Louis. "The blade was poisoned."

"There is no evidence, Sire, of that."

"I feel death close," said the King. "Send for my confessors."

His huntsman, Lasmartes, burst unceremoniously into the apartment. He hurried to the bedside and knelt by the bed.

"Sire," cried Lasmartes, "this must not be, this shall not be."

"It has happened, my good friend," said the King.

Lasmartes insisted on examining the wound in spite of the doctors' efforts to stop him. He had always been on very familiar terms with Louis, and during their hunting expeditions often behaved as though there was no difference in their rank.

179

"Why, Sire," cried Lasmartes, smiling broadly, "this is no fatal wound. In four days you and I will be bringing in a fine deer together."

"My good friend," said the King, "you seek to cheer me. There have been plots against me, and this is the result of one. The wound is small but the blade was poisoned. You and I have brought in our last deer. Farewell, my huntsman; it is only left for me to make my peace with God."

The Dauphin signed for Lasmartes to go, and the King called his son to his bedside.

"I leave you a Kingdom," he said, "which is greatly troubled. I pray that you will govern it better than I have. Let it be known that I forgive my murderer. Now . . . I beg of you, bring me a priest that I may make my peace with God."

One of the girls, who had been out with her chaperone, brought the news to the Parc aux Cerfs.

"Such excitement! I never saw the like. Crowds everywhere . . . people shouting at each other. I asked what it was all about. What do you think? The King has been assassinated."

Madame Bertrand turned pale, but she said nothing.

Louison stared at the girl who had just come, but she did not see her. She saw him . . . their Polish Count . . . with the knife in his body.

She could not speak; she could not think; she turned quietly away and hurried to her own apartments.

Madame Bertrand was too upset, contemplating the future, to notice her.

Louison shut herself in her room; she lay on her bed and there she remained for two days, refusing all food.

"She has a fever," said the others. "There is an epidemic of fevers. Madame Victoire had one; that was why the King went visiting her that day."

When the news was brought to the Marquise she was stunned.

Louis . . . dying! She could not believe it. She dared not. She had always believed that she must die first.

Her dear friend . . . dying! What would become of her when she was left to her enemies without his protection? It was like being thrown into a pit of hungry bandogs who had long thirsted for her blood.

The Abbé de Bernis, who had been her friend since the days when she had first come to Court and had been appointed by the King to prepare her for her role as King's mistress, now brought the news to her.

She wept with him and, losing her usual calm, grew hysterical.

"You must be prepared for anything that might happen," the Abbé told her. "And when it comes you must submit to Providence."

"I will go to him at once," she cried. "When he is ill, I should be at his side."

"His confessor is with him, Madame," said the Abbé. "There is no place for you at such a time."

She was aghast, realising the truth of this.

"I am his good friend. Our relationship is no longer a sinful one."

181

"I am afraid, Madame, that if you appeared his confessors would leave. He has asked for them to come to him. He does not ask for you."

Then she covered her face with her hands and wept silently. She saw this as the end of everything that had made her life worthwhile.

"Madame," the Abbé continued, "I pray you be of good cheer. I will keep you informed of everything that takes place. You may rely upon my friendship. I shall divide my services between my duties and my friendship for you."

"Thank you," she whispered. "You are my very good friend."

When he had left her, Madame du Hausset came to her to tell her that Dr Quesnay was waiting to see her.

He was brought to her at once, and she took both his hands in hers and lifted her ravaged face to his.

"Come, come," said Quesnay, "there is no reason for this grief. It is a scratch, nothing more, I tell you, nothing more."

"You think he will recover?"

"I am certain of it. There is a world of difference, Madame, between the sickness of a King and the sickness of a subject. Why, if he were not a king he would be well enough to hunt or dance at a ball in a day or so."

"You cheer me, my good friend. Is that your motive in speaking thus . . . to cheer me?"

"No, Madame, if I thought he was in danger I would say so. But he is not in danger, you may be assured. The

Dauphin is constantly with him . . . so are the priests. They are urging him to change his mode of life."

"You mean . . . they are trying to persuade him to cast me off?"

"I remember Metz, Madame."

"Yes. I know. Madame de Châteauroux, who had followed him to war, was dismissed from his presence and sent away in great humiliation. I would not allow that to happen to me. I would go before I could be sent."

"Do nothing rash," said the doctor. "Wait. It is always better to be cautious."

"Yes," said the Marquise, "I will wait. I know that in good time he will send for me. The Dauphin . . . his priests . . . they will drive him to depression. In a short while, I tell you, he will be sending for *me*. Yes, I will wait. It is only a matter of waiting. Then all will be as it was . . . as though that madman had never come near him."

The doctor smiled at her. He was very fond of her. He poured a powder into a glass and gave it to Madame du Hausset.

"Add a little water," he said, "and take it to your mistress. It will help her to sleep tonight and give her the rest she needs. And . . . take care of her. She needs your care now."

Madame du Hausset nodded and turned away that the doctor might not see her emotion of which he was fully aware.

Machault and d'Ayen made their way down to the guardroom where Damiens was being held.

The Duc d'Ayen was furiously angry because the attack had taken place when he, as Captain of the Guard, had been in the presence of the King and should have prevented it. He was determined to show the King and everyone else that he considered the attack the act of a traitor to whom he would show no mercy. The Duc d'Ayen, son of the Maréchal Duc de Noailles, was a supporter of the Jesuits, and he decided that if possible he would wring from Damiens information which would implicate the Jansenites.

Machault on the other hand was an enemy of the Jesuits, and he had made up his mind that Damiens was the tool of the Society of Jesus. He believed that this was quite clearly a plot to kill the King and put the Dauphin on the throne; and as the Dauphin had always come down very firmly on the side of the Jesuits this was a reasonable conclusion if Damiens was their agent.

Thus these two powerful men entered the cell of the unfortunate Damiens, each determined to wring a confession from him which would implicate a protagonist in the political conflict.

Damiens received them calmly. There was an enraptured smile on his face although he had already been roughly handled by the guards and was bruised and bleeding.

"Tell me this," said Machault, "was the blade poisoned?"

"I swear it was not poisoned," cried Damiens.

"How then could you hope to kill the King . . . with the small blade of a penknife?"

184

"I did not wish to kill the King, only to teach him a lesson."

"What lesson?"

"To tear himself from his evil ways and his evil counsellors, and wisely rule his people."

"Who ordered you to do this thing?" asked d'Ayen.

"None."

"That's a lie."

"It is no lie. I did it for God and the people."

"In the cause of religion?" said d'Ayen. "Tell me what you mean by that."

"The people are starving. They live in misery."

"You were paid to do this deed," Machault told him. "Who paid you?"

"I tell you I alone did it, for the glory of God and the people. I did not wish to kill. If I had wished to I could have done so."

"Did the Jesuits order you to do this thing?" asked Machault.

"I swear they did not."

"Then if not the Jesuits . . . the enemies of the Jesuits?" suggested d'Ayen.

"No one on earth ordered me. I did it for the glory of God."

"Why do you complain of poverty? Were you not serving in houses where you were given plenty to eat?"

"What is good for oneself only, is good for no one," answered Damiens.

"He has accomplices, depend upon it," said d'Ayen.

"And," murmured Machault, "we will discover them."

"You may do what you will to me," cried Damiens. "You may torture me . . . you may crucify me . . . I shall only sing with joy because I die as my Lord died."

"It is bluff," said Machault angrily. "Let us see if he is as good as his words."

He ordered that the prisoner be stripped and strapped to his bed, and braziers and hot irons were brought to the cell.

Machault and d'Ayen looked on while the flesh of the prisoner's thighs was torn with red-hot pincers; and although their victim lay sweating and groaning in his agony he would only say: "I did it . . . I alone . . . I did it for the glory of God and the people."

Louis ordered that the curtains be drawn about his bed, and he lay in gloomy contemplation.

It was thirteen years since he had lain close to death at Metz, thirteen years since his confessors had come to him and he had sworn that if he lived he would lead a better life. He had been repentant for some little time after his recovery; but very soon he had ignored his promises.

He had changed in thirteen years. In those days he had been devoted to Madame de Châteauroux; he had been faithful to his *maîtresse-en-titre*. Now he had lost count of the number of women who had administered to his pleasure; he could not even remember how many had passed through the Parc aux Cerfs.

He despised himself and his way of life; but he had grown cynical, and he was too intelligent easily to deceive himself, so that he did not believe he would truly repent.

Contemplating his hopes of a satisfactory future life made him very gloomy.

He had realised that his present indisposition had become more mental than physical, for now he was convinced that the blade had not been poisoned. The answers which the prisoner had given had been those of a fanatic.

All the same he must attempt to lead a better life. He must listen to the priests; he would have someone to preach at Versailles, and he would attend the services regularly. He would cease to visit the Parc aux Cerfs for a while; and he would not send for Madame de Pompadour. It was true that she was no longer his mistress in actual fact but she had been, and while he continued to treat her as his very good friend, the Church frowned on him and would not help him to repentance.

His doctors came to dress the wound.

They declared their pleasure that it was healing quickly.

"Heaven be praised, Sire," said one. "It was not a deep wound."

Louis answered in a tone of the utmost melancholy: "That wound went deeper than you think. It went to my heart."

The Dauphin seemed to grow in stature during those days. He was constantly at the King's bedside; he showed great regret and filial devotion, and none would have guessed, if they had not been fully aware of this,

187

what strained relations there had recently been between the King and his son.

The Dauphin seemed to forget these differences. He behaved with dignity as the temporary King of France, at the same time showing his reluctance for a role which could only be his on the death of his father.

He asked the King's advice on all matters, considered it gravely and behaved with such modesty that the ministers began to believe that the Dauphin would one day be the King France needed.

The people were fond of him. He had a reputation for piety, and they forgave him his one mistress, Madame Dadonville, to whom he was still faithful. The Dauphine was not an attractive woman, although it was generally conceded that with her piety, which matched that of the Dauphin, and her modest demeanour she would make a very good Queen of France one day.

But for all his virtues there were many who felt uneasy at the thought of his taking the crown. Intelligent he might be, pious he certainly was; but many feared that he would make a bigoted ruler; and if he came to power the Jesuits would come with him and would do their best to rule the state. The *Parlements* would therefore suffer a decline and the Place de Grève might be stained with the blood of martyrs.

A country where the philosophers were allowed to raise their voices was a healthier place than one which was in the rigid grip of the bigots. An indolent pleasure-loving King might be less of a menace than a stern one who was determined to let the bigots rule.

188

The Dauphin showed what could be expected from him when, fearing that the trial of Damiens might disclose evidence against the Jesuits, he ordered that it should not be an open one; moreover it was not to be conducted by the *Parlement* but by a secret commission.

Such a decision, while planned to protect the Jesuits, actually did them a great disservice, for the people, believing that the Dauphin wished to protect that community to which he had always given his support, were now convinced that the Jesuits were behind the plot to assassinate the King, and that Damiens was their tool.

They had been sullen when the King rode through their capital; there had been no shouts of "*Vive le Roi*"; but now that he was recovering from an attack which might have ended his life, a little of that lost affection returned.

The hungry people, ever ready to be inflamed, seeking excitement which would give them temporary relief from the boredom and squalor of their lives, were eager to riot. They looked for scapegoats, and now angry voices were heard in the capital shouting: "Down with the Jesuits!"

News spread rapidly through the city that the mob was on the march, its objective being the Jesuit College of Louis le Grand.

Terrified parents, whose sons were being educated there, rushed to the College to rescue their children. Two hundred boys were taken from the establishment, while crowds gathered about the convent, hurling insults at the Jesuits.

The Paris of that time was not yet inflamed by agitators to that pitch when it would pillage and murder, but its mood was ugly and the parents of the boys declared that their sons should not return to the College. This was a great blow for Louis le Grand, one of the wealthiest of the Jesuit institutions.

The Marquise was growing frantic. The days were passing and the King did not send for her; therefore she had no means of gaining access to his presence.

Her friends tried to console her. Quesnay was a constant visitor; so was the Abbé de Bernis, the Duc de Gontaut, the Prince de Soubise and the Duchesse de Mirepoix.

"Depend upon it," said Madame de Mirepoix, "he is at the moment in the hands of the Dauphin and his party. As soon as he escapes he will send for you."

"I thought so," said the Marquise, "but I must confess to you, my dear friend, that as the days pass, I grow more and more anxious."

"Then you must not be anxious. Anxiety is bad for you. You have kept your position all these years by your good sense; I do not think you have lost any of that excellent quality. In fact I should say that you have improved it."

Madame de Mirepoix was a gay companion, and the Marquise, who had long looked on her as a friend, referred to her affectionately as her *petit chat*.

"Now," she said, "I cannot tell you how happy it makes me to have my good friends about me. It is only at such times as these that we are able to recognise them. What should I do without you, *petit chat*, and my dear Bernis, Quesnay and the rest. But the loyalty of such people calls alarming attention to my false friends."

"Dear Madame, you refer to?"

"Neither d'Argenson nor Machault have called on me since the King was attacked. That is significant."

"Madame, d'Argenson was never your friend."

"That is true. I do not forget the part he played in the Choiseul-Beaupré affair. Perhaps one should not expect to see him here at such a time. But Machault! I thought he was my friend. Have I not constantly helped him to maintain his place! What does it mean? Why does he avoid me now?"

"It could mean this, Madame: he has thrown in his lot with your enemies. It may be that he believes the King may not live long, and wishes to ingratiate himself with the Dauphin."

"This is what it undoubtedly means. What a friend he has proved himself to be!"

"Madame, I implore you, be of good cheer. The King will recover and, when he is completely well, the first person he will need will be his dear Marquise."

At length Machault did call on the Marquise.

He had come to a decision. He had not dared discuss her with the King, and he felt uneasy while she remained at Versailles.

If she should regain her favour, his days were numbered; he was fully aware of that. He had come out too far into the open and shown himself her enemy, because he had believed during those first hours after the attack that the King was dying and that the Dauphin would be King in less than a week. Over-eager to show his willingness to serve the Dauphin, he had betrayed his attitude towards Madame de Pompadour.

He had acted a little too quickly; but he did not give up hope. If Madame de Pompadour could be induced to leave Court it might well be that the King would be resigned to her departure. Louis was a man of habit. Many believed that he visited the Marquise because she happened to be there. If she were not, he might soon forget her and spend his time with other friends.

At Metz, when the King was thought to be dying, the enemies of Madame de Châteauroux had arranged for her dismissal. Now was the time for similar bold action in the case of Madame de Pompadour.

Thus the Marquise, while receiving the comfort of her good friends, heard that Machault was on his way to visit her. She asked her friends to leave her alone, and braced herself to receive him.

"Well, Monsieur de Machault," she said when he stood before her, "it is long since I have seen you."

"Madame," answered the Keeper of the King's Seals, "it is with great sorrow that I come on my present mission."

"What is this mission?"

"I have to ask you to leave Versailles."

"*You* have to ask me!"

"I act on the instructions of the King," lied Machault.

The Marquise was so moved that she feared she would betray her feelings before this man whom she now knew to be her enemy. She bowed her head and said nothing.

"Believe me, Madame," went on Machault, "I act with great reluctance. You will remember what happened to Madame de Châteauroux at Metz. The King desires to change his mode of life and you, alas, are so much a part of that life on which he now wishes to turn his back."

"What is expected of me?" she asked, and she was horrified to hear the tremor in her voice.

"Madame, only that you leave Versailles without delay. Take my advice, go as far from Versailles as possible. You would be wiser to do this."

The Marquise did not answer. She stood still, not seeing the Keeper of the Seals; she was remembering her meeting with the King in the Forest of Sénart, those early days of their association, and the fortune-teller at the fair who, when she was nine years old, had told her she was a *morçeau du roi* and had from that time determined her destiny.

All that, to lead to such a moment as this! Now that she was no longer young, now that she was weak and ill, to be turned away from the only life which could ever have meaning for her!

Machault was bowing over her hand and taking his leave.

"Goodbye," she said. "*My friend!*"

★ ★ ★

Madame du Hausset came hurrying to her.

"Madame, dearest Marquise, what has happened? What has that man done?"

"He has given me my *congé*, Hausset. That is all. It is over. I am no longer the friend of the King."

"It is impossible, Madame."

"No, Hausset. He brought me word from the King. I think you should begin to pack at once. We are leaving Versailles."

"For where?"

"We will go to Paris."

"Paris! Madame, you know the temper of the people of Paris. They hate you."

"Perhaps when I have lost the love of the King, I shall lose the hate of the people of Paris."

"Oh, Madame . . . Madame . . . let me help you to your bed. You need rest. You will begin to cough again . . . and then . . ."

"And then . . . and then . . ." said the Marquise sadly. "What matters it, Hausset? How many weeks are left to me, do you think?"

"Many weeks, many years, if we take care, Madame."

"I have some good friends, Hausset. Perhaps the weeks ahead will try even them."

"There is someone at the door, Madame."

"Go and see who it is."

Madame du Hausset returned with Madame de Mirepoix.

"What does this mean?" asked the visitor.

"Sit down beside me, *petit chat*," said the Marquise. "I am leaving Versailles."

"Why?" demanded Madame de Mirepoix.

"Because, my dear, I have been ordered to go."

"The King? . . ."

Madame de Pompadour nodded.

"You have had your *lettre de cachet*?"

"It amounts to the same thing. Machault called on me an hour ago and told me that it is the King's wish that I leave at once."

"Machault! That fox!"

"He is the Keeper of the Seals."

"Thank Heaven he is the keeper of his own conscience. Tell me, have you had anything in writing from the King?"

"Nothing."

Madame de Mirepoix laughed loudly and ironically. "Depend upon it, this is a little plot of Monsieur de Machault's. Louis knows nothing of it. Would he dismiss you thus . . . without a word?"

"You know Louis. He would go to great lengths to avoid unpleasantness."

"Before this happened to him, was he not as affectionate towards you as ever?"

"He was."

"At first they frightened him with their talk of repentance. That meant he could not see you. Now he is getting better. You may be sure that in a few days he will be asking for you. Remember Madame de Châteauroux."

"Who was dismissed!"

"And who came back. Very soon it was the enemies of Madame de Châteauroux who were feeling uneasy."

Madame du Hausset came to announce that Dr Quesnay had called on the Marquise.

"What is this I hear?" he asked.

"My God," cried the Marquise, "so they are talking of it already?"

"Machault has been here," explained Madame de Mirepoix, "He says he comes from the King with orders for the Marquise to leave Versailles."

"Machault is like the fox at the dinner party," said the doctor, "who tells his companions that they are in danger and should quickly depart. Thus ensuring for himself a bigger share of what is on the table."

"The doctor is right," said Madame de Mirepoix. "Machault has had no authority from the King. He is acting entirely on his own account. Ignore him. Stay here. Remember, the one who quits the game has already lost it."

"Oh my friends, my dear friends," cried the Marquise, "what comfort you bring me . . . and, I believe, what is even better — sound advice. The King would never desert me; I am sure of that. Hausset, if anything has been packed, unpack it now. We are staying at Versailles."

Everyone was now convinced that the King was out of danger; but he remained melancholy. It seemed impossible to lure him from this mood. He would sit at a reception without speaking, staring into space. He had decided to mend his ways, to live a life of piety, but he was not enjoying by any means this new existence.

Courtiers would rack their brains for some witty comment which would amuse him. But, no matter how apt the *bon mot*, no smile appeared on the King's face; even the most brilliant comment could bring nothing more than a grunt of approval before Louis lapsed once more into depression.

Even Richelieu could hardly win a smile from the King. The accounts of his many amorous adventures fell flat on each occasion and, in spite of the Duc's attempt to tell stories which were more and more outrageous, he failed to amuse Louis.

It was two o'clock, and a small company was gathered in the King's private apartments where Louis, still convalescent in dressing-gown and night cap, presided. The Dauphin and Dauphine were present and, although it was time for dinner none could leave until the King gave his assent. He seemed to have forgotten the time, and stood, leaning on a stick, looking out of the window.

Richelieu was beside him trying desperately to entertain him with an account of one of his wilder experiences.

"This, Sire," he was saying, "was Madame de Popelinière. Her husband had discovered our intrigue and had determined to put a stop to it, so he housed her in Paris, set a guard over her, and believed her to be safe. Sire, there was no way into that house. It was well guarded by his faithful servants. Many, other than myself, would have admitted defeat and looked elsewhere."

The King yawned and continued to look out of the window.

Richelieu went on unperturbed: "And what did I do, Sire, you ask?"

"I did not ask," said the King.

"Sire, you are weak from this recent outrage, and I beg leave to save you fatigue by asking the question for you. What did that villain Richelieu do? Sire, he bought the house next door. He discovered the whereabouts of the lady's bedchamber. There was a magnificent fireplace in this room. In my room there was also a fireplace. I sent for workmen and in a very short time our fireplaces were changed into a door which was not visible to the casual observer and only known to ourselves. It was an excellent arrangement. It made calling on each other at any hour of the day or night so simple. Believe me, Sire, in Paris they are now selling models of Madame de Popelinière's fireplace!"

"I do believe you," said the King, "since I believe you capable of any villainy."

"Sire, I'll wager that, when you are feeling more like yourself, I will tell that story again and make you laugh."

"There have been many such stories," said the King. "I know full well that ladies consider becoming the mistress of the Duc de Richelieu one of the inevitable functions of Court life."

"Let us thank the saints that that is not said of the King, who is such a faithful lover of his *subjects*."

The King neither smiled nor reproved the Duc; he merely looked bored. Then he said: "I see the Dauphine is hungry. It is time you went to dinner, my dear."

198

"Thank you, Sire," the Dauphine said, and retired.

The King stared after her mournfully, and suddenly he seemed to come to a decision.

He looked about the company and saw that one of the ladies, the Duchesse de Brancas, was wearing a long cloak.

"Madame," he said to her, "will you lend me your cloak?"

Surprised she immediately took it off.

He put it about his shoulders and bowing turned away. Everyone in the room was staring at him as he made his way towards the door. The Dauphin followed him but, as they left the room Louis turned to his son and said: "I wish to be alone!"

The Dauphin bowed and returned to the others.

There was silence as he joined them. But there was no doubt in the mind of anyone as to where the King was going.

Madame du Hausset said: "Madame, there is a visitor to see you."

The Marquise started up; she could not restrain a cry of joy.

"My dear," said the King, "it has been too long since we met . . . far too long."

She knelt at his feet and was kissing his hands, which were wet with her tears. But almost immediately she had risen.

"But you are in your dressing-gown. And nothing but that cloak to protect you! And the weather as it is . . ."

199

"My dearest friend," said the King, "do not concern yourself for my welfare. I have recovered now."

"Praise be to the saints! Oh, Sire, it has been the most wretched time of my life."

"I so much regret that I have caused it."

"Nay, Sire, that matters not, for now I am happy again."

"Let us talk," said the King. "It would please me."

"Anything that pleases Your Majesty has always pleased me."

"I know, I know. They have been trying to make a monk of me."

She laughed; and he laughed with her.

"A king's life is not always a happy one," he said; "yet I think I prefer it to that of a monk."

"Your Majesty . . . a monk! Oh no! We could not allow that."

"I agree. We could not."

"And to see you again overwhelms me."

"You suffered, I believe, as I did."

"But you have come to visit me, and I am happy again."

"I escaped from the company," said the King. "I found them so completely dull. Now I am with you my spirits feel lightened. I can laugh again."

"Sire," said the Marquise, "may I invite you to sup with me this evening?"

"The invitation is accepted with alacrity."

"Then we will enjoy one of our intimate suppers. We shall invite only the most amusing. How glad I am that

I did not allow Monsieur de Machault to drive me from Versailles!"

"Machault attempted to do that?"

"He became very important, Sire. He all but shouted '*le Roi est mort*' — and was in great haste to pay his respects to the Dauphin."

"I am disappointed in Machault."

"He and d'Argenson together caused me great anxiety and some humiliation."

"That is unforgivable," said the King.

The Marquise's eyes began to gleam with triumph, but she said nothing more about her enemies. This moment was important — no reproaches, no recrimination, only plans for future pleasure.

But she saw that he had been unnerved by the experience, and her first task was to restore his confidence. Often he had appeared not to care that he had lost his people's favour; but the thought of their hating him so much that a section of them had decided on his assassination had deeply depressed him.

She hastened to dismiss that mood.

"You know, Sire," she said, "there have been many who wished to make you believe that this horrible act was done at the wish of the people. Nothing could be further from the truth. This man Damiens is simply a madman. There was no conspiracy."

"I wish I could be sure of that."

"But, Sire, it is obvious. When the people heard what had happened they were horrified. I sent my servants into Paris to discover what was happening, to talk to the people. There was no one who did not feel outraged by this deed. Only love was expressed towards yourself. Why, was not the Jesuit College of Louis le Grand in danger of being attacked! Paris was horrified by the deed. So was the *Parlement*."

"You comfort me as usual."

"And, Sire, it is as well that this has happened, because the greatest possible precautions will now be taken against a similar occurrence."

The King was nodding and smiling while the Marquise was making rapid plans. There must be an amusing evening such as the King had not enjoyed for a long time. A play perhaps. Not cards; perhaps he had decided not to gamble again. Not a ball. He was not well enough to dance. But he would enjoy a play; perhaps with herself taking the principal part.

Madame du Hausset heard the laughter of her mistress mingling with that of the King.

Madame la Marquise has genius, she thought; once more she has come safely through a difficult period.

And when the King returned to his apartment, everyone who saw him noticed that the gloom had left him and that he was smiling to himself.

The news spread rapidly. "The Marquise is back in favour, and the King is more devoted than ever."

D'Argenson and Machault heard the news and trembled.

There were two tasks before the Marquise now; she found no pleasure in them for she hated making enemies, but these two men had shown her quite clearly that if they were allowed to remain at Court they would always be a menace to her.

To secure the fall of d'Argenson had not been difficult; but the King had a great respect for the powers of Machault.

However, such insults as these two had levelled against her could not be overlooked, and the King, having been so promptly whisked out of his melancholia, was eager to reward the Marquise for making his life bright again.

It was true that France was at war, that she was facing a situation which was full of danger and she could use all her shrewd and experienced statesmen; even so, such insults to the Marquise could not be overlooked.

On the first day of February d'Argenson received his *lettre da cachet* from the King.

Monsieur d'Argenson, as your services are no longer necessary to me, I command you to send in your resignation of the Office of Secretary of State for War and other duties, and to retire to your estate at Ormes.

It was the dismissal which was dreaded by all who hoped to make their way at Court.

D'Argenson was furious. It had come at last. He knew that the Marquise would have been happier if it had come before. Now she had won. He was astonished because, less than a month ago, he thought he had won the battle between them.

Madame d'Argenson came to console him.

"This is not the end," she told him. "There is, after all, a life to be lived away from Versailles."

"Madame," he said. "I shall leave for Ormes as the King commands. It is unnecessary for you to give up your life here. You are not exiled."

Madame d'Argenson turned sadly away. She understood. He would have no need of her. His mistress, Madame d'Estrades, would share his exile.

Machault's *lettre* was differently worded and it was clear that Louis sent him away with some regret.

> Though assured of your probity, circumstances compel me to ask for your resignation. You will retain your salary and honours. You may rely on my friendship and protection, and may ask for favours for your children.

The King was clearly distressed at having to dismiss a man of whom he thought so highly. But this merely showed how deep was his regard for the Marquise. Machault's only fault, it seemed in Louis' eyes, was to have humiliated Madame de Pompadour and although, as Louis himself said, Machault was a man after his own heart, such a fault as he had committed against the King's dearest friend was enough to bring about his dismissal.

This was a lesson to all.

Any who sought to push the Marquise from her position would be a fool.

So, after the most uneasy days through which she had ever passed, the Marquise had emerged, more powerful than ever before.

Louis had soon forgotten his desire to lead a different sort of life, and it was not long before he was making his way to the Parc aux Cerfs.

Madame Bertrand greeted him with pleasure, declaring that this was one of the happiest days of her life. There was some truth in this, for she had been afraid that she might lose this very lucrative post.

"And today, Sire," she said, "you would wish to see? . . ."

Louis considered. "Tell me," he said. "How are they? What do they think of my long absence?"

"They think, Sire, that you have been away from the Court. That is what I told them. They have been eagerly awaiting an announcement of your return. They have asked me each day. They are well . . . except Louison. She has been unwell."

"I am sorry to hear that," said Louis, deciding that since she was unwell he would not ask to see her on this visit.

But while he was talking to Madame Bertrand, he heard someone at the door and turning saw Louison herself.

Madame Bertrand rose, stern and forbidding. The girls had no right to come into this room.

Louis saw that Louison had changed; she was less plump and her eyes seemed enormous. Yet she was more beautiful for a smile of happiness was on her face and she cried out: "So, my lord, my King, you are well again, and that murderer has not harmed you after all."

Madame Bertrand was speechless. Only the King, habitually gracious, gave no sign of his dismay that this girl had betrayed her knowledge of his identity.

Louison had rushed to him and thrown herself at his feet, sobbing wildly while she kissed his hand.

"Get up," said Madame Bertrand. "Go to your apartments at once."

Louison, continuing to sob out her joy, ignored the command. Madame Bertrand laid hands on the girl and roughly pulled her to her feet.

"You have gone mad," she said. "You do not know what you are saying. You have been suffering from visions."

"Do not be harsh with the child," said Louis. "Now my dear, calm yourself."

"I know . . . you are the King," sobbed Louison. "I saw letters in your pocket. When I heard that this scoundrel had tried to kill you . . . I nearly died."

"Come," said Louis, "you are distraught. Let me take you to your apartments and we will have a little supper there together. You shall tell me of your distress, which you feel no longer. That is how it shall be, eh?"

"You are back!" she cried. "You are well. Now I no longer wish to die."

The King signed to Madame Bertrand, and he himself went with Louison to her apartments.

He remained with her for several hours, during which supper was served to them.

When he left, Louison was greatly comforted.

Madame Bertrand was waiting for him when he was preparing to depart.

She was trembling with anxiety. "Sire," she cried, "I had no knowledge of that girl's wickedness."

"It is unfortunate," said Louis. "But I must blame myself. Carelessly I left my coat in a place where she was able to examine what was in my pockets."

"I have done my utmost to preserve Your Majesty's anonymity."

"I know it," said the King. "I do not wish these girls to leave here and talk of what has happened to them. The Polish Count . . . that was an excellent idea." Louis spread his hands and looked regretful.

"She must be sent away, Sire?"

"I see no alternative."

"She said she would go mad if she never saw you again."

"Mad," said the King. "She was hysterical tonight. I could well believe that there are seeds of madness in such a girl."

Madame Bertrand was silent, and the King went on: "You are a good woman, Madame Bertrand. You do your work well. I do not think it would be wise for me to find our little friend here when next I call."

Madame Bertrand bowed her head. She understood. That was to be feared with these little girls of the *faubourgs*; they had never learned restraint; when they wept and tore their hair and talked of suicide, the King found them distasteful. Such behaviour was so alien to the etiquette of Versailles in which he had been bred.

Damiens lay in his cell in the Conciergerie. He had been brought here from Versailles, and in spite of his pain he lay in a state of ecstasy.

His ankles and wrists were fettered; he could not lie down in comfort. He had suffered a great deal of torture since that windy day when, penknife in hand, he had approached the King.

They had tried hard to get a confession from him, but he had laughed in their faces and had told them nothing but the truth.

"I did it for the sake of the people and the glory of God," he continually repeated.

His trial had taken place in the Grande Chambre, where he had conducted himself with dignity. He told them frankly that he had no personal animosity towards the King, that he had merely wished to make a protest about his licentious behaviour and the condition of the people.

They had sentenced him to the most painful death they could conceive; he was to be drawn and quartered on the Place de Grève.

Ten thousand people crowded into the streets of Paris to see the end of Damiens. They were standing on the roofs; they were at every window.

There in the Place de Grève was Damiens, brought from his prison that he might suffer the utmost torment and watch the preparations for his barbarous execution.

So he watched for half an hour while the fire was lighted, the horses prepared and the bench made ready.

The crowd watched in horrified fascination. This was a sentence which had been commonplace in the days of Henri Quatre, when Ravaillac had suffered similarly for having killed that King; nowadays people had become more sensitive, more civilised; the philosophers had changed their ideas; and there were many who were unable to look on at this grisly spectacle.

Damiens groaned as his flesh was torn with red-hot pincers; this form of torture lasted for an hour as the lead was allowed slowly to drip into the wounds so as to cause the utmost pain and prolong the agony.

More dead than alive he was bound by iron rings to the quartering bench, and ropes were attached to his limbs and fastened to wild horses who were then driven in different directions.

But these did not do their work completely, and the executioner, in a sudden access of pity, severed the last quivering limb from the sufferer's body, which was then burned.

It was a sickening sight and the crowd was a silent one. Some said it was incredible that a spectacle of such barbarity could take place in the year 1757.

The King wished to hear no account of it. It was one of those unpleasant subjects which he always sought to avoid.

When he heard that a certain woman, hoping to please him, had sat close to the scene and watched every detail, he covered his face with his hands and cried out: "The disgusting creature!"

Thus ended the *affaire* Damiens.

And as the crowds were dispersing a carriage rattled through the streets of Paris. In it sat a white-faced, bewildered girl with a woman beside her.

Louison, on her way to a madhouse, would never again see the Parc aux Cerfs, nor the lover whom she had discovered to be the King of France.

CHAPTER
TWELVE

The Coming of Choiseul

The war was going badly for France. Although French soldiers were famed as being the best in the world, their leaders might be said to be the worst. This was largely due to the fact that they had been put in their high places, not because of their ability to fill them, but because, to please some charming person at home, the command had been granted to them.

France needed a strong man at the head of affairs; and the country was being ruled by a woman. She was an intelligent woman, a charming woman; cultured and artistic, no one doubted that she was clever within her limits. But she could not see beyond Versailles; her aim was not to secure France's position among the European nations but to hold her own in the esteem of the King. Moreover she was quite incapable of understanding the strategy needed in dangerous diplomatic relations with other countries.

Her friends desired honours. She loved her friends and wished to assure them of her friendship; therefore they received honours, and France lost battles.

The Prince de Soubise had shown his loyalty to her when she had found her position so precarious after the affair of Damiens, and as she wanted to show her gratitude, to the Prince de Soubise went the command of the Army.

Soubise was frivolous and effeminate, by no means the man for such responsibility, and he set out to war in anything but a military mood. Following the Army there must be numerous barbers; the fashion of Versailles made their constant service necessary, and Soubise and his kind had no intention of changing their habits merely because they were at war. The soldiers must be entertained; therefore travelling players followed the Army. There must be women, of course, and the soldiers were seen, in the towns through which they passed, their mistresses on their arms. The women needed the amenities of Paris; therefore there were milliners, *parfumeurs*, even dressmakers, and of course the inevitable hairdressers.

No officer would have thought of appearing on duty until his hair was frizzed and powdered. It had become a fashion at Court for the men to do embroidery; and many of the officers would be seen with their embroidery frames while their mistresses sat with them playing some musical instrument, singing to them, dancing for them, or perhaps merely sitting beside them also embroidering.

This, while being very colourful and almost as pleasant as being in Paris or Versailles, was not helpful to the winning of the war.

The hardy British and the Hanoverians were far less elegant, and far more military.

The incompetence of Soubise was revealed at Rossbach when Frederick's twenty thousand men wrung victory from the sixty thousand under the command of the Prince.

Frederick said afterwards: "The Army of the French seemed about to attack me, but it did not do me this honour and fled at the first discharge of our guns, without my being able to come up with it."

The conquered camp presented an extraordinary sight to Frederick's army. The barbers had fled, leaving wigs and powder behind them; the *parfumeurs* had abandoned their scent bottles, the officers their needlework, the women their fashionable garments.

There was no booty to appeal to the rough Prussian soldiers, who had no conception of the elegance of Paris and Versailles; perfume, curling tongs, and flimsy feminine garments meant little to them; the embroidery could only bewilder them; Prussians had not been brought up to handle the needle.

Frederick was kind to the prisoners he took, apologising for his inability to maintain them in the state to which they had been accustomed. "Gentlemen," he told them, "you must forgive my unpreparedness, for I did not expect you so soon — nor in such numbers."

Soubise in despair wrote to Louis: "I write to Your Majesty in my great despair. The rout of your Army is complete."

The news of the defeat at Rossbach was received in Paris with dismay; then the ironical Parisians began to laugh. They laughed at the King for allowing the Marquise to appoint his generals; and they laughed at Soubise for his incompetence.

As usual they expressed themselves in songs and epigrams; stories about Soubise and the Battle of Rossbach were circulated in the cafés.

Cartoons became popular. There was one portraying Soubise carrying a lantern looking for his Army, with the caption beneath: "Where is my Army? I believe someone has stolen it. I have mislaid it. Oh, praise the saints, there it is. Damnation! It is the enemy!"

There was another of Frederick looking cynically at Soubise in chains. Frederick was saying: "What prisoner is this? The Prince de Soubise! Release him at once. He is far more use to us when he commands the French."

But underlying the cynical comments was a great disquiet. "What are we doing on the side of Austria?" the people asked. "Have not the Austrians always been the enemies of France?"

The Dauphine went so far as to call on the Marquise.

"I pray you," she cried, "make no more generals, Madame."

But the Marquise had never felt so sure of her power as now. When she looked back and saw how she had come safely through the vicissitudes of Versailles, she had no doubt that she could bring France to victory. She even studied the maps and worked out plans of

214

action; and when Bernis, Minister for Foreign Affairs, overcome by the defeat of Rossbach, suggested suing for peace, and the King admitted that he was weary of war, the Marquise was still determined it should continue. She had placed herself at the head of the war party.

Those who left the game lost it, she decided.

The war was to go on.

Another of the generals of France was the Duc de Richelieu, who had been given his command by the King because of his power to amuse.

It may seem strange that this ageing *roué* should have sought to go to war, lover of elegance and luxury that he was. But he had his reasons. During his extravagant life he had built up a mound of debts; and although so far he had succeeded in keeping his creditors at bay, he realised now that he could not hope to do so indefinitely. He must recoup his fortunes. His idea was that he would go to war, plunder his enemies and with his booty return to Versailles a rich man.

Thus, while Soubise, idealistic perhaps but ingloriously incompetent, was displaying his weakness before the Prussians, Richelieu was making forays, not on the armies but on the civilian population.

Such methods, while followed with eagerness by certain of his officers, who themselves would take a proportion of the gains, created an alarming lack of discipline in the camp of the Duc de Richelieu; but eventually, having enough loot to satisfy himself and his creditors, Richelieu retired from the Army and,

215

returning to Court, set about building himself a magnificent house in Paris.

Paris, watching it grow in splendour every day, called it "Le Pavilion de Hanovre".

With the retirement of Richelieu, Louis de Bourbon (Comte de Clermont) took his place, and his election to this high post was received with ridicule throughout France. Fifty years old, he was the great-grandson of the famous Condé, and Abbé of Saint Germain-des-Prés. Although he had taken Holy Orders he was noted for his libertinism; he had however actually served with distinction under Maurice de Saxe, but quickly proved that, although he was a man who under the direction of a great commander could be a good soldier, he himself was quite unfitted to command.

Lacking foresight he could not see the main issue, being preoccupied with unimportant detail; and he failed at Crefield as Soubise had failed at Rossbach, for against him was Pitt's "Army of Operations" and Ferdinand of Brunswick's troops.

The French were in despair.

There had to be economy at Versailles to help meet the disastrous cost of the war. So a great show was made of curbing extravagance. Many of the building schemes of the King and the Marquise were suspended, and there were no theatrical performances; to banish boredom there was more intensive activity at the card table. There was little the King enjoyed so much as a game of cards played for high stakes, for while the Treasury was expected to meet his debts, he pocketed his winnings.

Yearning to lead the Army, the Dauphin looked on uneasily at the state of affairs. He had always fancied himself as a soldier, and he believed the time had come for someone to save France from disaster.

The Dauphine believed with her husband that he was that man.

She had always supported him wholeheartedly. Poor Marie-Josèphe, she suffered acutely. Madame Dadonville had given the Dauphin a son, and little Auguste Dadonville was a great joy to his father.

Still, Marie-Josèphe tried not to reproach her husband, and never referred to Madame Dadonville. As for the Dauphin he was aware of his wife's magnanimity, and felt a great desire to escape from it. How could he do this more gracefully than by going to the front?

He talked with his father about this matter.

"What is happening to our armies, father?" he said. "Our soldiers are going to pieces because of the inferiority of their leaders. What could inspire them more than to see your only legitimate son at their head — their own Dauphin?"

The King studied his son quizzically. The Dauphin had stood out against his father on more than one occasion. He had placed himself firmly on the side of the Jesuits; he had shown open criticism of Madame de Pompadour. True, at the time of the King's indisposition after the attack by Damiens, he had behaved with decorum — to a certain extent; but that could have been merely because he sensed the mood of the people, who at the time were showing unusual affection for his father.

No, the King did not like his son very much; he did not trust him.

Moreover Madame de Pompadour had already named the Duc de Broglie as the general to succeed Clermont.

"Your request moves me deeply," said the King slyly, "but you must not allow yourself to panic, my son. The war has gone against us, but activities have scarcely begun. Do not forget your position. You are heir to the throne. I could not allow you to place yourself in danger. Nay, my son, delighted as I am to know you are of a warlike nature to match your ancestors', I forbid you to leave Court."

The Dauphin went furiously from the King's apartments to those of the Dauphine.

"The destiny of France," he cried, "is in the hands of that woman."

There were many in the country who, with great apprehension, believed him to be right.

Perceiving France to be approaching one of the most disastrous hours of her destiny, the Abbé de Bernis, prevented by the Marquise from making peace, had two desires: one for his Cardinal's hat, the other to relinquish his post, or to call in an assistant.

Bernis had always believed that a Cardinal's hat was an umbrella to shelter a man from the storms which could threaten him.

218

He was scarcely an ambitious man and had had honours thrust upon him rather than having won them for himself. He had been born a poor man, but had made a fortune and would have been content with that. But since he had been selected by the King to teach the Marquise de Pompadour — Madame d'Etioles as she had been then — the graces of Versailles, the Marquise had selected him to be her friend, and thus he had become one of the most important ministers in France.

Like many of his compatriots he was an extremely sensual man, had become something of a rake, and was reputed to have indulged in a love affair with Madame Infanta, Louis' eldest daughter.

He was a man who found himself continually subdued by women. Madame Infanta had made her demands; now Madame de Pompadour arranged which path he should tread.

Yet he longed for peace because he was overwhelmed by the tragic position of his country, and he saw ahead not only defeat on the Continent but the loss of the French Colonial Empire to those zealous colonisers, the British. Already French possessions in India and Canada were in jeopardy.

Thus in spite of the Marquise he pleaded eloquently with the Council to sue for peace.

He pointed out that Clive was gaining the upper hand in India and that Louisiana and Canada were in dire need of help.

The Council wavered. Peace seemed the answer.

But the Marquise was not so easily defeated.

219

★　★　★

Madame de Pompadour sat with three of her women — her greatest friends. They all came from Lorraine, and were Madame de Mirepoix, Madame de Marsan and the Duchesse de Gramont.

Each of these women had profited by the friendship of the Marquise; Madame de Mirepoix being her *confidante*, Madame Marsan having been given the post of governess to the King's daughters, and the Duchesse de Gramont, like Madame de Mirepoix, sharing the Marquise's confidences; the Duchesse had not yet achieved the place she intended to have at Court, but she was the most ambitious of the three.

With her friends the Marquise discussed the weakness of Bernis and his flouting of her wishes by delivering that oration to the Council which had almost resulted in a plea for peace.

"I shall never forget, my little cat," said the Marquise, "that, after the Damiens affair, when I was preparing to leave Versailles, you told me that to quit the game was to lose it. That is what this coward Bernis is preparing to do now."

"You need a strong man at the head of affairs," said the Duchesse de Gramont.

"Indeed you are right," answered the Marquise. "But where are the strong men of France?"

"I know of one who now serves his country abroad and would welcome a chance to do so at home."

The Marquise was smiling at the Duchesse. She had no need to ask who that man was, being fully aware of

220

the devotion which existed between the Duchesse and her brother.

The Comte de Stainville had brought his sister to Court some years before. They were a devoted pair; too devoted, it was said.

Although the Duchesse had been a *chanoinesse* of a convent — a life for which she had no wish or aptitude — and the Comte de Stainville sought to make his way at Court, they lived openly together there to the astonishment of all who beheld them.

Stainville had been of immeasurable help to the Marquise in the Choiseul-Beaupré affair, and since then she had determined to make him her firm ally. His sister had become her friend, and he had his embassies. But it was natural that a man such as Stainville would look higher than an ambassadorial post; he would also like to be at Versailles with his sister. The virtuous and beautiful wife — with whom the Marquise had provided him — accompanied him on his mission, laid her immense fortune at his service, forgave him his many love affairs and was herself, besides being exceptionally virtuous, decidedly charming.

Stainville however believed no woman could equal his tall, flamboyant and ambitious sister; he had found an old and rich husband for her in the Duc de Gramont, whom she left soon after the marriage ceremony.

"Well?" said the Marquise, smiling.

"I refer, of course, to my brother," said the Duchesse. "He is eager for a chance to use his undoubted talents where they can best serve France."

The Marquise was thoughtful.

It was the answer, of course. Bring Stainville to Court, let him replace Bernis. He had once proved himself to be the faithful friend of the Marquise. Let him continue to do so.

The Comte de Stainville had returned from Austria to take the place of Bernis, who received his Cardinal's hat and was dismissed to Soissons. Stainville was created Duc de Choiseul, and under this bright and energetic man hope returned to France.

Choiseul was brilliant; no one denied it. He was ugly yet he could charm to such a degree that at any gathering he would become the central figure.

He was short of stature though shapely; his forehead was very high and broad, his eyes small, his hair red, and his lips thick, but it was the small *retroussé* nose which gave his face a comic look and would, on another man, have robbed him of dignity.

He was extremely witty — often cruelly so; his love affairs were as numerous as those of Richelieu, although there was no woman who held such a high place in his affections as his sister. He was very extravagant; fortunately for him his wife was one of the richest women in France. He was recklessly generous. Whoever called on him near dinner-time would be asked to stay to the meal. For this reason he kept two huge tables in his dining salon. The first was laid for thirty-five, and if there were more guests the second was immediately made ready.

Many said he was an atheist although he appeared occasionally at religious ceremonies; it was clear however that he was there for the sake of convention. He had a tremendous respect for the intellect, and he sought his true friends among the philosophers and the free-thinkers, who found a more ready welcome in his house than did the religious. He corresponded regularly with Voltaire; and was always eager to study new ideas.

He was a man of many parts, supremely confident in his own ability to make a name for himself and extricate France from the morass of failure in which she seemed fast to be sinking; he cared for the opinion of no one.

He made wild love to every woman whose charms appealed to him although these affairs were of short duration; and he made no attempt to conceal his relationship with his sister. Indeed he set a new fashion at Court. Many gallants, whose habit it was slavishly to follow any new fashion, began to profess a love for their sisters.

In some quarters Choiseul was ironically known as Ptolemy, after the Egyptian kings who married their sisters.

The Duc d'Ayen told Madame de Pompadour that he would very much like to follow the prevailing fashion, but he had three sisters and it was so hard to choose — they were all so unattractive.

Choiseul enjoyed criticism. He had the utmost confidence in himself and his future. He could spend half the night in pleasure, and next day bring his tremendous energy, not in the least impaired by the previous night's revelry, to bear on State affairs.

It was believed that, at times of stress, there often arose the man of the moment — a man of genius, in whose capable hands could be placed the helm of the Ship of State which appeared about to founder on the rocks of defeat, famine and perhaps revolution.

Louis believed he had found that man in the Duc de Choiseul.

CHAPTER
THIRTEEN

Mademoiselle de Romans

Louis sought desperately to forget the war and all its problems and, because he was Louis, he found his greatest consolation among the attractive young women whom Le Bel brought to him.

Most of these came to him by way of the Parc aux Cerfs but some pleased him so much that he took them from this establishment and set them up in houses of their own.

Mademoiselle Hainault was the daughter of a prosperous merchant. Her outstanding beauty had brought her to Le Bel's notice and, as even prosperous merchants saw great advantage in their daughters' being given to the King, her family put nothing in the way of her progress. They did insist however that this daughter of members of the respectable middle class should not be an inmate of the Parc aux Cerfs.

Having seen the girl, Louis found the parents' request reasonable. Thus Mademoiselle Hainault was given her own establishment and when — but not for some years — Louis tired of her, he provided a Marquis for a husband. In return she gave Louis two daughters.

Another girl who received special favours was the illegitimate daughter of the Vicomte de Ravel — Lucie-Magdeleine d'Estaing, who also gave the King two daughters.

Madame de Pompadour looked on benignly at these relationships, since they kept the King amused and gave her not the slightest tremor of apprehension. She knew that since the consequences of the Damiens outrage had brought disgrace to such powerful men as d'Argenson and Machault, it would have to be a very brave man or woman who would dare challenge her power.

But the ever-watchful Marquise began to notice that the King was not visiting his Parc aux Cerfs with the same eagerness as he had previously, and it occurred to her that he had had a surfeit of his *grisettes*.

If that were so, it could only mean that the danger could become imminent of a Court lady, with powerful friends behind her, winning the King's attention.

She feared that Le Bel, in searching for women who would please his master, might conceivably choose them according to his own taste. Might this not result in a stream of girls who had rather similar characteristics being brought to the Parc aux Cerfs? No wonder Louis was becoming jaded!

What must be found was a beauty of an entirely different kind, and the Marquise decided she would send out new scouts to discover her.

She sent for Sartines, the Lieutenant of the Police, and told him to search Paris for a girl who was beautiful but not conventionally so; she must have some startling quality in her appearance; she must be someone who was outstandingly different.

Sartines, realising that one of his most important duties, if he were a wise man, was to please the Marquise, set out on his search.

His was a difficult task, for the King's inexhaustible adventurings appeared to have led him to acquire all shapes and sizes.

One day when he was in a gaming-house, and talking idly to the proprietress, she spoke nostalgically of her childhood in Grenoble.

"Ah, Monsieur, if my parents could see me now! What a difference, eh . . . That quiet house in the square. Papa so strict, taking such care of his daughters . . . and what has happened? One of them comes to Paris to run a gaming-house."

Sartines nodded. She was a handsome woman and he had no wish to try his luck at the tables today. He invited her to drink with him and she accepted; but he could see that her thoughts were far away in a quiet house in a Grenoble square.

"Oh yes, Papa guarded us well. I . . . and my sister. Mind you, he would have to guard *her* well. I went to see them only a few months ago. Very respectable I had to become, Monsieur le Lieutenant. No mention of the gaming-house! Had I told them of that I should not have been allowed to see my sister. She is beautiful. I have never seen anyone quite like her. She is like one of the statues you see in the gardens. She is the tallest woman I ever saw."

"The tallest woman you ever saw . . ." murmured the Lieutenant hastily. "Tell me, how tall is Mademoiselle?"

"Mademoiselle de Romans is six feet tall, I swear. She is exactly like one of those stone goddesses. I always thought there could not be women quite like that — towering above other women, perfectly shaped, with black eyes and black hair. My sister is a goddess, Monsieur. If you saw her you would know why she is never allowed out without a chaperone."

"If I saw her, I am sure I should agree with you," said the Lieutenant with a smile.

He was determined to see her — and that without delay.

As soon as Sartines set eyes on Mademoiselle de Romans he was certain that the search which Madame de Pompadour had commanded him to make was ended.

He saw her in the company of her parents. Lawyer de Romans was quite clearly a stern and self-righteous man; but the Lieutenant did not experience any great qualms. The honours to be gained by becoming the King's mistress were equal to any which could come to Mademoiselle de Romans through any marriage she could make in Grenoble — that was if one counted honour by material gain, which the Lieutenant was sure Lawyer de Romans would.

He asked for an invitation to the house, saying that he came on very important business from Versailles.

The magic word "Versailles" immediately gained this and, as they sat over their wine, the Lieutenant said: "Your daughter must be the most beautiful girl in Grenoble, perhaps in France."

The lawyer looked pleased.

"What a precious possession!" went on the Lieutenant. "For it is clear that not only is she beautiful but virtuous."

"We have guarded her well," said the lawyer. "But Monsieur, shall we discuss your business?"

"She is my business, Monsieur de Romans. I want you to bring her to Versailles."

"For what purpose?"

"That would depend on your daughter. She could make a great position for herself at Court, Monsieur. It is a sin to hide one so outstanding in beauty and virtue from the world and keep from her those advantages which her merit would bring her."

Monsieur de Romans rested his elbows on the table and looked earnestly at the Lieutenant.

"My daughter has many suitors, Monsieur. There is none whom I have so far deemed worthy of her. I should need a very excellent proposition before I could consider your suggestion. I have my daughter's future to think of."

"You are a wise parent, Monsieur. Let us make a bargain. Let her be brought to Versailles — oh, with the utmost decorum of course. I can assure you that there would be no difficulty in bringing her to the notice of the King himself. Moreover I feel sure that, once His Majesty had set eyes on Mademoiselle de Romans, he would be so delighted with her beauty that he would make sure the excellent proposition, which you insist on, would not be denied her."

"It would have to be a *very* excellent proposition," said the lawyer.

"Let us arrange this. Have her brought to Versailles. If the . . . proposition is not to your taste, you can bring her back to her sequestered life. I am sure she will find a worthy husband of the *haute bourgeoisie* here in Grenoble. That would no doubt be very satisfactory for a young lady of her position in society — who is not possessed of great ambitions."

The lawyer's eyes gleamed with cupidity and determination.

His daughter was going to Versailles. He foresaw a brilliant future, for the sake of which he and her mother would smother those qualms they felt regarding their daughter's entering into an unsanctified union. Who knew, such a union might eventually lead to marriage with the *haute noblesse.* How different a future that would be from what could only be hers if she continued to live her sheltered life in Grenoble!

When the King saw her he was enchanted.

He said she was like a goddess. She was Minerva, so perfectly shaped, a woman to tower above all others in her physical perfection, a woman surely not of this earth.

Sartines informed the King that her father was a highly respectable lawyer and as such could not allow his daughter to become an inmate of the Parc aux Cerfs.

"Indeed not," said the King. "Arrange an establishment for her immediately. Let it be luxurious enough to please her parents, for I feel very grateful to them for having produced such a daughter."

She was under nineteen years of age and bewildered by the change of fortune which had come to her. She had been well educated, a fact which would have perturbed the Marquise had she been aware of it; and the tender charm of her royal lover soon overcame her reluctance. She was immediately put at ease by his gracious manners. She must forget, Louis told her, that he was the King. When they were together he was plain Louis de Bourbon who was falling more deeply in love every day with Mademoiselle de Romans.

Sartines had certainly succeeded in finding someone who was different from the pretty little toys who only pleased for a short time.

This intelligent young Amazon would, Louis believed, always have the power to delight him. He was certain that he would never tire of her.

She was gentle by nature and that appealed to him; she did not ask impossibilities although she did not forget that she was no *grisette*, but the daughter of a respectable lawyer.

Louis was eager to shower gifts upon her. She had her own magnificent carriage and rode about Paris in this, a figure of statuesque beauty. Because of her great height she did not wear her magnificent hair piled high, but low on her head. Very soon the women of Paris were following the new fashion and hair was being dressed *à la Romans*.

People wandered out to her charming house at Passy to look at her, to note what she was wearing, the way she did her hair.

She became known throughout Paris and Versailles as *la petite maîtresse*, a name given her partly ironically, since she was far from *petite*, partly to distinguish her from that *grande maîtresse*, Madame de Pompadour.

Madame de Pompadour smiled graciously on the newcomer, but after a while she began to wonder whether Sartines had been too assiduous in his duty when he had set out to find someone who was entirely different from all others.

Was she so wise to have given that order?

She heard, for she had informants in all quarters and naturally she would not overlook the establishment of Mademoiselle de Romans, that the King's *petite maîtresse* often received him reclining on a couch of taffeta, completely nude, but that her wonderful hair was so long that it made a rippling blue-black cloak through which her alabaster skin gleamed like the statues in the gardens of Versailles.

The Marquise winced. She must keep a vigilant eye on *la petite maîtresse*.

The Duc de Choiseul was delighted with the good fortunes which had come his way.

He had placed himself in charge of Foreign Affairs, War and the Navy; and since the country was at war, this meant that he was virtually the most important man in France.

He was of an optimistic nature and refused to be depressed by defeat; he had an unlimited belief in his own powers to rule, and, no matter what disaster befell France, he was certain that he, the great Choiseul, the man of the moment, would bring his country and himself gloriously through every ordeal.

He was completely given to the Austrian cause because he was of Lorraine and, since Maria Theresa's husband was the Duc de Lorraine, there was a certain family connexion between himself and the Imperial House of Austria. He was determined to maintain the alliance no matter how unpopular it was.

He was volatile and witty, and therefore a man who delighted the King. If the country's affairs were in an unsatisfactory state, Louis preferred the optimistic view; he liked to be with men who made him laugh. Choiseul, making light of France's troubles, making much of her happier prospects, brought contentment to Louis, and made it possible for him to continue with his pleasures, his conscience stilled.

Choiseul had brought about the third Treaty of Vienna in which he promised Maria Theresa the aid of a hundred thousand Frenchmen. The Treaty assured her that France would not sign a peace treaty until Frederick had returned Silesia to Austria. It was small wonder that Maria Theresa was delighted with the Treaty, particularly as, in return for these benefits, she was not asked to help France in her struggle against England. Choiseul had however received the pledge of

233

Elizabeth the Czarina to help France in the struggle against her enemies.

The Marquise persuaded the King that Choiseul was the most brilliant statesman France had known since the days of the Cardinals, Richelieu and Mazarin.

Meanwhile Choiseul carefully picked as his subordinates men whom he could trust to serve him. Many of his actions were bold rather than brilliant. He had attempted an invasion of England, in his enthusiasm forgetting the power of the English fleet. French squadrons were miserably defeated everywhere they attacked, and the result was disaster so great that the French could no longer be said to possess a home fleet.

Seventeen fifty-nine was a year of tragedy. In Canada the Marquis de Montcalm was beseeching the Government to send him help against the British. He died at Quebec in September of that year and, although General Wolfe the leader of the British troops died also, that battle ended in a resounding victory for the British.

Choiseul, realising that the war could not be won, sought to make peace with England, but Prime Minister Pitt was determined to continue the war.

The people were crying out against the Austrian alliance, and Choiseul, resilient as ever, dexterous as a conjurer, looked about him for a new rabbit to pull out of his hat.

He believed he had it.

He went to see his sister with whom he often discussed affairs. He had a great respect for her and his passionate devotion blinded him to many of her faults.

She received him affectionately.

He looked at her with admiration, his head on one side, seeing her as the beloved companion of his childhood whom he had brought to Court to be with him when they had very little money and only their noble lineage as assets.

"You are beautiful," he told her.

She drew him to her in an embrace. She was taller than he was and many of their enemies said that she was the more masculine of the two.

"Why does the King have to send for a lawyer's daughter when he could find what he wants at Court?" murmured Choiseul.

The Duchess laughed. "Ha! And how goes this great love affair with Venus?"

"Minerva, my dear Minerva. I had it from his Majesty's own lips. Mademoiselle de Romans is as superb as a goddess. She is Minerva herself."

"Minerva," said the Duchesse. "Now I should have thought Venus more suited to Louis' mood. Was not Minerva impervious to the claims of love?"

"There have been too many Venuses in Louis' life. Let him have his Minerva for a change. Change! It is all change. Richelieu has impressed upon him that variety is the sauce which makes the meal into a banquet. But you, my dear, remind me of Minerva, and I cannot see why . . ."

The Duchesse grimaced mildly. "*You* cannot see why. My dear Etienne, what ideas are you putting into my head? There is one who would see very well why. My dear, she is your great friend; she is also mine. You know why we must have our little Venuses from the dressmakers, our Minervas from the *bourgeoisie*. She would not tolerate one of *us* occupying that place which she guards so jealously although she can no longer occupy it."

"It would be dangerous . . . very dangerous to lose her friendship."

"It is due to it, my dear brother, that you are where you are today."

"And where I intend to stay!"

He was silent for a while; then putting his arm about her he led her to a couch where they sat down; and still embracing her he said: "I have a plan. The people are restive, as you know, and something must be done with the greatest speed. They are saying, 'The English are against us. The Prussians are against us; our friends are our old enemies the Austrians.' The people are losing heart becase they fear their enemies and do not trust their friends. I have an idea for a pact which I shall call the Family Compact."

She nodded, her smile full of admiration. "You are a genius, my dear."

He accepted the compliment lightly. He believed it no less than she did.

"Have you realised that a certain section of Europe is ruled by the Bourbon family? France, Spain, Naples and Parma. In times of stress families should stand together. I propose now to show the people of France that, contrary to the opinions of those pessimists among them, they have many friends in Europe. They are saying we have only one ally. Only one ally! If I make this pact — and make it I will — I will say to them: 'We have all the Bourbons of Europe as our friends. We stand together against all our enemies. One family. From Spain to Sicily I have but to beckon and they will come.'"

"And will they?"

Choiseul lifted his shoulders. "Our greatest need at the moment, sweet sister, is to pacify the people, to make them happy. One step at a time."

She smiled. "I see. We have come a long way from the poverty of our childhood, brother."

"And we will go much farther . . . both of us, my dearest . . . you and I. Our dear friend will not live for ever. She cannot live for ever."

"And then?"

"And then, and then . . ." murmured Choiseul, "it may be that the King will not have to look for his goddesses so far from his Court, eh?"

"But time is passing, Etienne."

"Time! What is time to us? We are immortal. I see no reason why you should not occupy the first place in the land. Others besides our dear friend cannot live for ever. I remember Madame de Maintenon."

"Etienne!"

Choiseul laid his hand lightly on his sister's lips.

"Silence, sweet one, for the moment. We can wait. We have learned to wait. Let us wait a little longer . . . only a little longer."

"Ambitious dreams, Etienne," she said.

"Great honours, my sister, invariably begin as ambitious dreams."

237

"The two of us together, brother! Is there any limit to the heights we can climb?"

"Only the summit is our limit, sister. Wait and see. The future is rosy for the Duc de Choiseul, and all the glory that shall ever be his he swears he will share with her whom he loves; beyond all others."

There were occasions when it was necessary, greatly to the King's regret, for him to visit Paris.

The people had now forgotten his brief return to favour when they thought him to be dying from the knife-thrust of Damiens. They did not call abuse at him as he rode their streets; they merely gave him sullen looks and silence. Indeed, such was his dignity that it was almost impossible to abuse him in his presence.

He sat in his carriage, erect, seemingly indifferent to the mood of his people.

Crowds gathered to see him pass, as they had ever done, and it was only when the carriage had rumbled on that the murmuring would break out.

As his carriage passed by the gardens of the Tuileries his eye was suddenly caught by a fair-haired child with her father, who was clearly an old soldier.

The girl was richly though by no means elegantly dressed, and her father was bending down to her. Louis could imagine the words he was saying to her. "See, there he is. There is the King."

The girl's beautiful blue eyes were wide with excitement. She pointed to the carriage. Louis leaned a little forward and bowed his head slightly in acknowledgement of her gesture.

He saw the glowing smile on her face.

A charming child, he thought. To see her has made the journey worthwhile.

She must be very young. He guessed she would be something under fourteen. Girls of that age seemed to him particularly delightful. They had a certain innocence which was lost later.

He wondered who she was, and thought how pleasant it would be to take her hands, embrace her and tell her that it made her King very happy to think that he had a subject such as she was.

On his return to Versailles, he sent for Le Bel.

"I saw a charming child in the Tuileries gardens today," he said.

"And Your Majesty wishes to make her acquaintance?"

"She was such a pretty creature, but odiously dressed. Her gown was pink and she wore jewellery, obviously false. I should like to see a child as pretty as that well dressed. She pointed at the carriage. I should like to have such a pretty child taught how to behave."

"If your Majesty will tell me her name . . ."

"I do not know her name. I but saw her as I passed the Tuileries."

"Sire, it will not be easy to find her if we do not know her name nor where she lives. There are many young girls who go to the Tuileries gardens."

"You give up too easily," said the King.

Le Bel sweated with apprehension. "Sire, I will search every street in Paris. If that child is to be found, I shall find her."

"In the meantime send for Sartines. We will ask his help."

Le Bel was displeased. He knew that Sartines had discovered Mademoiselle de Romans, but he was annoyed that the Lieutenant of Police should take on duties which previously he had considered his own — to be shared of course with the othet *valets de chambre*.

When Sartines arrived, clearly delighted to be called on the King's mission, Louis kept Le Bel with him while he explained what he expected from these two.

"Monsieur Sartines," he said, "you are a Lieutenant of Police. You should be able to bring me a young girl whom I saw today in the gardens of the Tuileries."

"She shall be brought to you immediately, Sire," said Sartines.

"When you find her," added the King, while Le Bel smiled sardonically.

"Le Bel, I suspect, despairs of finding her," said the King.

Sartines smiled. "We of the police have our methods."

"As I thought," said the King. "Perhaps you can teach some of them to Le Bel."

"His Majesty saw the child with her father in the Tuileries gardens," said Le Bel. "She is fair-haired, blue-eyed, under fourteen and very beautiful. Her father is an old soldier. That is all the description we have. But I have no doubt, Monsieur, with your efficient police methods you will have little difficulty in finding such a child among the crowds of Paris."

240

Sartines put his head on one side.

"This young lady was not in a carriage, Sire?"

"No, on foot," said the King.

"And she was well dressed?"

"In a hideous rose-coloured gown which fortunately could not disguise her grace. It was clearly a new gown."

"Then depend upon it," said Sartines, "if the family have no carriage they cannot be rich, and the young lady will wear the gown frequently on her journeys to the gardens. As she had no carriage it is very possible that she lives near the Tuileries gardens, for it is hardly likely that she would have walked far in this rose-coloured gown."

The King laughed and laid one hand on Sartines' shoulder, the other on Le Bel's.

"You see, Le Bel," he said, "how wise we were to call in the police. Go, my friends, work together. I do not wish to see my good friend Le Bel unhappy. Bring this child to me. Tell her parents that they will never regret putting her into my care."

The *valet de chambre* and the Lieutenant of Police bowed themselves out and set about their task.

Sartines was smiling contentedly; finding girls for the King was a more profitable business than hunting criminals for the law.

"The first one we'll ask is the lemonade-seller on the terrace," said Sartines. "If this girl is brought often to the gardens, he will be more likely to know her than anyone else. He is an old friend of mine."

The lemonade-seller did not seem very pleased to see his old friend Sartines.

He was obviously on the alert and had a look of guilt. Sartines was not proposing to worry him about whatever he might have on his conscience; he had come for information which the lemonade-man need not be afraid to give him.

"Good day to you, my friend. What heat, eh! A drink of lemonade? That is exactly what we need on a day such as this."

"Exactly," said Le Bel.

They sat on the steps of the terrace and drank the lemonade which was served to them.

"We want your help," Sartines began.

"Monsieur," protested the lemonade-seller, "I have done nothing. I cannot think why the police will not leave me in peace."

"It is not about yourself that we wish to question you."

"It is about a certain young lady," said Le Bel.

"Who is *he*?" asked the lemonade-seller suspiciously — indicating Le Bel.

"A gentleman of Versailles."

The lemonade-seller grinned. He told himself that he was a member of the police more likely, dressed up to look different.

Le Bel said impatiently: "Have you noticed a young lady — a child almost — who was here yesterday with her father? She was dressed very well in pink. The father was an old soldier and they came to see the King drive by."

The lemonade-seller screwed up his face. "What have they done?" he asked.

"Nothing for which they can be blamed."

The man shook his head. "I've got my business to attend to. It does not include gaping at the crowds."

"But surely you must watch for customers?"

Sartines had taken some coins from his pocket, and jingled them significantly.

The lemonade-seller's eyes glistened as he watched.

"But how do I come into this?" he asked.

"You are not concerned in it," said Sartines. "You are merely giving us information which we ask, and for which we are prepared to pay."

"Well, I did notice her, so there! Who could help it in that dress? They bought some of my lemonade. They always do when they come by."

"And you know who they are?"

The man hesitated, and Sartines slipped the coins into his hand.

"The father is Monsieur de Tiercelin," he said. "He thinks the world of that girl. So does Madame. They think no one is good enough to look at her."

"Thank you," said Sartines, and to Le Bel: "Come. It should not be difficult to find the home of Monsieur de Tiercelin which is close to the Tuileries."

It was not difficult. In less than half an hour after the encounter with the lemonade-seller they were being received into the Tiercelin home.

"Now," said Sartines, "it is your turn, Monsieur Le Bel."

The task before him was a commonplace one to Le Bel. He relished it. He rarely encountered parents who were not overjoyed when they discovered his mission; and in any case a little persuasion, a little foresight of the glorious future which awaited their daughters soon made them amenable to suggestions.

Monsieur and Madame de Tiercelin had led them into a small parlour which was somewhat ornate and quite hideous in eyes accustomed to the exquisite taste of Versailles.

"I will tell you quickly why I have come," said Le Bel. "I serve the King and come on his orders. His Majesty saw your daughter yesterday in the Tuileries gardens. He thought her charming and would like to make her acquaintance."

The Tiercelins looked at each other. They were clearly not surprised. They thought their daughter the most beautiful girl in Paris. It might have been that for this reason she had been taken to see the King pass by.

Madame de Tiercelin said: "Our daughter is very young."

"How old is she?" asked Le Bel.

"Twelve years old."

"The King has offered to undertake her education for a few years."

"Educate her . . . as a Court lady!"

"He will doubtless supervise her education himself."

The parents looked at each other, their eyes gleaming.

"Do you object to this offer which the King makes you? It is not a command, you know."

Madame de Tiercelin looked at her husband and nodded her approval.

"Our daughter is a very lovely child," began Monsieur de Tiercelin. "Already she has offers of marriage . . ."

"If you think that you can provide a more worthy husband for your daughter than the King eventually would, then you must make your own choice. His Majesty does not wish to cause you any unhappiness in this matter." Le Bel turned to Sartines. "Come, Monsieur, I see that Monsieur and Madame de Tiercelin have not heard of the great good fortune which can befall those in whom His Majesty takes a paternal interest. We have no instructions to inform them of this. We will take our leave."

Madame de Tiercelin was glaring at her husband as though she considered him a fool.

"Wait, Messieurs," she said.

Then Le Bel and Sartines knew that the case of Mademoiselle de Tiercelin was going to be as simple as most others.

Perhaps it was because Madeleine de Romans was pregnant — and the King always wished to avoid pregnant women — that he gave so much attention to Mademoiselle de Tiercelin.

She came to Versailles itself — a pert little creature, very lovely indeed to look at, divested of her hideous pink dress and wearing the garments which had been chosen for her.

She had been completely spoiled by her family, and therefore had little respect for the King. Fortunately for little Mademoiselle de Tiercelin he was in the mood to enjoy this.

The beautiful Mademoiselle de Romans was a dignified creature, and although she had never learned the etiquette of the nobility, a little tuition — as in the case of Madame de Pompadour — would quickly have put her at ease in Court circles. The King had no intention of marrying off his statuesque mistress; he was merely seeking a little diversion while she was indisposed and Mademoiselle de Tiercelin supplied that adequately.

Louis found the child so amusing that he said he himself would undertake her education for a while. This he did, teaching her many lessons in the *petits appartements*, even occasionally taking a meal with her.

It was an experience he had never had before, and it amused him to know that the Dauphin was even more shocked than usual.

But when Mademoiselle de Romans' boy was born he felt a wish to spend more time in her company and grew very fond of the child who resembled his "Belle Madeleine".

As for Madeleine de Romans, she was completely happy. She adored her little son and had a great affection for the King. She had not been a demanding woman when she had only herself to consider, but now that she had this beautiful boy she was determined to win for him the highest honours.

When the King came to visit her, while she was in bed with the child, he expressed his great pleasure to see her recovered from her ordeal and showed a further interest in the boy.

"I am so happy," she told him; "there is only one thing I need to make me perfectly so."

She looked so beautiful, with her black hair spread about her on the pillows, that Louis could not prevent himself from telling her passionately: "If it is in my power to grant it, I will do so."

"It is in your power," she told him.

"Then you have attained perfect happiness."

"Our son is shortly to be baptised," she said. "I wish him to be known by the name of Bourbon."

Louis hesitated. But he had given his word and, although he was quite capable of breaking a promise to his ministers, he found it very difficult to do so in the case of an exceptionally beautiful woman who pleaded so charmingly.

He stooped and kissed her.

"Take care," he said, "of Monsieur de Bourbon."

Her radiant smile was reward enough, he decided; and he continued to think of her after he left her.

Thus he was in no mood for petulant Mademoiselle de Tiercelin. A delightful child, he thought, but pert, far too pert. She needed discipline, which he found it hard to administer.

He sent for Le Bel when he returned to Versailles.

"I believe," he said, "that we promised Monsieur and Madame de Tiercelin that we would educate their daughter in a manner to fit her for the station she might one day be called upon to occupy."

"We did, Sire."

"Then pray make arrangements for her to leave for a convent where she will receive that education."

"It shall be done, Sire," said Le Bel.

The Court now knew that the King had temporarily tired of his naughty little playmate and had returned to the more dignified liaison with the statuesque Mademoiselle de Romans.

The dreams of Madeleine de Romans were centred in the boy with those dark blue eyes which, declared everyone who saw him, proclaimed him the son of the King.

She refused to let any of her servants bathe or dress him. He slept in her room and she herself fed him. She was terrified of allowing anyone to touch him, for how could any but herself understand how precious he was!

As she suckled him she would imagine the glories which would come to him. He had been baptised in the name of Bourbon, so she would induce the King to acknowledge him publicly as his natural son. In time she would persuade the King to legitimise him. Why should he not? Had not Louis Quatorze legitimised some of his illegitimate sons?

He would become a Comte, a Duc. He would have a safe place at Court. He would grow up so handsome that everyone would love him.

"My little one," she murmured, "your fortune is made. One day you will be one of the great men of

France . . ." She amended that. "One day you will be the greatest man in France."

She was so sure that her plans would materialise that she was determined he should be treated from the very beginning of his life as a royal Bourbon.

All her servants must follow her example and call the child Highness. Everyone must bow before approaching him, and as soon as he was old enough she took him driving in the Bois. He rode alone in the carriage, while she sat in the front with the driver, as a governess might have sat. She wished the world to know that she, his mother, was far beneath him socially.

This caused a great deal of comment and, as it was known that the boy had been baptised in the name of Bourbon, rumours were soon in circulation that the King had promised Mademoiselle de Romans to acknowledge her child as his son.

Madame du Hausset heard this news and hastened to bring it to the Marquise.

"It is a dangerous situation, Madame," she pointed out.

The Marquise was wistful. If only she had borne Louis a child such as this one was reputed to be!

"It has usually been his custom to marry them off when they become pregnant," mused the Marquise.

"Yes, Madame. There can be no doubt that his feelings for this one are different."

"It is a pity. What of this young Tiercelin?"

"She is now attending a school in Paris, Madame. She was sent there soon after the child was born."

"What is the child like? Is he as beautiful as his mother?"

"He is said to be very handsome, Madame, with a striking resemblance to His Majesty. Mademoiselle de Romans is so proud of him that she takes him to the Bois every afternoon and suckles him in public."

Madame de Pompadour was thoughtful for a few moments, then she said: "Hausset, this afternoon we will take a walk in the Bois."

The Marquise with Madame du Hausset left their carriage and walked under the trees.

It was a warm afternoon, but the Marquise wore a scarf, wound loosely round her neck, in which the lower half of her face was hidden. The wide-brimmed hat shaded her eyes.

There were not many people in the Bois that day; therefore Madame du Hausset had no difficulty in leading her mistress to that spot where Mademoiselle de Romans sat under a tree, suckling her baby.

Madame du Hausset approached the mother and child.

"Forgive me, Madame," she said, "but that is a very beautiful child."

Mademoiselle de Romans smiled dazzlingly. "Thank you," she said. "I entirely agree."

"My friend wants to see him. She is suffering from acute toothache at the moment."

"I am sorry to hear that," said Mademoiselle de Romans. "It can be so very painful." She looked at the Marquise who, covering her face more closely in the fold of the scarf, had approached. She held out the child and the Marquise bent to look at him.

"Delightful, delightful," she mumbled.

"Does he take after you or his father?" Madame du Hausset asked.

Mademoiselle de Romans could not suppress the satisfied smile which spread over her face.

"I am told that there can be no doubt whatever that he is his father's son," she said, smiling. "I am sure you would agree with me if I told you who he is."

"Have I the honour of his acquaintance?"

Again that smile showed itself at the corners of Mademoiselle de Romans' mouth. "I think," she said demurely, "that it is very likely that you have seen him."

"It was kind of you to show us the lovely little creature," added Madame du Hausset. "You must forgive us the intrusion."

"Mesdames, it was a pleasure indeed. You have been most kind."

As they went back to the carriage, Madame du Hausset knew that the Marquise was disturbed.

"Rumour does not lie about the child," she said. "He is indeed a perfect specimen. As for the mother, she is very beautiful."

Meanwhile Mademoiselle de Romans continued to smile.

She kissed the baby's dark head and whispered: "Did they think to deceive me? Did they think I did not recognise them? That was Madame de Pompadour herself with the faithful Madame du Hausset. And they came here to see your precious Highness. Now we

251

know it cannot be long. Did she not say you were a beautiful creature? Soon you will be publicly acknowledged, my precious. Then all the world will know that you are the son of the King — and once you are acknowledged, my darling, there will be no end to the honours I shall ask for you; and because you are quite irresistible you will get them."

It was a very contented Mademoiselle de Romans who sat with His Highness in the Bois that afternoon.

Mademoiselle de Romans found it very difficult to restrain her exuberance. She told her servants the reason for it.

"It cannot be long now before His Highness is legitimised," she said. "He has already won the approval of Madame de Pompadour. I believe His Majesty sent her to the Bois to see my son, to assure her that he is all his father believes him to be."

The servants were a little dubious. Madame de Pompadour would surely be a little envious of His Highness.

"Oh no," said Mademoiselle de Romans, "he is so disarming. People only have to look at him to love him."

"Madame," suggested her servants, "when His Highness is honoured, it will follow that his mother must be also."

Mademoiselle de Romans conceded that this must be so.

It was impossible for his fond mother to restrain her pride. When she took the child to the Bois and people stopped to admire him, she found herself explaining who he was, and why he was called Highness. She hinted that he was certainly soon to be recognised.

The whisper went round Paris. How beautiful is the King's *petite maîtresse*, and her son is surely one of the loveliest children in Paris. Did you know that he is about to be acknowledged as the King's son? The Marquise will have to look to her laurels, eh? *Petite maîtresse*, indeed. Depend upon it the mother of that child is aiming to be received at Versailles as *maîtresse-en-titre*.

The Marquise was strolling with the King in the gardens. They passed the Orangerie and were gazing at the Pièce d'Eau des Suisses when the Marquise said: "Mademoiselle de Romans is creating a little gossip in the capital, I fear."

The King's expression hardened slightly, but the Marquise was more sure of herself than she had been before the Damiens affair and she felt this to be a matter with which she must proceed, even at the risk of offending the King.

"The child is certainly beautiful," she went on. "One can understand her pride in him. But I think that the woman has lost her sense of proportion, and that can be so dangerous for herself . . . and others."

Louis paused and then said: "She has lately written several letters to me."

"Indeed! That is a little presumptuous."

"She has suddenly become obsessed with an idea that I intend to acknowledge the child."

"It would seem that she is trying to force Your Majesty to a decision. That is unwise of her."

"She is a proud mother," said the King almost tenderly.

"Pride can be dangerous. Perhaps it is a pity that Mademoiselle de Romans was never at Versailles. Here she might have learned to behave with decorum. Her conduct at present is . . . a little vulgar, do you not think so?"

"It was never so before the birth of the child," said the King. "I think we must blame the maternal feelings."

The Marquise was growing more and more apprehensive. The King was actually making excuses for the woman. This could mean only one thing. She *was* more than a *petite maîtresse* to him. He had not thought of casting her off. The Marquise knew the King well enough. Let Mademoiselle de Romans find him in the necessary indulgent mood and all her requests would be granted.

An outstandingly beautiful woman, who was not without education, mother of a child whose beauty was phenomenal. The Marquise could well believe that Mademoiselle de Romans might become another Marquise de Pompadour; she had all the necessary qualities to make her so.

"It is always a matter of acute grief to me," she said, "to hear Your Majesty's name being bandied about by the common people. I fear that in her enthusiasm for her child Mademoiselle de Romans is bringing about this unhappy state of affairs."

Louis nodded.

"Would Your Majesty allow me to explain to this woman . . . to let her know that she has placed you in a delicate position by her importuning and the unpleasant publicity which her conduct is drawing upon herself — and unforgivably — her King? You may trust my discretion. I think that if the young woman and her baby left Paris for a while, that would be a happy solution. They could return when the gossips have forgotten what an exhibition she made of herself."

The King had turned to admire the ornate Bassin de Neptune.

He was very fond of his belle Madeleine; he had an affection for the child; but she had changed since the birth, and she did provide a somewhat awkward situation at the moment.

He laid his hand on the arm of the Marquise. "I know, my dear," he said, "that I can safely leave this little affair in your hands."

"Thank you. I suggest a sojourn in a convent . . . not too far from Paris, so that Your Majesty could visit her, if you so wished."

"I think that is an excellent plan."

"Then I will proceed with it, and you need concern yourself with this affair no more. There are more pressing problems. Monsieur de Choiseul asked for an audience today. I see it is almost time for his arrival."

"Then let us return to the *Château*," said the King.

Mademoiselle de Romans had fed her baby and he was sleeping in his cradle when her servants came to tell her that a messenger from Versailles was below.

"It has come at last," cried Mademoiselle de Romans. "This is what I have been waiting for. I am summoned to Versailles. Did I not tell you?"

She turned to kiss the sleeping child. "Back soon, my precious Highness," she murmured. "You will soon be making a journey to Versailles."

She went downstairs. Waiting for her was a King's messenger. He was not alone, for with him had come several of the King's guards.

She was surprised but, being prepared for anything, she greeted the messenger warmly.

"I have a letter from the King," she was told.

She took it and read it.

She could not believe it. She read it again. She sat down feeling faint with fear. This was not the letter she had been expecting. This was one of those dreaded letters about which there was such controversy throughout France. The *lettre de cachet* which, for no given reason, could send a person into exile or to prison simply because that was the wish of the King.

It was now his wish that she should immediately leave for a convent outside the city, and there she should live in comfort until she received the King's orders to return to her house.

"There has been a mistake," she said. "This is not meant for me."

"You are Mademoiselle de Romans?"

"Yes . . . I am."

"Then this is addressed to you."

She seemed as if she would faint, and two of the guards caught her and helped her to a chair.

256

One of her servants had appeared, white-faced, in the doorway.

"Madame . . ." she screamed. "They are upstairs . . ."

But one of the guards said to her peremptorily: "Bring something to revive your mistress. She is fainting."

She felt consciousness coming back. She understood. The Marquise had done this. Oh, she had been a fool . . . a fool to boast of what was to be hers and the boy's. How could she have so far forgotten the obvious feelings of the Marquise! Powerful ministers had fallen before this woman; yet she, who was a simple woman from Grenoble, had set herself against her.

She had not wished to do that. She would never have attempted to oust the Marquise from the unique position she occupied at Court.

All she had asked for was recognition for her son.

And now . . . exile.

The two men who stood over her felt compassion for her. She was so beautiful, and because she was tall and would have seemed so composed, so able to take care of herself, she seemed the more pitiable.

"Madame," one of them murmured, "it is a very pleasant convent. They'll look after you well there."

"But," she began, "my son . . ."

"Come, Madame." The guards exchanged glances. "We ought to be going. Orders are for us to conduct you there. We have a carriage waiting."

"Let me write a reply to the King."

"Our orders are to take you there at once."

"I shall write to him from there."

"That's right," soothed one of the guards.

"I will go upstairs and get my son."

"Look here, Madame," said one of them.

But she had slipped past them and run up the stairs. They followed her as though they feared to let her out of their sight.

Two of her servants were in the nursery; they stared at her, with blank expressions which, while they told her nothing, filled her with a sudden fear which was so intense that she could not face it.

She ran to the cradle. It was empty.

"My son . . ." she cried. "My baby . . ."

The guards were at her side. "Madame," said one of them, taking her arm gently, "you couldn't take the little boy to the convent, you know."

"Where *is* my son . . . where . . . where . . . *where?*"

"Look, Madame, he is being taken great care of. We can assure you of that."

"I want him," she sobbed. "I want my baby."

The guards merely shook their heads and lowered their eyes. They were ashamed of the tears they feared they would shed.

But Mademoiselle de Romans would not have seen them; she had flung herself down beside the cradle and was crying for her baby.

CHAPTER
FOURTEEN

The Last Journey to Paris

The Seven Years War was over, peace had come at last, and the French were now at liberty to lick their wounds and look about them, to see what the long struggle, the loss of fighting men and materials, the crippling taxation, had brought them.

They could only see it as shattering defeat.

Canada was now completely in the hands of the British, and French interests in India had also been lost to Britain.

Choiseul's plan to placate the French with his Family Compact had proved to be disastrous to the Spanish, for with great delight, as soon as it was announced, Pitt had declared war on Spain, as a result of which she had been beaten by Portugal, Britain's ally, and Havana and Cuba had now passed into British possession. The French Navy was almost completely annihilated.

Pitt however, failing to receive the support of the Duke of Newcastle and the rest of the Whigs, was forced to resign; Lord Bute, who took his place, lacked

259

his genius, and thus in making peace the advantages to the British were not as great as they might have been.

However, Pitt was still in a position to demand the demolition of Dunkirk as a matter of principle and as an "external monument of the yoke imposed upon France".

But Bute's anxiety to end the war as quickly as possible led him to restore Martinique to France, and Cuba and the Philippines to Spain.

Frederick of Prussia had been left to fight Austria alone, but when he broke into Silesia there was peace between these two countries and a treaty was signed at Hubertsburg.

Britain was the only country which had come victoriously out of this long war. She had the whole of North America, a large slice of India, and a mastery over the trade of the world which was what she had always sought. Maria Theresa had gained a little but she was still receiving the subsidies from France which Choiseul's pro-Austrian Ministry had voted her. Frederick had Silesia, but he must return to Berlin which had been plundered by the Russians, so that much of the city's riches had been lost, and its population decreased.

But France? asked the suffering population of that sorrowful country; what had France to show for the Seven Years struggle? A lost Empire and Navy. An Army which had suffered so many defeats that it no longer believed in its power.

If the peace which had followed the War of the Austrian Succession was the "stupid peace", this was "the disgraceful peace".

Celebrations were ordered. France was at peace. Let the people rejoice. Let them look forward to better days ahead. A new statue of the King was set up close to the swing bridge of the Tuileries in the newly constructed Place Louis XV.

The people refused to celebrate. The weather was bad in any case, and the bunting was ruined by the teeming rain and torn down by the wind. It was as though the elements themselves were laughing at the French for being such fools as to pretend to rejoice.

Each morning new placards were discovered about the newly erected statue, and each was more malicious than the last.

Choiseul was closeted with the King and the Marquise in the Château de Choisy. The King looked depressed. No wonder, thought the Duc. The people of Paris grew more and more disrespectful every day. Only yesterday a placard had been affixed to the new statue, and on it was written:

By order of the Royal Mint it is declared that a poorly struck Louis shall be struck again.

Ominous words, and the King, for all his show of indifference, heartily disliked being made aware of the hatred of his subjects.

The Marquise looked haggard. She was finding it more and more difficult to disguise her illness. The Duc knew — he had his spies everywhere — that she had to add more and more padding as the weeks passed for

261

she was losing flesh fast. Her carefully applied cosmetics were a great help to her, but in the harsh morning light even they failed her.

His spies had told him that it was not only occasionally that she spat blood. The haemorrhages were becoming more and more frequent; they were accompanied by painful headaches which, when she retired to her apartments, forced her to spend hours on her bed.

The Marquise had been a good friend to him, Choiseul was thinking. As long as she lived that friendship must last. But he did not think it would be of much longer duration.

Then, dearest sister, he thought, the Choiseuls will be in complete command.

Glorious plans were waiting to be carried out. The Duchesse de Gramont should slip naturally into the place occupied by the Marquise. No, it would be an even more advantageous place because his sister would be ready to take on the dual role of mistress and friend. And when the Queen died, who could say what further glories might not await her? Madame de Maintenon was a shining example to all clever women; and when a clever woman had a strong brother behind her, a doting brother holding the reins of power firmly in his hands, who could say what might not happen?

Indeed there were great days ahead for the Choiseuls.

He should not grieve then to see the King concerned, the Marquise haggard and exhausted.

"Madame la Marquise," he said, "with the permission of His Majesty and yourself I will bring you a footstool."

"It is kind of you," said the Marquise sharply, "but I have no need of it."

"No?" said Choiseul. "So restful, I think."

"When one is tired, yes. I am not tired, Monsieur le Duc, at this hour in the morning."

The King smiled at the Marquise, and Choiseul was quick to notice the pity in his glance. "Madame la Marquise puts us to shame with her unflagging energy," he said kindly.

"None can compare with her, save only your august self," murmured Choiseul. "And how glad I am that this is so, for the news is not so good as it might be, Sire."

The King yawned, but there was apprehension behind the gesture. "What bad news now?" he asked.

"I think of the future, Sire. Those accursed enemies of ours across the Channel. Think of the position in which they now find themselves."

"Canada . . . India . . ." murmured the King.

Choiseul snapped his fingers. His optimistic nature refused to consider these defeats. "Think, Sire," he said, "of the resources which will be needed to defend these colonies. Our enemy will be open to attack at home. Why, very soon we shall be in a position to win back all that we have lost."

The Marquise was regarding the Duc with approving smiles. This was talk calculated to relieve the King of his melancholy. It did not seem important to her that, to make further war, the people must suffer more taxation; she seemed to forget that the Army was depleted, the Navy non-existent; she was obsessed by one duty: to amuse the King.

He was at the moment passing through a wretched time in his emotional affairs.

The Parc aux Cerfs was palling. The little *grisettes* had lost their appeal. Mademoiselle de Tiercelin had returned from her Paris school and had been given a little house not far from the *Château*; but she was demanding and extravagant; worse still she had quickly become pregnant and her time was near. The Marquise knew that the King was thinking of presenting her with her pension and her *congé*.

Mademoiselle de Romans was giving trouble. The King had a real affection for that young woman; but she offered him little comfort now. He called on her at the convent but she could only weep and implore him to give her back her child. In vain did he protest that the boy was being well cared for; she would look at him with those tragic, reproachful eyes, and behave as though there could be no joy in her life until her son was given back to her.

Louis felt that he could not face her reproaches; he knew that sooner or later he would give way, if he did. And the Marquise had taken such pains to terminate a matter which was becoming intolerable.

Give la belle Madeleine the boy, and there would again be that importuning, that boastfulness in public places, for she still referred to the child as Highness.

No, there was no comfort from the tragic Romans nor from the self-assured Tiercelin, who herself might become every bit as trying as Romans when her child was born.

Another matter gave the King concern. Choiseul was not the only one who was aware of the haggard looks of the Marquise, of the excessive padding beneath her gown.

One did not of course refer to a matter when one knew that to do so would create anxiety, so he must not tell her of his fears.

He wondered whether he would inquire of Madame du Hausset as to her mistress' health; but then he would receive assurances that it was "as good as ever". Dear faithful old Hausset would always do what her mistress expected of her. The King had turned his attention to Choiseul. "Has the state of the Army and Navy slipped your memory?"

"No, Sire. But I propose to build them up to such strength as has never been theirs before. I have plans here for new arsenals. As for the loss of Canada, we can be happy without Quebec. Here are further plans for the colonization of Guiana."

"It would seem to me," said the King, "that these schemes of yours are going to need money. Money means new taxes, Monsieur. Had you forgotten that?"

"I had not, Sire. And the people will pay the taxes when they know that French honour is at stake. I do not suggest new taxes. Only that we continue with the present ones for a few more years."

"The *Parlement* will never agree."

"I have sounded certain members already, Sire."

"And their reaction?"

"They threaten an Estates-General."

The Marquise held her breath in horror. She knew that the very mention of an Estates-General, that assembly of representatives of nobles, clergy and *bourgeoisie*, known as the Tiers Etat, was enough to infuriate the King.

Now his face had turned pale. "That," he said grimly, "I will never countenance."

The Marquise said quickly: "This is idle talk. There will certainly be no calling of an Estates-General. The right to decide can only belong to His Majesty. If, Monsieur de Choiseul, you are to prolong the taxation to enable us to make these reforms in the Army and the Navy, if you are to finance French Guiana, you must make the *Parlement* understand that it must either support you or be dismissed."

Choiseul bowed. The King smiled his approval at the Marquise's words.

"Madame," said Choiseul, "I am in complete agreement with you. I will go immediately to those ministers concerned and tell them of His Majesty's instructions."

"And if any one of them mentions an Estates-General," said the King, "tell him that I will not tolerate his presence here at Court."

Choiseul bowed and left the King and the Marquise together.

She turned to the King smiling: "I have the utmost confidence in Choiseul," she said.

"I too, my dear."

"It is merely because I sense Your Majesty's confidence that I feel my own," she said quickly. "You lead always; I follow. I think I often sense Your Majesty's thoughts; then they become mine."

"We think alike," said the King, "because we have been together so long."

She inclined her head slightly, and he thought: dear Marquise, how weary she is! Why does she not tell me of her sickness? Am I not her friend in truth?

"I will leave you now," he said, and he banished the compassion from his voice. "I have some documents to sign. Nothing . . . of importance. But they must be attended to."

He saw the relief momentarily in her eyes. There was consternation too. She would be thinking, what papers? Should I not be there to see these papers?

Weary as she was she was desperately afraid of missing something which she ought to know.

But he was determined. "Leave me now," he said. "We will meet shortly. We will then examine these plans of Choiseul's for his new colony."

She curtsied and left him.

Madame du Hausset was waiting for her.

"There is news," she cried as her mistress entered the apartment. "Mademoiselle de Tiercelin has given birth to a boy."

"A boy," said the Marquise in some dismay.

"A girl would certainly have been more comforting," agreed Madame du Hausset. "But she is no

Mademoiselle de Romans; she is more concerned with herself. This one will not be another little Highness. But I'm talking here, and you want to rest. Your bed is ready. Shall I help you undress?"

The Marquise nodded, and Madame du Hausset felt she could have wept as she undid the fastenings of the elaborate dress, and when it had been taken off and the padded garment removed from underneath, she looked at the wasted frame of the once lovely Madame de Pompadour.

"It will be more restful to get right into bed," said Madame du Hausset. "Is there anything you would like? Milk?"

The Marquise shook her head.

"If you try a little it would help to strengthen you."

"Oh Hausset, Hausset, I am so tired," said the Marquise.

"Yes . . . but you may rest now. Why do you not spend the remainder of the day in your bed? Are you not allowed to be a little indisposed sometimes?"

"He would miss me so. You know I never stay away from him longer than I can help."

"That was all very well once. Now you need your rest."

The Marquise began to cough, and lights of alarm sprang up in Madame du Hausset's eyes.

The cough subsided and the Marquise said: "I must tell the Duc de Choiseul never again to mention the Estates-General in the presence of the King. It upsets him. It makes him angry. He should not do it."

"Well, that is his trouble, Madame. Not yours."

"I would wish to see them friendly."

"Come, rest while you may, dear Madame."

The Marquise smiled, and as she did so the blood gushed from her mouth.

It was no use. She could not rise now. Even though she had arranged to be with the King that day, she must stay in bed, because she had not the strength to rise. There had never before been a haemorrhage such as this, and the time had come when it would be useless to attempt to hide the state of her health from the Court.

Madame du Hausset had changed the sheets, had put her into a clean bedgown, and had herself taken the news to the King.

The Marquise had insisted on knowing how he received it.

"I am afraid I wept, Madame," said Madame du Hausset. "I could not help it. And, Madame, he wept with me."

"Hausset, what do you know of this disease?"

"Only what I have seen with you, Madame."

"These coughs, these headaches, these fevers and night sweats . . . how long before they put an end to my life, Hausset?"

"You, Madame . . . talk of death! You who are so full of life. The beloved of the King. The First Minister of France. It is not for such as you to talk of death."

"I fancy I feel death close to me, Hausset. And I am not unhappy. If I died now I should die the King's very good friend. I would rather die now than be sent from him as once I feared to be. You remember, at the time of the Damiens affair when I thought that I should be dismissed, I was more unhappy than I am now. Dismissal from life cannot bring me such misery as dismissal from Court would have done."

"Madame, you talk too much. Preserve your strength, I implore you."

She shook her head. "Now, Hausset, I am going to do as I wish. It is as though a great burden has been taken from my shoulders. No more need to pretend. I am a sick woman. I am a dying woman. But I am no longer a woman with a secret."

"There is someone at the door."

"Go and see who it is, Hausset."

Madame du Hausset came back to the bed almost at once and said: "It is the Duchesse de Gramont. She has heard of your indisposition and comes to cheer you. I will tell her that you are too ill to see her."

"No, Hausset, bring her to me. I feel rested, lying here. But if I should cough, you must send her away . . . quickly . . . you understand?"

"Yes, Madame."

The Duchesse de Gramont came to the bed and threw herself to her knees.

"My dearest friend . . ." she said and there was a sob in her throat.

The Marquise did not question its sincerity. This woman was the sister of the Duc de Choiseul whom she trusted completely.

"You will soon be well," she said. "You must be well. How can the King be happy . . . how can France be happy without you!"

The Marquise smiled. "The King would grieve for me, I believe," she said. "France, never."

"But you will be with us — your gay self — very soon, I'll swear."

"Indeed I shall," said the Marquise.

How ill she looks! thought the Duchesse. She cannot live long. She must be near the end. That is blood at the side of her mouth. She is dying, and she knows it.

"We will give a ball to celebrate your recovery," said the Duchesse.

"It shall be a masque," said the Marquise. "I remember a masque at Versailles which was a very special occasion for me. I was a huntress . . ."

All will be changed when she has gone, thought the Duchesse. The King will seek consolation. And my brilliant brother and I will be there . . . his greatest friends. The Queen is seven years older than the King. Surely *she* cannot live long. A great future awaits us. Many women will now seek to become the King's mistress. But therein lies the difference between the Choiseuls and ordinary men and women. These creatures of the Court plan to be the King's mistress; I, and Etienne with me, plan that I shall be his wife.

Madame du Hausset came to the bedside. "His Majesty has sent word that he is on his way to visit you," she announced.

A radiant smile touched the face of the Marquise and she looked almost young again.

"You had better go, my dear," she said to the Duchesse. "He will not wish anyone else to be here."

The Duchesse bent over the bed and kissed the hot brow. She longed to stay; she wanted to see how the King behaved with this woman now. But the Marquise had conveyed her wish that she should leave, and the wishes of the Marquise were regarded as a command.

One day . . . soon . . . thought the Duchesse, I shall be the one to issue commands.

Louis took her hand and looked anxiously into her face.

"It grieves me," she said, "that you should see me thus. I am very ill, Louis."

"So at last you admit it."

"You have known?"

He nodded. "And suffered great anxiety."

"Yet you never spoke of my illness."

"Because I knew that it was your wish that I should not."

Her eyes filled with tears. They brimmed over on to her cheeks. "Forgive me," she said. "I am so weak now. It is not easy to control my tears. My dearest, I would have you know that the greatest happiness in my life has come from you."

He kissed the hand he still held. "As mine has from you." He was brisk suddenly as though he were afraid of this emotion between them. "I shall send my physicians to you. They will cure you."

"I have Quesnay," she said. "I could not have a better. He loves me. Love is the best doctor."

"Then," said the King, his voice trembling with emotion, "I should be your doctor, for none could give you more love than I."

272

"You have done me so much good. I feel better already. I will leave my bed. Perhaps, if Your Majesty invites me, I shall sup with you tonight."

"No," he said firmly. "You shall stay in bed."

"Dearest . . ."

"It is a command," he said, trying to smile. "I shall visit you frequently. I shall stay here at Choisy that I may do so."

She was deeply moved.

He sat by the bed for a long time; they did not speak, and neither noticed the silence. They were both recalling those days when he had hunted in the Forest of Sénart, and she had ridden by in her dainty carriages painted in those delicate colours which she made fashionable.

They were thinking of the ball at which he had recognised the fair huntress as the lady of the Forest of Sénart; on that night he had decided that they would be lovers.

That had happened twenty years ago. Twenty years of faithful devotion! It was the more remarkable that only for five of those years had she actually been his mistress.

The rest, which accompanied the sudden freedom from responsibilities, had a marked effect on the Marquise. Madame du Hausset hovered about her delightedly, watching her take a little milk.

Even Dr Quesnay, who was not given to optimism, was a little cheered. As for the King, he was certain that she would be well again.

"You see," said the Marquise, "all I needed was a little rest. I was overtired, nothing more."

As she appeared to be on the way to recovery, the King decided to return to Versailles where certain State matters demanded his attention.

"You must follow me, my dear," he said, "as soon as you are well enough. But, I beg you, do not leave your bed until you are quite ready to do so."

He took an affectionate farewell of her and left Choisy for Versailles.

When the Court had left, Madame du Hausset could not hide her relief. "Now, Madame," she said, "you will have a real rest. You will doze and read all through the day and sleep soundly at night."

The Marquise took the hand of her faithful friend and servant, and pressed it affectionately.

"First," she said, "I will make my will."

So during the days which followed the King's departure she busied herself with listing her possessions (which were vast) and deciding who should inherit them.

Her only relative was her brother, Abel, the Marquis de Marigny. She thought of her children, both of whom had died, and for whom she had intended to do so much.

Abel should have the greater part of her fortune, although there should be gifts of jewels and such valuable possessions as her pictures to Soubise, Choiseul, Gontaut and others. She wished that her mother had lived. Oh, but it would have been too harrowing for her to see this fatal disease gradually

274

taking a firmer grip on her daughter. Perhaps it was as well that Madame Poisson had died — and little Alexandrine also. Children of women such as herself might not be very kindly treated by the world when there was no one to protect them.

She was a very rich woman. Her income was some million and a half livres annually; she had magnificent establishments at Versailles, Fontainebleau, Paris and Compiègne. She had the *châteaux* of Marigny, St Remy, Aulnay, Brimborin, La Celle, Crécy, and of course the luxurious Bellevue. Petit Trianon, that exquisite *château* in miniature which she and Louis had planned together, was only half finished, and the Marquise knew that she would never entertain Louis in those charming little rooms.

She grew sleepy thinking of her *châteaux*, for each one could recall memories of certain occasions, so that they stood like signposts along the road, each one proclaiming some fresh triumph.

She was thinking now of Bellevue and the night when Louis had come to dine there — it was to be the first entertainment given in the new house. But the people — the angry people — had come marching to Bellevue, and she and her party had been forced to have the lights extinguished and take supper in a small house in the grounds, some little distance from the *château*.

She put her hand to her heart, recalling the terror of that occasion. Surely that heart had not leaped and bounded then as it did now.

She was suffocating.

"Hausset!" she called. "Hausset, come quickly."

★ ★ ★

When the King heard that the Marquise had become desperately ill again, he and the whole Court knew that she was dying.

It was a point of etiquette that only members of the royal family might die in the Château de Versailles, but Louis could not bear the thought of Madame de Pompadour's being far from him at such a time, so he gave orders that her rooms on the ground floor should be made ready to receive her.

When the news was brought to her that the King wished her to come to Versailles, she was so radiant that even Madame du Hausset believed that she would recover — at least for a time.

"You see, Hausset," she said, clinging to her friend with those arms which made Madame du Hausset want to weep every time she looked at them — for they had once been plump and rounded and were now almost fleshless — "you see how he loves me. We belong to each other. He makes me as royal as he is. Hausset, you see how great our friendship is."

She was carefully wrapped in blankets and carried out to a carriage in which she made a slow journey to Versailles. The people along the road came out to see her pass; they did not greet her with hostile shouts this time; they only looked on in silence.

Even they know, she thought, that this is my last journey.

In her old apartments at Versailles she lay in her bed. The doctors shook their heads over her; they could only pass her over to the priests.

276

She brooded on her sins and confessed them. Incidents of the past seemed to leap out of blurred pictures and make themselves vividly clear. She saw Charles Guillaume, her husband, imploring her to return to him and their family; she saw herself turning away from his pleas, knowing only her blind ambition. She thought of Alexandrine lying on her deathbed in the Convent of the Assumption, and she remembered Mademoiselle de Romans, crying for her son.

There were many spectres from the past to mock an ambitious woman.

Louis visited her several times a day, and her doctors asked him if he would break the news that she should prepare herself for Supreme Unction, as there was little time left.

He embraced her tenderly. It was their last farewell. She must now forget her King on earth, he told her, and prepare herself to meet an even greater King. And, because of the relationship between them, those who would grant her absolution insisted that they who had committed adultery should show their repentance by never again meeting on earth.

It was inevitable. The moment had come.

"Farewell, my dearest friend, farewell," said Louis with tears on his cheeks. "I envy you. You are going to your heavenly rest while I am left to a life which must seem empty because you will no longer be there to charm it."

For the last time they embraced, and Madame de Pompadour was left to the ministrations of her confessors.

★ ★ ★

Madame du Hausset signed to her servants to bring the clean clothes to the bed, but the Marquise smiled wanly and waved them away.

"No," she said. "It is not worthwhile. There is such a short time left."

The women looked at each other. They knew that she was right.

The priest came and prayed at her bedside and when he prepared to leave she said: "Wait a few more moments and we will go together."

He took her hand to bless her for the last time; she smiled and closed her eyes.

Before that day was ended she was dead.

That evening her body, shrouded in a white sheet, was placed on a stretcher and carried out of the Château de Versailles to the Hôtel des Reservoirs.

Louis himself insisted on making all the arrangements; he knew well, he said, that it was the last wish of the Marquise that she should be laid to rest in the Church of the Capucines in the Place de Vendôme, where her little Alexandrine now lay beside Madame Poisson.

Two days after her death the body of Madame de Pompadour left Versailles for the last time on its way to Paris.

It was a stormy April day and the rain was falling in torrents as the procession gathered at Notre Dame de Versailles preparatory to leaving for Paris.

With Champlost, one of his *valets de chambre*, beside him, Louis stood on a balcony hatless in the rain, staring after the cortège while it made its way down the Avenue de Paris. Tears flowed down his cheeks, and sobs shook his body, as memories of their long relationship assailed him. It was not easy to picture Versailles without the Marquise.

Champlost stood helplessly beside him, and Louis suddenly laid his hand on his arm. "Why Champlost," he said, "so you witness my grief. I shall never be completely happy again. I have lost one who has been my friend — the best friend I ever had — for twenty years. Twenty long years, Champlost."

"Sire, this is a grievous thing which has befallen us, and Your Majesty in particular, but you will catch a fever if you stand here thus, hatless in the rain."

The King looked up at the sullen skies, and the raindrops and the tears mingled on his cheeks.

"It is the only mark of respect I can show her now," he said.

The *cortège* was passing along the Avenue de Paris, and the King felt he could no longer bear to watch it.

He turned from the balcony and stepped into his private sitting-room. Champlost followed him respectfully.

The dignity of Versailles closed in on the King. Life must go on, even though the Marquise had departed.

Louis suddenly seemed to remember what etiquette demanded of him. He said almost lightly: "The poor Marquise is having bad weather for her journey to Paris."

CHAPTER
FIFTEEN

Marie-Josèphe

The death of Madame de Pompadour left the King desolate. He could find little comfort, and the intimate suppers which had once been so much a feature of life at Versailles became gloomy affairs, continued from habit rather than because they gave any particular pleasure. It was the Marquise who had arranged the entertainments, who had chosen the guests, who had given all her time to making sure that the King was continually entertained. And how could any of those uneducated little girls at the Parc aux Cerfs, however passionate, however voluptuous, make him forget for more than an hour or two all that he had lost with the passing of the Marquise.

Sometimes he would say: "That will amuse the Marquise. I must tell her . . ."

Then he would stop abruptly and turn away.

The Duchesse de Gramont was eagerly waiting to offer him comfort, but Louis turned from her in disgust, and Choiseul, fearing his sister's impatient exuberance, was forced to warn her to be very careful.

"Time," murmured the Duc, "it is time he needs. Give him a month or two to mourn her and he will be tired of mourning."

Meanwhile the King found a certain solace in the study of foreign affairs. He had little trust in any of his ministers; even Choiseul, he realised, was chiefly concerned with the well-being of Choiseul rather than that of France.

Perhaps one day, thought the King, it may be possible to retrieve our lost fortunes. If he could do that it might be that he would regain the affection of his people. He considered now what a victorious end to the Seven Years War might have meant. If France had emerged triumphant over her enemies, would the people perhaps have spoken his name with the respect they always showed to that other Bourbon, his ancestor, Henri Quatre?

He felt an enthusiasm which he had not known for years and which dulled the pain he experienced in the loss of the Marquise. He chose his secret agents — his, entirely his, unknown to anyone, even Choiseul — and dispatched them to the various Continental capitals. Their letters were seen by no one but himself.

He had come to a decision; his object should be the election to the Polish throne of a French Prince.

His grand-daughter Isabelle was betrothed to Joseph, heir to the Imperial throne. Madame Première, his daughter Louise-Elisabeth, had been right to insist on that betrothal. Poor Madame Première had died a few years before of the small-pox. The King did not wish to think of her. Death always depressed him deeply and

281

his main desire was to escape from the memory of that more important death.

Thus Louis shut himself away in his *petits appartements* and mourned the Marquise.

The case against the Jesuits was meanwhile growing to a climax. Not only in France were factions rising against them; they were considered to be a menace all over the world. It was said that they governed all Catholic countries, not openly but in secret; they had set up their colleges everywhere and sought to educate the young to their way of thinking, and thus strengthen their brotherhood. They had insinuated themselves into many of the Courts of Europe, chiefly as confessors to Kings and Queens, thus acquiring great ascendancy over those who governed.

Some years before, a rich Jesuit, Père La Vallette, who was the Superior of the Jesuits of Martinique, had lost many of his ships to English pirates. Being unable to maintain his industrial settlement, he became bankrupt to the tune of three million francs. His creditors were in a state of panic, and a number of them in Marseilles demanded that the Society should pay them the million francs owed by La Vallette.

The Society declared that it was not responsible for the debts of one of its members, whereupon the Marseilles merchants appealed to the *Parlement* of Paris, which ordered Père de Sacy, the General of the Jesuits, to settle La Vallette's debts.

The magistrates, who had sided with the Jansenites against the Jesuits in the many conflicts between the two, declared that this was more than a case of bankruptcy, and the affairs of the Society should be thoroughly investigated.

They declared that they had discovered the rules of the Society to be inconsistent with those of the Kingdom of France, and to be both disloyal and immoral. They ordered the colleges to be closed.

Those who supported the Jesuits, headed by the Dauphin and the Queen, made an immediate protest.

Choiseul and the Marquise had stood firmly on the side of the *Parlement*.

Madame de Pompadour had always considered the Jesuits a menace, but she had hated them more vehemently since their General, Père de Sacy, had refused to grant her absolution unless she left the Court. In the midst of this struggle she had died. Choiseul had determined on the expulsion of the Jesuits, but now that Madame de Pompadour was dead he had lost an ardent champion.

Louis was in no hurry to come to a decision. At the time of the investigation he sought to protect the Jesuits because he felt, as he had previously, that the *Parlement* was endeavouring to take his power from his hands. Eager as he was that France should not be in the power of the Pope — as the Jesuits wished her to be — he was equally determined that it was the King, not the *Parlement*, who should have the final say in the affairs of the country.

The *Parlement* had shown itself belligerent and, when he had attempted to oppose them over this matter of the Jesuits, had hinted that there should be an inquiry into the *acquits au comptant*. Louis knew that he could not face an inquiry into his private expenditure. The upkeep of the Parc aux Cerfs alone was excessive. There were young women who had been granted pensions and gifts; he had many children to maintain. Pretty little Mademoiselle Hainault had given him two delightful daughters, and it had cost a considerable amount to provide her with a pension and a husband in the Marquis de Montmelas. Adorable Lucie-Magdaleine d'Estaing, who was the natural daughter of the Vicomte de Ravel, had presented him with two charming daughters, Agnes-Lucie and Aphrodite-Lucie. He doted on his quartette of daughters, but they must be maintained in adequate comfort, and that cost money. There was the naughty little Mademoiselle de Tiercelin who was constantly demanding that her debts be paid. A life such as he led, although it presented him with variety and entertainment, also presented him with enormous bills. And he had no wish that the people should know the extent of his gallantries.

Already they talked of him as the Old Sultan, and exaggerated concerning the Parc aux Cerfs, which they called his harem; but until they had seen in black and white the cost of his pleasure, they must always doubt the authenticity of the stories they heard.

No, Louis could not allow his *acquits au comptant* to be made public and must submit to the blackmail of the *Parlement*.

The Dauphin, who had nothing to fear from an inquiry into his private life, threw himself wholeheartedly into the defence of the Jesuits.

He demanded an interview with the King and Choiseul.

Choiseul ignored the Dauphin; he knew that they could never be anything but enemies, and that it was useless to try to placate him.

He said to the King: "Sire, if you do not suppress the Jesuits you must suppress *Parlement*. And to suppress *Parlement* at this time would mean one thing: revolution."

The Dauphin intervened. "Why should we not suppress *Parlement*? Why should we not set up Provincial Estates? They would be selected from the nobility."

"And the clergy?" murmured Choiseul.

"Members of the clergy *and* the nobility," insisted the Dauphin.

Choiseul again addressed himself to the King. "Sire, whatever form the Dauphin's Provincial Estates took, it could only consist of *men*. One visualises their uniting, and standing together. They would be so powerful that they would usurp the power of the throne itself."

"Any who dared do that would be exiled," cried the Dauphin vehemently.

Choiseul burst into loud laughter. "Sire," he said turning to the King, "is it possible to exile the entire nation?"

"Monsieur de Choiseul is right," said the King. "There is no way out of this *impasse* but exile for the Jesuits."

The Dauphin turned on Choiseul with blazing eyes. "You have done this . . . you . . . with your schemes, with your ambitious dreams. You are an atheist . . . for all you make a show of attending sacred ceremonies. I wonder there is not some sign from Heaven . . ."

The expression on Choiseul's pug-dog face was insolent in the extreme. "A sign from Heaven?" he said, looking about him, out of the window and up at the sky. "I am no atheist, Monseigneur, but in the King's cultured Court we have grown away from superstition. Perhaps that is why, in those circles which lag behind us intellectually, we are mistaken for atheists."

"Choiseul," spluttered the Dauphin, "you forget . . . you forget to whom you speak . . ."

"I do not forget," said Choiseul becoming suddenly heated as the Dauphin, "that I may one day be unfortunate enough to be your subject, but I shall never serve you." He turned again to the King, his face white with the suddenness of his emotion. "Sire, have I your permission to retire?"

"You have it," said the King.

When he had gone, the Dauphin and the King faced each other, and Louis felt an unsuppressible distaste for this earnest son of his who even now, he believed, was supporting the Jesuits, not from any political angle but because he believed himself to be a representative of Holy Church.

The French would have a very bigoted King when this young man came to the throne. Indeed, thought Louis, I must live for a very long time; this poor son of mine has so much to learn.

"You . . . Your Majesty heard the insolence of that fellow!" the Dauphin stuttered. "I . . . I shall never forgive him."

Louis shook his head sadly. "My son," he said, "you have so offended Monsieur de Choiseul that you must forgive him everything."

With that the King turned and left the Dauphin, who could only stare after his departing figure in utter bewilderment.

By the end of that year which had seen the death of the Marquise, the Society of Jesuits was disbanded and no Jesuit could live in the Kingdom of France except as a private citizen.

The people of Paris went wild with joy; the Queen, the Dauphin and the Princesses were desolate; and the feud between Choiseul and the Dauphin grew.

To console the Dauphin the King decided to grant his son's lifelong ambition. The Dauphin had always wished to be a soldier and, although this had been denied him in time of war when his obvious aptitude for the life might have been some use to his country, he was now given his own regiment — known as the Royal Dauphin's Regiment — and threw himself with zest into his new life.

He spent weeks in camp with his soldiers and showed that he might have made a great career for himself in the Army. His austerity endeared him to his men, for they saw in him a leader always ready to share their discomforts.

During the manoeuvres the weather was bad and the Dauphin, unaccustomed to hardship, developed a particularly virulent cold. This he ignored, but the neglected cold persisted, and at the beginning of

October, when the military operations were concluded and he had joined the Court at Fontainebleau, the royal family was astonished to see how ill he was.

He had been plump but now he had lost all his spare flesh. It was believed that this was due to the violent unaccustomed exercise, but when the cough persisted, there were many who remembered the sickness of Madame de Pompadour and remarked that it would be strange if her old enemy the Dauphin should be similarly stricken.

Marie-Josèphe was very worried when she saw him.

"You must go to bed for a while," she insisted. "And you must let me nurse you. I was once told I was a good nurse."

"I remember the occasion well," said the Dauphin with feeling.

"Then you will not hesitate to place yourself in my hands?"

He said gently: "Then I was ill, Marie-Josèphe. Now I merely have a cold which I cannot throw off."

"The doctors shall bleed you," she said.

She found him docile; it was as though he wished to please her, to make up for the anxiety he had caused her.

She thought: he has changed. He is more gentle. He knows how I suffered, and he wants to make up for the misery he has caused me with that woman.

She wondered about the woman, but she did not ask.

She felt that there was something very precious about this period in her life and she would not have it spoilt in the smallest degree. She would try to forget the existence of Madame Dadonville and her little Auguste; and she would pray that the Dauphin would also forget.

She put on a simple white dress, thinking of that time when she had nursed him safely through the small-pox, when they had been so close together and she had believed that the bond between them was inviolate for ever.

I am happy, she thought; happier than I have ever been because when he is sick he comes to me. And I am a good nurse. Dr Pousse said so. Once again I will bring him back to health — and now that we are older, more mellow, the happiness we shall regain will last for the rest of our lives.

Marie-Josèphe sat at her husband's bedside. She was very worried because he did not get well. The cold persisted and it had grown worse.

"He suffers from pleurisy," said the doctors and they bled him again and again.

An ulcer had appeared on his upper lip. It was a malignant growth and no ointments would cure it, and although at times it seemed about to heal it always broke out again.

There came a day when he took the Dauphine's handkerchief to hold to his mouth after a fit of coughing, and when he handed it back to her it was stained with blood.

She remembered the sickness of Madame de Pompadour, and that she had seen the comely figure waste away almost to nothing. Thus was the Dauphin wasting before her eyes.

But she would save him. She was determined to; she loved him as she loved no one else in the world, and she would fight with all her skill to save him.

She remembered that wedding night when he had cried in her arms for the loss of his first wife. She had known at that time that he was a good man, a man of sensibility and deep feeling; then she, a frightened child, had become a woman determined to win what she desired, determined to hold it. And what she had desired was the love of her husband.

She believed she had won that in some measure. She had perhaps been too sure. That was why she had suffered so acutely when she had discovered his love for Madame Dadonville.

She remembered that tragedy — the loss of their eldest son, the Duc de Bourgogne, her little Louis Joseph, at the age of eleven. That had been a bitter blow to them both and to the child's grandparents. His death had been one of the really big sorrows of her married life; another son had died at the age of three months and that had been a bitter blow. The loss of these children, the affair of Madame Dadonville — they had marred what could have been such a happy life.

He had consoled her at the time of the Duc de Bourgogne's death. They had other children, he reminded her.

Yes, theirs had been a fruitful union. She had three sons: the Duc de Berry, the Duc de Provence and the Duc d'Artois; and two daughters, the Princesses

Clotilde and Elisabeth. And she had looked after them herself, because she had believed that she could give them more love and care than any governesses could.

The King had considered her in some amazement. "My daughter," he said, "you are an example to every wife and mother in France."

She fancied he spoke a little ironically, for she would seem very dull, very unattractive in his eyes; but at the same time she had glimpsed his genuine approval and affection.

But who should care for her child, but a mother? she asked herself. Who should nurse a husband in sickness, but a wife?

She prayed for long hours at night on her knees; she murmured prayers beneath her breath in the sickroom. But in spite of her unfailing care, in spite of her prayers, the Dauphin's condition did not improve.

The King sent for her, and when they were alone he put his arms about her and embraced her.

"My dear daughter," he said, "I am anxious."

"He is very ill, Sire," she answered.

"I am anxious for him and I am anxious for you."

"For me?"

"I do not think that you should spend so much time in the sickroom, my dear. You know what ails him. Oh my daughter, I see how disturbed you are. But you are brave — you are one of the bravest women in France, I believe — so I will speak the truth to you. I fear, daughter, that I shall not much longer have a son, nor you a husband."

She clenched her fist and her mouth was firm. "I shall nurse him back to health," she said. "I did it before when everyone despaired of his life. I shall do it again."

The King studied her affectionately. She had a strong will, this Marie-Josèphe. He was surprised now that he had ever thought her colourless. Because she was a good woman, that did not necessarily mean that she was a stupid one.

"My dear," he said emotionally, "you will. I know you will. But I want you to hear what the doctors have told me. They say that this disease of the lungs, from which my son is suffering, can be infectious. Those who live constantly in the heated sickroom could in time be smitten by it."

"My place is with him," she said.

"You exhaust yourself. Others could share this burden of nursing."

Her eyes were fierce. "It is no burden and none shall share it with me," she answered.

The King laid his hand on her shoulder.

"I shall join my prayers with yours, my child," he told her. He took her hand and kissed it. "Let us hope that the prayers of a sinful old man and the most virtuous young woman at Court may be answered."

Each day the Dauphin grew weaker, but he was uneasy if, when he opened his eyes, he did not see Marie-Josèphe.

"I am sorry," he told her one day, "sorry for the unhappiness I have caused you."

292

She shook her head. "You gave me great happiness," she said.

"I love you," he told her. "You, as no other . . ."

"Do you say so because you know it is what I long to hear?"

"I say it because it is the truth. It is long since I saw her. Oh Marie-Josèphe, how I wish I had been entirely faithful to you. You deserve so much more than I have given you."

She shook her head. "Please . . . please do not speak of it . . . Now we are together . . ."

"For the short time that is left," he began.

"No," she cried. "It shall not be a short time. I nursed you through small-pox. I will nurse you through this."

"Marie-Josèphe, always beside me when I need you. My nurse, my comforter, my wife, my love . . ."

"I am so happy," she said. "I wish that I could die at this moment."

He knew that he was dying. He had become very gentle, very patient.

How was it, the Court wondered, that a man who knew himself to be so near to death could face the future with such serenity.

The King answered the question. He said: "My son's life has been without reproach. He has no fear of what awaits him. If we had all lived as virtuously as he has lived, it would be so with us when we faced death."

The Court must stay at Fontainebleau because the Dauphin was too ill to be moved.

The Dauphin knew that it was on his account that they remained and he apologised, for he was aware that it must be the desire of most to return to the more comfortable and luxurious Versailles.

"I fear," he said, "that I am causing trouble to the Court. It is a pity that I am so long in dying."

He was eager to save his doctors work and would lie still, pretending to sleep that they might doze in their chairs as they, with the Dauphine, kept the nightly vigil at his bedside.

December had come and he would lie in his bed watching the snowflakes falling outside the windows. He knew he would not see the spring again.

The doctors came to the King and told him that the Dauphin's life was slowly ebbing away. Louis said: "My heart is troubled for the poor Dauphine. She insists on believing that he will live. Poor soul! I think she deliberately deceives herself because she cannot bear to think of life without him. She is exhausted. I do not want her to be with him at the end. It will be too painful, and I fear that she is on the verge of collapse. I shall go to her and insist on her resting awhile in her own apartments. When she has gone, let the Cardinal de la Rochefoucauld be brought to my son's bedside, to administer the last rites. Come, I will accompany you now to the sickroom."

He went there with the doctors and, approaching the Dauphine, he took her face in his hands and smiled gently at her. He saw the dark circles under her eyes and the marks of exhaustion.

"My child," he said, "I am going to issue a command. You are to go to your room. One of your women will bring you a soothing drink and then you will rest."

"I shall remain here," she said.

"The King speaks to you. He commands you to go to your room and rest."

"My father . . ."

The King's voice shook a little as he took her hand. "My daughter," he said, "obey me. It is my wish." He put his lips to her forehead.

"You will wake me if he asks for me . . ."

"Rest assured I will have you awakened at once."

So the Dauphine went to her room, and when she had gone the Cardinal de la Rochefoucauld came to the Dauphin's bedside to administer the last rites.

The King retired from the bedside and sat in one corner of the room. He could hear the strong voice of the Cardinal, the feeble responses of the Dauphin.

Death! thought the King. There is too much death at Versailles. It is little more than a year since I lost my dear Marquise, and now my only son . . .

Death! the spectre that haunts us all . . . Kings cannot hide from it. It beckons, and perforce one follows.

The voices had ceased. The King knew, before the Cardinal came towards him.

He stood up, and said: "It is over?"

"Yes, Sire. The Dauphin is dead."

Even into this sombre chamber etiquette had intruded. The Dauphine must be told. The new Dauphin must be proclaimed.

The King turned from the Cardinal and said in a loud voice: "Bring the Dauphin to me here."

In a few minutes the Duc de Berry was standing before him — shy, *gauche*, eleven years old. Louis looked at his son's eldest surviving boy and thought: God pity you who will one day be King of France.

"You know why I have sent for you?" he asked.

"Yes, Sire." The boy spoke in a whisper.

"You know that you are Dauphin of France?"

"Yes, Sire."

"There are many duties waiting for you, grandson. Some pleasant and some unpleasant. The first you must perform as Dauphin is, I hope, one of the saddest that will ever fall to your lot. Come with me now."

The King walked solemnly out of the chamber of death; the Dauphin, fitting his steps to those of his grandfather, looked bewildered rather than sorrowful.

Those courtiers and servants whom they passed bowed low, and the boy was aware that a new respect was accorded him.

They arrived at his mother's apartment, and the page announced: "His Majesty the King and His Royal Highness the Dauphin."

Marie-Josèphe started up from her bed, and her eyes went from the King to the figure of her eleven-year-old son who was now significantly ushered into her presence as the Dauphin of France.

296

★ ★ ★

What could be done to comfort a woman so stricken with grief? The King asked himself and his courtiers how he could lift Marie-Josèphe from the despondency into which she had fallen.

He could think of nothing he could give her but power.

He summoned her to his presence and talked to her.

"Daughter," he said, "I would not have you think that your position has been altered one jot by the death of my son. I still regard you as my beloved daughter."

She thanked him in her quiet, listless way.

He reminded her that she had mourned the customary two months and that she must not mourn for ever,

"Sire," she answered, "I shall mourn until I die."

"That will not be long delayed if you continue as you are now."

"Then I shall be happy, Sire. Alas for me, God has willed that I should survive him for whom I would have given a thousand lives. I hope that He will grant me the grace to spend the rest of my pilgrimage in preparing myself, in sincere penitence, to rejoin his soul in Heaven, where I do not doubt he is asking that same grace for me."

The King remembered how she had always advised the Dauphin, and he believed her to be an intelligent woman. That she was without gaiety and had little wit seemed unimportant. He himself was in no mood for wit or gaiety. He believed that he needed a companion, someone who could fill that empty space in his life which had been left by Madame de Pompadour.

There were many pretty girls and beautiful women eager to supply his physical needs. Could it be that this bereaved daughter-in-law could be his friend and *confidante*?"

He needed a woman friend. He trusted none of his ministers. He had always cared more for women than for men; only a woman, he believed, could give him disinterested friendship. Men were constantly thinking of their own advancement — as indeed were many women; but he was convinced that the divine spark of disinterested friendship could only come from a woman.

"My daughter," he said on impulse, "you have lost one who meant everything in your life. I have recently lost a very dear friend. We both suffer. Let us endeavour to help each other over this difficult period in our lives. Perhaps in seeking to soothe the other's grief we shall find a modicum of contentment. Let us be friends. We have much to talk of together. We must think of the future of your family. You will talk of them to me, and I will talk of matters of State which I used to discuss with my dear Marquise."

She was crying quietly. "Why, dear Sire and Father," she said, "I already feel a little happier than I did before. It is the prospect of being of some use to you."

"Then we are both a little happier. You shall occupy a suite of rooms immediately below my own. Be prepared to move into them at once."

She felt her spirits lifting because she was thinking of those meetings which had taken place in her husband's apartments. If the King had shown this friendship for her when her husband had been alive, how pleased he would have been! He had cultivated the friendship of his sisters because they had shared the King's confidence.

Was it possible that she, Marie-Josèphe, might discuss State policy with the King? If that were so, she would never forget her husband. She seemed to feel him beside her now, urging her to accept the friendship of the King, to comfort the King, to win his regard. Thus could she carry on the interrupted policies of her husband.

She thought of the Duc de Choiseul, who had been so insolent to the Dauphin not very long ago, at the time when the poor Jesuits had been suppressed.

Willingly, assiduously would she work as the late Dauphin had; she would do all that he had done; thus it could seem as though he lived on.

What would he have done, had he been alive and had the power?

CHAPTER SIXTEEN

Death at Versailles

At this time there was a great deal of excitement throughout France on account of the Calas affair which had
been dragging on for years, and concerning which Voltaire,
from his refuge at Ferney in Gex, had been thundering
forth his abuse of intolerance.

During the reign of pleasure-loving Louis XV, there
had been little persecution of Protestants in Paris and
the North, but in the South of France, which was
remote from the centre of culture, persecution had
gone on, and Protestants were tortured and executed.

The Calas family who were Protestants had become
prominent some three years previously. Monsieur Calas
was a wealthy merchant of Toulouse; his wife was a
noblewoman. They were the happy parents of several
children and they might have continued in happy
obscurity but for the fact that one of these, Louis, a
boy of seven, was greatly loved by a servant of the
household who was a Catholic.

This servant believed that, unless she could turn this
beloved child into a Catholic, his soul would be lost.
This being intolerable to her peace of mind she sought
to convert him, so she began by secretly taking him

with her to Mass; but later she dared to take him away from his family to a Catholic hairdresser and wigmaker in the town who agreed to hide him from his parents.

The loss of their little son brought great sorrow to the household, who sought for him in vain. But their uncertainty did not last long for, as it was a law of the Catholic Church that any child of seven or over was old enough to proclaim himself a Catholic, Louis did this, to the delight of the Catholic population of Toulouse and the consternation of his parents.

His father was summoned to appear before the Archbishop and ordered to pay certain sums of money for the boy's keep while he had been in hiding, and to pay for him to be brought up in a Catholic household. Little Louis was then ordered to write a letter to the Archbishop demanding that two of his sisters and a young brother be taken from their home to be educated with him as Catholics.

Louis had an elder brother, Marc Antoine, a stern Protestant and bachelor of law who was debarred from practising because, to do so, he needed a certificate proving that he was a Catholic; and naturally he could not obtain this unless he changed his religion.

The problem which confronted him — either to deny his faith or give up his profession — had so depressed him that he developed unwise drinking habits in order temporarily to relieve his depression.

One of his friends, a certain Lavaysse, was also a member of a Protestant family but, because he had been brought up by Jesuits, he had not found any difficulty in following the career he wanted. Lavaysse had belonged to the Navy in which he had excelled; and a rich relation had left him a plantation in Saint Domingo to which he was about to go.

Before leaving he called at the Calas house to say his farewells. He did not exactly boast but it was natural that the depressed Marc Antoine should compare his own career with that of the successful Lavaysse, and he suddenly left the company, went up to his room and hanged himself.

When his body was discovered, the family was horrified, not only at the loss of their son, but because it was the Catholic custom to take the body of a Protestant suicide — or suspected suicide — and drag it naked on a hurdle through the town. This was considered to be a stigma which would be attached to the rest of the family for years after the event.

The lamentations of the Calas family, when they cut down the body of Marc Antoine, attracted the attention of neighbours, who came into the house to see what was wrong.

"He has killed himself!" cried one.

Monsieur Calas, visualising the naked body of his son being subjected to humiliation, cried out: "No, no! It was not suicide."

"So . . . it was murder!"

One of the neighbours went into the streets and shouted: "Citizens, come quickly! Here is a Protestant family who have murdered their son."

Soon there was a crowd outside the house. They stormed into it, took the body of Marc Antoine, stripped it and dragged it through the streets. They seized every member of the Calas family and forcing them to march through the streets behind the body, they cried: "See! Here are Protestants who have strangled their own son."

The family was thrust into prison, and the Catholic priests concocted a case against them. Marc Antoine had declared his intention of becoming a Catholic, they said, and because of this his family had strangled him. Special services were held to eulogise Marc Antoine, for the priests saw an opportunity of inciting the citizens of Toulouse against the Protestants, and such opportunities were never ignored.

They declared that the Protestants held secret tribunals in which they decided to murder all of their number who expressed the wish to be converted to Catholicism. The people of Toulouse were called upon to show their love of the true faith, which meant that they must demand persecution of the Calas family.

The case of Calas might have been merely another which chained France to the dark ages of intolerance, but for the so-called atheist of Ferney who poured out his scorn for his fellow countrymen. "The judgement of this Protestant family," declared Voltaire, "is all the more Christian in that it is incapable of proof."

Calas, a man of sixty-four, was broken on the wheel. In the midst of his agony he was asked to confess, but he only declared his innocence and prayed for the forgiveness of his tormentors.

Voltaire, from Ferney on the borders of Switzerland — into which country he could escape should the French authorities decide to regard his outspokenness as treason — followed the case with great attention; he wrote to Madame Calas and asked her if she would swear to him that her husband was innocent.

Having received her reply in the affirmative, Voltaire then brought his genius into play. He was going to have the verdict against Calas reversed; not only that, he was going to put an end to religious persecution in France for all time.

He began by writing letters to Saint-Florentin, Duc de la Vrillière, who was known as the "Minister of the *lettres de cachet*" because he allowed his mistress to sell them at fifty louis each. Artfully Voltaire suggested that Saint-Florentin must feel as disturbed by this affair as he was. Saint-Florentin, thus brought into the limelight, while protesting that the *affaire* Calas was a matter for the Justiciary, was made uneasy because he felt that Voltaire was shining a light on the prisons which were full of those who, because some person of influence had wished them out of the way, had received their *lettres de cachet*.

The campaign was fierce and long. That was what Voltaire intended it should be. The wits and *savants* took it up; the injustice of the punishment meted out to Monsieur Calas was discussed among the writers and philosophers.

Choiseul watched not without pleasure. He was on the side of Voltaire, eager as ever to see the Church in a subordinate position.

The force of public opinion stirred up by the fiery writings of Voltaire brought about the release from prison of Madame Calas who immediately left Toulouse to find refuge at Ferney.

This took place immediately before the expulsion of the Jesuits; and Choiseul, eager to score a trick against Saint-Florentin, released a certain young man from service in the galleys. This was Fabre, whose father had been sentenced to serve there. Fabre had made possible his father's escape by taking his place.

When this was discovered there had been a certain outcry and a demand that such a saintly young man should be given his liberty. Saint-Florentin had retorted that Fabre had defied the law and, since he had placed himself in a position to take over his father's service, he should do so.

Choiseul now stepped in. He had an eye for public approval. The Calas case had aroused deep feeling throughout France and he felt that a large public opinion was in favour of tolerance.

He therefore ordered that Fabre be given his freedom. Saint-Florentin was furious, but he could do nothing against the all-powerful Choiseul.

Meanwhile Voltaire's pamphlets continued to be received in Paris, and when he heard that the Toulouse *Parlement* was planning to re-arrest Madame Calas he suggested she go to Paris, which was more liberal-minded than any city in France, and there plead her cause.

While Madame Calas was travelling to Paris, Saint-Florentin made a great effort to discredit Voltaire and with him his ally Choiseul.

He employed a talented writer, Fréron, to write an article, which was supposed to have appeared in an English paper, attacking the King.

Choiseul's spies however had brought him information that this was about to be launched in Paris; whereupon Voltaire's venomous pen produced such attacks on Fréron as to make that man quiver with rage and terror, and Voltaire had little difficulty in proving the article to be a forgery.

The Toulouse *Parlement* meanwhile had busied itself to bring another case against the Protestants; and when a young girl was found dead in a well, her father, a Monsieur Sirven who was a Protestant, was accused of murdering her because, the *Parlement* declared, it was a custom of Protestants to murder their children.

However, Voltaire's invective and the knowledge that the all-powerful Choiseul was supporting him, encouraged others to be bold.

It was proved that the only witness in the case was a small child, who had been alternately bribed and threatened to say that she had seen Monsieur Sirven throw his daughter into the well. The truth was discovered to be that the child had been taken from her parents and put into a nunnery to learn to become a Catholic. The child had fretted for her parents and home, and because of this had been ill-treated. When she showed signs of madness she was sent home where, fearful that she should be taken back to the nunnery, she killed herself by jumping down the well.

Voltaire immediately offered refuge to the Sirven family who hastened to cross the mountains of the Cevennes and reached Ferney.

306

The fiery writer made the most of this and received visitors from all over the world to whom he made the Sirvens tell the story of their wrongs.

His writings had been circulated abroad, and the result was that England and Russia, probably to humiliate France, started to raise funds for the persecuted Protestants in that bigoted country.

Choiseul stepped in. He knew that he was striking a formidable blow at the Jesuits. He demanded that the *Parlement* of Toulouse give up the papers appertaining to the Calas case, and that it be tried in Paris.

He himself received Madame Calas and her daughters, treated them with the utmost respect, assuring them that he would be their advocate; he even put them into a carriage and had them driven round to see the wonders of the capital.

All Paris was impressed by the dignified demeanour of Madame Calas, and Choiseul knew that he had the people behind him.

All this had happened before the death of the Dauphin, and the Dauphine knew that her husband had been watching the Calas case with the utmost interest.

In the tragedy which had overtaken her she had forgotten that the case was still awaiting judgement.

Now, after the King had told her that he wished to be her friend, the news was brought to her that a verdict had been given in this case in favour of Madame Calas, who was given money and once more allowed to use the family escutcheon. This was tantamount to a declaration that her husband had been wrongfully executed.

Voltaire was exultant. He had proved the power of the pen. From that year, 1765, there were to be no more persecutions of Protestants in France.

When the Dauphine heard the way events were moving she made up her mind.

This was a further blow at that bigotry which the Dauphin had supported. Voltaire, who was called an atheist, Choiseul, who went to church merely because etiquette demanded that he should, had struck a blow against all that the Dauphin had worked for.

If she had had any doubts before, the Dauphine was now determined. She was going to stop grieving for her husband, and work as he would have worked. She would not rest until she had driven the Duc de Choiseul from the position he now held.

Having quickly become aware of the Dauphine's animosity, the Duc de Choiseul was uneasy. He sought out his sister and suggested that they take a turn in the gardens, explaining to her that what he had to say should be said out of doors.

When they paused by the fountain, he said:

"I feel apprehensive about the Dauphine."

"That little fool!"

"Yes," murmured Choiseul.

"I always thought her mild as milk," said the Duchess de Gramont. "Now she is not even that. She is weak as water."

"Have you noticed the King's affection for her?"

"The King!"

Choiseul laughed merrily. "He has not decided to make her his mistress, if that is what you are thinking," he said. "But he is going through a dismal period. He still thinks of the Marquise and imagines he needs comforting. The Dauphine, like the virtuous widow she is, mourns for her husband. So they put their heads together and become maudlin over their lost loved ones. It makes a bond."

"Bah!" said the Duchesse. "He'll be tired of that in a week or so."

"Perhaps, but a great deal can happen in a week or so. And since Madame Calas has been re-instated she has determined to attack me."

"As a gnat might try to attack a bull."

"There are small insects whose sting contains poison, remember."

"What do you propose to do?"

"Curb the King's love for his little daughter-in-law. Wipe the scales of pity from his eyes. Let him see her as she really is. In other words bring back the healthy contempt he has always had for her and the now sainted Dauphin."

"How will you do this?"

"Give him another little friend."

"And you have chosen her?"

"We both chose her long ago. Tell me, has he shown any interest?"

"But little. The only woman he seems to be interested in now is young Etiennette Muselier. I heard she was pregnant."

"Such a woman need not disturb us."

"No, but she satisfies him in his present mood."

"And he shows no interest in you?"

"No more than he does any other at Court. That Esparbès woman is very alert."

"We must certainly watch her. I believe at this moment that Louis could be lured into a liaison and continue it through habit. You know it was largely habit with Pompadour."

"What do you suggest?"

"This. Tonight I will do my utmost to see that he drinks deep. After the *coucher* be ready to slip up to his bedchamber by way of the private staircase."

"And Le Bel, Champlost and the rest?"

"Leave them to me. Le Bel is the only one we need consider. I will tell him that I have heard of a beautiful creature who would interest the King. While he is off on the hunt, you will slip into the royal bedchamber."

"And then?"

Choiseul burst into loud laughter. "Then, sister, the matter will be in your capable hands." He was serious immediately. "And remember this. We must lure him from the Dauphine. I mean to relegate her to obscurity. In a short time, if we work together, she will have no more power at Court than the Queen. If she is allowed to gain influence with the King she will frustrate all my plans. Tonight, sister, you must succeed."

"Never fear, brother. You remember when we were both young and talked of making our fortunes, when we planned in our poverty-stricken *château* . . ."

310

"Which," mused the Duc, "you called Château Ennui."

She nodded and went on: "I always said that when I wanted something I would get it."

Choiseul smiled fondly at his sister. He did not see that she was big, raw-boned, coarse-complexioned and lacking in those feminine charms which the King found so appealing; he only saw the woman he most admired in the world and who he believed could not fail.

Louis lay drowsily in bed. The *coucher* was over, the curtains drawn.

He felt desolate. Today he had seen a funeral pass when he was out hunting. Funerals had a morbid fascination for him. Often he would stop a *cortège* and ask what had caused the death.

Today he had received an answer which had made him very uneasy: "Hunger, Sire."

He had galloped quickly from that spot, but the hunt had been spoiled for him.

He was growing old, he supposed. He could not pass over what was unpleasant as easily as he once had. It was due to these deaths around him. The Marquise. His own son.

It was small wonder that he had needed little persuasion to drink too heartily.

He was not sorry that he had. It might be conducive to sleep.

He was aware of a movement in the room, a rustle of the bedcurtains.

"Who is there?" he demanded.

The curtains were drawn aside, and a far from charming woman looked down at him. She was smiling lasciviously. He thought her most unattractive, her hair loose, her dressing-gown open to disclose the flimsy bedgown.

"Madame de Gramont," he said coolly, trying to emerge from the fumes of alcohol which made him feel so drowsy, "what do you want?"

"I found it impossible to stay away any longer, Sire." She had come closer.

"You have a request to make?"

He heard her throaty laughter, and perhaps because she believed he was going to command her to go away, and she was determined to stay, she leaped upon him and seized him in her strong arms.

He thought wildly for a moment that she had come to assassinate him, but Madame de Gramont was making her intentions clear; those suffocating hugs were meant to portray affection, those great masculine hands, desire.

"I pray you," he began, "in the morning . . ."

But she was a determined woman, and he struggled a little, but not very much. It was a piquant situation, quite unique in his experience, and he felt too languid to do anything but allow himself to rise to the occasion.

The King was still a little bewildered in the morning, and at the *lever* he whispered to the Duc de Richelieu, who was handing him his shirt: "Last night I was ravished in my bed. I must tell Choiseul to keep his sister in better order."

312

Richelieu was alert. "Could not Your Majesty have called for help?"

"The attack came so suddenly, and she was so overpowering. There seemed no alternative but to submit."

This was serious, thought Richelieu. Choiseul had his hands firmly on the reins of Government; if his sister took the place of Madame de Pompadour there would be a sphere of influence about the King which it would be impossible to penetrate. Richelieu was not without his ambitions.

He would seek out that enchanting little Esparbès. Gramont could stand little chance against that dainty creature, and the rape of the King could only succeed if it were accompanied by indifference in an intoxicated victim and an element of surprise.

Madame d'Esparbès was plump and frivolous, *petite* and very feminine.

"Was there ever a woman made in more direct contrast to the ravisher of Your Majesty?" whispered Richelieu.

Louis watched the young Comtesse; she was leaning her arms on the table, peeling cherries. They were very white, and perfectly formed; it was said that Madame d'Esparbès had the most beautiful arms at Court.

Louis felt listless, but he realised that he must do something to escape from the Duchesse de Gramont. He could dismiss the woman from Court, but that would offend Choiseul, and he looked upon the Duc as the most clever of his ministers and one whom he could not afford to do without.

The simplest way, Louis supposed, watching the plump tapering fingers with the cherries, was to install someone else in that place which Madame de Gramont coveted.

Inwardly he shivered. It had been an unusual experience and for that he did not entirely regret it. But robbed of the element of surprise and novelty it could only have been repulsive; and he must find immediate protection from that rapacious woman.

Madame d'Esparbès was giving him one of her dewy smiles. She was a sensual little animal; he had heard of her adventures with others. He believed that she would be quite amusing.

He returned the smile and with a gesture invited her to change her place for the one beside him.

When supper was over he had made arrangements that she was to come to his bedroom immediately after the *coucher*.

Le Bel would stand on guard so that, should unwelcome visitors approach, they could be told that the King was engaged.

Thus he felt safe from the attentions of the Duchesse, and he was mildly pleased to have the kittenish d'Esparbès nestling against him.

"Oh, Sire," she cried, "tonight I have reached the summit of my dreams."

"I know," said the King, "that you are a lady of great experience. I believe you have slept with every one of my subjects."

314

Madame d'Esparbès dimpled. "Oh, Sire!" she murmured.

"There is the Duc de Choiseul, for one," pursued the King.

"But Sire, he is so powerful."

"And the Duc de Richelieu is another."

"He is so witty, Sire."

"Monsieur de Monville also."

"Such *beautiful* legs!"

"I agree that Choiseul has power, Richelieu wit, and Monville shapely legs. But what of the far from prepossessing Duc d'Aumont?"

"Oh, Sire, he is so devoted to Your Majesty."

The King began to laugh. Madame d'Esparbès laughed with him. This was success. Anyone who could make the King laugh, especially during this period of depression, would be welcomed to share his company.

But neither the rivalry between the Duchesse de Gramont and Madame d'Esparbès, nor the antagonism which existed between the Dauphine and the Duc de Choiseul could enliven the *ennui* into which the King had fallen — and the Court with him. The intimate supper parties were dull affairs. There were no private theatrical performances; the Marquise was sadly missed, not only by the King.

Louis was continually reminded that he was growing old. He could not stop talking of death, and when any member of the Court died, he wanted to hear all the details. If the deceased were younger than he was, the Court could be prepared for hours of gloom.

315

The Queen's father, Stanislas, had died; and the Queen had grieved for him ever since.

"He was the person in the world who loved me best," she told her women. "I shall mourn him for the rest of my life. My only consolation is that he is happier than I am and would not wish to return to this sad world."

The King, who had made tentative movements towards a reconciliation with the Queen, left her alone after the death of Stanislas. He wanted to be with those who helped him to forget the proximity of death.

It seemed that Marie Leczinska did not recover from the death of her father. Her health declined each day; her skin grew yellow and her once plump body seemed to be wasting away, although she retained her abnormal appetite. The doctors were nonplussed; they could put no name to her malady but *coma vigil*.

The Court decided that the next to die would be the Queen.

Choiseul's brain was busy. When the Queen died he must endeavour to arrange a marriage for the King. Sadly he was beginning to realise that Louis would never accept the Duchesse de Gramont as a wife. The whole Court was laughing about the rape of the King, for Richelieu had naturally made sure that such an opportunity of showering ridicule on Choiseul and his sister should not be missed.

If the Queen should die, and it was impossible to hope for a marriage between the King and the Duchesse de Gramont, Choiseul would attempt to strengthen the bonds between France and Austria. The

Archduchess Elisabeth, daughter of Maria Theresa, was highly eligible.

But he would not as much as hint at this matter while the Queen still lived; even with his sister he would not discuss it, because he knew that she had not yet given up all hope of marrying the King herself. Alas, it would be a little more difficult to force the King into marriage than forcing him to accept her for one night in his bed.

Choiseul's hopes of a royal marriage for his sister were very dim.

He was even a little worried about his own position. The Dauphine was worming her way into the King's confidence, and he was fully aware that she had some sentimental notion of her duty towards her dead husband which made her work assiduously for his, Choiseul's dismissal.

A short while ago he would have laughed at the possibility; now he was not so confident.

He often found that the Dauphine shared his conferences with the King, as Madame de Pompadour had done, which was a disconcerting state of affairs, for while he had counted on the support of the Marquise he could count with equal certainty on the opposition of the Dauphine.

Nevertheless he did not waver in his somewhat arrogant attitude, and refused to admit that he considered the Dauphin a worthy adversary.

Then suddenly he ceased to feel anxious concerning the Dauphine.

The trio were in the King's private apartment and Choiseul had determined to bring to the King's notice a matter which had long been on his mind.

The Dauphine sat with her back to the window, and thus her face was in shadow. The King was seated at the table with Choiseul opposite him.

They had discussed various State matters, when Choiseul said boldly: "Sire, the Dauphin will soon be of an age to marry."

He did not glance at the Dauphine but he was aware that she was alert.

"Oh," said the King, "he is young yet. Not thirteen, I believe. How old is Berry, my dear?"

"Not quite thirteen," said his mother.

"About three more years before a marriage could be consummated," mused the King. "And even then . . ."

The Dauphine shot a malignant glance at Choiseul. "My son is younger than his years in some matters," she said. "I would not wish him to be hurried into marriage."

Choiseul lifted his hands in a characteristic gesture. "But, Sire," he said, "when one considers the marriages of Dauphins one must think of France rather than the age of the bridegroom."

"That's true," said the King. "Whom have you in mind?"

"The daughter of the Empress, Sire. Such a marriage would strengthen the bonds between France and Austria. There could be nothing more desirable."

Choiseul noticed that the Dauphine had clenched her hands and was drumming them impatiently on the table.

"There is more than one daughter, I believe."

"I had in mind the youngest, Marie Antoinette," said Choiseul. "She is near the Dauphin's age and, I have heard, very beautiful and charming."

The King was nodding slowly when the Dauphine rose suddenly from her chair.

"I should never agree to such a marriage," she said.

"My dear . . ." began the King in tender reproach.

Choiseul had also risen to his feet. He leaned across the table. "Madame," he said, "I implore you to think of France . . . and waive your prejudices."

"I have a wife in mind for my son," said the Dauphine, speaking rapidly, almost breathlessly. "I would wish to see him allied to a daughter of the House of Saxony. She would be more like himself than this Austrian. The people would not like an Austrian marriage. My son's cousin is now eight years old . . ."

Choiseul interrupted: "It would mean too long a wait before the consummation."

"There is time."

"Madame, in matters of State there is never too much time."

The Dauphine turned from Choiseul to the King. "Sire," she said, "I ask you to save my son from this . . . distasteful marriage."

"Sire," blazed Choiseul, "it is fortunate that none but ourselves can hear the words of Madame la Dauphine. Marie Antoinette is admirable in every detail. I implore Your Majesty to give me permission to send the Dauphin's portrait to the Empress and to beg her to allow us to have that of her daughter."

"You go too fast, Choiseul," said the King; and as he spoke the Dauphine sank to her chair. She was overcome by a paroxysm of coughing.

The King hurried to her side. "My dear," he said, "you are ill. You are very ill . . ."

The Dauphine nodded and lay back in her chair, her body still racked by coughing.

The King half turned but did not look at Choiseul. Louis was shaken; he had thought that his daughter-in-law had looked wan for some time, but that that was due to her mourning for her husband. Now he could not meet the expression he feared to find on Choiseul's face. The Duc would draw his conclusions as to the meaning of this bout of coughing, and he would be unable to hide his satisfaction and triumph.

Here was Death — inescapable Death come to haunt him again. He would read in Choiseul's eyes that Death was his ally, standing by, eagerly waiting to rid him of an enemy.

"Send for her confidential woman," he said over his shoulder.

Choiseul strode to the door to do his bidding.

The woman came into the room, alarmed.

"Take the Dauphine to her apartments," said the King. "I think she should be put to bed, and there she should rest awhile."

"Yes, Sire."

The King went to the woman and laid his hand on her arm.

"She has had a bad turn. Has she been in this condition before?"

"There have been occasions, Sire."

"Recently?"

"Yes, Your Majesty."

"I was not told."

"It was Madame la Dauphine's desire that none should be told, Sire."

"Now take her to her apartments. I will send physicians to her."

He went to the Dauphine who was lying back in her chair, her eyes half closed.

"Come, my dear," he said. "Here is your woman. She will take you to your bed. I shall visit you there."

The Dauphine rose unsteadily to her feet. The eagerly watching Choiseul saw that her face had that flushed look which he had noticed in the Dauphin's; he saw too that she had lost a good deal of weight in the last weeks.

He had seen two people look like that recently. One was the Dauphin, the other the Marquise de Pompadour. Was it possible that the pulmonary scourge was about to afflict her?

When she had gone the King turned to him.

"Leave me now," he said. "I wish to be alone, for a great fear has come to me and I have no more heart for business just now."

Alone the King paced up and down his apartment.

"Madame la Marquise," he murmured, "I would that you were with me now. You would know how to comfort me. I have seen you die, my dearest friend, and I have felt the bitter loneliness which followed. I have seen my son die. I did not love him, but at least he was my son, my only son. And today I have seen Death in the face of the Dauphine. Death . . . It is all about me. The Queen is slowly dying, poor woman. Am I to lose all who have lived about me for so many years? Marquise . . . why did you leave me? Who can comfort me now you are gone?"

Was there not some woman — someone who combined beauty with understanding?

If there were, she was hard to find. The little *grisettes* of the Parc aux Cerfs had lost their power to charm. When he entered the place he sometimes wondered what would happen to him if he died in the midst of his pleasures, with all his sins upon him. He had to face the fact that he was no longer as virile as he had once been. His visits to the Parc aux Cerfs among those young uninhibited creatures often exhausted him.

He wanted a friend who was also a mistress. She must have all the qualities of the Pompadour, and the beauty which had been hers in the first weeks of their acquaintance. But where could he find her? Did she exist?

The Duchesse de Gramont had none of her qualities; Madame d'Esparbès hardly any.

Was it possible that one day he would find her? Could he then settle down to serenity when occasions like this one would not depress him so completely?

Somewhere in Paris, in France, such a woman existed. He would be ready to cherish her for the rest of his life and richly reward the one who brought her to him.

★   ★   ★

Choiseul had the satisfaction of knowing his enemy grew weaker every day.

The Dauphine was no longer well enough to share the King's counsels. All through that winter she was seen to be suffering from the complaint which had ended her husband's life.

The doctors shook their heads over her. One who nursed a patient as she did the Dauphin, insisting on doing every menial task herself, ran great risks of being infected. And this is what had happened. She had survived the small-pox when she had nursed him; but this time she was not to escape.

The doctors were right. With the coming of spring the Dauphine died.

Her passing seemed to bring her great contentment for, as she said, she had no desire to live after her husband had died, and now she was to join him and this had been her greatest wish since he had departed this life.

The next victim, said the courtiers, would be the Queen.

Then, thought Choiseul, we will get the King married again. A new and lively Queen will change everything at Court. She will sweep away melancholy and if she is an Austrian bride she will be my friend. Choiseul had begun to think that he was destined to remain in power for the rest of his life. Even fortune favoured him. As soon as the Dauphine had begun to oppose him she had been stricken with illness and shortly after conveniently removed from his path. That was a sign, he told his sister.

"And the King shows no indication of his fondness for you?"

The Duchesse declared vehemently: "It is that foolish d'Esparbès. She is constantly with him. Her very absurdity makes him laugh."

"When a woman makes the King laugh, that is dangerous for that woman's enemies."

"Even though there is ridicule in his laughter?"

"Louis so desperately seeks laughter that he is prepared to accept any kind. My dearest, I think it is time we arranged the dismissal of that woman. She is a fool, I know. But let us not be too complacent."

Before he could plan a campaign against her, Madame d'Esparbès visited him and indicated that she wished him to give a command in the Army to a relative of hers.

Choiseul insolently refused this; whereupon she told him to beware. "Very soon," she said, "you will use all your efforts to please me. Everything I ask, you will be eager to give me."

"That," said Choiseul, "is an interesting prophecy. How long, I wonder, before we shall know whether it is to be fulfilled?"

She swept angrily away, and when he was alone some of Choiseul's bravado deserted him. He believed she must feel very sure of herself to speak as she did. Could it be that the King, out of sheer boredom, was going to give her what she was clearly demanding and have her accepted at Court as *maîtresse-en-titre*?

He must be stopped at once.

Choiseul considered the methods which had been used so successfully by Madame de Pompadour, and he proposed to use similar ones. He was quite unscrupulous and immediately drew up an account of what he believed had happened when the King spent the night with Madame d'Esparbès. This he took to the King and told him that it had been written by a friend of Madame d'Esparbès whom she had secreted in a closet next to the bedchamber. In this account it was stated that the King had failed as a lover in spite of the use of an aphrodisiac.

Louis, who was almost as terrified of impotence as he was of death, was furiously angry.

So, thought Choiseul slyly, his guess had not been far from the truth, for only if this was so could the King be quite so furious.

"I cannot be blamed for growing old," he said coldly, "but I could be blamed if I continued to receive people who allowed such foolish gossip to be circulated about my Court."

Choiseul bowed his head.

He could not resist an open rebuff to Madame d'Esparbès. Passing her on the staircase in the ceremonial promenade, he said to her in a loud voice so that all could hear: "Well, *ma petite*, and how does the *affaire* progress?"

The King, who heard this, was horrified and it was noticed how coldly he received Madame d'Esparbès.

Everyone knew that that lady need no longer be feared as a rival for the position of *maîtresse-en-titre*.

All except the lady herself were certain of her downfall. She however was surprised when, immediately after the promenade, a letter was brought to her apartments. She was to leave Court at once for the estates of Monsieur d'Esparbès, her husband's father, since her presence was no longer required at Court.

Bewildered and powerless to protest or even to ask the reason for her dismissal, she departed.

During the following summer Marie Leczinska died.

Louis, who had certainly not loved her, was very sad as he went to her room and quietly kissed her cold forehead.

Yet another death! This was not going to relieve the depression.

The King would sit at the table in the *petits appartements* and say nothing; and since the King was silent, so were the guests.

What a contrast to those days when Madame de Pompadour had dominated the company and gaiety and wit had prevailed!

The King closed the Parc aux Cerfs. He had no heart for such pleasures, he told Le Bel. Moreover, as Death seemed to have become a permanent guest at the *château*, he was considering living a reformed life.

"For who knows, my friend," he said, "where Death will strike next?"

Le Bel said: "It will not be Your Majesty. Your Majesty has surely discovered the secret of eternal youth."

"Do not think to please me with such blatant falsehoods," said the King abruptly.

And Le Bel looked solemn. He saw great profits lost to him, and he sighed for the days when it was his duty to search Paris and Versailles for charming girls to please the King.

The Court too was solemn. A repentant King meant a dull Court. Who knew what would happen in the King's present mood! He might people the Court with priests and insist that religious services take the place of balls and banquets.

Louis might feel the need to repent. His friends did not. For them it was more than probable that there were many years of delicious sin on Earth left to them before they began to consider preparing themselves for the life to come.

Why, said some pessimists, he might even marry the Duchesse de Gramont. The lady was irrepressible. The whole Court knew of what had been called the rape of the King. If that could happen to him, might he not be led unresisting into marriage?

Something must be done. A new mistress must be found. She must be so gay, so enchanting, that she would be able to charm the King from his present mood.

Somewhere in France she existed, and it was the desire of every ambitious and pleasure-loving man at Court to find her.

None of the candidates aroused more than a flicker of interest in the King, and then one day Le Bel was cornered by a man who assured him that he would end the search.

This man was a hanger-on at Court, a man who had taken part in many a shady adventure, who lived by his wits and owned an establishment in which he trained beautiful young women to be suitable mistresses for men in high places, and then concluded profitable transactions.

This man was the Comte du Barry.

CHAPTER SEVENTEEN

Madame du Barry

Jean Baptiste du Barry, rake, rogue, adventurer, was feeling very pleased with himself as he left Le Bel. He was by nature an optimist: he could not have succeeded in his way of life if he had not been so. He lived by the expediency of the moment and his unwavering belief in the future.

He was now certain that, although many powerful men at Court — headed by Choiseul — had failed to provide the King with a mistress, he, living on the fringe of the Court, a man with an unsavoury past and a doubtful future, was going to succeed.

"This time," he said to himself, "there shall be no failure. The woman is mine. Ha! From Jean Baptiste Comte du Barry, to Louis de Bourbon King of France. Not such a great step for her as some might think!"

Le Bel was not very enthusiastic; du Barry would admit that. He could only believe that the Comte might provide the King with amusement for a night or so.

"Oh no, no, my friend," murmured Jean Baptiste. "I will provide him with the successor to Madame de Pompadour."

He could not prevent himself from laughing aloud. Once before he had come near to success. Had they forgotten that? He certainly had not. But for Madame de Pompadour he would have succeeded too.

He would not count that a great failure. Many men, even at Court, had found a formidable adversary in that woman; but now she was where she could not foil the plans of Jean Baptiste du Barry. And that clever purveyor of woman had a creature to offer who greatly excelled even la belle Dorothée.

Yes, he was certain of that. Jeanne was the most delicious creature who had ever fallen into his hands.

Dorothée also had been delightful after he had trained her. *After*, of course. They all owed so much to Jean Baptiste.

He had secured a meeting between the King and Dorothée as he now proposed to arrange between Jeanne and the King. The King had been delighted with the lovely Dorothée.

"Perhaps for one night . . . two nights," Le Bel had hinted.

One night! Two nights! Girls were well brought up in the establishment of Monsieur le Comte du Barry. La belle Dorothée was no little bird for the *trébuchet*, no candidate for the Parc aux Cerfs. He had meant her to reign at Court, and so she would have done, daughter of a Strasbourg water-carrier though she was, but for Madame de Pompadour.

That woman! She was clever, he would grant that; but she would not have succeeded against the Comte du Barry except for the fact that he could not approach the King, and she was beside him every hour of the day.

She did not do the damage herself. She would not soil her aristocratic hands (aristocratic! snorted Jean Baptiste. Was the daughter of a meat-contractor in Paris so much superior to one of a water-carrier in Strasbourg?). No; others told the King that la belle Dorothée had been the mistress of a man who was suffering from a painful disease, the very mention of which, considering the life he led, could throw the King into a panic.

So that was the end of la belle Dorothée. Perhaps he had asked too quickly for that diplomatic post in Cologne. Well, he had more experience now, more *finesse*; and there was no Madame de Pompadour to sweep a possible rival out of the way. There was only weary Le Bel (showing his age, poor fellow) eagerly looking for someone, anywhere, who could amuse the King.

So Jeanne was going to succeed where Dorothée had failed. Jeanne had the vitality, and when he told her she would be wild with joy. He pondered. Should he try to restrain her? Perhaps. Perhaps not. When he thought of Jeanne in her most abandoned mood and imagined her with the King, he could but hover between hilarious laughter and apprehension. So much depended on the mood of the King.

Louis was surrounded by ladies who failed to please him, so perhaps one who was certainly no fine lady would be exactly what he needed. And Jeanne (surely he did not exaggerate when he called her the most

331

beautiful girl in Paris) was experienced. She had entertained so many men in her amatory life that she would surely know how best to please the King. Jeanne was perfect for the role. She was not very young — nearly twenty-five in fact — although they would say she was twenty-two. Even so that was not exactly young. Yet she remained so fresh that it was extraordinary. It was not only because of that perfect skin; it was something within herself, some inner delight in being alive and well, and able to amuse, some perpetual joy which never seemed to desert her whatever befell her. She retained it even during their quarrels, and they had had some violent ones. (He trembled now to remember an occasion when she had packed her valise and left his house. Thank God he had found her and brought her back.) He was sure it had been hers during those days of poverty in Vaucouleurs, and in that depressing de la Garde establishment where she worked for a while. It was Jeanne herself — bubbling over with good spirits, happy to possess life no matter where she lived it.

Perhaps it was this quality in her, rather than her startling beauty, which made her so outstanding, so certainly a person who could bring good fortune to herself and her benefactor.

He pictured himself swaggering about Versailles and Paris. All those who had warned him that he would end up destitute would be forced to eat their words. He would have some surprises to show them at home in Lévignac, where they still looked upon him as a ne'er-do-well, in spite of the letters he wrote to them from Paris.

He was no longer young; he was ready to accept that sad fact, for he was midway between forty and fifty. He may not have accumulated wealth so far, but he had acquired wisdom and experience, and in a matter of months from now his fortune would be made. Jeanne would make it.

There had been a time when he had been rich. That was twenty years ago when he had been clever enough to make a wealthy marriage. The family had thought that Catharine Ursula Dalmas de Vernongrèse would come to the tumbledown old *château* in Lévignac, use her money to renovate the place and buy some of the land which they had lost during previous generations, thus bringing back to the du Barry family the dignity of the past.

It was for this very reason that the marriage had been arranged for their eldest son.

Jean Baptiste had had other ideas. He had married Catharine to win her fortune for himself, not to give it to his family.

He admitted now that he had been incautious, but then he had lacked the experience which he had now acquired. He had tried to double his fortune at the gambling tables and very soon Catharine's money had gone the way of that of the du Barrys.

That was years ago and, since Catharine was now as poor as his own family, there was no need for them to stay together, so they had parted and Jean Baptiste had come to Paris to make another fortune.

And now, as once he had seen Catharine as the woman who would make him a rich man through marriage, he saw Jeanne who was to bring him to the same happy state through the infatuation of the King.

Catharine had been one of the richest girls in Toulouse; Jeanne was the most beautiful in Paris.

She was his to mould and use to his advantage as Catharine had been. A man grows wiser in twenty years, and this time he would succeed.

Nearly twenty-five years before, in the village of Vaucouleurs, Jeanne Bécu (now known as Mademoiselle Vaubarnier) had been born on an August day in the year 1743.

Jeanne was the illegitimate daughter of Anne Bécu, and no one was sure who was her father. Not that anyone cared very much. Some declared it was one of the soldiers who had been billeted in the village. Anne had a lover among them. Others said it was the cook in the village inn. Anne was often in and out of the kitchens there. Others said that of course it was one of the Picpus monks, for Anne went to the convent regularly to sew for them, and she had been seen behaving with Jean Jacques Gomard — Frère Ange to his community — in a manner which should not be expected between monk and visiting seamstress.

When Jeanne was four years old she accompanied her mother to Paris where Anne had found work as a cook in the house of a beautiful courtesan known as Francesca.

334

Anne was delighted with her new situation especially when Jeanne, whose beauty was already remarkable, attracted the attention of Francesca's lover, Monsieur Billard-Dumonceau who, being an amateur artist, desired to paint the child's portrait.

"You must lend me Jeanne for a time," he told Anne. "I will take her to my house, for I am going to paint her. You will have nothing to fear; she will be returned to you safely."

Anne Bécu had no fear. She looked upon Monsieur Billard-Dumonceau as her benefactor; moreover she had formed a strong friendship with a fellow servant at Mademoiselle Francesca's; this was Nicolas Rançon. They had become lovers, but because they were both advancing into middle age they were contemplating entering into a more settled relationship.

When the Abbé Arnaud, who called on Monsieur Dumonceau, saw Jeanne, he took her on to his knee and asked her who she was.

Without embarrassment she told him. He said she was the loveliest little girl he had ever seen, and added that it was regrettable that she was without education.

Monsieur Billard-Dumonceau considered this, and eventually decided that he would have her educated; consequently she was sent to the Convent of Sainte Aure which had originally been a charity school for the daughters of the poor and criminal classes. Recently it had been decided that the girls who were brought there should not necessarily be in need of care, protection and correction; they might be the daughters of poor yet respectable people who had been selected to receive some sort of education.

In this place, where it was considered a sin to laugh, Jeanne remained until she was fifteen years old, Monsieur Billard-Dumonceau having paid the fees which would keep her there until that time. He had by then forgotten the charming little girl who had interested him, and as her fees were no longer paid Jeanne was sent home to her mother.

So out into the streets of Paris came Jeanne, more lovely than ever in her early womanhood, her golden curls released from the hood and forehead band which, in the Convent, had restricted them, her blue eyes alert for adventure.

And the adventures which befell Jeanne were inevitable.

She had begun as apprentice to a hairdresser only to become the hairdresser's mistress and so enslave him that he wished to marry her. His mother had quickly sent Jeanne away.

She had then become "reader" to Madame de la Garde, the widow of a rich tax-farmer, but the widow had two sons and Jeanne's relationship with them, being discovered by the widow, resulted in her instant dismissal.

Her next post was in the millinery and dressmaking establishment of Monsieur Labille in the Rue Neuve des Petits Champs; and from the moment she stepped into that scented and luxurious establishment she knew that she would find its manners and customs more congenial than anything she had encountered before.

Her duties were by no means arduous, for the Sieur Labille quickly decided that she would be of more use as a salesgirl than in the back rooms, making hats and gowns.

She changed her name to Mademoiselle Lange; and in the perfumed showroom she waited on noblewomen and the men who accompanied them on their shopping expeditions. Many a gentleman came to Labille's to assist his women friends to choose a gown or hat. It was slyly said that the gowns and hats of Monsieur Labille had a great attraction for the male sex.

Now a wider life stretched before Jeanne. She was intoxicated by the splendour about her. She could not resist the fascinating manners, the charming compliments of these gentlemen who were quite different from Monsieur Lametz, the hairdresser, and even from the sons of Madame de la Garde who, she realised now, had both been a little self-important and patronising towards their mother's young reader.

Monsieur Labille wanted the whole world to know how he looked after his girls. They must live in; they must be in their beds at an early hour. They must go regularly to Mass. He was not averse however to their delivering a purchase to a house as a special favour and, if they were petted and made much of and stayed a little longer than necessary, Monsieur Labille might shake his finger and deliver a lecture, but he could not be harsh with his girls. He doted on them; so could he blame others for doing so?

He realised that of all his girls Mademoiselle Jeanne Lange was the most adorable; and so he lived in fear that one day some young man would carry her off and she would grace the establishment no longer. He could do nothing to protect her from the admiration of his customers; after all, in her ability to attract lay her great value to him.

Jeanne very soon had her lovers — rich young men on the fringe of the Court who brought good business to the shop. The chief of these was Radix de Sainte-Foix, a very rich young man who was a farmer-general and Navy-contractor.

The mistress of such a rich young man was quickly noticed and very soon Mademoiselle Lange became known in many layers of Paris society, because Radix de Sainte-Foix enjoyed taking Jeanne about with him and observing the admiration and envy she aroused (and the envy he himself did). Jeanne's life was full of lighthearted gaiety. All her spare time was spent in the company of this doting lover, until one day he took her to the house of Madame Duquesnoy.

This woman — who called herself the Marquise — posed as a noblewoman who had lost her fortune and was attempting to retrieve it by running a gaming-house for her friends. She was determined to keep this exclusive, so she said, and members were closely scrutinised before they were allowed to join her circle.

Sainte-Foix determined to take Jeanne there. But, he explained, Mademoiselle Lange, salesgirl at Labille's, would certainly not be admitted. Not that he was the sort of man who would let such a trifle stand in his way. He was going to give her a new name and a new personality. To begin with she was to be Mademoiselle

Beauvarnier. Did she not think that more aristocratic than Lange? And she was not to mention her connexion with Labille's.

Jeanne was ever ready for some new adventure, and as Mademoiselle Beauvarnier she frequented the *salon* of the self-styled Marquise Duquesnoy.

Jean Baptiste du Barry was a frequent visitor, being interested in Madame Duquesnoy's methods, which were similar to his own. Like herself he entertained lavishly; he had his gaming tables, and he introduced attractive young women to men, allowing them to use rooms in his house.

But he would be more successful than Madame Duquesnoy, he decided, because he trained his girls himself. He could take any little *grisette* and turn her into a mistress fit for a petty nobleman.

He was constantly looking out for suitable entrants to his establishment; and no sooner had he set eyes on Jeanne than he decided that he would mould her most advantageously.

Jeanne had never met anyone like Jean Baptiste du Barry. Glib and suave, he could with ease assume the manners of Versailles — so at least it seemed to a girl who knew nothing of such manners. At last she had met a real nobleman and she was fascinated.

She was wasted . . . wasted, declared Jean Baptiste. Such beauty to be thrown away in a shop! He had never heard anything like it. Jeanne must leave Labille's immediately.

And where should she go? she asked. Where would she find work as easy and pleasant as that which she did at Labille's?

"Work!" cried Jean Baptiste. "You should never work. Others should work for you. You shall come to my house. There you shall live as . . . Madame du Barry."

"You mean you would marry me?"

"Willingly — if I had not already a wife. But we will not let such a trifle deter us. Come, my child, I will make a lady of you. Who knows, one day I may take you to Versailles."

It was too gloriously glittering. She would consult with her mother and Aunt Hélène, she told her new admirer.

He was a little disturbed, but to show his goodwill he offered to give the Rançons lodging in his house if Jeanne would leave Labille's and come to him.

That decided Jeanne and her family. She had at last fulfilled the promise of her youth. She was the mistress of a nobleman.

For four years Jeanne lived in the house of the Comte du Barry. During that time he sought to make a lady of her; a feat which, Jeanne assured him, was quite impossible, and with which opinion he came to agree.

First of all he changed her name. He did not like Beauvarnier. He thought Vaubarnier more distinctive. Jeanne, happily accepting the new name, quickly summed up the character of her new lover. He was boastful; he was not entirely to be trusted; but she grew fond of him and she realised that he was doing a great deal for her. Her mother and stepfather were delighted to be lodged in such a magnificent house and that, they said, made the liaison so respectable, even though the Comte had many mistresses, and they were all kept in the house. They were all attractive — they would have been of no use to him otherwise — and he enjoyed watching them appear at his evening parties, when they were expected to entertain the guests. He put no restraint on the extent of the admiration which was offered to them and made his visitors pay handsomely for such privileges.

Often Jean Baptiste would take her to a ball at the Opera House and entertainments at the house of noblemen; she was always singled out for her remarkable beauty which became by no means impaired by the life she led. Others might wilt and fade — not so Jeanne. She had an unusual vitality and imperturbability; she was invariably good-tempered; she appeared to live entirely in the present and be without the slightest concern for the future.

Even the Duc de Richelieu when he saw her was attracted.

Perhaps it was the attentions of such a highly placed nobleman of the Court which gave Jean Baptiste grandiose ideas.

He had long desired a diplomatic post at Court, but although he had made many supplications to the Duc de Choiseul, he had been unsuccessful; and he was still suffering from the slight he had received at the time of the La Belle Dorothée incident when he had asked for a post in Cologne and been so promptly refused it.

He would find some way of being received at Court; and he believed it would be through Jeanne.

She was so ready to fall in with his plans that he was sure that if she ever had an opportunity she would work for him. She had been very kind to his son Adolphe who sometimes lived with them, for she was fond of children and they of her. Adolphe, in his early teens, looked upon her as an elder sister, and she was delighted with their relationship; and Jean Baptiste knew too that if she ever had the power she would not forget to help Adolphe.

Why should she not bring good to them all? She regarded herself as a member of the family. She was even known in some quarters as Madame du Barry.

"The good of one is the good of all," said Jean Baptiste.

That was why he was so excited because Le Bel had agreed to meet Jeanne.

He returned to the house before she did, and he was uneasy — as he always was when she was out alone; and when she arrived he fiercely demanded to know where she had been.

"Taking a glass of wine with Madame Gourdan," she told him; she was invariably frank.

"Taking a glass of wine with that old bawd! You must be mad. At such a time . . . at such a time. This could ruin everything. What did she want of you?"

"Only to offer me shelter if I decided to leave your house."

"Impudence. Ha! She knows you would not be so foolish."

"I left you once," Jeanne reminded him.

He strode to her, put his arms about her and held her tightly. "Do not even speak of it," he cried.

"Well, I did not agree to go to her," she said soothingly.

"I should think not . . . when Fortune is about to smile on you as she never has before."

"And who is Fortune . . . this time?" she asked.

"One whose name I will not mention lest you laugh me to scorn for a pretentious old fool. Le Bel is coming to supper with us. I want you to sparkle for him. I want you to dazzle him. Jeanne, this is the most important night of your life."

She was accustomed to his flights of fancy. She was fond of him; she wanted to please him; so she promised him that she would be as charming as she knew how to be to his friend Le Bel.

"Le Bel," said Louis, "you are not attending. What is on your mind?"

"A thousand apologies, Sire." Le Bel helped the King into his coat. "My thoughts were with a certain . . . woman."

"At your age, Le Bel!" said Louis smiling.

"Such a woman, Sire. I have never seen the like before."

The King yawned. "I remember the last one you brought here."

"This, Sire, is quite a different type, I can say, with honesty, that neither I nor Your Majesty has ever seen such a beauty."

"I fear I am growing tired of such pleasures," murmured the King. "My doctors advise me to be more moderate."

"Yet . . . I should like to show her to Your Majesty."

"I am in no mood for more of your *grisettes*."

"Sire, she is no *grisette*. She is the sister-in-law of the Comte du Barry. The loveliest creature I ever set eyes on. And her husband, I have heard, is quite complacent. He never bothers his wife and is quite happy to know that she is universally adored."

"I have rarely known you so eulogistic, Le Bel."

"Sire, wait until you have seen her!"

"I do not think I wish to see her."

"I know, Sire, these girls are brought to you, and you are too kind, too courteous to turn them away when they disappoint you. But I should like to show you this one. You would only need to look. I have invited her to my apartments tomorrow night. If Your Majesty would consent to be hidden in the apartment, you could see this woman for yourself, and if you did not like what you saw she would be dismissed and need never know that you have seen her."

"This is a new game you have invented for me to play," said the King.

"Sire, does it appeal?"

"Not overmuch. But I believe that your taste is not what it once was. I do not believe that this creature has anything more to offer than a hundred others. So I will put you to the test."

"Tomorrow night, Sire. I'll wager you will change your mind."

"Do not let the woman know she is observed. She should not be warned to be on her best behaviour. I would see her as she really is."

Le Bel bowed his head.

So Jeanne was taken to that fateful supper party in the company of Jean Baptiste who called himself her brother-in-law. It was a very gay party, and Jeanne, supping for the first time within the Palace of Versailles, was as excited as a child.

She wore a dress which far surpassed in elegance any she had ever had. However, she quickly forgot Jean Baptiste's instructions about her behaviour and, since the guests kept filling her glass with wine, she very soon became her abandoned self.

Jeanne could, at such times, throw off her ladylike manners as lightly as though they were a cloak Jean Baptiste had wrapped about her. She could become what she once was — what neither he nor the stern nuns of Sainte Aure had been able to eradicate — a lighthearted, generous and vital girl of the lower class of Paris.

Louis was seated on a chair behind curtains through which he could see without being seen and which had been placed over a door so that he could, if the proceedings became tedious, quietly open the door and slip away.

From the first he had thought her very lovely and had determined that for her beauty alone she should spend the night with him; but when he saw her throw aside the manners which had been so clearly grafted on, when he heard that loud and abandoned laughter, the epithets of the streets, the ability to laugh at everything, he found himself watching, alert, while a smile curved his lips.

She was of the streets of Paris no doubt, but she was quite different from any of the little girls who had found their way to the Parc aux Cerfs. She was unique in her character as well as in that perfect face and form.

He was torn between the desire to remain and watch, and to go into the room and send all the others away that he and she might be alone.

Le Bel was right; this girl had something that others of her class lacked. He would amend that: she had something which he had never discovered in anyone before.

He was excited as he had not been for years. He felt happy as he had not been since the death of Madame de Pompadour.

Was he so old? Fifty-eight. Why, in the presence of that girl he could feel twenty!

Louis parted the curtains and stepped into the room.

Everyone about the table rose, except Jeanne. Louis felt exultant. It was characteristic of her that she should not rise.

He ignored them all and went to her.

"Madame," he said, "as none of these people will present *you* to me, may I present *myself* to you?"

"Why, of course you can," said Jeanne. "Do you want to join the party?"

"Madame is kind," he said.

"Oh, that's all right," said Jeanne. "One more makes little difference."

She was studying him with pleasure. She saw an ageing man who even now was very handsome. He was more distinguished-looking than any man in this room; and he was looking at her with . . . Oh, well, Jeanne knew that look. She had seen it many times before.

Le Bel was stammering: "Madame du Barry, you are in the presence of His Majesty."

"Well!" cried Jeanne laughing loudly, "I thought I had seen your face somewhere before."

There was an awed silence in the room. Then the King began to laugh.

"I am so glad," he said. "That makes us seem less like strangers, does it not?"

"Oh, there's a joke for you!" said Jeanne. "I never thought of the King and me as strangers."

"It is a thought which makes me desolate," said Louis. "We must make nonsense of it by becoming friends."

"You're a nice man, Your . . ." She turned to Le Bel and Jean Baptiste, and she cared nothing to see that they were positively writhing in their embarrassment. "What do I call him?" she said.

Le Bel began to stammer, but the King took her hand. "Call him your friend," he said; "that would please him more than any other name."

Jeanne raised her beautiful eyes to the ceiling. She said as though to someone up there: "The King is my friend. Well, I never thought to see the day . . ."

"Nor I," said Louis, "when I should meet someone who gave me such pleasure merely to look at and listen to."

Jeanne had turned to the others as though to say: "Listen to him!"

But Louis had waved his hand.

"Madame du Barry and I would prefer to be alone," he said.

"The King has a new *grisette*," said Choiseul to his sister. "A very low creature. I give her to the end of the week."

"Then clearly we need not bother ourselves about her."

"Oh no," murmured the Duc. "She is of the lowest type. The King's taste does not improve with age."

"Yet," said the Duchesse, "I have noticed that Louis looks happier than he has for a long time. He was very gay at the promenade today, and he had an air as though he were watching the clock, eager to be gone to some rendezvous."

"I will send for Le Bel and ask him about the woman," said the Duc.

"Do so now; I am less complacent than you. It is due to something I have seen in Louis' face."

Choiseul sent for the *valet de chambre*.

"Now, Le Bel," he said, "who is this new little bird who sings, so gaily in the *trébuchet*?"

348

"You refer, Monsieur le Duc, to Madame du Barry?"

"Madame du Barry! Is she the wife of that disreputable creature who pestered me in the past?"

"His sister-in-law, Monsieur le Duc."

"And you brought her to the King?"

"Monsieur le Duc, I have my duty to perform."

"I wish it would lead you to look a little higher than the gutters of Paris."

"Monsieur, she is the sister-in-law of the Comte du Barry. One could hardly describe her as from the gutter."

"The Comte du Barry? He is no Comte. He should be forced to abandon a title to which he has no right. I hear the woman is low . . . very low . . ."

"Very low, Monsieur le Duc."

"Such a woman could not possibly amuse His Majesty for more than a night or two."

"She could not, Monsieur le Duc."

Choiseul bowed his head. "Very well. But Le Bel, you could consult me before you bring these very low creatures to the attention of His Majesty."

"In future, Monsieur le Duc, that is what I will do."

Le Bel retired. He was more perturbed than he would have wished Choiseul and his sister to see. He had not for years known the King so pleased with a woman.

Choiseul was not the only member of the Court who was disturbed.

Richelieu, who knew from personal experience how attractive Jeanne could be, had been ready enough to see her brought to the King for a few nights; he would not have objected to her staying in the secret apartments of Versailles for a week — but no longer.

It was incredible that Louis could become so infatuated. Admittedly the girl possessed rare beauty, but her speech belonged to the *faubourgs* and nowhere else; yet since it issued from those charming lips the King seemed to find every word she uttered comparable with the wit of a Richelieu or a Voltaire.

He was quite enraptured. She had already been presented with many precious jewels; and the whole Court was expected to make much of her. She appeared at the intimate supper parties in the *petits appartements*, although of course, never having been presented, she must not appear in the State apartments.

At these parties the King was as merry as he had been in those days when Madame de Pompadour had been there to gratify all his wishes and to provide him with elegant and witty entertainment.

It was an extraordinary phenomenon, but the fifty-eight-year-old Louis was in love, as he had not been since the days of his boyhood.

Madame de Pompadour had been his dear friend, but she had never enjoyed the health which was clearly Madame du Barry's. She was not a sensual woman as Madame du Barry was. It was obvious that this young woman of the outstanding beauty and vitality was as experienced as the King himself in the art of making love.

Richelieu sought to point out to Louis — in a perfectly respectful manner — that he was behaving like a callow youth.

350

"It is impossible for me to see, Sire," he said, "why you should feel so enamoured of this woman. Oh, she is beautiful, but so are many others."

"You must be blind," said the King, "if you compare her beauty with that of others."

"Yet," murmured Richelieu, "it is said that *love* makes us blind."

The King was too happy to be irritated, and that gave Richelieu the courage to go on.

"What has she, Sire, which others lack?"

"The secret of making me forget I am an old man. She, so young, has taught me much I did not know before."

"Your Majesty was never in a brothel, that is obvious," said Richelieu with some asperity.

And still Louis did not reprove him.

"I know," he said, "I am not the first. I believe I have succeeded Sainte-Foix."

"Your Majesty succeeded Sainte-Foix as you succeeded Pharamond."

The King merely laughed at this allusion to one of the first Kings of the Franks, who lived in the fifth century.

Then it was clear to Richelieu that Louis did not care how many lovers Madame du Barry had had; he did not care how humble were her origins. He was so happy that he had found a woman who possessed all that he sought, a woman who could make him laugh again, forget he was fifty-eight years old; a woman who could make him feel young and gay because he was in love.

★ ★ ★

Choiseul's uneasiness grew. He had seen how precarious his position had become during the King's friendship with the Dauphine; he was not prepared to allow another woman to come between him and the King.

How wise Madame de Pompadour had been to keep him supplied with uneducated little beauties while she remained his friend and adviser. But what was this woman, more than an uneducated *grisette*? The King must be in his dotage.

As for the Duchesse de Gramont, she was furious.

"If he keeps this woman with him," she declared, "every Court lady will consider herself to be insulted."

Choiseul was not the man to let himself be easily defeated. He could use his tremendous energies to discredit a woman such as Madame du Barry, as readily as he would to settle some political dispute.

"She is clearly a wanton," he told his sister. "Du Barry keeps what is tantamount to a brothel. It should not be difficult to discover such facts about her that the King will have to dismiss her from Court."

"Then let us immediately begin our search," cried the Duchesse.

It was not long before they had discovered a very important piece of information. The woman was not Madame du Barry at all; she was Mademoiselle Bécu, Rançon, Lange, Beauvarnier or Vaubarnier.

This was the most damaging evidence against her, because the King had emphatically declared, after the death of the Queen, that he would have no mistress at Court who was not a married woman. He had no intention of allowing any woman to lure him to marriage, as Madame de Maintenon had lured his great-grandfather.

The first step was to summon Le Bel.

Le Bel had changed since Jeanne had come to Court, for he realised that by bringing her to Louis' notice he had incurred the annoyance of the all-powerful Duc de Choiseul and his sister, and Le Bel knew very well what that could mean.

Both Choiseul and his sister left Le Bel in little doubt that they considered the offence he had committed a major transgression against Court etiquette, against the King and, most heinous of all, against themselves.

"Idiot!" cried Choiseul. "You are more than an idiot, you are a knave."

"I trust I have not deeply offended you, Monsieur le Duc," began Le Bel.

"Do not look at me in such alarm. I am wondering what His Majesty will say when he hears what you have done."

"I . . . Monsieur I but obey His Majesty's orders."

"Not content," went on the Duc turning to his sister, "with bringing a common prostitute to His Majesty's notice, this man has brought one who is also an unmarried woman."

"It is unforgivable."

"Monsieur le Duc . . . Madame la Duchesse . . . there has been some mistake. This woman . . . she is the sister-in-law of the Comte du Barry. She is married to his brother . . ."

"Married to the brother of the Comte du Barry!" snorted Choiseul. "I tell you this woman is Jeanne Bécu, or Rançon or Lange or Beauvarnier or Vaubarnier. A pleasant type, to need so many names! But there is one title to which she has no right. She has never been married, and you . . . idiot, dolt, knave, have offended against the King's strict rule."

"Monsieur le Duc," cried Le Bel trembling, "if this is so . . ."

"*If* this is so? It is so. I have made it my business to discover the truth about this woman. She is an unmarried woman, and if you value your position at Court you will get rid of her . . . quickly, and extricate the King from this impossible situation into which you have thrust him."

"I will do all in my power . . ."

"It is to be hoped, for your sake, that you will," said the Duchesse slyly.

"And with all speed," added Choiseul.

Le Bel immediately called on Jean Baptiste.

"What is wrong?" asked Jean Baptiste. "You look as if you have lost a fortune."

"Worse! I am in danger of losing my place at Court."

"What is this? Calm yourself."

"Jeanne is *not* Madame du Barry. She is not married."

"But, Monsieur Le Bel."

"It is useless to lie," said Le Bel firmly. "The Duc de Choiseul has his spies everywhere. He knows she is not married to your brother."

Jean Baptiste was taken aback. "Well?" he said.

"You fool! You've deceived the King. Do you not know that he does not take unmarried mistresses?"

"We will get her married."

"The point is that she was not married when you said she was."

"A trifle."

"It will be the end of her chances at Court."

"Listen," said Jean Baptiste, "I will get her married immediately. I have a brother who is a bachelor. He will marry her and that will allow us to snap our fingers in the pug's face of Monsieur le Duc."

Le Bel hesitated. He greatly feared Choiseul, and wished that he had never brought Jeanne to Court. He could only win back the Duc's approval by ridding the Court of her.

He made up his mind that he would do what the Duc wished him to.

He said firmly: "I must go to the King at once and tell him the truth."

Le Bel begged for a private audience.

Louis looked at him with some concern. The man had changed visibly in the last week or so. He seemed furtive, afraid.

"What ails you?" asked Louis. "You will have to take better care of your health. You remind me of that man who dropped dead a week or so ago. You remember the one I mean. He had your looks. Take care, Le Bel."

"Sire, I am in good enough health. But I greatly fear I have offended you, in bringing Madame du Barry to your notice."

"Then you must be suffering from madness. I was never more pleased."

"This woman is not what you think her to be. She is no Comtesse."

Louis smiled. "I am quite ready to believe that."

"Sire, her mother was a cook."

"How interesting," said Louis. "I hope she shares her mother's skill. You know my interest in the culinary art. Is this yet another pleasure we may explore together?"

"A cook, Sire . . . a cook . . ." wailed Le Bel. "The daughter of a cook received at Versailles!"

Louis burst out laughing. How many years is it, pondered Le Bel, since he laughed like that. He would never let the woman go.

"You concern yourself overmuch with small distinctions," he was saying. "A Comtesse . . . a cook. I am a King, Le Bel, and I have so far to look down on both cooks and Comtesses that it is difficult for me to distinguish how far they are from each other."

"Your Majesty is pleased to jest, but I have not told you everything. There is something even more disgraceful."

Louis' face clouded. He was beginning to be annoyed with the sly reference to Jeanne's past. He did not care to examine the past — either his or hers — all he cared was that she was making his present life tolerable.

"I do not wish to hear it," he said.

"Sire, I must tell you."

Le Bel went on, ignoring Louis' look of astonishment. "Forgive me, Sire, but this woman is not married."

The King hesitated.

356

Then he shrugged his shoulders. "So much the worse," he said. "But that is easily remedied. Let her be married at once." He began to laugh. "It would certainly be as well in this case that I am given no opportunity to commit any act of folly."

Le Bel could only stare at the King. Yet he was not seeing the King. Louis in love, benign and happy, was not to be feared in the same way as the Duc de Choiseul and his sister.

Le Bel dared not go to them and tell them that the King had merely said: "Then let her be married."

"Sire, you cannot . . . you must not . . ." wailed Le Bel. Louis looked incredulous for a few moments, then he said sharply: "You exceed your duties."

"But Sire, this . . . this low woman . . . this un-married woman."

Louis' face turned scarlet. He picked up a pair of tongs and brandished them. He was like a young lover ready to defend his mistress.

"You tempt me," he cried, "to strike you with these. Leave my presence at once."

Le Bel staggered; his face was purple now, his mouth twitching, and Louis was ashamed of his unaccustomed display of anger.

"Go to your apartments," he said kindly. "You need rest. You are growing old, Le Bel. As I was . . . until Madame du Barry came to cheer me. Go along now. You have taken to heart matters which are not of the slightest importance."

Le Bel bowed and left the King.

He went to his apartments. He had discovered something. The King was in love as he had not been for years. He was going to keep Madame du Barry at Court. She was to be recognised as *maîtresse-en-titre*. At last the place of Madame de Pompadour had been filled.

And Choiseul? He would remain his enemy.

"Go to your apartments and rest," the King had said. Rest! With Choiseul ready for revenge?

The next day, after a restless night, Le Bel had a stroke. He lived only for a few hours.

He died of shock, said the Court. The shock of seeing the *ex-grisette* whom he had brought to the *trébuchet*, about to fill the place of Madame de Pompadour.

Meanwhile Jean Baptiste lost no time in bringing to Paris his unmarried brother, the Chevalier Guillaume du Barry, that a marriage might take place between him and Mademoiselle de Vaubarnier (Jean Baptiste had added the *de* to her name by this time).

The Chevalier Guillaume was far from unwilling. He was promised that he would be amply rewarded for his services, and he was glad of any excitement which would take him away, if only temporarily, from the tumbledown old *château* in Lévignac where he and his sisters lived under the despotic rule of their mother.

Jean Baptiste was delighted with the way his plans were working out. The King's demand that Jeanne should be married pointed to one fact: Louis had evidently decided that Jeanne was to be received at

Court, and this was tantamount to recognising her as *maîtresse-en-titre*.

Jeanne was being prepared to follow in the footprints of Madame de Pompadour, which to all earnest observers were still visibly leading from the valleys of obscurity to the summit of power.

Determined that his interests should not be forgotten he brought from Lévignac to Paris, with his brother Guillaume, his sister, Fanchon, so that she might become Jeanne's companion at Court and thus look after the interests of the family.

Fanchon was middle-aged, slightly lame but shrewd; and she had a great affection for her adventurous brother and was very grateful to him for rescuing her from the dreary life at the family *château*.

Jean Baptiste then busied himself with providing a forged birth certificate for Jeanne, in which he not only described her as the legitimate daughter of Jean-Jacques Gomard de Vaubarnier but deducted a few years from her age. Jeanne was twenty-five, which was not really very young, so he would make her out to be twenty-two.

As for the Chevalier Guillaume, he became the *"Haut et puissant Seigneur, Messire Guillaume, Comte du Barry, Capitaine des Troupes Détachées de la Marine"*.

"Everybody," said Jean Baptiste, "is now happy."

Guillaume could return home amply rewarded, Fanchon would have a place at Court, and Jeanne need have no qualms about masquerading under a false name as she was now in truth, Madame du Barry. The

King was delighted, because he need no longer concern himself with this little point of etiquette and could enjoy the company of his mistress in peace.

But there were many who were far from content. And chief of these was, of course, Choiseul.

CHAPTER
EIGHTEEN

The Presentation of Madame du Barry

Richelieu was watching events closely. He was an old man, but as in his love affairs he continued with zest, so it was in his political ambitions.

Choiseul was a fool. Pride was his vulnerable spot and it would bring him to disaster, prophesied Richelieu. He had declared himself against the new mistress from the beginning and he would not change his attitude towards her. If he had been a wise man he would at least have pretended to do this.

The King was deeply enamoured, and Choiseul was fully aware how strong had been his attachment to Madame de Pompadour. He should consider: this woman was young and healthy; the King was old and prone to melancholy. Madame du Barry had the same chance as Pompadour had had of keeping her place.

It was the ambition of every man at Court to provide the King with a mistress who would be a friend and not forget her sponsor. Therefore a wise man, who had been unable to provide the King with a mistress, would seek to make himself the friend of the woman whom someone else had procured.

Thus the Duc de Richelieu made up his mind that he would become the friend of Madame du Barry. Not only that, he would gather together certain of his friends and they would stand by her; their object being to oust Choiseul and his friends from the positions they occupied, and take them themselves.

He discussed this matter with his nephew, the Duc d'Aiguillon who, realising that this would mean great political advancement for himself, considered it an excellent idea.

"Our first duty," said Richelieu, "is to show ourselves agreeable to the favourite. Not too agreeable, you understand. Distantly so. But we are eager to be her friend. We sympathise with her against the churlish Choiseul. We will sound Vauguyon. You know how he loathes Choiseul and longs to see him dismissed."

The Duc d'Aiguillon agreed, and the campaign began.

It was not difficult to make friends with Madame du Barry, because she was ready to bestow her smiles on any who asked for them and, being delighted with the manner in which her life was going, she bore no rancour towards anyone. She had even tried to soothe the fury of the Duc de Choiseul.

He had been quite insulting. "Madame," he had said, "it is useless for you try your wiles on me. *My* friends are ladies."

She was temporarily angry; then she shrugged aside her anger. "Poor old Duc," she said to Fanchon, "he is worried about me, is he not?"

Fanchon advised caution, but Jeanne was not by nature cautious; and Fanchon was mollified to some extent by the friendly overtures of Richelieu and the Duc d'Aiguillon.

"Not," said Fanchon, "that we do not understand the motive behind this show of friendship. But friends, no matter how they come, are welcome."

Richelieu, on his way to the King's Chapel, saw the Duc de Choiseul ahead of him.

The rain had started to come down heavily and Richelieu, who had suspected a sudden shower, had armed himself with an umbrella. Choiseul who was not similarly provided was caught in the downpour.

Richelieu drew level with Choiseul.

"Allow me," he said, his eyes gleaming, "to offer you the shelter of my umbrella."

Choiseul surveyed Richelieu with that air of amused tolerance he often showed towards those whom he suspected of being his enemies, and who — so he wished to convey — worried him no more than a fly buzzing about him.

"That is good of you," he murmured.

As together they walked towards the chapel several people noticed them, and both were aware of the amused glances.

"What do they think?" murmured Choiseul, "seeing us two thus linked together?"

"They think we are two heads under one bonnet?"

"Ah," said Choiseul, "I have heard it said that two heads can be better than one."

363

"I am sure," answered Richelieu, "that there is truth in that statement."

They entered the chapel and attended the service.

When they came out the sun was shining and many courtiers kept within earshot of the two Ducs because the affair of the umbrella had been astonishing and it was believed that it could only mean a *rapprochement* between these two rivals.

If Richelieu joined forces with Choiseul and they stood together against Madame du Barry, even adored as she was by the King, she would have a very stormy passage ahead of her.

Richelieu gave the Duc his sly smile. Choiseul responded. His voice rang out clearly: "I am grateful to you for keeping me dry. Now the weather is fair, and I need not sue for further favours. And my way does not lie in the same direction as yours."

Richelieu replied: "You are right, Monsieur de Choiseul, the weather is fair indeed, and therefore you do not need the protection I can offer. Should it change however, you may depend upon me. I am your good friend."

The words seemed fraught with significance. They could mean that Richelieu and Choiseul were joining forces. On the other hand they could have been spoken ironically; and considering the nature of the two Ducs this seemed more likely.

Richelieu went immediately to the King.

"Sire," he said, "you are the happiest of God's creatures on this showery day. You are in love, and the object of your love has more than good looks, she has good temper. Forgive the presumption, Sire, but you are not only the happiest King but the happiest man in the world."

Love had brought a little naïvety back to Louis' character and Richelieu was reminded of the young boy he remembered, married at fifteen to a Queen whom he had then believed to be the most beautiful woman in the world.

Now he smiled at Richelieu, pleased because he liked to hear Madame du Barry praised.

"There is one little lack which Your Majesty must adjust. This charming lady is always relegated to the secret apartments, and is therefore debarred from enjoying Your Majesty's company on all occasions. Thus will it be, Sire, until the lady is presented."

The King laid his hand on Richelieu's arm.

"You have spoken my thoughts aloud," he said. "I intend Madame du Barry to be presented in the near future."

Richelieu's smile was very sly indeed. He heard his own voice echoing in his memory — You may depend upon it, Monsieur de Choiseul, I am your good friend.

The Duchesse de Gramont stormed into her brother's apartments.

"So now," she said, "she is to be presented at Court. They will be bringing in the fishwives from Les Halles and presenting them at Court next. Brother, this must not happen."

"We must take every step to prevent it."

365

The Duchesse gripped her brother's arm. "Once she is presented, she will be as Madame de Pompadour. She will take charge of affairs. We rose to our present position because the Pompadour was our friend. What will happen to us when we have another, as powerful as Pompadour . . . our enemy!"

"This woman is no Pompadour. For all her *bourgeoise* origins Pompadour was an intelligent woman. This woman has nothing but her health, her good looks and her vulgarity."

"But the King is older, do not forget. He is in his dotage."

"Sister, we will fight this woman. Think how far we have come. We have stood firm against Prussia and Britain. Shall we fail at the whim of Madame du Barry?"

"I fear her more than all the states of Europe."

"You lose heart too quickly. We will have her dismissed in a few weeks. But we must go warily . . . step by step. This presentation must not take place."

"You know, do you not, that Richelieu is standing behind her?"

"Richelieu! That double-faced old rogue. But he is an old man."

"D'Aiguillon supports him."

"D'Aiguillon! The brave soldier! D'Aiguillon the fool. What are you thinking of, sister, to consider such a man?"

"I fear, brother, that they are beginning to form a party around her. You can depend upon it, the King will support those who support her."

"I admit that could happen. But it must not. While she has not been presented and cannot be openly acknowledged she is no great danger. But it is of the utmost importance that she shall never be presented."

"The King has determined on it. Richelieu and d'Aiguillon support it. And she is naturally eager for it. I cannot see how it will be avoided."

"Then you do not know your brother as well as I thought you did, sister. We could implore the King not to commit this folly, and he would not listen to us. But if ridicule were our advocate it might be different. We might shame the King into forbidding the presentation although we could not persuade him to take such a step."

"Ridicule," said the Duchesse. "But we have tried that. He is so besottedly in love that he is impervious to ridicule."

"You will see. I have already arranged with the *chansonniers*, and very soon songs will be heard about Madame du Barry in every Paris *café*."

The Duchesse nodded.

"That is not all," went on the Duc. "The lady's past will not bear investigation, as you know."

"But the King does not object to her low birth."

"Oh, she would have been adequate for the old Parc aux Cerfs, as she is for the *trébuchet*. But Louis must see that there is a difference between these establishments and the Galerie des Glaces."

"You have some suggestion?"

The Duc nodded. "I am dispatching a trusted friend this very day to a lady who is very well known in Paris . . . and at the Court. I refer to Madame Gourdan of the Maison Gourdan."

Madame Gourdan rested her elbows on the table and smiled beguilingly at her visitor.

She knew he came from Versailles, and she was always pleased to welcome such clients to her house. She was well known in the *Château* and was often called upon to supply girls to entertain the company at some lavish banquet. Such were very profitable transactions, and so good for the name of her house.

Madame Gourdan, who was something of a wit, often described herself as Purveyor to the Royal Château of Versailles. Such a reputation she said was so very much appreciated by the merchants of Paris.

"I come," said her visitor, "from a person of such eminence that I may not disclose his name."

Ah, thought Madame Gourdan, His Majesty without doubt.

Her diamond bracelets glittered on her arms; her podgy hands, jewel-covered, smoothed the rich black satin of her gown.

"The Maison Gourdan is at his service. You would like to see some of my most beautiful girls, eh Monsieur?"

"No. I have come to obtain your signature on a document."

Madame Gourdan's expression changed. She did not like documents which must be signed. They invariably brought trouble.

"You had better explain your business," she said sharply, "for I am at a loss to understand it."

"I believe you knew a young woman named Mademoiselle Vaubarnier or Mademoiselle de Lange."

Madame Gourdan nodded. "One of the loveliest girls I ever saw."

"You knew her well, Madame?"

"Not as well as I should have liked."

"She worked here in your establishment, did she not?"

"Now you have touched on one of the greatest disappointments of my career. I would have taken her ... Well, Monsieur, I should have been a fool not to. And I assure you, Monsieur, I am no fool. One does not successfully run a house such as this if one is."

"So she did not work in this house?"

Madame Gourdan shook her head.

"But I have a paper here which says that she did."

"Then that paper lies. Who said it?"

"You did ... Madame."

"I did!"

"It says here that Mademoiselle Vaubarnier or Mademoiselle Lange at one time worked in 'my house, the Maison Gourdan'."

"Let me see this." She had leaped to her feet and was looking over his shoulder. "There is nothing to show I wrote that."

"There would be, Madame, if you put your name here."

"I see," said Madame Gourdan, narrowing her eyes.

"Madame, your signature to this paper is desired by a man of great authority. He does not ask you to give it.

He will pay for it. So much will he pay that even you who, I see, are a very successful woman, would be astonished."

She continued to look at him through narrowed eyes.

"Come, here is a pen. Sign, and a fortune is yours. Not only that. There would be other privileges . . ."

She folded her arms and looked at him belligerently. So the rumours had not lied, she was thinking. Jeanne had found her way to Versailles. This could mean only one thing: Jeanne was going to be acknowledged by the King.

She laughed suddenly.

"You are going to bargain with me," sighed the man. "Come . . . tell me your price. What do you ask?"

"Monsieur, this is what I ask: that you take that paper and get out of my house. I sell girls, not lies. You are asking me to dishonour my profession."

He opened his mouth to protest. But Madame Gourdan had called to her Negro eunuch who could have lifted the visitor in his strong arms as though he were a baby.

"Show this gentleman out," she said.

When he had gone she sat down and began to laugh. So Jeanne . . . little Jeanne . . . was on the way to becoming the most important woman in France.

Choiseul and his sister must therefore manage without the help of Madame Gourdan; and this, he assured her, they could very well do, although he admitted it would have been very helpful if he could have had the woman's signature to that paper.

370

They would now merely *suggest* that she had lived in the Maison Gourdan before coming to Court. That would be accepted by some who wished to believe it was true.

"It is easy to spread tales which are damaging, about the successful," he said, "because they are so much envied, and those who envy are so delighted to believe the worst. Our little du Barry has a multitude of enemies — many among those who have never set eyes upon her."

So the rumours were started, persisted in, embellished. Nothing was too scandalous to be recounted about Madame du Barry.

In the streets and the *cafés* they were not only talking of her, they were singing about her, and one of the most popular ballads was that which Choiseul had had based on that old folk song *La Bourbonnaise*.

Quelle merveille!
Une fille de rien,
Une fille de rien,
Quelle merveille!
Donne au Roi de l'amour,
Est à la Cour!

Elle est gentille;
Elle a les yeux fripons;
Elle a les yeux fripons;
Elle est gentille;
Elle excite avec art
Un vieux paillard.

En maison bonne,
Elle a pris de leçons,
Elle a pris de leçons,
En maison bonne,
Chez Gourdan, chez Brisson,
Elle en sait long.

Que de postures!
Elle a lu Arétin,
Elle a lu Arétin;
Que de postures!
Elle fait en tous sens
Prendre les sens.

Le Roi s'écrie:
L'Ange, le beau talent!
L'Ange, le beau talent!
Viens sur mon trône,
Je veux te couronner,
Je veux te couronner.

These songs were sung beneath the windows of the *Château* itself. The King heard them, Madame du Barry herself heard them.

Louis watched her, as she sat with her head on one side listening.

He was prepared for anger, but she only laughed. She began to tap out the rhythm and Louis stared in astonishment as Madame du Barry herself sang *La Bourbonnaise*.

"You are a very unusual woman," he said.

"But how so?" she asked.

"To sing that song."

"I like the tune.

"'*Quelle merveille! Une fille de rien . . .*'" she sang. She laughed. "It is true . . . that part at least. That is what I am: '*une fille de rien*'."

"I will tell you what you are," said Louis emotionally; "you are the gentlest-tempered woman in the world. Madame de Pompadour would have discovered the writer of that song and insisted on his sojourn in the Bastille."

"Ah," Jeanne replied, "but Madame de Pompadour was a great lady. And I am only: '*Une fille de rien*'."

There had rarely been such controversy at Court as there was over the presentation of Madame du Barry, for in spite of the King's eagerness and determination that the presentation should take place, there was a powerful section against this.

Choiseul and his sister naturally led this section, but it contained other powerful adherents.

The Dauphin, a *gauche* boy of about fifteen, very much under the influence of his Aunt Adelaide, had been induced to show his contempt for Madame du Barry on more than one occasion; and although he was but a boy, it was remembered at Court that Louis was nearly sixty, and when he died that boy would be King.

The Princesse Adelaide also, although she had now very little influence at Court, was nevertheless the King's daughter.

So, although Louis very much desired this presentation, he continually found that obstacles were put in the way of its taking place.

Anyone but the imperturbable du Barry might have felt that she was destined never to take the place of Madame de Pompadour, but Jeanne merely shrugged aside the difficulties which were placed in her way, bore few grudges against her enemies, took her lessons in deportment from Vestris, the most celebrated dancing master in France, and continued to delight the King.

Richelieu had now come out into the open as her ardent supporter, and had himself ordered her Court dress. Marigny, the brother of Madame de Pompadour, had also given proof of his support, and ordered that the *châteaux* of Bellevue, Marly and Choisy should be redecorated in readiness for the new favourite.

This was gratifying but, until a sponsor could be found, Jeanne could not be presented, and in spite of the fact that the King himself wished that sponsor to be found, it was exceedingly difficult to discover a woman who would undertake the task.

The Baronne de Montmorency offered her services, but she insisted that for such a task she would need generous reward. The sum she asked for was quite fantastic, and Louis angrily declined her services, since to accept them at that price would have been an insult to Madame du Barry.

The next candidate was the Comtesse de Béarn. The price she asked was more moderate, so it was accepted. But when it was heard that she had undertaken the task, she was boycotted so severely by the Choiseul faction, treated with such disdain by the Dauphin and the Princesse Adelaide — and naturally by Victoire and Sophie — that she was alarmed and at the last moment pretended to have sprained her ankle.

The ceremony was postponed.

Madame d'Alogny next offered her services. Adelaide was very annoyed. This woman had seen the anger which the conduct of the Comtesse de Béarn had aroused, yet brazenly she came forward to do what Madame de Béarn's good sense had prevented her from doing.

"I will show her," Adelaide told her sisters, "what it means to flout me."

She then showed her sisters and the Court so successfully that for some time poor Madame d'Alogny wished not only that she had never agreed to present Madame du Barry but that she had never been born.

At a ceremony when Madame d'Alogny was received by Adelaide and it was necessary for her to kneel, kiss the hem of the Princesse's gown and wait for permission to rise, Adelaide merely walked away from her, leaving her kneeling there unable, in accordance with the etiquette of Versailles, to rise, since the permission had not been given.

To find herself in such a position was like living in a nightmare. Madame d'Alogny did not know what to do, but remained kneeling while the company looked on at her with raised eyebrows until, overcome with shame, she rose and shuffled away.

She knew that she would be similarly humiliated on future occasions if she persisted in her plans to present Madame du Barry at Court.

She therefore declared that, in spite of the generous remuneration, she could not do it.

The King was furious; even Jeanne began to wonder whether she would ever be presented. Louis, however, was not going to allow his desires to be frustrated. He sent for the Comtesse de Béarn and told her that she would formally present Madame du Barry to him whether she liked the task or not.

Madame de Béarn assured the Court that she had received orders and dared not disobey them. She prayed they would not blame her therefore, because she was obliged to carry out this uncongenial task.

In this case, said the Choiseul faction, there is no help for it. Madame du Barry will be presented.

Then, a few days after Madame de Béarn had been forced to accept the task imposed upon her, the King had an accident in the hunting field.

When Adelaide saw his body being brought to the *Château* on a stretcher she called to her sister: "This is the judgement of Providence. God has decided that Madame du Barry shall never be presented at Court."

The Princesses installed themselves in the sickroom, and when Jeanne presented herself Adelaide faced her triumphantly.

"Madame," she said, "the King is dying. It is time he made his peace with God, and to do that he does not need your help."

Victoire and Sophie nodded beside her, and Jeanne, with tears in her eyes, for she believed what they said was true, was turned away.

However, the King was not seriously hurt and as soon as he was conscious he dismissed the Princesses from his room and sent for Madame du Barry to come and comfort him.

Louis was more determined than ever that Jeanne should be presented, so that she should be with him on all occasions.

On the great day crowds left Paris for Versailles. They wanted to see the arrival of Madame du Barry for her presentation. It was a brilliant occasion and the dazzling Court dress of the men and women was reflected by the mirrors in the Galerie des Glaces, while Louis, his arm still in a sling, awaited the arrival of his mistress.

Beside the King stood Richelieu, and a little distance away Choiseul and his sister, the royal Princesses and all their supporters.

There had been so many ominous hitches that many people superstitiously believed that even now the ceremony would not take place.

It was time for Madame du Barry to arrive, but she had not come. No one could ever remember a lady, about to be presented, being late before.

Choiseul was smiling complacently. His sister murmured that it was to be expected. What did street-girls know of Court manners?

The King was growing flushed and uneasy. Richelieu was imploring him to be patient. All those in the great Galerie waited as the minutes ticked away and still Madame du Barry did not appear.

The King was about to call off the proceedings. He was angry. Even Jeanne could not behave like this with impunity. The excitement was intense. What would happen when and if she did arrive? Would the King act towards her coldly, deliver a public reprimand?

The King and Richelieu were looking more and more gloomy, Choiseul more and more delighted.

And then she came; and when he looked at her — surely the most beautiful sight he had ever beheld — all the King's irritation vanished.

Her fair hair — that wonderful golden hair — was dressed high on her head. Her blue satin dress showed her perfect figure to advantage; she was wearing the hundred thousand livres' worth of diamonds which the King had sent her on the previous day; and she glowed with high spirits, confidence and gaiety.

She would have knelt before the King, but Louis could not allow that, and when tenderly he took her hand and smiled into her radiant face, it was as though everyone in the Galerie drew a deep breath.

The presentation had taken place.

The King was holding her hand, leading her to the Princesses.

Even Adelaide dared do nothing but graciously acknowledge her.

Vestris had done his work well. She did all that was required of her with the grace of a woman who might have known all her life that one day she would be the central figure in such a ceremony.

"You were so late . . ." murmured the King.

"I made the hairdresser do my hair again," she whispered. I knew you would want me to look my best."

Louis' eyes misted. Was she not enchanting? This girl from he did not care to know where — who could keep the King of France waiting for such a reason?

At last he had someone who could take the place in his affections which had been Madame de Pompadour's.

Jeanne du Barry had now been presented. She was established in the eyes of all as the King's *maîtresse-en-titre*.

Madame du Barry now had her suite of rooms — bedroom, library and reception room — connected by a secret staircase with the King's apartments.

She selected her ladies with the help of the King and Richelieu; and the chief of these was the Maréchale de Mirepoix, Madame de Pompadour's "little cat".

The King had grown fond of this woman whom he had met so often in the company of Madame de Pompadour; she was not only witty and amusing, but very shrewd. It was true that being a friend of the Marquise she had also been on good terms with the Choiseuls; but she was now in debt and, bearing no resentment against Madame du Barry, was ready to be her friend since such friendship would bring a comfortable income. Thus she blithely skipped from

379

the side of the Choiseul faction to that of Madame du Barry.

The Marquise de l'Hôpital and the Comtesse de Valentinois were equally ready to give their support to the rising star; so that Jeanne found herself surrounded by women who were ready to advise her as to the ways of life at Versailles.

She had now grown fond of Fanchon, whom she had nicknamed Chon, finding in her sister-in-law one whose shrewd judgement she could trust more than any other's. Chon brought her astute mind to work for the du Barrys, and Jeanne was a member of the family now.

The situation had its irony. In the streets Choiseul's *chansons* were being sung, his cruel stories being repeated, but the Church party, who hated Choiseul, blaming him for the suppression of the Jesuits, believed that Madame du Barry was a possible ally. Thus many priests appeared at Court to do honour to the favourite, blithely waving aside the facts of her present carnality and the rumours of her past.

Jeanne accepted everything with great good humour and occasional comments which made courtiers either wince or stifle their laughter.

The King had shown his devotion by presenting her with the Château de Luciennes not far from Marly; and he took her out to show her the exquisite little house which was being built at Trianon.

There was no doubt that the recipient of that little treasure would be Madame du Barry for, instead of tiring of her as so many people had been sure he must, Louis grew more and more devoted every day.

On one occasion at table the King dropped his toothpick, and Jeanne characteristically did not wait for a servant to pick it up; she herself leaped from her chair and went down on her hands and knees, crawling under the table to retrieve it.

Flushed and laughing she held it up. "Here it is," she said.

Louis looked at her; at such moments she could appear more delightful than when she was dressed for some State occasion, and he was suddenly overcome with emotion.

Forgetful of the onlookers he left his chair and knelt beside her.

"It is not for you to kneel to me," he said, that all might hear. "It is I who should kneel to you . . . and thus shall it always be between us two."

Never, said the Court, had the King been so enamoured of a woman as he was of Madame du Barry.

CHAPTER
NINETEEN

Choiseul and Madame du Barry

The entire Court was watching the battle between the Choiseuls and Madame du Barry, and bets were made as to who would eventually win. The King was undoubtedly enamoured of his new mistress; but the Duc de Choiseul was the most brilliant statesman in France.

Choiseul was to blame for the conflict. In those first months Jeanne du Barry was ready to forget past insults and be friends. In her frank way she had not hesitated to make overtures of friendship; she had even been prepared to treat the Duc with coquetry. It was all of no avail. He had shown clearly that her beauty left him cold, that her vulgarity shocked him and that however enamoured the King became, he, Choiseul, would remain her enemy.

Jeanne eventually gave way to an expletive which was repeated around the Court. Never, it was said, had such an expression been heard in the stately rooms. What did Jeanne care! She had reached her position by being perfectly natural and she was not going to begin changing her ways now.

With the vulgarity went the kindest heart in Versailles. Jeanne found it difficult to hate anyone, and even her animosity towards the Duc de Choiseul was sporadic.

"Oh well," she would in effect say to Chon, "I suppose he did want that sister of his to take my place. It must be a bit of a disappointment to them. You can understand how they felt about me. Poor old Choiseul! Poor old Gramont."

"Do not be too lenient with them," warned Chon. "Pity makes for softness and, believe me, you cannot afford to be soft with enemies as venomous as those two."

Jeanne had already gained a reputation for generosity. She had sought out Monsieur Billard-Dumonceau, the benefactor of her childhood, and had rewarded him. Jean Baptiste was very satisfied with the way in which his affairs were going for, although he had received no appointments at Court, he had been granted several large sums of money and was able to indulge his hobby of gambling as never before; Jeanne had brought his son, Adolphe, to Court and was planning to make a grand marriage for him.

She had, it was true, decided that she would take revenge on Madame de la Garde for turning her out of her house, and called on her one day with the express purpose of doing so, but when she saw the old woman's trepidation, she relented suddenly.

After all, thought Jeanne, I really was all that she said I was, and I ought to be grateful to her for turning me out of her house.

So instead of parading her glory before the old woman in a vaguely threatening manner as she had intended to do, she found herself promising to use her power in another direction and put honours in the way of her sons.

That was typical of Jeanne. She could never completely throw off the aura of the streets of Paris, and she loved humanity; while she could bestow pardon for past offences right and left, she found it very difficult to harbour resentment. Planning revenge seemed to her such a waste of time when there were so many more exciting things to be done.

So she went her way, ignoring her enemies until that greatest of all forced her to notice him.

"Oh dear," she would groan, "here comes old pug-face." And she would turn away in a manner which was not in accordance with Versailles etiquette. She would grimace and put her tongue out at his back in a manner which might have been accepted in the Saint-Antoine district but which seemed extraordinary in the Galerie des Glaces.

Meanwhile the Choiseuls continued to have songs written about her. The Duc's spies discovered all the details of her early life; they were exaggerated and put into songs which were sung in the streets.

Her loud laughter, her expletives, her expressions would seem to confirm the stories of her beginnings.

Card-playing was a ceremony at Versailles — until Madame du Barry came.

She would sit holding her cards, chuckling over them or cursing them, in a manner which had never before been heard within the walls of the *Château*.

On one occasion, when she lost to the King, she cried: "You're a cheat. That's what you are!"

The stunned silence which greeted this remark did not deter her. She continued to sit there with what her enemies called the gutter-grin on her face.

The King however merely smiled and gaily explained how he had beaten her.

"Liar!" she cried affectionately.

And Louis seemed to think that it was the height of bliss to hear from those vulgar but voluptuous lips that he was a cheat and a liar.

Others were less kind.

Once when she threw her cards on the table she cried in her brand of vulgar slang: "I am cooked!"

Choiseul, who was standing close to her, murmured: "You should be a better judge of *that* state than the rest of us, Madame."

And Jeanne, realising the reference to her mother's occupation, sat back in her chair and gave vent to loud laughter.

It was very difficult, thought Choiseul, to discountenance such a creature, whose very vulgarity endowed her with an unconquerable resilience.

However she discovered among her household servants a cook who bore an extraordinary likeness to Choiseul.

There was the same pug-dog face, the same air of nonchalance.

"Why," she said to Chon, "it is like having the Duc in my household, and that is something I cannot tolerate."

She talked about the cook as her "Choiseul" and compared him with the King's Choiseul.

There came a day when she dismissed the man, and that night at one of the intimate supper parties she told the King what she had done.

"I have dismissed my 'Choiseul'," she cried. "When are you going to dismiss yours?"

All those who heard looked upon that as a direct declaration of war.

The Choiseuls retaliated by introducing to the Court a young Creole of great beauty who had recently married into their family. She had been a Mademoiselle de Raby, and it was soon realised by all that the Choiseuls intended that she should replace Jeanne du Barry.

Jeanne was a little shaken when she saw this young woman who was a statuesque beauty and perfectly groomed in the ways of Versailles.

Chon implored her to take care.

Madame de Mirepoix, whose feelings were not entirely mercenary — for it was impossible to live near Jeanne, continually reminded of her generosity, and not feel affection for her — advised her, as she had advised Madame de Pompadour in her moments of fear, that she must not panic but fight.

"Then, dear Comtesse," she said, "you have nothing to be afraid of. If I myself am sad it is not because I think the Choiseuls will succeed in this plot but because of the alarm they are causing you."

Jeanne, in her forthright way, went to the King and asked: "What do you think of this Creole, Lafrance?"

Because it was a habit of his to apply nicknames to those about him, she had retaliated by giving him one: Lafrance. It suited him, she said; and he was not averse to accepting it from her lips.

"Do I see anxiety in your beautiful eyes?" asked the King with a laugh.

"Do I see lust for the Creole in yours?" she demanded.

"If you did," said Louis, "which you do not, it would not mean that I should wish you to leave me."

Jeanne smiled. "No, of course it would not. I would not want you to feel that I should whimper if you wanted a change now and then. As long as you come back to me, of course."

He smiled at her. "You would have to find me someone to compare — just a little — with yourself, before I should feel tempted. As for this woman, I cannot think of her without thinking at the same time of the Duchesse de Gramont. Never would I allow that woman to have any say in my affairs."

Jeanne was contented. She knew, before the Choiseuls realised this, that the affair of the Creole was going to be a failure.

The Choiseuls were furious. They had presented their protégée to the King and, although he had been courteous enough, he had shown her no more attention than etiquette demanded.

The Duchesse de Gramont was less able to control her anger than her brother was, and as the procession descended the great staircase to pay court to the Dauphin, she pushed her way forward so that she was immediately behind Jeanne.

As Jeanne was about to make her curtsy to the Dauphin, who had not hesitated to show his disapproval and dislike of her, Madame de Gramont put her foot on the train of Jeanne's dress.

Jeanne, midway in her curtsy, sprang up and watched her train as it was ripped away from her gown.

She was angry, partly because the King was present and to please him she had been trying to learn something of the Versailles manners.

Now she was ready to put her hands on her hips and let out a stream of invective against the Duchesse. But suddenly she caught the eyes of the King upon her. He was flashing a message to her which she read as: there is only one way to behave, so that the Duchesse will seem more ill-mannered than you.

Then Jeanne understood that etiquette demanded she should behave as though the incident had not happened and she still had a train to her dress.

She turned to the Dauphin, swept him a deep curtsy and passed on, leaving her train behind her.

There were significant glances. The girl from the *faubourgs* was learning.

But it seemed the Duchesse was not; that little incident earned her dismissal from Court for a period.

Had she not been the sister of the powerful Choiseul she would have been banished for ever.

Jeanne continued to be plagued. The Comte de Lauraguais, a friend of the Choiseuls, sought to humiliate her by a gesture which was typical of his set.

This noble went to the house of Madame Gourdan and acquired a very beautiful young girl as his mistress. He bought a house for her, gave her fine clothes, money and jewellery; and the manner in which he did all this made the Court realise that he had some motive in view other than his infatuation with the girl.

When he named her the Comtesse du Tonneau his meaning was understood. For a *tonneau* and a *baril* had almost the same meaning; and it was easy to confuse Barry with *baril*.

His punishment for this escapade brought him banishment from Court; nor did Madame Gourdan escape censure. She was not allowed to send any of her girls to the entertainments at Fontainebleau, and this was a great loss to her financially, and unjust because, having no knowledge of the Comte's intentions, she was not in the least to blame.

Jeanne herself bore little resentment and very soon arranged that the ban should be lifted from Madame de Gourdan; but she was beginning to be affected by the solemnity of her surroundings, and it was noticed that in public she behaved with a restraint and decorum which would have seemed incredible a short time before.

In private with Louis she did not change her manners at all; and this was how the King wished her to be.

As it became apparent that Madame du Barry had come to Court to stay, a party began to be formed with her as its centre. It was naturally one which was in complete opposition to the Choiseul party, and as it was headed by Richelieu and his nephew, the Duc d'Aiguillon, it clearly had one purpose — the overthrow of Choiseul.

The Duc de Vauguyon and René de Maupéou joined this party, which became known as the *Barriens*.

A new year had begun; and the battle between the King's mistress and the First Minister was still being waged fiercely.

The King had presented that exquisite little house, which he and Madame de Pompadour had begun together, to Madame du Barry; and there at Petit Trianon Louis was able to retire from the Court and live the life of a country nobleman.

Both the King and Jeanne were enchanted by the place; here they convinced themselves that they lived in the utmost simplicity. They received their intimate friends in the little reception suite overlooking the Jardin Français, and pretended to dispense even with servants when they installed the *table volante*, that most ingenious invention of Loriot's, with its four side tables which descended to the floor below when a further course was required (as they descended a piece of metal in the shape of a rose would slip into place where these tables had been). When they had been reloaded and were ready to make the ascension to the *salle à manger*, the metal rose would gently open and slide away while the tables loaded with food would appear in its place.

This interesting invention was a constant delight to Louis.

"Here," he said, "we may live in absolute privacy in our Petit Trianon."

That the King should wish to live thus with his mistress would seem to be an indication that, far from tiring of her, he was slipping into a relationship somewhat similar to that which he had enjoyed with Madame de Pompadour.

The Court believed that sooner or later either Madame du Barry or Choiseul would be dismissed. They knew too that both were equally determined to be victorious.

Thus the battle was watched with eager interest.

Madame du Barry might have her Trianon, but Choiseul had recently arranged that the Dauphin should marry the youngest daughter of the Empress Maria Theresa.

Choiseul's friends declared that when the Archduchess Marie Antoinette arrived in France the power of Madame du Barry would begin to wane; for Marie Antoinette must be the firm ally of Choiseul since he, more than anyone, had been responsible for her marriage.

The Dauphin hated the mistress; so did Madame Adelaide — and naturally her sisters. When the

Dauphine became aware of the circumstances and added her influence to theirs, could the du Barry continue to keep her position?

"Lafrance," cried Madame du Barry, as she entered the King's apartment, "I have decided what you shall give me for my New Year's gift."

Louis smiled. She was so full of vitality, that merely to look at her seemed to make him forget he was sixty.

"Well?" he said.

"I will tell you. You are fond of Madame de Mirepoix?"

"That is so," the King agreed.

"Then all is well. She has so many debts that she despairs of ever paying them. She suffers great anxiety. Now I want my New Year's gift to be the *Loges de Nantes* so that I can give these to her. If she had them, all her troubles would be over. Please say you will give me these as my New Year's gift."

The King looked grave. The *Loges de Nantes* were the rents which came from the stalls and booths which were set up in Nantes and represented a considerable income. They had, until her recent death, been in the possession of the Duchesse de Lauranguais.

He shook his head. "I greatly fear Madame de Mirepoix cannot have them, as I have already bestowed them."

Jeanne's face flushed. "But I have already promised her that they shall be hers!"

The King lifted his shoulders and walked to the window.

392

Jeanne stamped her foot. "You must tell this person that you have changed your mind."

"But," said Louis coolly, "I have not changed my mind."

Jeanne looked at him and for once he saw all the gaiety drained from her face.

He came to her side quickly. "You are the best-hearted woman in the world," he said. "Do not look so sad. How like you to ask for a New Year's gift which you could bestow on someone else. Now I will tell you on whom I have already bestowed the *Loges de Nantes:* on someone of whom I happen to be very fond indeed. Her name? The Comtesse du Barry."

Jeanne burst into loud laughter, and threw her arms about the King.

"So you were but teasing me. And Madame de Mirepoix gets her *loges*. Oh, Lafrance, I was frightened for the minute!"

He looked at her tenderly. Frightened? Not because she herself might be losing her popularity. No! Scared that poor Madame de Mirepoix should not receive her rents.

Shortly after that she asked for the return of the Comtesse de Gramont.

"Do I hear rightly?" asked the King.

"Well," cried Jeanne, "there's the pug-dog going about the Court looking as though he has lost his bitch. I like dogs, as does Your Majesty."

"Do you not know that man is your most bitter enemy? And if you have a greater it is his sister."

"Oh, let us have her back. In any case she does more harm to me in the country than she does at Versailles. I like to keep my enemies in view."

"You are very different from Madame de Pompadour. She would never have allowed the Duchesse de Gramont to come back to Court."

"Oh . . . the Pompadour. I could never be like her, so what's the use of trying? I can only be what I am."

"The kindest-hearted lady in the world," said Louis.

So the Duchesse de Gramont returned to Court, and Choiseul told his friends that he and his sister would have preferred her to remain in exile than to know that her return had been brought about through the grace of Madame du Barry.

"Still," said Choiseul, "perhaps the woman will leave Court when the Dauphine arrives. For the Dauphine will be so embarrassed to find such as Madame du Barry installed at the Court of France."

When Richelieu told Jeanne what Choiseul had said, her reply was an expletive which amused the old Duc so much that he had to go about the Court telling everyone what Madame du Barry had said.

The new Dauphine arrived in France — little more than a child; she was a dainty creature, with reddish hair and a very fair complexion. Louis was delighted with her and rode out into the Forest of Compiègne to greet her.

The Choiseuls were delighted; they looked upon this charming young girl as their closest ally and one who would work with them for the downfall of the du Barry.

But if they thought that the King, in his interest in his grand-daughter-in-law, would forget Madame du Barry, they were mistaken.

Jeanne sat down with the royal party to supper at Muette, and the two women took stock of each other.

Jeanne laughed inwardly. Poof! she thought. Red-haired and sandy-skinned! Her eyelashes are so light you can scarcely see them. Why, if she were not the daughter of an Empress no one would take any notice of her.

The Dauphine had been schooled by her mother, so when the King asked her opinion of the Comtesse du Barry she was immediately aware of his desire for a favourable reply.

"I find her both charming and amiable," said the Dauphine; and the King patted her hand and told her that he was certain he and she were going to be the best of friends.

The festivities which accompanied the marriage of the heir to the throne were naturally dazzling. The firework displays were magnificent and the road from Paris to Versailles was thick with the crowds on their way to see the sights. It was said that Louis was determined to imitate the splendour of his grandfather.

Ah, said the agitators, but times were different then. Now there was a shortage of grain in France. Why? It was blamed on bad harvests, but was it due to those who hoarded grain? Was the King guiltless?

Some began to calculate the cost of the festivities, and they were discovered to be somewhere in the neighbourhood of twenty million livres.

Twenty million livres, when there were thousands in the capital alone who could not afford to buy bread! Pamphlets were published. One, *Reflections on the Nuptials of His Highness the Dauphin*, circulated throughout Paris, gave an account of the cost of the entertainments which had been given to celebrate the marriage.

While the people waited to see the sights they grumbled together.

A banquet was given at the Hôtel de Ville, to be followed by a display of fireworks in the Place Louis XV, and during this display some scaffolding caught fire and this spread to nearby buildings. Panic ensued and in their endeavours to escape many people were trampled underfoot. Eight hundred people were injured on that night, two hundred of them fatally.

It was a grim scene when daylight disclosed what had occurred on that tragic spot, stained with the blood of the dead and injured. People stood about in groups talking of the disaster. They grumbled about such lavish displays; they talked of the price of bread and the extravagance of these wedding celebrations.

Why should the people starve when the aristocrats lived in luxury? That was the question which was being asked on that very spot which in the near future was to be renamed the Place de la Révolution.

CHAPTER
TWENTY

The Defeat of Choiseul

There was now a powerful party to stand against Choiseul, and at its very heart was Madame du Barry. Jeanne listened to what they told her she must do; Richelieu, Aiguillon, Maupéou, the Abbé Terray were all advising her. "Persuade the King to this . . . to that."

The King listened to her, for Louis at sixty was beginning to long more and more for peace; and Jean Baptiste and his sister Chon were continually warning Madame du Barry that either Choiseul must go or she would.

Thus it was that the odds were growing against Choiseul.

The Duc, otherwise so shrewd, entrenched himself in his nobility and refused to believe that a *fille de rien* could ever be important to the crown of France. Madame de Pompadour was at least *bourgeoise*; she was a woman of education to compare with that of members of the Court; therefore he had quickly realised that it was wiser to be on her side than against her; but he refused to consider Madame du Barry worthy of his attention.

Choiseul was now being blamed for the failure of the Seven Years War — most unfairly, for the war had been a disaster before he had come to power. It was remembered that he had spent thirty million livres in an endeavour to establish a settlement in Guiana, for which purpose he had sent out twelve thousand people from Alsace and Lorraine. Almost every one of those would-be-colonists had died.

"Why," asked the *Barriens*, "should this man Choiseul be regarded as a great statesman, essential to France? Look at his record."

It was true that he had annexed Corsica, but to do this he had used an immense amount of public funds, which must come from the poverty-stricken people. They forgot too how he had strengthened the Army and Navy.

As Madame du Barry became more important to the King, so the disgrace of Choiseul became more certain.

Meanwhile Aiguillon had become involved with the magistrates of Rennes by his arrest of La Chalotais, the Attorney-General who had worked against the Jesuits and had been scornful of the weak manner in which Breton affairs were conducted.

It was a sign of the times that every French province had now begun to ask what was happening to the liberty of the people; and when the Duc d'Aiguillon sought to force obedience from the Breton *Parlement*, the *Parlement* of Paris rose in support of its Breton counterpart.

Louis was finding himself drawn into conflict with his *Parlements*.

It was when La Chalotais wrote a letter of complaint against Aiguillon to the King that Aiguillon ordered the arrest of Chalotais. The *Parlement* then brought a counter-charge against Aiguillon accusing him of embezzling public monies; and with this charge against him, and because the *Parlement* refused to try La Chalotais, Aiguillon came to Paris to ask for vindication there.

Louis presided at his trial, for which members of the *Parlement* came to Versailles.

The King however was eager to escape from the restraint put upon the monarchy by the *Parlement*, and after two sittings he destroyed the documents involving Aiguillon and declared the Duc immune from further accusations.

The *Parlement* left Versailles and in Paris made a declaration that in spite of the King Aiguillon should be "deprived of his rights and privileges as a peer until he should be purged of the suspicions which stained his honour".

This was a direct insult to Louis, a reminder that *Parlement* was now more powerful than the monarchy. There could be nothing more likely to inflame the wrath of one who had always believed in the Divine Right of Kings.

As Choiseul must take his stand on the side of the *Parlement*, the *Barriens* saw a means of ridding themselves of the Minister and his friends and slipping into power themselves.

The Chancellor Maupéou placed himself on the side of the King, in spite of the fact that he had been given his post by Choiseul; but he believed that only with the dismissal of Choiseul could he achieve the power he sought. Therefore, although until this moment he had feigned loyalty to Choiseul, now that Choiseul appeared to be in decline he no longer felt the need to do so.

Maupéou had joined the *Barriens*, and the party discussed its policy which should receive the support of the King through Madame du Barry.

In the streets of Paris the struggle between King and *Parlement* was growing. There was change in the air. Louis had been hated for so long that few remembered those days when he had been known as *Le Bien-Aimé*.

The songsters and rhymesters were busy. There was a new prayer ironically shouted in the *cafés*:

"Our Father, who art at Versailles, honoured be thy name; thy Kingdom is undone; thy will is as little done on Earth as it is in Heaven; give us back our daily bread which thou hast taken away. Forgive thy Parliaments, who have supported thy interests, as thou forgivest thy ministers who have sold them. Be not led into temptation by the du Barry, but deliver us from the demon Chancellor. Amen."

All Paris was agog to see the magnificent carriage which the Duc d'Aiguillon had presented to Madame

400

du Barry, presumably as an acknowledgement for the King's support in his recent trial.

The arms of the du Barrys were set in the centre of four gold panels, and two doves, representing the King and his mistress, were depicted nestling in a bed of roses.

All agreed that there could never have been such a luxurious carriage; beside it those of the Dauphine looked cheap.

The cost of the magnificent vehicle was discovered to be somewhere in the neighbourhood of fifty-two thousand livres.

"Fifty-two thousand livres on a carriage!" said the people. "When we cannot afford to pay two sous for bread!"

Choiseul could now clearly see disaster looming ahead, and he believed that nothing but war could save him from dismissal, because then he would be indispensable to his country.

He commenced secret negotiations with Spain hoping that that country would provoke England into war over a dispute which had sprung up between the two countries concerning the Falkland Islands. But with the recent example of how disastrous war could be, the Spanish were in no mood to precipitate themselves into hostilities merely to save Choiseul, and they hesitated.

Choiseul was cornered. He had no alternative but to disclose his intentions, and he was immediately accused by the Abbé Terray, Aiguillon and Maupéou of trying to provoke war.

Choiseul fought desperately for his position. He sought an interview with the King, during which he assured him that if he would exile Maupéou and Terray the *Parlement* would cease to make trouble. On the other hand the Chancellor, the Abbé and Aiguillon told the King that the only way to avoid trouble was to dismiss Choiseul.

Jeanne du Barry was instructed by her friends that now was the moment to press for the dismissal of her enemy.

This she did, and the result was that a letter was written to Choiseul.

Even so, Louis could not bring himself to have it delivered. He remembered that for twelve years Choiseul had been head of the Government, and during those years France, considering the state in which she had been when Choiseul took office, had not fared as badly as might have been expected.

But the *Barriens* were pressing him and he was feeling too bored with the situation, anxious for only one thing: to leave the politics of Versailles for the peaceful life of Petit Trianon, with Madame du Barry to amuse and pander to his pleasure.

It was eleven o'clock on the morning of Christmas Eve 1770 when the Duc de Vrillière called on Choiseul.

"Ah," said Choiseul, "welcome, my friend."

He spoke ironically, knowing full well that Vrillière was no friend of his.

"I bring a letter from His Majesty," said Vrillière.

Choiseul knew as he took the letter that the ex-salesgirl of Labille's had beaten the shrewd statesman. Was it not typical of affairs at the Court of Louis XV?

He was determined not to show his despair to Vrillière.

He took the letter and read it.

Cousin, the dissatisfaction caused me by your services forces me to banish you to Chanteloup, whither you will repair in twenty-four hours. I should have sent you farther off but for the particular regard I have for Madame de Choiseul in whose health I feel great interest. Take care your conduct does not force me to change my mind. Whereupon I pray God, cousin, to have you in His holy keeping.

Louis.

Chanteloup! thought Choiseul. Far away from the glittering world of Versailles. So this was the end of that glorious career, begun under the favour of Madame de Pompadour, lost under the disfavour of Madame du Barry.

The lesson was one which a man of his intelligence should have learned; always be the friend of the King's reigning mistress.

"Monsieur le Duc," said Vrillière, "I deeply regret that I have been selected for this unpleasant duty."

Choiseul laughed loudly. "Monsieur le Duc," he answered, "I know full well that you would have found it hard to discover a task more congenial to you."

Vrillière bowed, and Choiseul saw the smile of satisfaction which played about his mouth. Thus would those, who had been wiser than he had and decided to enrol as *Barriens*, be smiling today.

He sent his servants to bring his wife to him.

She came and stood before him, a question in her eyes. She had a lovely face, thought the Duc; he had not served her well.

She had brought him rare faithfulness as well as a fortune. And even now it was the King's regard for her which meant that he would not have to go farther away than Chanteloup. She had rejected the King's attentions for the sake of a husband who had never pretended to be faithful to her and who made no secret of loving his sister more than he loved his wife.

"What is wrong, Etienne?" she asked now. "You look as though you are facing ruin."

"I am facing ruin."

She took the letter from his hand and read it.

"Well?" he said.

"There are places in the world as beautiful as Versailles," she said. "I think Chanteloup is one of them."

"No reproaches?" he asked. "We are to live as exiles, and it could have been otherwise. If I had made friends with that low creature . . . if I had smiled and fawned on her . . ."

She shook her head. "She is no longer of any importance to us, Etienne!"

"Is she not?" He laughed suddenly. "I shall not forget her. I shall remember her . . . at Chanteloup."

"Could you not live your life and let her live hers?"

He took her by the shoulders. "You are too gentle, my dear. Men such as I only live when they fight. The battle is not over."

He released her and turned away from her because the Duchesse de Gramont had come into the room.

"Can it be?" she demanded.

He held out the letter to her.

She read it, threw it to the floor and stamped on it. "That low creature has done this!"

"She has," said Choiseul, "and so have we; but the battle is not yet over. We will make a retreat to Chanteloup and wage war on her from there. Remember, Louis is past sixty. Think of the life he has led. The Dauphine is my friend, and the Dauphine will command our genial but lethargic Dauphin. Oh no, the battle is not yet lost. Come, let us go to dinner. I fancy it will taste as good to exiles as to those who remain at Court . . . for a little longer."

Choiseul with his wife and sister left Versailles for Chanteloup.

Through the capital they drove, followed by numerous carriages containing their followers and possessions.

The citizens watched them.

"There goes a great man," they said. "He is dismissed because Madame du Barry says he must go."

Choiseul knew their thoughts and smiled benignly on them. He was certain that it would not be long before he was returning.

To Chanteloup, he thought; there we will hold a court which will be almost as luxurious as that of Versailles, and perhaps more brilliant; there shall be made welcome the philosophers, the most brilliant of the writers; there shall be written songs and satires; and one day, not far distant, it would be Madame du Barry who drove from Versailles in disgrace while the Choiseuls came back in their glory.

With the dismissal of Choiseul the *Parlement* had lost its most powerful supporter.

Maupéou was doing his best to persuade the King that the power of the *Parlement* should be curbed and a new system set in motion.

Louis however, having at last given way to persuasion over the dismissal of Choiseul, was undecided.

Madame du Barry was called upon to help him make the decision, and this she did by having placed in her apartments a large Vandyke picture of Charles I. Her excuse for doing this was that the Barrys were related to an Irish family, the Earls of Barrymore, who were vaguely connected with the Stuarts. Thus, said Jeanne du Barry, the gentleman in the picture was a connexion of hers.

But the real reason that picture had been installed was that it might be a perpetual reminder to Louis of what happened to a King who had been in conflict with his Parliament.

As the situation worsened and the *Barriens* determined that something must quickly be done, Jeanne was told to remind the King verbally of what had happened to Charles I.

This she did, putting her arms about Louis, saying: "This picture has become to me as a warning. Oh, Louis, dismiss your *Parlement*. Remember it was a *Parlement* which cut off that fellow's head."

Louis turned to look at the tragic King depicted on the canvas.

He remembered the stares of the people, the sullen mutterings, the state of his country.

He gave an order, and on that cold January night his musketeers visited the homes of all magistrates to deliver *lettres de cachet* which they must accept, or agree to a new set of rules which should be laid down by the King.

They refused to comply and accepted the *lettres de cachet*; and a new Government was formed under the Triumvirate of Aiguillon as Foreign Minister, Maupéou as Chancellor and Terray as Comptroller-General.

Louis spoke to its members on its inauguration, saying: "I order you to commence your duties. I forbid any deliberation contrary to my wishes and any presentations in favour of my former *Parlement*, for I shall never change."

The clouds of revolution had begun to take definite form over the land of France.

CHAPTER
TWENTY-ONE

The End of the Road

The King and his mistress gave themselves up to pleasure, but Louis felt old age creeping upon him. There were times when *ennui* caught up with him and he could not throw it off; he thought a great deal about death, for so many people who had shared his life had died. If he heard of anyone's dying he would demand to know the details of the disease and their manner of passing; he would often stop a funeral *cortège* of strangers and ask for these details. Then he would brood on them and would find them even more depressing.

Life would have been intolerable but for Madame du Barry, who was constantly at his side, bright and gay, full of vitality, always seeming to know exactly what he needed to disperse his gloom. Thus he relied upon her, and grew uneasy if she were not at hand.

When she was honoured he was delighted, and when Gustavus the Crown Prince of Sweden visited the French Court and treated Madame du Barry as though she were Queen of France, giving her as a parting gift a collar for her dog, which was inset with diamonds and contained a thirty-six-inch chain made entirely of rubies, he was more pleased than she was.

He liked to see the animal wearing his collar and chain, and Madame du Barry and the dog were often observed walking with the King in the gardens, her dog almost as glittering a personage as herself.

They both delighted in their animals; Louis, who had from childhood days always loved cats, was on one occasion more angry than his courtiers had ever seen him when he discovered some of them intoxicating his cat with wine that they might watch the creature's antics.

This shared love of animals, of botany and of cooking was mutually enjoyable. She was to him the most satisfactory person at Court.

But Madame du Barry had been warned by her friends that Madame de Pompadour had kept her place by finding young girls who would please the King. Jeanne had always known that she would be a fool to ignore her successful predecessor's example, so occasionally she procured a beautiful young woman whom she presented to Louis.

As for Louis, he was not greatly interested but, since his dear Madame du Barry had taken such pains for his pleasure, he felt it would be a breach of etiquette to explain that he was feeling his age and found her adequate to meet his needs.

So occasionally Madame du Barry would archly leave him alone with some little friend of hers — always making sure that the companion of the evening should be possessed of more beauty than brains.

Marie Antoinette and the Dauphin were as tiresome towards Madame du Barry as the Dauphin's father and Marie-Josèphe had been towards Madame de Pompadour. The flighty young Dauphine had refused to acknowledge Madame du Barry by not speaking to her at receptions, thus creating a very awkward *contretemps* because, until spoken to by the Dauphine, Madame du Barry herself must not, according to the demands of etiquette, make any remarks.

The Dauphine had been very obstinate, and only stern admonitions from her mother, the Empress (strained relations with France were imminent at that important time when the division of Poland was being considered) forced the frivolous young woman to fall in with the King's wishes. As a result she made the comment *"Il y a bien du monde aujourd'hui à Versailles"*, which was soon quoted in various intonations throughout the Court — that pointless comment which had to be spoken to prevent strained relations between two countries!

The Dauphin was a disappointment to his grandfather — a great shuffling boy without any Court graces, spending more time making locks or with his workmen who were engaged in building operations, than in more courtly occupations. He had scarcely a word to say, and had a distressing habit of grunting when spoken to — and escaping from polite society as soon as it was possible.

Louis much preferred the Dauphine, although he was very annoyed with her over her attitude to Madame du Barry.

His daughters, led by Adelaide, had done a great deal to magnify the trouble between the Dauphine and Madame du Barry; Louise-Marie, the youngest, had now achieved an ambition, which had long been hers, and gone to Saint-Denis to become a Carmelite. Perhaps it was as well. One more daughter away, in a place where she was unable to plague her family and remind her father that he had not fulfilled his duties towards his daughters!

One day when the King was playing cards in Madame du Barry's room, Chauvelin, one of the most notorious rakes at Court who was standing by Madame du Barry's chair advising her on her hand, suddenly fell forward.

"What is wrong with Chauvelin?" asked the King shrilly.

Several of the men examined him.

"Chauvelin is dead, Sire," was the answer.

Louis stood up and stared at his old friend. Then abruptly he left the apartment.

Madame du Barry followed him, and when they were alone he turned to her, his eyes wide with horror. "You know the life he has led," he said. "And he was struck down without warning!"

He was badly shaken and asked to be left alone.

At such times it was necessary to plan some diversion which would draw the King out of his depression.

Unfortunately it was not easy, for shortly after the death of Chauvelin, the Abbé de la Ville came to thank the King for giving him a post at the Foreign Office, and as he was admitted he had an apoplectic fit in Louis' presence from which he did not recover. The Maréchal d'Armentières collapsed during a *lever* and died; and while the King was brooding on this, news was brought that Sorba, the Genoese Ambassador, had died without warning.

Louis, fearful of the life which he believed would follow that on Earth, and knowing that before he could repent he must give up Madame du Barry, fell deeper into melancholy. Give up the only one who could bring him any comfort! He could not do it.

And one day while he was hunting in the Forest of Compiègne a storm arose, and a tree very close to the King was struck by lightning; Louis believed that he had been warned.

Something must be done, decided Madame du Barry. She would arrange that they should leave for Petit Trianon. When they were there together he would forget his fears of death.

In the Petit Trianon Jeanne du Barry awaited the return of the King from the hunt.

She felt a little uneasy, which was strange for a person of her high spirits. The King's looks had alarmed her when he had set out on the hunt that morning.

She had wanted to ask him not to go, but she had realised that her power over the King was partly due to her lack of interference. It was April, a time of sunshine and showers. The countryside was beautiful, and surely Petit Trianon was the loveliest place to be in at this time of year.

What worried her? It was foolish. It was a little note in the Almanach de Liège which had been pointed out to her.

"In April a great lady who is the favourite of fortune will be called upon to play her last role."

She had not liked the sound of that. Yet she reminded herself that she had many enemies who might have inserted it, knowing that it would cause her more apprehension than any of the cruel songs they sang about her.

The King was looking his age; the Dauphine did dislike her so, and the Dauphine would rule France once the King was dead; there was no doubt of that.

"Poof!" said Madame du Barry. "What is wrong with me? Shall I mope because the King looked less robust this morning, and the month is April?"

There was so much to be happy about. Could a woman ever have been more pleased with life?

She had looked after those she loved; she had done her best to placate her enemies.

Choiseul continued to plague her from Chanteloup.

"A pox on Choiseul!" she cried. "A pox on these gloomy thoughts!"

But Chon was coming into the room and her face looked drawn.

"The King has returned from the hunt," she said. "I fear he is ill."

Jeanne would allow no one but his servant Laborde to sit with her by his bed, and the King slept fitfully, his hand in hers.

"I fear," she whispered to Laborde, "that His Majesty has a fever. If he is no better in the morning we will send for Lemoine."

Lemoine, First Physician in Ordinary, arrived in the morning.

He examined the King and smiled at the anxious Madame du Barry. "It is nothing much," he told her. "His Majesty has a slight fever, but there is no danger."

Jeanne du Barry knelt by the King's bed and kissed his hand when Lemoine had left them. She went on kissing that hand.

Louis touched the golden hair.

"What is it?" he asked.

"I was afraid . . ." she said. "So much afraid. And now Lemoine says there is nothing to fear."

"Ah, Jeanne," said the King, "how you depend upon me!"

She was more serious than he had ever seen her. "You think I am afraid because I should be turned out of the Court!" She pursed her lips and allowed a coarse epithet to escape. "What do I care for the Court! I have riches now. I should never starve. It is not the loss of my King I fear. But the loss of my man."

And with that she sprang up suddenly and ran from the room.

Louis looked after her. No one had ever behaved thus to him before; but then nobody ever did behave like Jeanne.

He touched his cheeks. There were tears on them. Was it because he was so weak or because he was so moved?

★ ★ ★

The surgeon La Martinière arrived in the afternoon of that day, and when he had examined the King he said: "Sire, you cannot stay at Petit Trianon. We must have you moved at once to Versailles."

"But why?" said the King. "I suffer only from a slight fever." La Martinière did not answer for a moment. Then he said that the ceilings of the Petit Trianon were too low, and were not suitable; the King needed the large airy State bedroom of Versailles.

Louis turned wearily on his side and said nothing.

Jeanne shook La Martinière by the arm.

"But why?" she demanded. "Why should he be taken from here? He is not seriously ill. I can nurse him. I and Laborde. It will not be good for him to be moved."

"Madame, I am his doctor," La Martinière reminded her.

"But the very knowledge that you are moving him to Versailles will upset him. Don't you see that? It will make him think he is very ill."

"Madame, the King is very ill."

"Nonsense! Monsieur Lemoine says . . ."

"I say that the King is ill and that he must go to Versailles."

"And if I do not agree? . . ."

La Martinière smiled and said quietly: "I repeat, Madame, I am the King's doctor."

A servant came to announce that the carriage was already at the door.

"Very good," said La Martinière. "His Majesty must have a heavy cloak over his dressing-gown. Orders have already gone to the *Château* that his bed is to be prepared."

He went from the room, passing Jeanne as though she were not there. Jeanne turned to Chon who had been in the room and had heard the conversation between the King's mistress and his doctor.

"You . . . you heard what he said?" stammered Jeanne.

Chon nodded. It was significant. It pointed to two facts. The King was ill — ill enough for death to be feared; and Jeanne had already lost the importance which had been hers yesterday.

The tension in the *Château* was increasing. Messages were sent to Choiseul at Chanteloup — messages of hope. The *Barriens* were alarmed, knowing they would automatically fall with the King.

News spread through the Palace. The King had been bled once . . . twice . . . and there was talk of a third bleeding.

It could not be long now before Madame du Barry was dismissed, for the King must make his peace with God, and the priests would not allow him to do that while his mistress was with him.

Doctors were arriving at Versailles from all over France, and there were now fourteen of them about the King's bedside. They were waylaid by those who were eager for news as they bustled in and out of the State apartments.

And then, as La Martinière bent over the King, he noticed the rash and recognised it for what it was.

He said nothing to the King but beckoned to the doctors who were present. They came forward one by one to examine the King; they said nothing, but the looks they gave each other were significant.

La Martinière led them away from the bed.

"I think," he said, "that the family should be informed that the King is suffering from small-pox."

The Dauphin received the news very solemnly. He did not show that it filled him with apprehension.

His sprightly wife watched him in exasperation. One would have thought a young man of Louis' age would have wanted to be King. What sort of man had she married? He was *gauche*, preferring his locksmith's to feminine company. He was impotent, so what chance had they of providing an heir to the throne?

Contemplating the future, even the frivolous Dauphine felt faintly uneasy.

Marie Antoinette sent all her attendants away because she feared they might sense this fear which had come to herself and her husband. They must not be allowed to know that it existed; she was determined on that.

She went to her husband and laid her hand on his shoulder.

"You will have to do your best when it comes," she said.

He grunted, but she knew him well enough now to understand the emotion behind the grunt.

"There will be two of us," she said with a smile which illumined her face.

417

He stood up abruptly and, brushing past her, went to the window. "We are too young to be King and Queen of France," he said. "We have too much to learn."

She watched him standing at the window, looking along the Avenue towards the sullen city of Paris.

Adelaide rang for Victoire, and Victoire rang for Sophie.

When her two younger sisters stood before her, Adelaide said: "I have news for you. Our father is suffering from small-pox."

Victoire opened her mouth, and Sophie, watching her, did the same. They kept their eyes on Adelaide's face, for they knew that she would tell them what they must do.

"We shall nurse him," she said.

Victoire began to shiver then because she feared the small-pox. Sophie, looking from one sister to the other, was uncertain what to do.

"There is danger," cried Adelaide, "but we will face it. We will nurse him as our brother's wife nursed the Dauphin through small-pox."

"Our brother was younger than our father is, when he recovered his health," said Victoire.

"I shall nurse him. *I* shall see that he grows well again." Adelaide took a step closer to her sisters. "We shall not stay in the room while that *putain* is there. If she appears we shall tiptoe out without a word. You understand me? There is no room in the King's bedchamber for that low woman and the Princesses of France."

418

★ ★ ★

A hasty meeting of priests took place in the *Château*.

What should be done now? The King had contracted small-pox. Small-pox at sixty-four! Consider the life he had led. What were the chances of his survival?

"The last rites should be performed. The King should be shrived," was one opinion.

"We cannot do that until Madame du Barry is sent away."

"Then she must be sent away."

"Have you forgotten that we owe the dismissal of Choiseul to the favourite? Choiseul abolished the Jesuits. Choiseul was the enemy of the Church party. How can we have the favourite sent from Court when she is the enemy of Choiseul?"

"But the King should receive the last rites . . ."

They were in a quandary.

They could only wait. Everything depended on the sick King. If he recovered, those who had sent Madame du Barry away would be very unpopular. They must remember Madame de Châteauroux at Metz.

So the men of the Church waited.

Louis stirred in his bed and asked for Madame du Barry.

"Let her come to me without delay."

The message was brought to her by La Martinière himself.

"You know, Madame," he said, "from what disease he is suffering?"

She nodded.

"You run great danger from contact with him. You know that?"

"Of course I know it," she answered.

"We could tell His Majesty that you are indisposed, that you had felt the need to go to Petit Trianon to rest."

She swung round and faced him, her hands on her hips, all Court veneer suddenly thrown off.

"What do you take me for?" she demanded. "He would know then, would he not, what was wrong with him? He must not be told. He must not guess. Once he knows, he will die. Do I not know him better than any of you? He has thought often of sickness and death — too often. It was always my pleasure to put an end to those thoughts. If he knows he has small-pox, that will be the end of him. Believe me."

"Then Madame," said La Martinière, "what do you propose to do?"

She stood up to her full height. Never had she looked more beautiful, never had she shown more clearly that she came from the streets of Paris.

"I'll tell you what I shall do. I shall go in there . . . And I shall be with him. I shall nurse him. I . . . and I alone. Because, Monsieur, that is what he will want. That is what he will expect. And if it is not done, he will know the reason why."

With that she stalked from the room.

And when La Martinière returned to the King's bedroom he found Madame du Barry seated at the bedside. The King had his hand in hers; she was laughing, telling him some joke, and her cheek was against his.

There were occasions when she was forced to rest, and when she announced that she would retire the three Princesses informed by their spies glided into the room like three white-clad ghosts. They said nothing as they passed Madame du Barry; indeed they looked beyond her as though they did not see her.

She thought of them — careless of their safety as they tended their father.

She remembered what she had heard of the wildness of Madame Adelaide, and she felt tender towards her now as she, with her docile sisters, undertook all the menial tasks of the sickroom.

Louis was amused. He looked forward to the periods when Madame du Barry would take over the duties of the sickroom and Loque, Coche and Graille would tiptoe out in single file.

Did ever a man have three such daughters? he asked himself. He was sure now that they were a little mad.

But on the eighth day he looked at his hands and saw the spots there.

He held them up to the light and called to his physicians.

"Look," he said.

The doctors nodded sombrely.

"It is no surprise to you, I see," said the King. "Yet you have been telling me that I am not ill, and that you will cure me. Yet you know that I suffer from the small-pox!"

The doctors were silent, and Louis continued to stare at his hands in despair.

From the moment that there was no longer any need to keep this matter secret, the news spread through the *Château*; it spread through Versailles to Paris, and throughout France.

The King has small-pox. He is sixty-four. Consider the life he has led! This is the end.

And in the *Château* itself many hastened to assure the Dauphin and the Dauphine of their loyalty.

So the moment has come, thought Louis. I am more fortunate than some. I have time to repent.

He commanded that the Archbishop of Paris should be brought to him, and when the man arrived he said: "I have a long journey before me and I must be prepared."

"Sire," said the Archbishop, "you should make your peace with God; but before you confess your sins, I must remind you that there is one, who has shared so many of them with you, whose presence at Court is an affront to God."

"You refer to the one who has given me my greatest comfort."

"I refer, Sire, to the woman who impedes your way to salvation."

"Who is that at the door?" asked Louis.

"It is Madame du Barry herself, Sire."

The King saw her hurrying to the bedside. There was an infinite sorrow in her face; he had never seen her so drawn and haggard.

"You must not come too near," he said. "It is the small-pox."

She nodded.

"You knew?" he said. "You have nursed me all these days . . . knowing?"

"I did not wish you to know. I am furiously angry with those who told you."

"My own observation told me," he replied. "You see it has spread to my hands. My dear, this is our last meeting."

"No," she said.

"You must go away from Court," he insisted. "There is no place for you here now."

"While you are here, my place is here."

"I am so soon to leave."

"You're a liar," she said half smiling.

He smiled with her.

"Dearest," he begged her, "go now. Go away from the Court. You should not be near me. I trust your wonderfully good health has saved you. You have a long life before you. And I am about to go. I must make my peace with God. I have so many sins to account for."

She did not speak. He must receive the last rites. He must confess and be forgiven. She knew that death had given her the *congé* which Choiseul had attempted and failed to give.

She shook her head and the tears, spilling from those beautiful blue eyes, rolled down on to her cheeks.

"If I recover," said Louis, "the first thing I shall do is to send for you."

She put her fingers to her lips in an attempt at gaiety. Do not let them hear you say that, she was warning him; they will never grant you absolution if they do.

But she would never come back. She knew it as he did. He was dying.

"Go now, my dear one," he said again, "and have the Duc d'Aiguillon sent to me. He and his Duchesse are your friends. I want you to go to their *château* at Rueil. You will be safe there. You need to be safe."

"Goodbye, my King," she sobbed.

Then she turned and left him.

So this is the end, he thought.

And his thoughts went back over his life. He thought of another old man who on his death-bed had held a five-year-old child in his arms and told him he would soon be King. That old man was Louis Quatorze, and he himself had been the five-year-old boy.

For fifty-nine years he had been King of France. And what had he made of those years? What was he leaving behind him?

Now that he was dying events took on a greater significance. Was that because now he forced himself to look at them, whereas previously he had always turned away?

Vividly he remembered that period of riots in Paris, when the people had said he stole their children so that he — or his favourites — might bathe in their blood. How he had hated the people of Paris then! That was when he had built the road from Versailles to Compiègne, so that he could avoid visiting his capital except on State occasions.

The road to Compiègne! It should never have been made. He should have gone back to Paris . . . again and again. He should have won the love of the people of Paris, not their hatred. Won it? There was a time, when they had called him Well-Beloved, when it had been his. He should have served his subjects. Instead of fine *châteaux*, instead of extravagant *fêtes*, instead of establishments such as the Parc aux Cerfs, there should have been bread for the people, abolition of unfair taxes — a happy country.

He saw his life winding back behind him like a road he had traversed . . . the long and evil road to Compiègne.

And what of the legacy he had left to his grandson? Poor, shuffling, *gauche* Louis XVI! How would he ride the storm which his grandfather, so concerned with his pleasures, had been too selfish to prepare for?

He had seen trouble ahead. He had smelt revolution in the air like the smell of smoke from a distant fire. There had been occasions when it had seemed very near.

But he had always consoled himself.

There is trouble brewing, he had thought. It will come some time. The people are changing. They no longer believe in the Divine Right of Kings. The philosophers, these writers — they are bringing new ideas to the people.

425

There will be trouble one day. Oh, but not in my time. *Après moi le déluge.*

He wanted to go back. He wanted to live his life again. He wanted to ask pardon of so many people but, oddly enough, chiefly of his grandson.

There were tears in his eyes. He needed laughter, gaiety. He wanted to dispel melancholy thoughts.

He called a page to his bed.

"Send for Madame du Barry," he commanded.

"Sire," the page replied, "she has left Versailles."

"So soon," he murmured and closed his eyes.

In the Cour de Marbre the drums sounded as the Viaticum was carried through the Chapel to the King's bedroom. With it came the Dauphin and the Dauphine and other members of the royal family; but only the Princesses Adelaide, Victoire and Sophie accompanied the priests into the chamber of death.

Those who waited heard the ringing tones of the Grand Almoner and the feeble responses of the King.

"His Majesty asks God to grant pardon for his sins and the scandalous example he has set his people. If he should be spared he swears he will spend his time penitently improving the lot of his people."

The King lay back on his pillow greatly relieved. That fate, which he had always feared, had not been his. He was to die but his sins had been forgiven.

Outside the *Château* the crowd waited. In Paris there was almost a festive air. The citizens were already talking of the new King, who was young and, so they had heard, not interested in women. He was quiet too and kind.

Would to God, they said, that the old one had died years ago, and the new one had been our King.

They already had a name for him. Louis the Longed For.

Everything, they said, would be different when he came to the throne.

There was one woman who waited in the crowd about the *Château*. She was six feet tall and very beautiful. She was the wife of an officer named de Cavanac, but before her marriage she had been Mademoiselle de Romans.

For years she had been searching for the son who had been taken from her; she believed now that she would find him, for when the King was dead there would be no one to care if that boy bore a striking resemblance to his father.

Madame de Cavanac believed that Louis XVI, who was said to be so kind, would help her to find her lost boy.

So she waited in the crowds, tense, expectant. She had loved the dying man; but she longed for the return of her lost child.

The Duc de Bouillon stood in the doorway of the bedchamber.

"Messieurs," he said, "the King is dead."

There was a brief silence; and then the silence was no more.

The stampede had begun.

The ladies and gentlemen of the Court were all eager to show how quickly they had rallied to the new King and Queen. Through the State rooms, through the anterooms, they ran to fall at the feet of Louis XVI and Marie Antoinette.

Bibliography

Pierre Gaxotte. Translated from the French by J. Lewis May. *Louis the Fifteenth and his Times.*

G. P. Gooch, CH, DLitt, FBA. *Louis XV. The Monarchy in Decline.*

Lieut-Colonel Andrew C. P. Haggard, DSO. *The Real Louis XV.* (2 volumes.)

Casimir Stryienski. Translated from the French by H. N. Dickinson. *The National History of France: The Eighteenth Century.*

Iain D. B. Pilkington. *The King's Pleasure. The Story of Louis XV.*

Lieut-Colonel Andrew C. P. Haggard, DSO. *Women of the Revolutionary Era, or Some Who Stirred France.*

Nesta H. Webster. *The French Revolution. A study in Democracy.*

Stefan Zweig. *Marie Antoinette.*

Ian Dunlop. With a foreword by Sir Arthur Bryant. *Versailles.*

Robert B. Douglas. *Memoirs of Madame du Barry.*

The Life and Times of Madame du Barry.

Karl Von Schumacher. Translated by Dorothy M. Richardson. *The Du Barry.*

Pidansat de Mairobert. Edited with an introduction by Eveline Cruickshanks. *Memoirs of Madame du Barry*.

An Abridgement of Louis Sébastien Mercier's "Le Tableau de Paris". Translated and edited with a preface and notes by Helen Simpson. *The Waiting City*.

Georges Cain. *Nooks and Corners of Old Paris*.

G. Lenôtre. Translated by H. Noel Williams. *Paris in the Revolution*.

William Henry Hudson. *France*.

Bidou. *Paris*.

M. Guizot. Translated by Robert Black, MA. *The History of France*.

Louis Adolphe Thiers. Translated with notes and illustrations from the most authentic sources by Frederick Shoberl. *The History of the French Revolution* (5 volumes).

Thomas Carlyle. *The French Revolution*.

Baron Ferdinand Rothschild. *Personal Characters from French History*.

C. A. Sainte-Beuve. *Portraits of the 18th Century*.

The Homecoming

Norah Lofts

Sybilla's husband was home from the wars — but he had brought his mistress with him

Sir Godfrey Tallboys had come home from the Crusades. Home to Knight's Acre. But the long years had brought many changes — and not only to his estate. His wife Sybilla, exhausted with struggling to keep poverty at bay, had grown old before her time. And with Sir Godfrey's return, there was yet another change at Knight's Acre. With him was the Moorish slave girl who had saved his life in Spain . . . Tana, beautiful and beguiling, had been his mistress in those years away — and now she was expecting his child.

Aflame with all the jealous passions of the East, Tana saw Sybilla as the obstacle to her desire. Her arrival was to alter the fortunes of the quiet Suffolk house. And in a way none of them could have possibly foreseen . . .

ISBN 978-0-7531-8832-3 (hb)
ISBN 978-0-7531-8833-0 (pb)

Louis the Well-Beloved

Jean Plaidy

France eagerly awaits the day the young King, Louis XV, comes of age and breaks free from the rule of his ministers. The country hopes Louis will bring back glory and prosperity to France. However, he is too preoccupied with the thrills of hunting and gambling to notice the power struggle going on in his own court. Soon, the King is introduced to the pleasures of mistresses and a succession of lovers follow. From the gentle persuasions of Madame de Mailley to her overtly ambitious sister, Madame Vintimille, France stands by and watches a King ruled by his women . . .

ISBN 978-0-7531-8840-8 (hb)
ISBN 978-0-7531-8841-5 (pb)

Pargeters

Norah Lofts

Pargeting is a highly skilled trade. And Pargeters is the name given to the Suffolk home of John Mercer in honour of Adam Woodley, the craftsman who had decorated it so lovingly.

Over two generations, and throughout the turbulent years of the Civil War, Pargeters comes to stand as a symbol of unity for a household divided by conflicting political loyalties and abandoned by its menfolk. And it is the mistress of Pargeters, Sarah Woodley-Mercer — a woman of unflinching courage and quiet strength — who holds the small household together in this troubled time, battling against all odds to secure the home she loves and will not readily give up . . .

ISBN 978-0-7531-8560-5 (hb)
ISBN 978-0-7531-8561-2 (pb)

The Prince of Darkness

Jean Plaidy

The untimely death of Richard the Lionheart has left his nephew Arthur and his younger brother John in contest for the throne of England. Reluctantly the barons choose John, and so begin years of rule by a ruthless and greedy tyrant.

Despite his reputation, John still managed to seduce the young and beautiful Isabella of Angoulême. But in taking her as his bride he makes an enemy for life. And in the tempestuous years that follow many men come to believe that the house of Anjou is tainted by the Devil's blood, that the loathsome monarch is himself Evil incarnate, the very Prince of Darkness.

ISBN 978-0-7531-8582-7 (hb)
ISBN 978-0-7531-8583-4 (pb)